21st Century Practical College English

复旦卓越·英语系列

U0116855

翟象俊，1939年出生。1962年毕业于复旦大学外文系英美语言文学专业，1966年在复旦大学研究生毕业。曾任复旦大学英语部主任兼外文系副主任、教授、硕士生导师。享受国务院特殊津贴。现为上海市翻译家协会副会长。曾参与《英汉大词典》、《英汉双解英语短语动词词典》的编写。主编《大学英语》（精读）（获国家优秀教材特等奖）及"九五"国家重点教材《21世纪大学英语》（获国家优秀教材二等奖）；译著有《乱世佳人》、《钱商》和《阿马罗神父的罪恶》及英、美作家海明威、霍桑、贝克特等人的中短篇小说多种。

余建中，1955年出生，复旦大学外文学院教授。现任教育部大学外语教学指导委员会委员、全国大学外语教学研究会副会长。代表译著和主编的教材有：《朗文英汉双解英语成语词典》（主译），《21世纪大学英语》（主要编者、部分分册主编），《大学英语综合教程》（全新版）（主编之一），《新世纪文科英语教程》（主编）等。曾获上海市育才奖、宝钢教育奖等。

陈永捷，教授，博士生导师。1953年出生。现任上海交通大学外国语学院副院长、全国大学外语教学研究会副会长、上海市大学英语教学研究会理事长。主编《实用英语综合教程》系列教材，获1998年上海市教委优秀教材二等奖。为《大学核心英语》（修订版）、《21世纪大学英语》和《新视野大学英语》的主要编者之一，《21世纪大学英语听力》（第四册）、《新视野大学英语》（读写第四级）主编，并负责《实用英语综合教程》（第三版1—3册）的修订。1995年获宝钢教育奖。

普通高等教育"十一五"国家级规划教材

2007年上海普通高校优秀教材一等奖

21st Century Practical College English

21世纪大学实用英语

总 主 编　翟象俊　余建中　陈永捷

Student's Book

综合教程（第一册）

本册主编　翟象俊　余建中　陈永捷　梁正溜

复旦大学出版社

内 容 提 要

　　《21世纪大学实用英语》系列教材根据《高职高专教育英语课程教学基本要求》以及我国高职高专人才培养特点和教学改革的成果编写而成,突出教学内容的实用性和针对性,将语言基础能力的培养与实际涉外交际能力的训练有机地结合起来,以满足21世纪全球化社会经济发展对高职高专人才的要求。

　　本套教材包括《综合教程》、《综合练习》、《教学参考书》(每一种分为基础教程和1-4册)及配套的音带、多媒体课件、电子教案等。本套教材供高职高专院校普通英语教学使用。

　　本书为《综合教程》第一册,共8个单元,每个单元均包括听说、读写和实用技能训练三大板块的内容。听说部分围绕每单元的主题,并结合高职高专学生学习生活和毕业后工作实际需要,进行听力与口语方面的专门训练。读写板块包括 Text A (精读),Text B(泛读)和 Text C(扩展阅读),并配有相应的练习。实用技能训练部分根据高职高专教育的特点,提供以提高职业技能和素质为目标的实用训练,包括 Grammar Review, Practical Writing 和 Basic Reading Skills 等内容。

《21世纪大学实用英语》编写人员

总主编

翟象俊　余建中　陈永捷

编委会（以姓氏笔画为序）

朱金花　余建中　宋　梅　张益明　陈永捷

陈明娟　周明芳　季佩英　姜荷梅　秦　凯

袁轶锋　顾伯清　梁正溜　梁育全　翟象俊

本册主编

翟象俊　余建中　陈永捷　梁正溜

本册副主编

何善秀

本册主要编写人员（以姓氏笔画为序）

余建中　何善秀　宋娜娜　宋　梅　张益明

张　颖　陈永捷　陈　进　袁轶锋　梁正溜

黄　莺　翟象俊　Amy Goldman, Ph.D.

前　言

　　《21 世纪大学实用英语》系列教材根据教育部颁发的《高职高专教育英语课程教学基本要求》编写,包括《综合教程》、《综合练习》、《教学参考书》(每一种分为基础教程和 1—4 册)及配套的音带、多媒体课件、电子教案和网络课程等。本套教材供高职高专普通英语教学使用。《综合教程》第一册的起点词汇量为 1 000 词,《基础教程》的起点词汇量为 600 词。一般以第一册作为起点,基础稍弱的学生也可以从《基础教程》学起,而基础较好的学生则可以将第二册作为起点。

　　《综合教程》每册 8 个单元,每个单元包括三大板块(听说板块、读写板块和实用板块)和导语。本册中"听说板块"围绕每单元的主题,并结合高职高专学生学习生活和毕业后工作实际需要,对学生进行听力与口语方面的专门训练。"读写板块"由同一题材的三篇文章组成:Text A 为精读材料,配有课文前的热身练习,课文后的口语、阅读理解、词汇、结构、翻译等技能训练;Text B 为泛读材料;Text C 为扩展阅读材料,课后也均配有与课文相关的练习。"实用板块"则根据高职高专英语教学的特点,提供以提高职业技能和素质为目标的实用训练,包括语法复习、实用写作和基本阅读技能等内容。为方便教学,实用板块穿插于每一单元中。

　　《综合练习》每册 8 个单元,每个单元包括两个部分。第一部分是根据《综合教程》各个单元中 Text A 和 Text B 的内容而设计的相关练习,并配合各单元的主题,增加 2—3 篇快速阅读短文;第二部分结合高等学校英语应用能力考试(Practical English Test for Colleges)的要求设计练习试题,所有题型和题量均以 B、A 两级考试大纲和样题为依据。此外,按照期中、期末的学制安排,《综合练习》还包含期中、期末考试练习卷各一份,最后还附有一份 PRETCO 模拟试卷。

　　《教学参考书》每册 8 个单元,每个单元根据《综合教程》的相关内容配以教法推荐、背景知识、课文译文、课文逐段详解及相应例句(全部例句均配中文译文)、练习答案。另外还附有《综合练习》中的练习答案和录音原文。

　　《21 世纪大学实用英语》吸取了现行国内外同类教材的优点,以我国高职高专人才培养特点和教学改革的成果为依据,突出教学内容的实用性和针对性,将语言基础能力与实际涉外交际能力的培养有机地结合起来,以满足 21 世纪全球化社会经济发展对高职高专人才的要求。具体说来,本套教材具有以下几个特点:

1. 注重培养听说能力。本教材根据高等教育英语教学内容和课程体系改革的要求,与时俱进,以"听、说"为重点,将听、说题材与课文主题保持一致,把听、说、读、写、译的技能训练有机地结合起来,使学生的听、说训练贯穿于课程教学的始终。

2. 着眼于提高学生的职业技能和素质。本教材根据高等教育英语教学的特点,提供相关的实用训练,力求使学生通过切合实际的学习过程打下一定的基础,在日常或涉外工作时能更加熟练地掌握和使用英语。

3. 选材广泛,注重"跨文化"知识的教学。本教材注重选材内容的趣味性、信息性和实用性,语言的规范性和文体的多样性,不仅重视英语语言基础知识和基本技能的训练,还同时注意将文化内容与语言材料相融合,介绍西方文化背景。

4. 强调教学的整体性。本教材将听、说内容与读、写内容相结合,将精读、泛读和扩展阅读融为一体,把听、说、读、写、译五种技能的训练和培养围绕着同一主题展开,形成一个有机的整体。

5. 将"教、学、练、考"融为一体。除了与课文内容相关的练习和期中、期末练习试卷以外,本教材还配有专门针对高等学校英语应用能力考试的习题和题解,以期让学生在巩固所学内容的同时,能够适应各种英语能力考试。

6. 拓展教学时空,实现教材的立体化。本教材包括配套的音带、多媒体学习课件、电子教案及网络课程等,以期充分利用多媒体和网络化现代教学手段,立体、互动地引导学生开发各种学习潜能。

《21 世纪大学实用英语》的主干教材由复旦大学、上海交通大学、上海商学院等高校的翟象俊教授、余建中教授、陈永捷教授、梁正溜教授、姜荷梅副教授等主编。上海及其他省市多所高等院校的资深专家共同参加了编写工作。

编　者

2006 年 7 月

使 用 说 明

　　本书为《21 世纪大学实用英语综合教程》第一册。全书共 8 个单元,供一学期使用。

　　每一单元包括内容简介(Preview),听说(Listening and Speaking),读写(Reading and Writing)三部分。

　　内容简介用简单易懂的语言对整个单元作总体介绍,以使学生对面临的学习任务有所了解。

　　听说部分共设 10 个练习。练习一的主要内容是一篇口语体的短文,要求学生边听短文边做听写填空练习。练习二则要求教师与学生共同总结短文内容和相关表达方式,然后让学生用所学的词汇和句型进行口头表述。练习三为两段二人或多人会话,要求学生先做听写填空练习,然后根据会话内容回答问题。练习四主要是给学生创造一个活用所学内容的机会。上述四个练习一般须在课堂内完成。练习五至练习十是为了让学生巩固以上所学内容而设的,可以由学生通过自主学习在课外完成,但是教师可以请部分学生在下一单元开始前就练习十的内容进行演讲。

　　读写部分的内容比较广泛,共配有三篇课文和相关练习及其他实用练习。

　　课文 A 为精读材料。教师在教学过程中,应该充分利用课文前的 Starter。该练习能够起到引入课文、活跃气氛、启发思想的作用。本书 Text A 和 Text B 后的生词表将单词、词组和专有名词分别列出,这两篇课文后还分别有 Notes on the Text,这主要是为了方便教学,同时也方便学生预习或自习。配合 Text A 的练习共包括 Reading Aloud, Understanding the Text, Reading Analysis, Vocabulary, Structure, Translation, Grammar Review, Practical Writing 等项。

　　Reading Aloud 练习选择部分课文段落供学生朗读、背诵。

　　Understanding the Text 主要采用问答形式,该练习可以作为学生预习课文的思考题,也可结合课文讲解进行。

　　Reading Analysis 主要使用表格归纳、解析课文的结构和段落大意。教师可以在讲解课文前后根据学生的预习情况让学生当场完成分析任务。当然,教师也可以把本练习作为回家作业,让学生课后完成。

Vocabulary 练习主要针对课文中出现的常用词和词组,帮助学生掌握它们的用法。教学大纲以外的词和词组一般不出现在这一练习中。

Structure 选取课文中最为有用的英语句子结构或表达方式,教师应该在课堂上通过诸如句型转换、完成句子、翻译、造句等形式,让学生切实学会使用它们。

Translation 一般可以作为学生的回家作业。翻译练习的主要目的是让学生将课文中的词语和表达方式准确地应用到句子中去。

Grammar Review 以系统复习英语语法为主,练习重点放在学生容易混淆、容易出错的语法现象上。教师可以在课堂上花适当时间讲解这部分内容,或者根据学生的具体情况掠过语法复习。

Practical Writing 是根据学生今后工作需要而编写的实用写作训练,内容较多,其中的大部分练习应该由学生在课后完成。教师除了定期抽查学生的写作练习外,还应该在课堂上多讲一些范文或实例,以帮助学生学习写作要点。

Text B 和 **Text C** 为泛读材料,其中 Text B 及其阅读理解和词汇等练习需要在课堂上处理,Text C 可以作为课外阅读材料。

Basic Reading Skills 是每个单元的最后一项内容,主要讲解一些基本的英语阅读技能并配有相应的练习。

一般来说,课堂上处理本书一个单元应花 8 节课时间,具体做法可参见教师用书的相关部分。

编　者

2006 年 7 月

CONTENTS

Practical Writing	Text B	Text C	Basic Reading Skills
Registration Forms	What I Hope to Gain from a College Education	Devlin's Advice	Reading for the Main Idea: Topic Sentence (1)
Book Order Forms	Don't Eat the Tomatoes; They're Poisonous!	Ups and Downs	Reading for the Main Idea: Telling the Difference Between a General Idea and Details
Application Forms	His Life's Work	The Odd Couple	Understanding Signal Words (1)
Business/Name Cards	Exercise: What Can It Do for You?	Walk, Don't Run	Understanding Signal Words (2)
Greeting Cards	The Golden Carambola Tree	A Dinner of Smells	Understanding Signal Words (3)
Thank-you Notes	From Crutches to a World-class Runner	Socrates	Understanding Signal Words (4)
Notes of Congratulation	Blameless	A Lady Named Lill	Reading for the Main Idea: Topic Sentence (2)
Notices	Maintaining Progress in Your English Studies	Successful Language Learners	Reading for the Main Idea: Topic Sentence (3)

UNIT 1

Highlights

Preview

This is the first unit of Book One. In the Listening and Speaking section, you will learn how to start a conversation with other people and how to talk about yourself. In the Reading and Writing section, Text A tells us about the transition the author experienced from high school to college; Text B tells us what the writer wants from his college education; Text C includes some advice from a former college student.

Listening & Speaking

Introducing Yourself

1 You're going to meet two new college students. Listen to them talk about themselves and fill in the blanks with the missing information.

Hello! _____ is Zhang Hong and I'm eighteen years old. I _____ a small town in Hebei. It's a nice place with a big lake and many small hills. _____ are doctors. I'm the _____ in the family.

I'm very happy to _____ you here at this college. I hope we'll be _____.

Hi! _____ Li Qiang and I'm nineteen. I come from Tianjin. I like _____ and _____ very much. I listen to music every day and often go to _____ on weekends. I enjoy _____ very much. I'm very happy to have the opportunity to _____ with you. I'm sure we'll get along and become good friends.

2 Now introduce yourself to your class telling them your name, your age, where you come from, when you began to learn English and what you like to do on weekends.

Getting to Know People

3

1) *Before you listen to the first conversation, read the following words and expressions which may be new to you.*

by the way	顺便问一下,顺便谈一下
department	系
major	主修科目,专业
management	管理
terrific	极好的,了不起的
come on	快;走吧

Listen to the conversation twice and fill in the blanks with the missing words.

Li Ming: We're having great weather, _____?

Wang Ying: We sure are. By the way, I'm Wang Ying.

Li Ming: Hello. _____ Li Ming.

Wang Ying: Which department _____, Li Ming?

Li Ming: I'm in the Department of Computer Science. I'm from Beijing.

Wang Ying: Really? _____ meet you! I'm also from Beijing. My major is Hotel Management.

Li Ming: That's terrific. My classmate Jun Jun is over there. She's from Shanghai. Come on, _____ meet her.

Now listen to the conversation again and answer the following questions.

1. Which department is Li Ming in?
2. Where is Li Ming from?
3. Which department is Wang Ying in?
4. Where is Wang Ying from?
5. What does Li Ming want Wang Ying to do?

2) *Before you listen to the second conversation, read the following words which may be new to you.*

apartment	房间
baggage	行李
upstairs	往楼上

Listen to the conversation twice and fill in the blanks with the missing words.

Li Ming: Jun Jun, I'd like you to meet my new friend Wang Ying.

Jun Jun: _____, Wang Ying. My name is Zhang Xiaojun, but everybody calls me Jun Jun.

Wang Ying: How do you do, Jun Jun?

Jun Jun: How do you do?

Li Ming: Wang Ying is in the Department of Hotel Management. She is from Beijing and has just arrived.

Jun Jun: _____?

Li Ming & Wang Ying: Yes.

Jun Jun: Have you found your apartment, Wang Ying?

Wang Ying: Yes, I've been told it's on the 3rd floor of this building.

Jun Jun: That's good. _____.

Wang Ying: _____. I can do it myself.

Jun Jun: If there's anything we can do for you, we'll be happy to help.

Wang Ying: _____.

Now listen to the conversation again and answer the following questions.

1. What is Jun Jun's real name?
2. Of the three people talking to each other, which two come from the same city?
3. Where is Wang Ying's apartment?
4. What does Jun Jun want to help Wang Ying do?
5. What will Wang Ying do if she is in need of help?

4 Form a dialogue with one of your classmates, telling each other your names, where you come from, your majors and your departments. You can use the sentences given below.

> Which department are you in?
>
> What's your major?
>
> Where do you come from?
>
> My major is....
>
> I'm glad to meet you!
>
> It's a pleasure to meet you.
>
> How do you do?

Listening Practice

5 Listen to people speaking and decide what they are talking about.

1. A) Study.   B) College.
   C) Weather.   D) Hometown.
2. A) Weather.   B) Study.
   C) Hobby (业余爱好).   D) Exercise.
3. A) Exercise.   B) Weather.
   C) Study.   D) Courses.
4. A) School.   B) Classmate.
   C) Department.   D) Study.
5. A) Hobby.   B) Courses.
   C) College.   D) Exam.

6 Listen to the following questions and choose the appropriate answers.

1. A) Sorry, I don't know.   B) It starts at eight.
   C) Yes, I like it.   D) It's very interesting.

2. A) It's over there.   B) Yes, thank you.
   C) It's very nice.   D) No, sorry.
3. A) I'm in the Physics Department.
   B) Yes, I am.
   C) No. I'm not majoring in Computer Science.
   D) Yes. We're in the same department.
4. A) In the park.   B) In my pocket.
   C) On the third floor of the shop.   D) It's 9:30.
5. A) Yes, I did.   B) Yes, of course.
   C) No, I didn't.   D) Oh, I failed.

7 Listen to the following short dialogues and choose the appropriate answers.

1. A) $25.   B) $13.
   C) $30.   D) $26.
2. A) $70.4.   B) $14.7.
   C) $17.4.   D) $14.
3. A) $14.50.   B) $40.50.
   C) $4.   D) $4.50.
4. A) Five years.   B) Six and a half years.
   C) Six years.   D) Half a year.
5. A) $4.   B) $10.
   C) $40.   D) $30.

8 Listen to the following talk and fill in the blanks with the missing words. The talk is given twice.

People go to college for many reasons. Some go to college to _____ who they are and what they want to become. Others go to college to follow their _____.

For me, going to college gives me the opportunity to have new _____. At college I have to organize my time and the way I spend my money. I also have to _____ myself. What I like best here is that I can make full use of the _____, which has so many books, newspapers and magazines.

Becoming a college student has also given me the opportunity to meet many friends. Here I have new classmates from _____ places. I have not only made friends with them, but have also learnt a lot from them.

The most important reason for me to be a college student is to follow my dream. All my life I have dreamed of _____ a good teacher. I like children and I want to _____ by teaching.

(174 *words*)

9 Listen to the talk again and then answer the following questions orally.

1. Why do people go to college?
2. Why does the speaker go to college?
3. What does the speaker like best about college?
4. What is the speaker's most important reason for going to college?
5. What is the speaker's dream?

10 Tell your classmates three reasons why you want to be a college student, using the following words and expressions.

first of all
secondly
finally

Reading & Writing

Text A

Starter

For many people, college life is a new experience. They feel excited and at the same time a bit worried. How did you feel when you first got to college? Name three things that you felt excited about and three things you felt a bit worried about.

Things I felt excited about when I first got to college:
1.
2.
3.

Things I felt a bit worried about when I first got to college:
1.
2.
3.

Discuss your response with a classmate. You and your classmate may have different responses.

Now read the following passage and try to find out what worried the writer when he first got to college.

1. _____

2. _____

3. _____

4. _____

Text

College — A Transition Point in My Life

Author Unknown

When I first entered college as a freshman, I was afraid that I was not able to do well in my studies. I was afraid of being off by myself, away from my family for the first time. Here I was surrounded by people I did not know and who did not know me. I

5   would have to make friends with them and perhaps also compete with them for grades in courses I would take. Were they smarter than I was? Could I keep up with them? Would they accept me?

2   I soon learned that my life was now up to me. I had to set a study program if I wanted to succeed in my courses. I had to regu-

10   late the time I spent studying and the time I spent socializing. I had to decide when to go to bed, when and what to eat, when and what to drink, and with whom to be friendly. These questions I had to answer for myself.

3   At first, life was a bit difficult. I made mistakes in how I

15   used my time. I spent too much time making friends. I also made some mistakes in how I chose my first friends in college.

4   Shortly, however, I had my life under control. I managed to go to class on time, do my first assignments and hand them in, and pass my first exams with fairly good grades. In addition, I

20   made a few friends with whom I felt comfortable and with whom I could share my fears. I set up a routine that was really my own — a routine that met my needs.

25   *5*   As a result, I began to look upon myself from a different perspective. I began to see my-

self as a person responsible for myself and responsible for my friends and family. It felt good to make my own decisions and see those decisions turn out to be wise ones. I guess that this is all part of what people call "growing up."   30

6   What did life have in store for me? At that stage in my life, I really was not certain where I would ultimately go in life and what I would do with the years ahead of me. But I knew that I would be able to handle what was ahead because I had successfully jumped   35 this important hurdle in my life: I had made the transition from a person dependent on my family for emotional support to a person who was responsible for myself.

(416 *words*)

New Words

◆transition /træn'zɪʃn / *n.*	(instance of) changing from one state or condition to another 过渡;转变
*enter /'entə / *vt.*	go or come into (a place) 进入
*freshman / 'freʃmən/ *n.*	a student in the first year of high school or university (中学或大学)一年级学生
*surround /sə'raʊnd / *vt.*	be or move into position all around (sb. or sth.) 包围;围住;环绕
*compete /kəm'piːt / *vi.*	try to win sth. by defeating others who are trying to do the same 竞争;对抗
*course /kɔːs / *n.*	a series of lessons or studies in a particular subject 课程;科目
*smart /smɑːt/ *a.*	clever 聪明的
*succeed /sək'siːd / *vi.*	do what one is trying to do; achieve the desired end 成功;达到目的
★regulate /'regjʊleɪt/ *vt.*	control (time, speed, etc.) so that it functions as desired 调整;调节(时间、速度等)
◆socialize / 'səʊʃəlaɪz/ *vi.*	meet people socially 与人交往;交际
*shortly /'ʃɔːtlɪ/ *ad.*	in a short time; not long; soon 不久;很快
*however /haʊ'evə/ *conj.*	nevertheless; yet 然而;可是
*control /kən'trəʊl/ *n.*	the ability or power to make sb. or sth. do what

	you want 控制；支配
* manage /ˈmænɪdʒ/ *vt.*	succeed in doing (sth.) 设法做到
★assignment /əˈsaɪnmənt/ *n.*	task or duty assigned to sb.; a piece of work that a student is asked to do (分派的)任务；(指定的)作业
* addition /əˈdɪʃn/ *n.*	adding; person or thing added 加；增加的人(或物)
* comfortable /ˈkʌmfətəbl/ *a.*	feeling physically relaxed and satisfied; feeling free from anxiety 舒适的；安逸的；无忧无虑的
* share /ʃeə/ *vt.*	have or use (sth.) with others; tell (sb.) about (sth.) 与别人分享(或合用)(某物)；把(某事)告诉(某人)
* fear /fɪə/ *n.*	unpleasant feeling when danger is close; feeling of being afraid 恐惧；害怕
★routine /ruːˈtiːn/ *n.*	fixed and regular way of doing things 惯常的程序；常规
◆perspective /pəˈspektɪv/ *n.*	a way of looking at things and forming a judgement (观察问题的)视角；观点
* responsible /rɪˈspɒnsəbl/ *a.*	[*for*] legally or morally obliged to take care of sb. or sth. or to carry out a duty, and liable to be blamed if one fails (法律上或道义上)需负责任的,承担责任的
* decision /dɪˈsɪʒn/ *n.*	sth. that is decided 决定
* wise /waɪz/ *a.*	having or showing good judgement 英明的；明智的
* stage /steɪdʒ/ *n.*	a part of an activity or a period of development 阶段,时期
★ultimately /ˈʌltɪmətlɪ/ *ad.*	in the end; finally 最后,最终
* ahead /əˈhed/ *ad.* & [一般作表语] *a.*	further forward in space or time 在前面,在前头
* handle /ˈhændl/ *vt.*	deal with; manage; control 处理,应付；管理；操纵,控制
* successfully /səkˈsesfəlɪ/ *ad.*	成功地
◆hurdle /ˈhɜːdl/ *n.*	[fig.] difficulty to be overcome; obstacle 难关；

障碍

| ★dependent /dɪˈpendənt/ a. | [on, upon] needing support from sb. or sth. 依靠的;依赖的 |
| * emotional /ɪˈməʊʃənl/ a. | of the emotions 情感的 |

生词量	总词数	生词率	B 级词(*)	A 级词(★)	纲外词(◆)
32	416	7.7%	23	5	4

Phrases & Expressions

by oneself	alone 单独地,独自地
keep up with	move or progress at the same rate as 跟上
be up to	be left to (sb.) to decide 取决于…的,须由…决定的
for oneself	unaided; without help 独自地;依靠自己
at first	at or in the beginning 起先,开始时
have sth. under control	have sth. managed, dealt with, or kept in order successfully 使某事恢复正常;使某事处于控制之下
in addition	as sth. extra; besides 另外;加之
set up	establish 建立
as a result	coming or happening as a natural consequence 结果
look on/upon	regard (sb. or sth.) in the specified way (以特定目光或情绪)看;看待
turn out	prove to be 证明是
grow up	reach the stage of full development; become adult or mature 长大;成长;成熟
in store	about to happen; waiting 即将发生;等待着
ahead of	in front of 在…前面

Notes on the Text

1. I was afraid of being off by myself, away from my family for the first time. 我害怕独自一人在外,因为我是第一次远离家人。off 意为 away(离开)。

2. Here I was surrounded by people I did not know and who did not know me. 在这里,周围都是我不认识的人,而他们也不认识我。people 后有两个定语从句:

（whom）I did not know 和 who did not know me。

3. I had to decide when to go to bed, when…：本课文使用了较多连接副词和连接代词。这类副词和代词可以用于动词、介词或一些固定的短语之后。除本句中的副词 *when* 和代词 *what* 和 *whom* 外，类似的实例还有第三段中的副词 *how*，第四段中的代词 *whom*，第五段中的代词 *what*，第六段中的副词 *where* 和代词 *what*。

4. These questions I had to answer for myself. 这些问题我都得自己回答。本倒装句中的 These questions 是动词 answer 的宾语，置于句首是为了与上文衔接更紧密。

5. I set up a routine that was really my own —·a routine that met my needs. 我建立了一种真正属于我自己的常规——一种满足了我的需要的常规。破折号后的 a routine that met my needs 系同位语，强调和补充说明上文的 a routine。

6. I began to see myself as a person responsible for myself and responsible for my friends and family. 我开始把自己看作是一个对自己负责也对朋友和家人负责的人。… a person responsible for myself…：短语作定语时，一般置于其所修饰的名词之后。相同的例子还有第六段中 a person dependent on my family…。

7. It felt good to make my own decisions and see those decisions turn out to be wise ones. 凡事由我自己作决定并看到这些决定最终证明是明智的决定，这种感觉很好。本句中 It 是形式主语，真正的主语是后面的 to make… and see…这两个不定式短语。动词 see, hear, feel 等后面用作宾语补语的不定式通常不带 to。felt 是连系动词，意为"给人某种感觉"。又如：How does it feel to be a college student?

8. At that stage in my life, I really was not certain where I would ultimately go in life and what I would do with the years ahead of me. 在人生的这一阶段，我真的不能确定我的人生之路最终将会走向何方，我真的不知道在以后的几年中我会做什么。was not certain 后跟了分别由 where 和 what 引导的从句。

9. But I knew that I would be able to handle what was ahead because I had successfully jumped this important hurdle in my life: I had made the transition from a person dependent on my family for emotional support to a person who was responsible for myself. 但我知道，我能应对未来，因为我已经成功地跃过了我生命中的这一重要难关：我已经完成了从一个依赖家人给予感情支持的人向一个对自己负责的人的过渡。

Exercises

Reading Aloud

1 Read the following paragraphs until you have learned them by heart.

When I first entered college as a freshman, I was afraid that I was not able to do well in my studies. I was afraid of being off by myself, away from my family for the first time. Here I was surrounded by people I did not know and who did not know me. I would have to make friends with them and perhaps also compete with them for grades in courses I would take. Were they smarter than I was? Could I keep up with them? Would they accept me?

I soon learned that my life was now up to me. I had to set a study program if I wanted to succeed in my courses. I had to regulate the time I spent studying and the time I spent socializing. I had to decide when to go to bed, when and what to eat, when and what to drink, and with whom to be friendly. These questions I had to answer for myself.

Understanding the Text

2 Answer the following questions.

1. What was the writer afraid of when he first became a college student?
2. What are the three questions he had about his classmates and himself?
3. What did the writer have to do in order to do well in his studies?
4. What mistakes did the writer make at first?
5. What happened to him shortly after?
6. What other things did the writer do in addition to his studies?
7. How did the writer begin to see himself as a result?
8. What did he think of his future at that time?
9. Why was the writer so sure about himself and his own future?
10. What does the expression "this important hurdle in my life" mean?

3 Topics for Discussion.

1. What do you think of the writer's "transition" from a person dependent on his family to a person responsible for himself? Do you want to do the same as the writer has done?

2. The transition from high school to college can be difficult for some young people. What are your difficulties and how are you going to overcome (克服) them?

Reading Analysis

4 Read Text A again and complete the following table.

Paragraph	Topic	Topic Sentence	Supporting Details
1	Afraid of not being able to do well in my studies	When I first entered college as a freshman, I was afraid that I was not able to do well in my studies.	1. Afraid of being _____ 2. Surrounded by people I didn't know and who didn't know me 3. Have to make friends with them and also compete with them
2	My life was now up to me.	_____ _____ _____	1. Set _____ 2. Regulate _____ 3. Decide when to go to bed 4. Decide what to eat and drink 5. Decide with whom to be friendly

Paragraph	Topic	Topic Sentence	Supporting Details
3	Life was a bit difficult.	_____ _____ _____	1. Made mistakes in _____ 2. Made some mistakes _____
4	Had my life _____	Shortly, however, I had my life under control.	1. Went to class 2. Did my first assignments and handed them in 3. Passed _____ 4. Made _____ 5. Set up _____
5	Look upon _____	_____ _____	See myself as a person _____ for _____ and responsible for _____
6	Life in store for me	But I know that I would be able to handle what was ahead.	Reason: _____ _____ _____

Now retell the main idea of the passage by using the information in the table you have completed.

Vocabulary

5 Fill in the blanks with the words given below. Change the forms where necessary.

comfortable	enter	fear	handle	however	manage
responsible	share	shortly	smart	succeed	surround

1. George is a very _____ boy; he is one of the best students in his class.

2. You have to work hard if you want to _____ in your courses.

3. _____ after you left, a girl came into our office looking for you.

4. At first, the course was a bit difficult for me but I _____ to pass the final exam with a fairly good grade.

5. Mary is my best friend and I always _____ my secrets(秘密) with her.

6. The lost traveler was filled with _____ when he saw a bear(熊)running toward him.

7. When you're away from your family, you have to be _____ for yourself.

8. At first, he was afraid of being off by himself. Shortly, _____, he became used to living alone.

9. Children in China _____ school at the age of 6 or 7 and must study there for at least nine years.

10. The earth is _____ by air, which makes up its atmosphere(大气层).

11. If you can't _____ the job, I'll get someone else to do it.

12. John was so _____ and warm in bed that he didn't want to get up.

6 Fill in the blanks with the expressions given below. Change the forms where necessary.

as a result	at first	be up to	grow up	in addition
keep up with	make friends with	set up	turn out	under control

1. You can ask him for advice but the final choice _____ you.

2. Everything is developing(发展) so quickly in today's world that I am afraid I can't _____ all the changes.

3. The brave sailors(海员) managed to keep their boat _____ during the storm.

4. If _____ you don't succeed, try, try again.

5. The boy said that he wanted to be a computer scientist(科学家) when he _____.

6. Today young people from different countries can easily _____ one another through email.

7. Mark wanted to finish his homework in two hours, but it _____ to be harder than he thought.

8. Tom fell and broke his leg. _____, he would have to be away from school for a month or two.

9. A new school has been _____ there.

10. _____, I have something else to do this weekend.

Structure

7 Complete the following sentences by translating the Chinese into English.

Model:

> I had to decide **when to** go to bed, **when** and **what to** eat, **when** and **what to** drink, and with **whom to** be friendly.
>
> At that stage in my life, I really was not sure **where** I would ultimately go in life and **what** I would do with the years ahead of me.

1. My friend told me _____ long ago, but I have forgotten it now. (如何玩这个游戏)

2. The taxi driver asked me _____. (我要去什么地方)

3. Henry was not sure _____. (他们会不会接受他)

4. Tom always tells others _____, but seldom does it himself. (做何事,如何做)

5. As a college student now, you have to know _____. (爱什么人,不爱什么人)

6. I am not certain _____. (他什么时候作出那个决定的)

8 Study the following example. Then, with the verb provided translate each of the sentences into English using the "V + Object + as" structure.

Model:

> I began to **see** myself **as** a person responsible for myself and responsible for my friends and family.

1. 我把李民看作我最好的朋友,我们有同样的爱好和兴趣。(see)

_____

2. 他们把数学老师视为他们最好的教师。(look upon)

_____

3. 我们把这地方视为我们的家。(think of)

_____

4. 他们把自己的大学生活看作一生中最幸福的几年。(look on)

_____

Translation

9 Translate the following sentences into English.

1. 约翰既聪明又有责任心。他喜欢跟别人交朋友。

_____

2. 我已经决定竞争这个新岗位。你也可以竞争。你自己决定吧。

_____

3. 医生来后不久就设法把我父亲的病控制住了。

_____

4. 作为新生,我们大部分人都不知道等待着我们的大学生活会是怎样的,但是我们都知道我们必须把学习搞好。

_____

5. 要在大学里取得成功,我们必须跟上其他的学生并且制定一个适合我们需要的常规。

_____

6. 虽然上星期的作业比我想象的难,我还是按时交上去了。

_____

Grammar Review

动词时态(Verb Tenses)(1)

The Simple Present Tense and the Simple Past Tense(一般现在时和一般过去时)

英语中,不同时间发生的动作或存在的状态,要用不同的动词形式来表示。这种不同的动词形式称作时态。动作发生或状态存在的时间有现在、过去、将来和过去将来四种,而发生或存在的方式也有一般、进行、完成和完成进行四种。这样组合起来,英语就有 16 种时态,其中最常用的是 12 种,其动词基本形式(以 make 为例)列表如下:

方式 时 间	一般	进行	完成	完成进行

现在	make
	makes
		am
		is making
		are
			have
			    made
			has
				have
				    been making
				has

过去	made	was making were	had made	had been making

将来	shall
	    make
	will
		shall
		    be making
		will
			shall
			    have made
			will	

过去将来	should make would			

一般现在时(**The Simple Present Tense**)

用　　法	例　　　句
1. 表示经常发生的动作或现在的存在状态	I usually <u>get</u> up at six in summer. 我夏天通常6点钟起床。 They <u>are</u> students of the Department of Computer Science. 他们是计算机系的学生。
2. 表示客观事实或普遍真理	The earth <u>moves</u> around the sun. 地球绕着太阳运转。 A friend in need <u>is</u> a friend indeed. 患难朋友才是真朋友。

用　　法	例　　　　句
3.表示主语的特征、性格、能力等	Some of my classmates speak English very well. 我的几个同学英语说得很好。 My brother is good with his hands. 我兄弟的手很灵巧。
4.在时间状语从句和条件状语从句中表示将来	It won't be long before we meet again. 我们不久就会再见面的。 If you come tomorrow, I'll go swimming with you. 如果你明天来,我就和你一起去游泳。

一般过去时(The Simple Past Tense)

用　　法	例　　　　句
1. 表示过去某一时间的动作或状态	When I first entered college as a freshman, I was afraid that I was not able to do well in my studies. 作为一名一年级学生初进大学时,我担心自己学业上搞不好。 At first, life was a bit difficult. 开始时,生活有点艰难。
2. 表示过去经常或反复发生的动作或存在的状态	In the first month or two, I spent too much time making friends. 在最初的一两个月里,我在交朋友上花的时间太多了。 When he was in high school, Tom often made his own decisions. 在中学时,汤姆经常自己作决定。

用　　法	例　　　　句
3.在主句用过去时态的时间状语从句和条件状语从句中表示将来	Mary said she would come if she <u>had</u> time. 玛丽说如果有时间她就会来。 He said he wanted to be a teacher when he <u>graduated</u> from college. 他说大学毕业后他想当一名教师。

10 Fill in the blanks with the given verbs in their proper tenses.

be	can	feel	have	make	manage	meet	set

Shortly, however, I (1)＿＿＿＿＿＿ my life under control. I (2)＿＿＿＿＿＿ to go to class on time, do my first assignments and hand them in, and pass my first exams with fairly good grades. In addition, I (3)＿＿＿＿＿＿ a few friends with whom I (4)＿＿＿＿＿＿ comfortable and with whom I (5)＿＿＿＿＿＿ share my fears. I (6)＿＿＿＿＿＿ up a routine that (7)＿＿＿＿＿＿ really my own — a routine that (8)＿＿＿＿＿＿ my needs.

earn	enjoy	get	go	like	live
live	run	train	want	watch	work

Joe Sutton is a professional boxer(职业拳击手). He (1)＿＿＿＿＿＿ his job. He (2)＿＿＿＿＿＿ very hard and (3)＿＿＿＿＿＿ a lot of money. He (4)＿＿＿＿＿＿ in a small town but (5)＿＿＿＿＿＿ in London. He (6)＿＿＿＿＿＿ a very healthy life. He (7)＿＿＿＿＿＿ to bed early, (8)＿＿＿＿＿＿ up early and (9)＿＿＿＿＿＿ twenty kilometers every morning. His friends (10)＿＿＿＿＿＿ all his fights on TV. They (11)＿＿＿＿＿＿ boxing and (12)＿＿＿＿＿＿ Joe Sutton to be the world champion(冠军).

Practical Writing

Registration Forms

11 The following is part of a student registration form. Fill in the form with the information given below in Chinese. Some parts have been done for you.

王大海　女　现年 17 岁　河南省开封市人　生于 1988 年 5 月 17 日

联系地址:中国河南省开封市北京路 68 号(2008 年 6 月 30 日前有效)

电话:86-378-6263693   传真:86-378-6263693   邮编: 475002

电子邮件地址:wangdahai@ 163. com

Student Registration Form

PLEASE PRINT OR TYPE ALL INFORMATION

NAME		
Last name（Family name）	First	Middle

PRESENT MAILING ADDRESS		
Street and number *No.* 68 *BEIJING ROAD*	Good until: （Month-Day-Year） *06/30/2008*	
City	State/Province(省)	Zip/Postal code(邮编)
Country（if not US）	Telephone number（including area/country code）	
E-mail address	Fax number（including area/country code）（传真号） 86-378-6263693	

Sex	☐ Male(男) ☐ Female(女)				
Date of birth	Month	*MAY*	Day	____ ____	Year	____ ____

说明:1. last name 姓, first name 名。

2. 英语地址的习惯写法是"从小到大":室/号→胡同/弄堂→街道/路→省/
市→国家。

12 Fill in the following form with your own information.

Information Request Service

Complete this form NOW to get more information about the college and
departments that interest you.

Your Details

Please complete in BLOCK CAPITALS and in English

Title (Dr, Mr, Miss, Mrs, Ms)   Nationality

_____   _____

First name   Home address

_____   _____

Last name   _____

_____   _____

Date of birth   Telephone

_____   _____

E-mail address

_____

Text B

What I Hope to Gain from a College Education

Alexis Walton

After graduation from high school, I plan to do several things. The most important thing I plan to do is to go to college. Other than a degree, from a college education I plan to pursue higher learning, to begin a career, and to make history in my family.

2   The first thing I hope to gain from a college education is   **5** higher learning. Learning goes far beyond a high school education and is very necessary in today's society. It allows us to be familiar with our environment and everyone in it, and it allows us to maintain assurance of ourselves. A lot of us would be lost without any learning at all, and our world would be very confused. One must learn   **10**

to do such things as applying math skills as well as being responsible and independent. I know that a college education would allow me to acquire these abilities.

15

3   Secondly, I hope to begin a career as a result of my college education. As a college student, I plan to study chemical engineering. After taking all the classes necessary for this major and completing them successfully, I hope I'll be able to begin a career as a chemical engineer.

20

4   Making history in my family is yet another important thing I hope to gain from my college education. Neither of my parents graduated from college, nor did any of my three brothers, but they did, however, graduate from high school. Taking a look back has motivated me to reach farther. I plan to make history in my family by being the first to get a college education.

25

5   Pursuing higher learning, beginning a career, and making history in my family are things I hope to gain from my college education. It is very important that I accomplish these goals so that I will have continued success. I know all of these things and many more are possible. If I believe it, then I can achieve it.

(325 *words*)

New Words

* gain /geɪn/ *vt.*   get (sth. desired), esp. as a result of one's efforts; obtain; win 得到;获得;赢得

* education /ˌedʒuːˈkeɪʃn/ *n.*   training and teaching, esp. of young people in schools and colleges, etc. 教育

* graduation /ˌgrædʒʊˈeɪʃn/ *n.*   graduating from a university, high school, etc. (大学、中学等)毕业

* plan /plæn/ *vt.*   make plans (to do sth.); intend 计划;打算

* degree /dɪˈɡriː/ n. 学位;程度;度数

★pursue /pəˈsjuː/ vt. 追求;从事

* career /kəˈrɪə/ n. a job or profession one chooses or does for the whole or part of one's working life 职业;生涯

* allow /əˈlaʊ/ vt. permit (sb./sth.) to do sth. 允许;容许

* familiar /fəˈmɪlɪə/ a. [with] having a good knowledge of sth. 熟悉的;通晓的

* environment /ɪnˈvaɪərənmənt/ n. 环境

★maintain /meɪnˈteɪn/ vt. cause (sth.) to continue; keep (sth.) in existence at the same level, etc. 保持;维持

◆assurance /əˈʃʊərəns/ n. confident belief in one's own abilities and powers 把握;信心

* confuse /kənˈfjuːz/ vt. make (sb.) unable to think clearly; puzzle; put (sth.) into disorder 把(某人)弄糊涂;使困惑;使混乱,搞乱

* apply /əˈplaɪ/ vt. make practical use of (sth.) 应用;运用

* skill /skɪl/ n. ability to do sth. well 技能;技艺;技巧

* independent /ˌɪndɪˈpendənt/ a. not dependent (on other people or things) 独立的;自主的

◆acquire /əˈkwaɪə/ vt. gain (sth.) by one's own ability, efforts or behavior (通过自己的能力或努力)获得;学到

* ability /əˈbɪlətɪ/ n. skill, strength, etc. needed (to do sth.) 能力

◆secondly /ˈsekəndlɪ/ ad. in the second place 第二;其次

★chemical /ˈkemɪkl/ a. of or relating to chemistry 化学的

* engineering /ˌendʒɪˈnɪərɪŋ/ n. practical application of scientific knowledge in the planning and making of engines, machines, etc. 工程

* major /ˈmeɪdʒə/ n. principal subject or course of study at college or university (大学生的)主修科目;专业

* complete /kəmˈpliːt/ vt. finish 完成

* engineer /ˌendʒɪˈnɪə/ n. 工程师

* graduate /ˈɡrædʒʊeɪt/ vi. complete a course for a degree or diploma 毕业

★motivate /ˈməʊtɪveɪt/ vt. stimulate the interest of (sb.); cause (sb.) to want to do sth. 激起(某人的)兴趣;激发(某

★accomplish /əˈkɒmplɪʃ/ *vt.*   complete（sth.）successfully；achieve 完成；实现

∗ goal /gəʊl/ *n.*   aim；purpose 目标；目的

∗ continue /kənˈtɪnjuː/ *vi.*   keep on（doing sth.）；not stop（doing sth.）继续（做某事）；不停

∗ success /səkˈses/ *n.*   act or fact of succeeding 成功

∗ achieve /əˈtʃiːv/ *vt.*   get or reach（sth.）；complete（sth.）successfully 得到；达到；完成，实现

生词量	总词数	生词率	B 级词（∗）	A 级词（★）	纲外词（◆）
31	325	9.5%	23	5	3

Phrases & Expressions

other than   apart from；except 除了

higher learning   高等教育；大学水平的学识

make history   do sth. important that will be recorded and remembered 创造历史；做出值得纪念的事情

go beyond   exceed 超过

as a result of   because of 作为…的结果；由于

Proper Name

Alexis Walton /əˈleksɪs ˈwɔːltn/   亚历克西斯·沃尔顿

Notes on the Text

1. Other than a degree, from a college education I plan to pursue higher learning, to begin a career, and to make history in my family. 除了获得一个学位，我还计划从大学教育中追求更高深的知识，开始一种职业生涯，并在我的家庭中创造历史。

2. Learning goes far beyond a high school education and is very necessary in today's society. 知识远远不止是获得中学教育，知识在今天的社会是非常必要的。

3. One must learn to do such things as applying math skills as well as being responsible and independent. 一个人不仅要成为负责、独立的人，还必须学会做像应用数学技能这样的事情。

4. Making history in my family is yet another important thing I hope to gain from a college education. 在我的家庭中创造历史是我希望从大学教育中得到的又一样重要的东西。yet 与 another 连用表示"再、还、又"之意。又如:Play the tape yet another time. 把磁带再放一遍。(指第三遍以上)

5. Neither of my parents graduated from college, nor did any of my three brothers, but they did, however, graduate from high school. 我的父母都不是大学毕业生,我的三个兄弟也都不是大学毕业生,可是他们都是高中毕业生。在 … but they did, however, graduate from high school 中,did 表示强调。

6. I know all of these things and many more are possible. 我知道所有这些事情和更多的事情都是可能实现的。

Exercises

13 Answer the following questions.

1. What is the most important thing the writer wants to do after graduation from high school?
2. What are the goals the writer wants to achieve by going to college?
3. Why does the writer think that higher learning is necessary in today's society?
4. What kind of ability does the writer hope to acquire from going to college?
5. What does the writer plan to study and what career does he hope to follow?
6. What can be learned about the writer's family from the text?
7. Why is it very important for him to accomplish his goals?
8. Does the writer think it possible for him to achieve his goals?

14 Fill in the following blanks with the words or expressions given below. Change the form where necessary.

accomplish	achieve	acquire	apply	complete
environment	gain	graduate	plan	skill

1. Reading and writing are two different _____.
2. Knowledge(知识) _____ by learning and skill is gained by practice.

3. John _____ to open a bookshop near our college this autumn.

4. After graduation, Henry wants a job in which he can _____ his math skills.

5. We often hear it said that the best way to _____ a foreign language is to live in the country where it is spoken.

6. Formal education has several stages that follow one another. Usually students need to _____ one stage before they continue to the next.

7. As a parent, Henry is trying to create(创造) a happy home _____ for his children to grow up in.

8. He _____ full marks in the English examination.

9. I hope to begin a career as an engineer after I _____ from this college.

10. Alexis thinks he will be able to handle what is ahead of him and _____ his goals in life.

15 Fill in the blanks with the expressions given below. Change the form where necessary.

as a result of	as well as	be familiar with	go beyond
make history	other than	such... as	so that

1. Henry hurried out _____ he could get to class in time.

2. What they were talking about _____ my knowledge so I just listened to them without saying anything.

3. _____ the bad weather, I had to stay at home all day yesterday.

4. _____ you _____ the students in Class Two?

5. Alexis has _____ in his family by being the first to get a college education.

6. A college education allows me to get a degree, but _____ that, it also allows me to be a responsible and independent person.

7. In the first year at college, we take _____ courses _____ math, physics, English and politics.

8. Mary works in a restaurant in the evenings _____ doing a full-time job during the day.

Text C

Devlin's Advice(忠告)

Keith Devlin

Dear New Student:

1   What *awaits*(等待) you in the coming years — your college years? And what awaits you after your graduation from college?

2   For an entering college student, the *likelihood*(可能性) is that the job you will be doing ten years from now does not yet *exist* (存在). You will be doing something that at present no one is doing, or hardly anyone.

3   How can you possibly prepare for such a future?

4   My strongest advice would be to *value*(珍视) the *breadth* (宽度,广度) of the education *available*(可得到的) to you. The key to being successful in the world of today or tomorrow is an ability to learn.

5   At high school you had a teacher. But when you are out at work you will *probably*(很可能) have to *go it alone*(自个儿干). College is a *half-way house*(中途歇脚的客栈;过渡场所). The professors are there to help and guide you. But as teachers, the most important thing they are trying to "teach" you is how to learn. For example, your mathematics professor is not there to teach you mathematics. He or she is there to show you how to learn mathematics, and to help you in the *process*(过程). That's a big difference from high school.

6   My second piece of advice is to work hardest at those *subjects*(科目) you don't like or think you can never do. For many students, the subject that they don't like is mathematics. But for many career *paths*(道路), mathematics is what they need to know in order to be successful. For *construction*(建筑) workers and engineers, *geometry* (几何学) is what you need to know. For future teachers , it is *statistics* (统计学) that you need to see if your

tests are fair to your students. Even for someone who just wants to be a stay-at-home mom, *calculations*(计算) are needed to keep a *household*(家庭).
In fact, what I am saying applies to all of you when you find yourself faced with any subject. Colleges and universities don't have all those graduation *requirements* (要求) in order to make you suffer. They are there to help you *broaden*(开阔) your mind, and to prepare you to live your life to the fullest.

7   My final piece of advice is to enjoy your life at college. I often hear people say that college is not the real world; that the *purpose*(目的) of your college years is to prepare you for your life "in the real world" in the future. That's not right. You won't stop living in the next few years. Your time at college or university is not *pre-life*(为以后作准备的生活). It's several years of your life. It is the "real world." So enjoy your time as a student and live your new "real life" to the full.

(449 *words*)

Comprehension of the Text

16 Choose the best answer for each of the following multiple choice questions.

1. The writer has written this letter to students who have just _____.
   A) entered college
   B) finished their college education
   C) entered high school
   D) finished their high school education

2. What is the writer's view about the jobs students of today will do in the future?
   A) There will not be enough jobs for everyone.
   B) There will be too many jobs, but too few people to do them.
   C) Most of the jobs will be new to the students.

D) Most of the jobs will be too difficult for the students to do.

3. How many different pieces of advice has the writer given to new students?

A) 2.   B) 3.   C) 4.   D) 5.

4. According to the writer, which is the most important advice for new students?

A) Learn how to learn.

B) Enjoy life at college.

C) Be interested in all subjects at college.

D) Go to class on time.

5. A university professor is different from a high school teacher in that _____.

A) he knows more about the subjects he teaches

B) he tries to help students learn by themselves

C) he likes mathematics more than high school teachers do

D) he enjoys teaching more than anyone else

6. The reason why the writer talks about mathematics when he gives his second piece of advice is that _____.

A) mathematics is far more useful than any other subject

B) mathematics is the most difficult to study

C) the writer himself is a teacher of mathematics

D) many students do not like mathematics at all

7. In the sentence "Colleges and universities don't have all those graduation requirements in order to make you suffer," the word "suffer" means _____.

A) get hurt

B) fall ill

C) work very hard

D) experience pain or difficulty

8. The writer is against the view that "college is not the real world" because

_____.

A) it is fun to be in college

B) nobody can enjoy college life to the full

C) college life is also part of students' lives

D) college life is more or less the same as high school life

Basic Reading Skills

Reading for the Main Idea: Topic Sentence (1)

英语段落的中心思想常用主题句表达。所谓主题句就是概括说明某一段落中心思想的句子。因此,能迅速识别段落的主题句有助于读者很好地理解段落的中心思想。主题句通常出现在段落的开头。如 A 篇课文的第二段:

<u>I soon learned that my life was now up to me.</u> I had to set a study program if I were to succeed in my courses. I had to regulate the time I spent studying and the time I spent socializing. I had to decide when to go to bed, when and what to eat, when and what to drink, and with whom to be friendly. These questions I had to answer for myself.

这一段的第一句是主题句,说明作者很快认识到,进了大学后,现在的生活就取决于自己了。接下来的三句则说明怎样取决于自己。最后一句说明这些问题都必须自己回答,再一次强调了主题句所表达的思想。

再如 A 篇课文的第三段:

<u>At first, life was a bit difficult.</u> I made mistakes in how I used my time. I spent too much time making friends. I also made some mistakes in how I chose my first friends in college.

这一段的第一句是主题句,说明一开始,并非一切顺利,生活有点困难。怎么个困难法呢? 后三句则做了具体说明。

17 Read Text B again and identify the topic sentence of each paragraph.

Fun Time

Humor

More Intelligent(聪明) in Dreams

When a student failed to solve a math problem in class, he expressed his regret to his teacher.

"I remember solving the problem in my dream last night, but for the time being I've forgotten it. What can that mean?"

"It means that you are more intelligent in dreams than when you are awake," the teacher explained.

Absent-minded Professors

One absent-minded(心不在焉的) professor walked to the edge of a wide river, and far across on the other side he saw another absent-minded professor. The first professor called loudly, "Hello! How do I get to the other side of the river?" The second professor on the far side of the river shouted back, "Hello! You are already on the other side of the river."

UNIT 2

Highlights

Preview

Listening & Speaking
Offering Help

Expressing Willingness
   to Help

Listening Practice

Reading & Writing
Text A

He Helped the Blind

Grammar Review

Verb Tenses (2)

Practical Writing

Book Order Form

Text B

Don't Eat the Tomatoes;
   They're Poisonous!

Text C

Ups and Downs

Basic Reading Skills

Reading for the Main Idea:
   Telling the Difference Between
   a General Idea and Details

Preview

This unit tells about people who invented new things and helped the development of our society. In the Listening and Speaking section, you will learn how to offer help and express willingness to help. In the Reading and Writing section, Text A tells the story of the blind young man who invented the Braille system. Text B tells how tomatoes become part of the American diet. Text C records briefly the beginning of aviation started by the Wright brothers.

Listening & Speaking

Offering Help

1 A librarian is going to provide you with some information about the use of the library. Listen to the short talk carefully and fill in the blanks with the missing words.

This is our library. It's well stocked (藏书). It's open _____. You can borrow all the books in the library except the rarest (珍奇的) ones, or those that _____ only here. You can borrow them for several days to several months, but must return them _____, or you'll be charged (罚款) for overdue (过期的) books. It's bad form (行为) to write in public books or mistreat (破坏) them _____. To use the library, you will have to show your student ID (学生证). By the way, you can go online (上网) here _____, or read your textbooks _____ in the evening. Enjoy your reading!

2 Now help one of your classmates to use the library for the first time. Try to use the language you have just learned in Exercise 1.

Expressing Willingness to Help

3

1) *Before you listen to the first conversation, read the following words and expressions which may be new to you.*

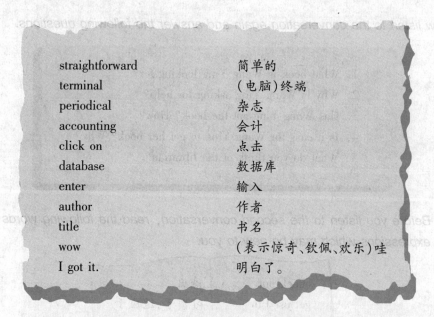

straightforward	简单的
terminal	(电脑)终端
periodical	杂志
accounting	会计
click on	点击
database	数据库
enter	输入
author	作者
title	书名
wow	(表示惊奇、钦佩、欢乐)哇
I got it.	明白了。

Listen to the conversation twice and fill in the blanks with the missing words.

Wang Ying: Excuse me.

Librarian: Yes? Is there anything _____?

Wang Ying: This is my first time in the library. Can you show me _____?

Librarian: Sure. It's fairly straightforward. Let's go over to a terminal and _____.

Wang Ying: Thanks.

Librarian: Here _____. Are you looking for a book or a periodical?

Wang Ying: A book on accounting.

Librarian: Now you can _____ the books database.

Wang Ying: Now what?

Librarian: You can enter _____ or the title of the book.

Wang Ying: OK. Wow! I got it. Thanks again _____.

Librarian: _____.

Now listen to the conversation again and answer the following questions.

1. What book is Wang Ying looking for?
2. Why is Wang Ying asking for help?
3. Has Wang Ying got the book? How?
4. Is it easy for Wang Ying to get her book? Why?
5. What do you think of the librarian?

2) *Before you listen to the second conversation, read the following words and expressions which may be new to you.*

check out	借出
get used to	习惯于,适应于
See you around.	回头见。

Listen to the conversation twice and fill in the blanks with the missing words.

Li Ming: _____ .
Wang Ying: Most of them, but a couple were checked out.
Li Ming: _____ ?
Wang Ying: Well, it was my first time, and I was a bit slow learning it.
Li Ming: It takes a little getting used to. _____ .
Wang Ying: That's very kind of you, but I think I can manage.
Li Ming: _____ .
Wang Ying: Thanks.
Li Ming: _____ !
Wang Ying: You too. Bye.
Li Ming: See you around.

Now listen to the conversation again and answer the following questions.

> 1. Where has Wang Ying been?
> 2. Did Wang Ying get all the books she needed?
> 3. Did Wang Ying use the computer? What happened?
> 4. What did Li Ming try to do?
> 5. What did Li Ming say about Wang Ying?

4 Make a dialogue with one of your classmates, stating a problem, expressing willingness to help, asking someone to do something and offering help. You can use the structures given below for the task.

> Would you like me to (do)...?
> I could (do)... (for you), if you like.
> Do you want me to (do)...?
> Is there anything I can do for you?
> If there's anything I can do, I'd be happy to help.
> Can I do anything?
> Can I help?

Listening Practice

5 Listen to people talking and decide what they are talking about.

1. A) Cake.   B) Peace.
   C) Coke.   D) Help.
2. A) Weather.   B) Lunch.
   C) Work.   D) Time.
3. A) A method.   B) A trip.
   C) A place.   D) A city.
4. A) Work.   B) Money.

C) Help.   D) Life.

5. A) A book.   B) A plan.

C) A play.   D) A film.

6 Listen to five questions and choose the appropriate answers.

1. A) Yes, please.   B) Not too bad.

C) No, have a seat.   D) Oh, pretty good.

2. A) What a pity!   B) Oh, not at all.

C) It's a pleasure.   D) That's all right.

3. A) Yes, I do.   B) No, thanks.

C) Yes, I like it.   D) No, it was a lie.

4. A) Well, I'm glad to be of help.   B) That's very kind of you.

C) That's for sure.   D) I'm ready.

5. A) I tried, but no one answered.   B) That's what I want to say.

C) Me, too.   D) You bet.

7 Listen to five short dialogues and choose the appropriate answers.

1. A) Continuing to watch TV.   B) Reading in the library.

C) Going to the cinema.   D) As usual.

2. A) Right way.   B) Surely he is.

C) He's not sure.   D) Certainly not.

3. A) An accountant.   B) A technician.

C) A salesman.   D) A scientist.

4. A) The woman got a surprise.   B) The man got a surprise.

C) The woman got sick.   D) The man got sick.

5. A) Because he caught a cold.   B) Because he made a mistake.

C) Because he missed the party.   D) Because he failed to pass the exam.

8 Listen to the following short talk and fill in the blanks with the missing words. The talk is given twice.

Men have lived together in groups since the very earliest times. Each group tried to keep together and to find _____ that would keep the group going after its old members were _____ .

In order for the group and its values to survive(幸存), it was _____ for the older members to teach children all that they had learned so that they could solve the problems they would _____ . Young people had to be trained to carry on the customs(习俗), knowledge, and skills of the group. So the _____ of "education" existed(存在) long before there were actual schools.

But when letters were _____ , schools became a necessity. Special(专门的) _____ was required to master(掌握) the symbols(符号). And the existence(存在) of these symbols made it possible to accumulate(积累) and transmit(传递) knowledge on a scale(规模) that had never been _____ before.

Ordinary(普通的) life in the group did not provide(提供) this type of _____ . So a special organization(组织) was needed to take over the _____ of providing it. And this was the _____ .

Nobody knows _____ the first schools appeared. We do know that they appeared in Egypt(埃及) and perhaps in _____ and in some other countries 5,000 to 6,000 years ago.

(197 *words*)

9 Listen to the talk again and then answer the following questions orally.

1. Why did the older members want to teach their children?
2. What was the earliest idea of "education"?
3. When was it necessary to build schools in human history?
4. When was the first school built?
5. What is the topic of the talk?

10 Have a free discussion on the topic given below.

To live is to give.

Reading & Writing

Text A

The development of society is powered by inventions and discoveries. Looking back into history, we may find a number of them have changed people's lives greatly. Can you name three inventions or discoveries that you think are the most important in human history?

Three inventions or discoveries that you think are the most important in human history:
1.
2.
3.

Now compare your response with a classmate, and explain why you think they are the most important.

Text

He Helped the Blind

Jeanne K. Grieser

B lind and wanting to read — those were the realities of Louis Braille's life. The desire to read easily led to the Braille system. January 4 is Braille Day. That day honors the blind. But we should also remember Louis and what he achieved by age 15.

2 Louis Braille was born on January 4, 1809, in France. He   5
lived with his parents, two older sisters, and one older brother in a

small, stone house in Coupvray.

	A	B	C	D
E	F	G	H
I	J	K	L
M	N	O	P
Q	R	S	T
U	V	W	X
Y	Z		
and	for	of	the

3   Three-year-old Louis went to his father's work-shop. Louis's father was a saddle maker who made items out of leather. Imitating his father, Louis tried to cut a piece of leather with a small knife. His hand slipped, and the point of the knife went into his eye. The doctors took care of him the best they could, but the injured eye got infected. Then the infection spread to his good eye. Louis became blind.

4   Louis went to a public school and learned by listening to the teacher. To do his homework, his sister and a friend read the assignments to him. Soon Louis was at the top of his class.

5   One day, the pastor of Louis's church came to Louis's house and told his parents of a school for the blind in Paris. Louis's parents decided to send him to the school when he was nine years old.

6   Louis wanted very much to read. The school had only 14 books for blind people; the books were big and heavy. The letters were large and raised; one book took a long time to read. Louis thought there must be a better way to read.

7   When Louis was 12, Charles Barbier, a French Army officer, came to the school. Barbier developed an alphabet code used by army soldiers. The code was used to deliver messages to the soldiers at night. It was made up of dots and dashes. It kept the messages secret even if the enemy would see them, but the code was too complicated for the blind. Louis thought the code was slow and the dashes took up too much space. Only one or two sentences fit on a page.

8   Over the next three years, Louis worked to simplify the

code. On a vacation at home, Louis, age 15, picked up a blunt awl. Aha! An idea came to him. He made the alphabet using only six dots. Different dots were raised for different letters. Later, he made a system for numbers and music.

9 Today, Braille is in nearly every language around the world. Louis Braille, at age 15, changed the lives of blind people when he created the six-dot Braille system. It is fitting that January 4, Louis's birthday, is considered Braille Day, in honor of the blind.

45

(454 *words*)

New Words

* blind /blaɪnd/ *a.*		unable to see 瞎的,盲的
* reality /rɪ'ælətɪ/ *n.*		all that is real; quality or state of being real 现实,实际;真实,真实性
* desire /dɪ'zaɪə/ *n.*		longing; strong wish 渴望;愿望
* system /'sɪstəm/ *n.*		group of things or parts working together as a whole; set of ideas, theories, principles, etc. according to which sth. is done 系统;制度;体系
* honor /'ɒnə/ *n.*		great (public) respect, good opinion, etc. shown to sb.; good character or reputation 崇敬;敬意;荣誉;名誉
vt.		show great respect or honor to 向…表示敬意;给…以荣誉
★workshop /'wɜːkʃɒp/ *n.*		车间;工场;作坊
◆saddle /'sædl/ *n.*		鞍;马鞍;鞍具
* item /'aɪtəm/ *n.*		single article or unit in a list; single piece of news 条,项;项目;条款;(新闻等的)一条,一则
◆leather /'leðə/ *n.*		皮革
* imitate /'ɪmɪteɪt/ *vt.*		copy the speech, actions, etc. of (sb.); take or follow as an example 模仿,仿效,学…的样
◆slip /slɪp/ *vi.*		滑;滑落;溜;悄悄地走
* injure /'ɪndʒə/ *vt.*		hurt; harm 伤害;损害
★infect /ɪn'fekt/ *vt.*		cause (sb./sth.) to be affected (by a disease,

	germs, etc.) 传染;感染
◆infection /ɪnˈfekʃn/ *n.*	传染;感染
*spread /spred/ *v.*	(cause sth. to) become (more) widely known, felt or suffered(使)传开;传染;(使)蔓延
*public /ˈpʌblɪk/ *a.*	公立的;公众的,公共的;公开的
n.	公众,民众
◆pastor /ˈpɑːstə/ *n.*	牧师
*church /tʃɜːtʃ/ *n.*	教堂;[C-]教会
◆French /frentʃ/ *a.*	法国的;法国人的;法语的
n.	法语
*officer /ˈɒfɪsə/ *n.*	person appointed to command others in the army, navy, air force, etc. 军官
*develop /dɪˈveləp/ *v.*	制订;研制;(使)形成;(使)成长;(使)发育;发展
★alphabet /ˈælfəbet/ *n.*	字母表
*code /kəʊd/ *n.*	(system of) words, letters, symbols, etc. that represent others, used for secret messages or for presenting or recording information briefly 密码;电码;代码
◆soldier /ˈsəʊldʒə/ *n.*	士兵
*deliver /dɪˈlɪvə/ *vt.*	传送(信息等);投递(信件等);发表(演说等)
★dot /dɒt/ *n.*	点,圆点
★dash /dæʃ/ *n.*	(莫尔斯电码的)划,长划;破折号(即—);猛冲,飞奔
*secret /ˈsiːkrɪt/ *a.*	not known by others 秘密的
n.	fact, decision, etc. that is kept secret 秘密
*enemy /ˈenəmɪ/ *n.*	敌人
★complicated /ˈkɒmplɪkeɪtɪd/ *a.*	(结构)复杂的;难懂的
*fit /fɪt/ *vi.*	被容纳;(服装等)合身,合适;适合;适应
a.	适合的;健康的
◆simplify /ˈsɪmplɪfaɪ/ *vt.*	make (sth.) easy to do or understand; make simple 使简易;使简明;简化
★vacation /vəˈkeɪʃn/ *n.*	time when a school, etc. is closed to students; holiday 假期;休假

◆blunt /blʌnt/ *a.*   without a sharp edge or a point 钝的

◆awl /ɔːl/ *n.*   small pointed tool for making holes, esp. in leather or wood 锥子

◆aha /ɑːˈhɑː/ *int.*   (used esp. to show surprise or satisfaction) 啊哈 (表示惊讶、得意等)

* nearly /ˈnɪəlɪ/ *ad.*   almost; very close to 几乎, 差不多

* create /kriːˈeɪt/ *vt.*   make (sth. new or original); have (sth.) as a result; produce 创造; 创作; 引起; 产生

生词量	总词数	生词率	B 级词(*)	A 级词(★)	纲外词(◆)
38	454	8.4%	20	7	11

Phrases & Expressions

lead to	have (sth.) as its result 导致
make… out of…	produce… using… as material 用…制造出…
take care of	look after; be responsible for 照料; 负责
make up	form, compose or constitute 组成, 构成
take up	fill or occupy (the specified time or space) 占去(时间或地方)
pick up	take hold of and lift 拿起; 捡起; 提起
come to	(of an idea) occur to (sb.) (指主意)被想起
in honor of	out of respect for 出于对…的敬意

Proper Names

Jeanne K. Grieser /ˈdʒiːn keɪ ˈɡriːzə/	珍尼·K·格里泽
Louis Braille /lwiː ˈbreɪl/	路易·布莱叶
France /frɑːns/	法兰西, 法国
Coupvray /ˈkuːpfreɪ/	库普弗雷(法国城市)
Paris /ˈpærɪs/	巴黎(法国首都)
Charles Barbier /ˈtʃɑːlz bɑrˈbjeɪ/	查尔斯·巴比埃

Notes on the Text

1. The desire to read easily led to the Braille system. 实现轻松阅读的愿望导致了布

莱叶盲字体系的产生。该句的主语部分是 the desire to read easily。

2. We should also remember Louis and what he achieved by age 15. 我们还应该记住路易和他在 15 岁时取得的成就。remember 后有两个宾语：Louis 和 what he achieved by age 15。第二个宾语是由 what 引导的名词从句。

3. Imitating his father, Louis tried to cut a piece of leather with a small knife. 路易学着父亲的样子，试着用小刀割一块皮革。Imitating his father 是分词短语，用作状语。分词短语作状语时，它逻辑上的主语一般必须与句子的主语一致。课文中类似的用法还有：He made the alphabet using only six dots. (Para. 8)

4. The doctors took care of him the best they could, but the injured eye got infected. 医生们竭尽全力为他医治，但那只受伤的眼睛受到了感染。the best 是副词 well 的最高级形式。the best they could = as well as they could。

5. Louis's parents decided to send him to the school when he was nine years old. 路易的父母决定把他送到那所学校去，当时他 9 岁。时间状语从句 when he was nine years old 放在了主句的后面。课文中同样的结构还有 Louis Braille, at age 15, changed the lives of blind people when he created the six-dot Braille system. 路易·布莱叶在 15 岁时创造了六圆点布莱叶体系，从而改变了盲人的生活。(Para. 9)

6. It kept the messages secret even if the enemy would see them, but the code was too complicated for the blind. 即使敌人看到信息，电码也能使它保密。但这种电码对盲人来说太复杂了。

7. On a vacation at home, Louis, age 15, picked up a blunt awl. 在家中度假的某一天，15 岁的路易捡起了一把钝锥子。age 15 是插在主语和谓语中间的一个修饰语，修饰 Louis。

8. It is fitting that January 4, Louis's birthday, is considered Braille Day, in honor of the blind. 把路易的生日 1 月 4 日定为向盲人表示敬意的布莱叶日是非常恰当的。Louis's birthday 是 January 4 的同位语。

Exercises

Reading Aloud

1 Read the following paragraphs until you have learned them by heart.

When Louis was 12, Charles Barbier, a French Army officer, came to the school.

Barbier developed an alphabet code used by army soldiers. The code was used to deliver messages to the soldiers at night. It was made up of dots and dashes. It kept the messages secret if the enemy saw them, but the code was too complicated for the blind. Louis thought the code was slow and the dashes took up too much space. Only one or two sentences fit on a page.

Over the next three years, Louis worked to simplify the code. On a vacation at home, Louis, age 15, picked up a blunt awl. Aha! An idea came to him. He made the alphabet using only six dots. Different dots were raised for different letters. Later, he made a system for numbers and music.

Understanding the Text

2 **Answer the following questions.**

1. Who was Louis Braille?
2. Why is January 4 named Braille Day?
3. How many people were there in Louis's family?
4. How did Louis become blind?
5. As a blind child, did Louis give up his school education? How could he keep up with studies in school?
6. What did Louis's parents decide to do when he was nine years old?
7. What were the books for the blind like in the school in Paris?
8. What was the alphabet code used by army soldiers made up of?
9. Why was the code no good for the blind?
10. How long did it take Louis to develop his Braille system?
11. How does the Braille system work?

3 **Topics for Discussion.**

1. "Louis Braille, at age 15, changed the lives of blind people when he created the six-dot Braille system." Now discuss with your classmates what changes this system can bring to a blind person's life.
2. "Necessity is the mother of invention." Do you agree that Braille's story proves this saying? Do you know any other examples that prove the truth of this saying?

Reading Analysis

4 Read Text A again and complete the following table.

Part	Topic	Paragraph	Main Idea
I	Opening remarks	1	January 4 is Braille Day in honor of _____ and _____ .
II	Louis Braille's invention of Braille system	2	Louis Braille was born on _____, in _____ .
		3	Louis became blind when he was _____ _____ years old.
		4	Louis went to school and was at _____ _____ .
		5	Louis's parents decided to _____ .
		6	Louis was not satisfied with the books for blind people and wanted _____ .
		7	The _____ developed by Charles Barbier did not fit the blind.
		8	At age _____, Louis developed his own _____ on a vacation at home.
III	Closing remarks	9	Louis Braille's creation changed _____ _____ .

Now retell the main idea of the passage by using the information in the table you have completed.

Vocabulary

5 Fill in the blanks with the words given below. Change the forms where necessary.

reality	desire	honor	imitate	injure	infect
spread	develop	deliver	secret	create	nearly

1. As a young man, he has a strong _____ for success.
2. The plan must remain _____ until next month.
3. On Memorial Day(阵亡将士纪念日) the American people _____ those soldiers who died in wars.
4. My finger was _____ when I tried to collect the broken glass by hand.
5. We were happy that her dream of marrying Fred finally became a _____.
6. My classmates all laughed when I _____ our teacher.
7. The book says that modern music was first _____ in Italy.
8. The boy could earn(赚得) a little money by _____ newspapers.
9. Jane stayed home on Monday so that her cold would not _____ to others in the office.
10. Your throat(咽喉) looks _____. I think you should take some medicine.
11. Do you believe that God _____ the world in six days?
12. It took us _____ two hours to get there.

6 Fill in the blanks with the expressions given below. Change the forms where necessary.

lead to	make sth. out of	take care of	be made up of
take up	come to	in honor of	pick up

1. It suddenly _____ me that I should have left a message on his desk.
2. Please _____ that piece of paper you've just dropped on the floor.
3. I don't think quarrels will ever _____ any good results.
4. My friend agreed to _____ my dog while I'm on vacation.

5. The students are planning a big party _____ their retiring (将退休的) teacher.

6. Human beings learned to _____ tools _____ stones thousands of years ago.

7. Don't you think watching TV _____ too much of your time?

8. A team _____ 15 doctors and 25 nurses was sent to the flooded area (水灾地区).

Structure

7 Complete the following sentences by translating the Chinese in brackets into English.

Model：

> Louis Braille was born **on** January 4, 1809, **in** France.

1. The Wright brothers made their first powered flight _____ _____. (1903 年 12 月 17 日在美国)

2. The peace talks between the two enemy countries began _____ _____. (1961 年 6 月 28 日在第三方国家)

3. I shall never forget the tragedy (悲剧) that happened _____ _____. (2001 年 9 月 11 日在纽约)

4. The well-known American writer died _____. (1941 年 1 月 13 日在巴黎)

Model：

> **Imitating** his father, Louis tried to cut a piece of leather with a small knife.

1. _____, John became an engineer after he finished college. (跟随他的哥哥)

2. _____, Louis decided to create a better way of reading for the blind. (自己非常想读书)

3. _____, John tried hard to find the answer to the question. (敲着脑袋)

4. _____, I set up a study program to regulate the time I spend on study and on socializing. (学着做一个对自己负责的人)

8 Translate the following sentences into English using the "main clause + when..." structure.

Models:

> 1) Louis's parents decided to send him to the school when he was nine years old.
>
> 2) Louis Braille changed the lives of blind people when he created the six-dot Braille system.

1. 记着到那儿以后给我写信。

_____

2. 把自己的恐惧告诉妈妈之后,玛丽感觉好多了。

_____

3. 在城里迷路时,我幸运地找到了一位警察。

_____

4. 当他受伤的眼睛受到感染,接着又传给那只好的眼睛时,他就成了盲人。

_____

Translation

9 Translate the following sentences into English.

1. 你可以把信息转变成(transfer... into)由点、划组成的密码来使它保密。

_____

2. 刀从她湿漉漉的手中滑落,扎伤了她脚边的小宠物(pet)。

_____

3. 选择10月1日,中华人民共和国的诞生日,作为国庆节是非常恰当的。

_____

4. 在乡下度假时,我拍摄了一些美丽的建筑物的照片,比如这所公立学校和它旁边的小教堂。

_____

5. 创造的愿望是十分重要的。如果我们只是模仿别人,那就很难发展新事物了。

_____

6. 消息在传达给军官之前就在士兵中间传开了。

_____

Grammar Review

动词时态(Verb Tenses)(2)

The Present Progressive and the Past Progressive(现在进行时和过去进行时)

现在进行时表示说话时正在进行的动作,也可表示现阶段正在进行的动作。现在进行时由助动词 be 的现在时形式(am, is, are)加-ing 分词构成。

过去进行时表示过去某一时刻正在进行的动作,或过去某一段时间内正在进行的动作。过去进行时由助动词 be 的过去时形式(was, were)加-ing 分词构成。

现在进行时(**The Present Progressive Tense**)

用　　法	例　　　　句
1. 表示说话时正在进行的动作	I'm looking for my umbrella right now. 我此刻正在找我的雨伞。 She is cooking dinner at this moment. 她此时正在做饭。
2. 表示现阶段正在进行的动作,虽然此时此刻这个动作也许并没有进行	He is studying Chinese in Beijing. 他目前在北京学习汉语。 The students are preparing for the examination. 学生们正在准备考试。
3. 表示按计划安排近期内即将发生的动作	He is leaving for Beijing tomorrow morning. 他打算明晨动身去北京。 I'm going to Hainan for the winter holiday. 我打算去海南过寒假。
4. 表示刚过去的动作	You don't believe it? I'm telling the truth. 你不相信吗? 我刚才说的都是实话。 I don't know what you are talking about. 我不明白你刚才在讲什么。

用　　法	例　　句
5. 表示现阶段经常发生的动作,常与 always, forever, constantly, continually 等连用,往往带有感情色彩(如不满、厌烦等)	I've lost my key again. I'm always losing things. 我又把钥匙给弄丢了。我总是丢东西。 He is constantly leaving things around. 他老是乱扔东西。
6. be 用于进行时态,表示一时的表现	Jenny is being a good girl today. 詹妮今天很乖。(可能平时很淘气) He's being silly by saying so. 他这样说是在犯傻。(平时不一定傻)

过去进行时(**The Past Progressive Tense**)

用　　法	例　　句
1. 表示过去某一时刻正在进行的动作	I was sleeping at 2:00 yesterday afternoon. 昨天下午两点钟的时候我正在睡觉。 I was watching TV when she came to see me. 她来看我的时候,我正在看电视。
2. 表示两个过去的动作同时进行	Susan was cooking dinner while Robert was fixing the car. 罗伯特在修车的时候苏珊正在做饭。 They were playing basketball while I was doing my homework. 他们在打篮球而我在做作业。
3. 表示一个动作发生时另一个过去动作仍在进行	Was it still raining when you came in? 你进来的时候还在下雨吗? He lost his keys when he was playing football. 他在踢足球的时候丢了钥匙。

10 Complete each of the following sentences with the correct form of the word given.

1. — Where are you?
   — I'm upstairs. I _____ (have) a bath.

2. One day, I _____ (drive) in England when I suddenly _____ (realize) I was on the wrong side of the road.

3. The river _____ (flow) very fast today — much faster than usual.

4. I _____ (live) with my grandparents when I _____ (enter) high school.

5. Hurry up! The train just _____ (come) in.

6. I _____ (make) dinner last night when the phone _____ (ring).

7. Mr. Cameron _____ (leave) China in a few weeks, so you have plenty of time to talk with him.

8. My brother _____ (play) basketball when he _____ (break) his arm.

9. He _____ (work) in a chemical factory these days.

10. I _____ (watch) TV when all the lights _____ (go) out.

11. You _____ always _____ (watch) TV. You should do something more active.

12. I don't understand why he _____ (be) so selfish. He isn't usually like that.

Practical Writing

Book Order Forms

11 The following is part of a book order form. Fill in the form with the information given below in Chinese. Some parts have been done for you.

李思嘉要在贝思得书店订购三本书,其书名和单价分别为:

1. *Getting Ahead*   ¥12.00
2. *New Interchange* (Book One)   ¥39.90
3. *International Business English*   ¥22.00

她的个人信息如下:
联系地址:中国湖南省长沙市解放路118号   邮编:410003
单位电话:86-731-6949979   家庭电话:86-731-6953478

电子邮件地址:lisijia66@ yahoo. com. cn   传真:86-(0)731-6949978

Book Order Form

Please fill in the information needed.

Name:	
Address:	
City:	
State/Province:	*Hunan*
Country:	
Zip Code:	
Home Phone:	86-731-6953478
Office Phone:	
Fax:	
E-mail:	

No.	Title (书名)	Quantity (数量)	Unit Price (单价)	Total (总价)
1		1	¥12.00	
2	*New Interchange* (*Book One*)			
3			¥22.00	
Total				

12 Select three books from the following list and fill in the book order form with your own information.

Title	Unit Price
Jane Eyre《简爱》	¥7.80
Gone with the Wind《飘》	¥11.90

Title	Unit Price
Pride and Prejudice《傲慢与偏见》	￥4.80
Tess of the D'Urbervilles《苔丝》	￥6.30
The Godfather《教父》	￥7.80
Rebecca《蝴蝶梦》	￥6.80
Little Women《小妇人》	￥8.50
A Farewell to Arms《永别了,武器》	￥3.50

Please fill in the information needed.

Name: _____		Date: _____	
Address: _____			
City: _____	State/Province: _____	Zip Code: _____	Phone: _____
E-mail Address: _____			

Books				
No.	Title	Unit	Quantity	Total
1				
2				
3				
Total				

Text B

Don't Eat the Tomatoes; They're Poisonous!

Michael Williams

The first tomatoes were found growing wild by Indians in Peru and Ecuador thousands of years ago. The Indians brought the tomato plant with them when they moved north to Central America. The Spanish soldiers, who conquered Mexico in the early 1500s took tomato plants to Spain.   5

2 The tomato soon made its way across Europe, but the English were wary of it. They thought it was pretty to look at but believed it was not meant to be eaten. English doctors warned patients that tomatoes were poisonous and would bring death to anybody who ate one.   10

3 For hundreds of years, both the English and the Americans would decorate their homes with tomato plants, but they never dared to eat the vegetable. This myth might still prevail today had it not been for a New Jersey man named Robert Johnson.

4 In 1808, Johnson returned from South America with a large   15
quantity of tomato plants. He had hoped to sell them to the American market. He gave the plants to local farmers and offered a prize for the largest tomato grown. But the tomato was still rejected in his hometown of Salem, New Jersey, and everywhere else as well. Johnson decided to take a desperate measure. He publicly an-   20
nounced he would stand on the steps of the local courthouse and eat a basket of tomatoes in public.

5 The townsfolk were shocked. Johnson's doctor warned he would foam at the mouth, then fall down and die in a few minutes.

6 Finally, the important day arrived. Two thousand people   25
surrounded the courthouse to watch a man kill himself (or so they thought). The crowd fell into a dead silence as Johnson, dressed

in a bright suit, walked up the steps of the
courthouse. When the clock struck noon,
30 he picked up a tomato and held it up. He
then talked to the crowd.

7   "Friends, I will now eat my first
tomato."

8   When he took his first bite, a
35 woman in the crowd shrieked and fainted.
After finishing the tomato, Johnson picked up another and started
eating it. Another woman in the crowd fainted.

9   Soon the basket was empty. The crowd exploded in applause. Robert Johnson became a hero. In less than five years,
40 the tomato became a major crop in America.

10   Today, over 50,000,000 bushels of tomatoes are produced
each year. Over 40,000,000 cases of tomato juice are consumed as
well as millions of bottles of catsup. The tomato might never have
become a part of the American diet had it not been for Robert
45 Johnson's desperate measure.

(424 *words*)

New Words

* tomato /təˈmɑːtəʊ/ *n.*	番茄,西红柿
◆poisonous /ˈpɔɪzənəs/ *a.*	containing poison 有毒的
◆Indian /ˈɪndɪən/ *n.*	印第安人;印度人
a.	印第安人的;印度的;印度人的
* central /ˈsentrəl/ *a.*	of, at, near or forming the center of sth. 中心的; 中央的;中部的;在中心的
* Spanish /ˈspænɪʃ/ *a.*	of Spain; of the people of Spain or their language 西班牙的;西班牙人的;西班牙语的
n.	the language of Spain 西班牙语
◆conquer /ˈkɒŋkə/ *vt.*	gain control of (a country, etc.) by force 征服
◆wary /ˈweərɪ/ *a.*	cautious; careful 谨慎的;小心的;谨防的
* pretty /ˈprɪtɪ/ *a.*	pleasant to look at; pleasing and attractive 漂亮 的,秀丽的

	ad.	fairly or moderately 相当；颇
* warn /wɔːn/	*vt.*	give (sb.) notice of sth., esp. possible danger or unpleasant consequences 警告；告诫
* patient /ˈpeɪʃənt/	*n.*	person who is receiving medical treatment, esp. in hospital 病人
	a.	忍耐的；有耐心的
* death /deθ/	*n.*	dying or being killed 死；死亡
★ decorate /ˈdekəreɪt/	*vt.*	make (sth.) (more) beautiful by adding ornaments to it 装饰
◆ myth /mɪθ/	*n.*	神话；杜撰出来(或不可能)的人(或事物)
★ prevail /prɪˈveɪl/	*vi.*	exist or happen generally; be widespread 普遍存在(或发生)；盛行；流行
* quantity /ˈkwɒntətɪ/	*n.*	number or amount, esp. a large one 量，数量；大量
* local /ˈləʊkl/	*a.*	belonging to a particular place or district 地方性的；当地的，本地的
* prize /praɪz/	*n.*	award given to winner of a competition, race, etc. 奖赏；奖金；奖品
* reject /rɪˈdʒekt/	*vt.*	refuse to accept 拒绝；拒绝接受
◆ desperate /ˈdespərət/	*a.*	绝望的；孤注一掷的，拼命的
* measure /ˈmeʒə/	*n.*	action taken to achieve a purpose 措施；办法
	vt.	量，测量；估量，衡量
* announce /əˈnaʊns/	*vt.*	make known publicly 宣布，宣告
* courthouse /ˈkɔːthaʊs/	*n.*	place where trials or other law cases are held; [AmE] county administrative building 法庭；法院；[美]县政府办公楼
◆ townsfolk /ˈtaʊnzfəʊk/	*n.*	people of a town 镇民
★ shock /ʃɒk/	*vt.*	使震惊，使惊愕
	n.	冲击；震动；震惊
◆ foam /fəʊm/	*vi.*	吐白沫；起泡沫
* minute /ˈmɪnɪt/	*n.*	one sixtieth of an hour, equal to 60 seconds; very short time 分，分钟；片刻，一会儿
* finally /ˈfaɪnəlɪ/	*ad.*	in the end; coming last 最终；最后
* silence /ˈsaɪləns/	*n.*	condition of being quiet or silent; absence of

	sound 寂静;无声;沉默
* strike /straɪk/ *vt.*	打,击,敲;(时钟等)敲响报(时)
n.	罢工
★bite /baɪt/ *v. /n.*	咬,叮
◆shriek /ʃriːk/ *vi.*	utter a shrill scream 尖叫
* faint /feɪnt/ *vi.*	lose consciousness (because of heat, shock, loss of blood, etc.)(因受热、受惊、失血等)昏厥,晕倒
* explode /ɪkˈspləʊd/ *v.*	(cause sth. to) burst with a loud noise; blow up (使)爆炸;(使)爆发
★applause /əˈplɔːz/ *n.*	approval expressed by clapping the hands and shouting 鼓掌;欢呼;喝彩
* hero /ˈhɪərəʊ/ *n.*	person who is admired by many for his noble qualities or his bravery; chief male character in a story, poem, play, etc.英雄;男主角;男主人公
◆bushel /ˈbʊʃəl/ *n.*	蒲式耳(谷物、水果、蔬菜等的容量单位,1 蒲式耳在英国等于 36.368 升,在美国等于 35.238 升)
* produce /prəˈdjuːs/ *vt.*	create (sth.) by making, manufacturing, growing, etc.; cause to occur; create; bear or yield 制造;生产;出产;引起;产生;生育
* case /keɪs/ *n.*	container of any kind for holding things 箱;盒;容器
★juice /dʒuːs/ *n.*	liquid obtained from fruit, vegetables, meat, etc.; drink made from this(水果、蔬菜、肉的)汁;果汁;果汁饮料
★consume /kənˈsjuːm/ *vt.*	use up 消耗,花费,耗尽
* million /ˈmɪljən/ *n.*	1,000,000; one thousand thousands 百万
◆catsup /ˈkætsəp/ *n.*	调味番茄酱
◆diet /ˈdaɪət/ *n.*	the kind of food that sb. eats each day; selection of food for changing one's weight, improving one's health, etc.日常饮食,日常食物;(有助于减肥等的)特种饮食,规定饮食

生词量	总词数	生词率	B级词(＊)	A级词(★)	纲外词(◆)
43	424	10%	24	7	12

Phrases & Expressions

make one's way	go forward; slowly become successful 前进,向前进;取得成功
as well	in addition; also, too 也,又,还
in public	openly 当众;公开地
walk up	走上
hold up	raise; lift 举起;抬起

Proper Names

Michael Williams /ˈmaɪkəl ˈwɪljəmz/	迈克尔·威廉斯
Peru /pəˈruː/	秘鲁(南美洲西部国家)
Ecuador /ˈekwədɔː(r)/	厄瓜多尔(南美洲西北部国家)
Central America	中美洲
Mexico /ˈmeksɪkəu/	墨西哥(拉丁美洲国家)
Spain /speɪn/	西班牙(欧洲西南部国家)
Europe /ˈjuərəp/	欧洲
New Jersey /njuːˈdʒɜːzɪ/	新泽西州(美国东部一州)
Robert Johnson /ˈrɒbət ˈdʒɒnsən/	罗伯特·约翰逊
Salem /ˈseɪləm/	塞勒姆(美国新泽西州城镇)

Notes on the Text

1. The first tomatoes were found growing wild by Indians in Peru and Ecuador thousands of years ago. 最早的番茄是几千年前印第安人在秘鲁和厄瓜多尔发现的野生番茄。

2. The Spanish soldiers, who conquered Mexico in the early 1500s took tomato plants to Spain. 在 16 世纪初期征服了墨西哥的西班牙士兵又把这种植物带到了西班牙。who conquered Mexico in the early 1500s 是一个非限定性定语从句,修饰 the Spanish soldiers。

3. They thought it was pretty to look at but believed it was not meant to be eaten. 他们

认为番茄看上去很漂亮,但却不是供人食用的。

4. This myth might still prevail today had it not been for a New Jersey man named Robert Johnson. 如果不是有一个名叫罗伯特·约翰逊的新泽西人,这一荒诞说法可能至今还在流行。这是一个虚拟语气的句子,had it not been 相当于 if it hadn't been。课文中类似的结构还有 The tomato might never have become a part of the American diet had it not been for Robert Johnson's desperate measure. 如果不是罗伯特·约翰逊那孤注一掷的措施,也许番茄永远也不会成为美国人饮食的一部分。(Para. 9)

5. Two thousand people surrounded the courthouse to watch a man kill himself (or so they thought). 两千人围在县政府办公楼周围来看一个人自杀(或者说他们认为他是自杀)。or so they thought = or they thought so。

6. The crowd fell into a dead silence as Johnson, dressed in a bright suit, walked up the steps of the courthouse. 当约翰逊身穿一套色彩鲜亮的西装走上县政府办公楼的台阶时,人群突然陷入一片死一般的寂静。

7. Over 40,000,000 cases of tomato juice are consumed as well as millions of bottles of catsup. 人们消费的番茄汁超过了 4 000 万箱,番茄酱几百万瓶。

Exercises

13 Answer the following questions.

1. Who found the first tomatoes and where did they find them?
2. What did the English think of the tomato?
3. How were tomatoes used before they were eaten by people?
4. What measure did Johnson first take to make Americans accept the tomato?
5. Why did Johnson decide to eat a basket of tomatoes in public?
6. Were people interested in Johnson's announcement? How do you know?
7. What happened when he took his first bite?
8. What did the crowd do when they saw the basket emptied?
9. How are tomatoes used today?

14 Fill in the blanks with the words given below. Change the forms where necessary.

poisonous	warn	decorate	quantity	local	reject
measure	shock	strike	announce	faint	consume

1. The children were much more careful after I _____ them of the danger of fire.

2. When the singer _____ his decision to leave the band(乐队), his followers were all surprised.

3. My doctor has asked me to eat a specific(特定的) _____ of fruit and vegetables every day.

4. That's the trouble with those big cars — they _____ too much fuel(燃料).

5. Mrs. Green, the oldest person in town, is dearly loved by the _____ people.

6. Unlike (不像) the other rooms in your house, the children's room can be _____ with more colors.

7. Why did you _____ the job offer? You will never find a better job.

8. The news surprised Ann so much that she _____.

9. I can't tell which mushroom(蘑菇) is _____ just by smelling it.

10. "He hit me, so I _____ him back," the boy answered.

11. What new _____ are being taken to prevent(防止) this kind of thing from happening again?

12. Those people in the house were _____ by the sudden exploding sound outside.

15 Fill in the blanks with the expressions given below. Change the forms where necessary.

make one's way	as well	fall into
walk up	hold up	in public

1. Jim always tries to embarrass(使难堪) me _____.

2. After the long walk I'm feeling tired, and thirsty _____.

3. Led by a guide, the climbers _____ to the mountain top.

4. As the hillside(山坡) was covered with snow, we had to _____ carefully.

5. The visitors _____ silence when they saw the poor village.

6. The teacher _____ the picture so that the students at the back could see it.

Text C

Ups and Downs

Jeanne K. Grieser

Y ou fly a thousand miles to visit Grandma; you fly to see the *ocean*(海洋). Can you *imagine*(想象) how long a trip like that would take if airplanes weren't around? On the highway, a person can drive about 65 miles in an hour; but an airplane can fly up
5 to 500 miles an hour! That's quite a difference! August 19 has been set aside to *observe*(庆祝) *aviation*(航空). Let's find out why.

2   On April 16, 1867, Wilbur Wright was born in Indiana. Four years later on August 19, 1871, Wilbur's brother Orville was born in Ohio. Wilbur and Orville were close to each other. In fact, their
10 voices even sounded alike!

3   Wilbur and Orville didn't have any special training in science or engineering, but they enjoyed taking *mechanical*(机械的) things apart to see how they worked. They studied birds and *insects*(昆虫) in flight. From their *observations*(观察) of how birds fly, they built a
15 huge *kite*(风筝) and began to test its flight. After the successful test, Wilbur and Orville built a larger, man-carrying *glider*(滑翔机). They wanted to experiment in private so they took their glider to an isolated *beach*(海滩) near Kitty Hawk, North Carolina. Since they were far from home, they set up a tent to live in.

20 4   Wilbur and Orville made yearly trips to Kitty Hawk to test their gliders. In 1902, they had made more than 700 successful glider flights. Now they needed to find an engine that would be light and powerful enough to get a plane off the ground.

5 Since the automobile *manufacturers*(汽车制造商) wouldn't build the engine, the brothers talked to Charles Taylor. Together they designed and built a 12 to 16 horsepower engine and *propeller*(螺旋桨). In one year, the project was finished.   25

6 On December 17, 1903, the Wright   30
brothers' powered flight was a success at
Kitty Hawk. Orville was the pilot, and he stayed in the air for 12 seconds. The first flying machine was called "The Wright Flyer." The wings looked like a box kite. The pilot had to lie face down over the wing in a type of *cradle*(摇篮). He moved his body from   35
side to side to change the plane's direction.

7 The brothers took turns and made three more flights that day. Then a gust of wind blew the flying machine over and completely destroyed it. Wilbur and Orville returned home and built another glider that was stronger and had a more powerful motor. On   40
September 20, 1904, Wilbur flew the Flyer II in the first circular flight over a *pasture*(牧场) in Ohio. The flight lasted 1 minute and 36 seconds.

8 Since that time, airplanes have become larger, faster, and safer. Now over 800 million people travel by airplane each year. To   45
recognize(表彰) the Wright brothers' *contribution*(贡献) to aviation, National Aviation Day is observed on August 19. After reading this article, do you know why this date was chosen?

(474 *words*)

Comprehension of the Text

16 Choose the best answer for each of the following multiple choice questions.

1. From the passage, we know that an airplane can fly as fast as _____.
   A) 65 miles/hour   B) 130 miles/hour
   C) 360 miles/hour   D) 500 miles/hour
2. What do we know about Wilbur and Orville from the passage?

A) They were born in the same house.

B) They spent a lot of time together.

C) They looked like each other very much.

D) They had the same manner of speaking.

3. What was the first thing they built to fly?

A) A huge kite.   B) A glider.

C) The Wright Flyer.   D) The Flyer Ⅱ.

4. They chose the beach near Kitty Hawk to test their gliders because

_____.

A) it was far away from their home

B) there was strong wind on the beach

C) they wanted to keep their experiment secret

D) they could set up a tent on the beach

5. In which year did the Wright brothers make their first powered flight?

A) 1902.   B) 1903.

C) 1904.   D) 1905.

6. When flying "The Wright Flyer", the pilot must _____.

A) stay in the air for at least 12 seconds

B) move his body from side to side in the cradle

C) lie face down over the wing in a type of cradle

D) change the plane's direction all the time

7. Flyer II was better than "The Wright Flyer" in all of the following aspects(方面)

except _____.

A) it had a stronger body

B) its engine was more powerful

C) it could stay longer in the air

D) it could change directions more easily

8. August 19 is set aside to observe aviation because it was the day when

_____.

A) Wilbur Wright was born

B) Orville Wright was born

C) the Wright brothers tested their first glider

D) the Wright brothers made their first powered flight

Basic Reading Skills

Reading for the Main Idea: Telling the Difference Between the General Idea and Details

识别段落主题句的一个方法是识别哪个句子是概括性的,哪些句子表达的是细节。比如在下面的几个句子中:

Barbier developed an alphabet code used by army soldiers.

The code was used to deliver messages to the soldiers at night.

It was made up of dots and dashes. It kept the messages secret if the enemy saw them, but the code was too complicated for the blind.

Louis thought the code was slow and the dashes took up too much space.

Only one or two sentences fit on a page.

第一句是概括性的,其余的句子是有关该 code 的种种细节。

再比如 A 篇课文第八段:

Over the next three years, Louis worked to simplify the code. On a vacation at home, Louis, age 15, picked up a blunt awl. Aha! An idea came to him. He made the alphabet using only six dots. Different dots were raised for different letters. Later, he made a system for numbers and music.

第一句是概括性的,其余的句子是 Louis 如何 worked to simplify the code 的细节。

17 Read the following paragraph from Text B and identify which sentence gives a general idea and which sentences give details.

The tomato soon made its way across Europe, but the English were wary of it. They thought it was pretty to look at but believed it was not meant to be eaten. English doctors warned patients that tomatoes were poisonous and would bring death to anybody who ate one.

UNIT

3

Highlights

Preview

This is the third unit of Book One. In the Listening and Speaking section, you will learn the importance of saying "thank you." In the Reading and Writing section, the writer of Text A expresses his gratitude to his mother in a letter on Mother's Day, thanking her for all she has done for him; Text B tells the story of a man who managed to raise his seven children alone after his wife died; Text C tells how a couple of opposite personalities can still live a happy life as long as they have love.

Listening & Speaking

Why to Say "Thank You."

1 You are going to listen to a short talk on the importance of saying "thank you." Listen to the talk carefully and fill in the blanks with the missing words.

The two most important words in the English language are "thank you." Unfortunately, they are seldom heard. When was _____ you said "thank you"? Saying "thank you" shows how you value(尊重) the other person and the social relationship _____. To say "thank you" is to express gratitude(感激). Gratitude is the _____. Getting into the habit of saying "thank you" must begin right away to _____. Take today to email, call or visit your friends, family, business associates(同事), or spouses(配偶), _____ who haven't received a thank-you note from you recently. Tell them _____!

2 Now tell your classmates about your last experience saying "thank you" — when, where and how you said it.

Expressing Gratitude

3

1) *Before you listen to the first conversation, read the following words and expressions which may be new to you.*

mobile phone	手机
How are you doing?	[口] = How are you?
What's up?	什么事?
Don't mention it.	不用谢。
deserve	值得

Listen to the conversation twice and fill in the blanks with the missing words.

Li Ming: (*The mobile phone rings.*) Hello?

Wang Ying: Li Ming? Wang Ying. How are you doing?

Li Ming: Oh, hi, Wang Ying. _____?

Wang Ying: I'm just calling to thank you again for the gift _____
_____ at the party yesterday.

Li Ming: Oh, don't mention it.

Wang Ying: It _____.

Li Ming: You deserve it. I hope _____.

Wang Ying: Oh, very much.

Li Ming: I wish you _____ in the world again.

Wang Ying: Thank you, I know you do. That's _____.

Li Ming: Well, let me know if I can be _____.

Wang Ying: OK. And thanks again. Bye.

Li Ming: See you.

Now listen to the conversation again and answer the following questions.

1. What did Wang Ying thank Li Ming for?
2. When was the party?
3. What did Wang Ying think of the gift?
4. Why did Wang Ying make the phone call?
5. What do you think of Li Ming?

2) *Before you listen to the second conversation*, *read the following words and expressions which may be new to you*.

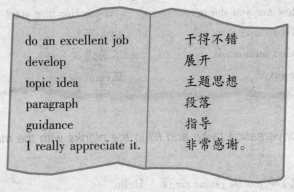

do an excellent job	干得不错
develop	展开
topic idea	主题思想
paragraph	段落
guidance	指导
I really appreciate it.	非常感谢。

Listen to the conversation twice and fill in the blanks with the missing words.

Instructor: Say, Li Ming, you did an excellent job _____

_____.

Li Ming: Oh, really?

Instructor: Yes. I really like the way _____.

Li Ming: Oh, thanks. _____ without your help.

I really appreciate it.

Instructor: It was my pleasure. _____.

Li Ming: Don't worry. _____!

Now listen to the conversation again and answer the following questions.

1. Whom did Li Ming meet?
2. What was Li Ming praised for?
3. What did Li Ming thank his instructor for?
4. What did the instructor encourage Li Ming to do?
5. What did Li Ming say?

4 As you know, there are many different situations that call for an expression of thanks. The following list contains the most common situations. Make a dialogue with one of your classmates, in which you express gratitude.

1. for a gift;	A. Thank you.
2. for a favor(好事);	B. Thank you very much.
3. for an offer of help;	C. That was very nice of you.
4. for a compliment (恭维) and a	D. I appreciate it / your help.
wish of success;	E. Thanks, anyway.
5. when asked about health;	
6. for an invitation(邀请);	A. You're welcome.
7. when leaving a party or social	B. (I'm) Glad I could help.
gathering;	C. It was nothing.
8. for services, such as being waited	D. My pleasure.
on in a store or restaurant.	E. Anytime.

Listening Practice

5 Listen to people speaking and decide what they are talking about.

1. A) Teaching.   B) Driving.
 C) Learning.   D) Swimming.

2. A) A shirt.   B) A skirt.
 C) A coat.   D) A tie.

3. A) An exam.   B) A gift.
 C) A party.   D) A trip.

4. A) A mobile phone.   B) A birthday party.
 C) A watch.   D) A new bicycle.

5. A) A job.   B) A letter.
 C) A company.   D) A report.

6 Listen to five questions and choose the appropriate answers.

1. A) Surely I will.   B) Yes, please do.
    C) It was my pleasure.   D) Thanks, but I have to go.

2. A) Yes, we haven't been for ages.   B) There you go.
    C) Here we are.   D) Go ahead.

3. A) This coming weekend.   B) I really appreciate it.
    C) The usual crowd.   D) What if it rains?

4. A) I had enough.   B) It's lunch time.
    C) It's a coffee break.   D) Oh, I'd love to, thanks.

5. A) Who's that?   B) What's that?
    C) Who's who?   D) Which's which?

7 Listen to five short dialogues and choose the appropriate answers.

1. A) To read.   B) To move.
    C) To travel.   D) To relax(放松).

2. A) A dinner.   B) A movie.
    C) A party.   D) A trip.

3. A) By bus.   B) By taxi.
    C) By train.   D) By plane.

4. A) The party has just begun.   B) The party is unusual.
    C) The party is over.   D) The party is late.

5. A) In a supermarket.   B) In a restaurant.
    C) At the airport.   D) At the bank.

8 Listen to the following short talk and fill in the blanks with the missing words. The talk is given twice.

I was on my way out of the bank one day when a kind elderly lady held the door open for me. I responded with _____ and said, "Thank You!" "_____?" she asked. Afraid that I may have offended(冒犯) her, I meekly (和蔼地) responded, "Thank you." "That's what I thought I heard," she replied, adding she had heard those words so seldom _____.

On a similar recent occasion, I was getting change from a cashier(收银员) at the grocery(杂货) store and thanked her for _____. I thought she was going to cry. No one was behind me _____, so I asked her if everything was _____. She told me that it had been a very rough(糟糕的) day and that my expression of appreciation struck a cord(心弦) _____. She asked me if I knew why so many people seemed so inconsiderate(不体谅人的) these days. We simply don't think enough about _____ of expressing gratitude. I personally believe that if we were more thoughtful, we all would be _____.

(180 *words*)

9 Listen to the talk again and then answer the following questions orally.

1. What did the elderly lady do at the door of the bank?
2. What was she surprised to hear?
3. Why was the cashier so moved at the grocery store?
4. What did the cashier complain about?
5. What seems to be the problem in today's society?

10 Have a free discussion on the topic below.

We all would be more thankful if we were more thoughtful.

Reading & Writing

Text A

Starter

Our parents have not only given us our lives, but also done everything possible to make sure that we are well fed, well clothed and well educated while we grow up. No language in this world can fully express our gratitude for what our parents have done for us. Tell three unforgettable things that your parents did for you.

Three unforgettable things that your parents did for you:
1.
2.
3.

Text

Thanks, Mom, for All You Have Done

Bob Burns

We tend to get caught up in everyday business and concerns and forget some of the things that are most important. Too few of us stop and take the time to say "thank you" to our mothers.

2   With a letter to my mother on the occasion of Mother's Day, I'm going to take a minute to reflect. Feel free to use any of this in   5 greeting your own mother on Sunday, May 10. Happy Mother's Day to all.

Dear Mom,

3 This letter, I know, is long past due. I know you'll forgive the tardiness, you always do.

4 There are so many reasons to say thank you, it's hard to begin. I'll always remember you were there when you were needed.

5 When I was a child, as happens with young boys, there were cuts and bumps and scrapes that always felt better when tended by you.

6 You kept me on the straight path, one I think I still walk.

7 There was nothing quite so humbling as standing outside my elementary school classroom and seeing you come walking down the hall. You were working at the school and I often managed to get sent outside class for something. Your chiding was gentle, but right to the point.

8 I also remember that even after I grew bigger than you, you weren't afraid to remind me who was in charge. For that I thank you.

9 You did all the things that mothers do — the laundry, the cooking and cleaning — all without complaint or objection. But you were never too busy to help with a problem, or just give a hand.

10 You let me learn the basics in the kitchen, and during the time I was on my own it kept me from going hungry.

11 You taught by example and for that I am grateful. I can see how much easier it is with my own daughter to be the best model I can be. You did that for me.

12 Your children are grown now, your grandchildren, almost. You can look back with pride now and know you can rest. As mothers are judged, you stand with the best.

13 God bless you, Mom.

(358 *words*)

New Words

◆mom /mɒm/ *n.*　　　　　　　　[US infml] mother 妈;妈妈

*tend /tend/ *vi.*　　　　　　　　[后接不定式]往往会;易于

　　　　　　vt.　　　　　　　　look after; take care of 照料;护理

*everyday /'evrɪdeɪ/ *a.*　　　　used or happening daily 每天的,每天发生的;日常的

*business /'bɪznɪs/ *n.*　　　　　matter; affair; buying and selling; commerce; trade; firm; shop 事务;事;买卖;商业;生意;商行;商店

*concern /kən's3:n/ *n.*　　　　关心;忧虑,挂念;关切的事;感兴趣的事;[常作 ~ s]事物

★occasion /ə'keɪʒn/ *n.*　　　　particular time (at which an event takes place); suitable or right time (for sth.); opportunity(事情发生的)时刻,时候;场合;时机;机会

*reflect /rɪ'flekt/ *v.*　　　　　深思;反省;反射(光、热、声等);反映

*greet /gri:t/ *vt.*　　　　　　　问候,迎接;招待

★due /dju:/ *a.*　　　　　　　　到期的;应到的;应付的

*forgive /fə'gɪv/ *vt.*　　　　　excuse (sth.); no longer be angry about (sth.); excuse or pardon (sb. who has done sth. wrong) 原谅;饶恕;宽恕

◆tardiness /'tɑ:dɪnɪs/ *n.*　　　缓慢;迟;拖延

*reason /ri:zn/ *n.*　　　　　　cause 原因,理由

◆bump /bʌmp/ *n.*　　　　　　swelling on the body, esp. one caused by a blow 肿块

◆scrape /skreɪp/ *n.*　　　　　injury or mark made by scraping 擦伤;擦痕

*path /pɑ:θ/ *n.*　　　　　　　small narrow way through or across a place 小路;小径

★humble /'hʌmbl/ *a.*　　　　(of a person, his position in society, etc.) low in rank; unimportant; not having a high opinion of oneself; not proud 地位低下的;卑贱的;谦逊的;谦虚的

　　　　　　vt.　　　　　　　make (sb./sth./oneself) humble; lower the rank or self-importance of 使谦恭;羞辱;降低…的地

位;使卑贱

★elementary /ˌelɪˈmentrɪ/ *a.*　of or in the beginning stages (of a course of study); dealing with the simplest facts (of a subject); basic 初级的;基础的;基本的

＊hall /hɔːl/ *n.*　会堂,礼堂,大厅;门厅;[美](大楼)的过道,走廊

◆chiding /ˈtʃaɪdɪŋ/ *n.*　责备;责骂

＊gentle /ˈdʒentl/ *a.*　mild; kind; not rough, violent or severe 温和的;慈祥的;温柔的;和婉的

＊remind /rɪˈmaɪnd/ *vt.*　cause to remember 提醒;使想起

＊charge /tʃɑːdʒ/ *n.*　掌管;照管;价钱,费用;控告,指控;电荷,充电

＊laundry /ˈlɔːndrɪ/ *n.*　dirty clothes, sheets, etc. waiting to be washed; washed (and dried) clothes; place where clothes, sheets, etc. are washed 待洗衣物;已洗好的衣物;洗衣店,洗衣房

★complaint /kəmˈpleɪnt/ *n.*　complaining; reason for complaining; statement of complaining 抱怨,诉苦;怨言;抱怨的缘由;申诉,投诉;控诉;控告

★objection /əbˈdʒekʃn/ *n.*　statement of dislike or disapproval 反对;异议

＊basic /ˈbeɪsɪk/ *a.*　forming a base or starting point; fundamental 基础的;基本的

　　　　　　　n.　[~ s] simplest but most important parts (of an activity, etc.)基本原理;基本因素;基本的东西

＊grateful /ˈgreɪtfl/ *a.*　being, or showing oneself to be, full of thanks; thankful 感激的;感谢的

＊model /ˈmɒdl/ *n.*　模范,榜样;模型;样式;模特儿

◆grandchild /ˈgræntʃaɪld/ *n.*　daughter or son of one's child(外)孙女;孙子;外孙

＊pride /praɪd/ *n.*　feeling of pleasure or satisfaction which one gets from doing sth. well, from owning sth. excellent or widely admired, etc.得意,自豪

＊judge /dʒʌdʒ/ *vt.*　判断,估计;评价;审判;裁决

　　　　　　　n.　法官,审判员;仲裁人;裁判员;鉴定人

◆bless /bles/ *vt.*　grant health, happiness and success to 赐福,保佑

生词量	总词数	生词率	B 级词(*)	A 级词(★)	纲外词(◆)
32	358	8.9%	19	6	7

Phrases & Expressions

be/get caught up in	be/get absorbed or involved in 被卷入;陷入
on the occasion of	at the time of (a certain event) 在…之际
feel free (to do sth.)	[infml] (used to tell sb. that they can do sth.) 随意; 请便;欢迎
to the point	(in a way that is) relevant and appropriate 切题的 (地);切中的(地);中肯的(地)
in charge (of sb./sth.)	in a position of control or command (over sb./sth.) 主 管;负责;指挥
give/lend a (helping) hand	give help 给予帮助,助一臂之力
on one's own	alone; with no help from others 独自一人;独力地;单 独地
look back	think about one's past 回顾,回忆

Proper Names

Bob Burns /bɒb ˈbɜːnz/	鲍勃·伯恩斯
Mother's Day	(美国、加拿大等的)母亲节(5 月的第二个星期日)

Notes on the Text

1. Thanks, Mom, for All You Have Done 谢谢你,妈妈,为了你所做的一切。标题中的 You Have Done 是修饰 all 的定语从句,前面省略了关系代词 that。

2. We tend to get caught up in everyday business and concerns and forget some of the things that are most important. 我们往往被日常事务缠住而忘记一些最为重要的事情。get caught up 是被动语态,get 作联系动词,相当于 be。相同的例子还有第 7 段中的 get sent outside class。that are the most important 是定语从句,修饰 the things。

3. Feel free to use any of this in greeting your own mother on Sunday, May 10. 在 5 月 10 日星期天问候你的母亲时请随意用这封信中的任何句子。本句是祈使句,用动词原形,表示劝告、建议、命令等语气。

4. This letter, I know, is long past due. 我知道,这封信早就该写了。本句中 I

know 是插入成分。due 表示到期的,past due 过期了。

5. When I was a child, as happens with young boys, there were cuts and bumps and scrapes that always felt better when tended by you. 我小的时候,如同所有的小男孩一样,身上总有些割破的伤口、碰撞造成的肿块和擦伤,但有你照料,我总会感到好一些。本句中 as happens with young boys 是一个由关系代词 as 引导的非限制性定语从句,修饰整个句子。that always felt better when (they were) tended by you 是定语从句,felt 也作联系动词,意思是"感觉、觉得"。when (they were) tended by you 时间状语从句中省略了主语和 be 动词。在英语中,如果状语从句的主语和主句的主句一致,且后面跟有 be 动词,则可以省略从句中相同的主语和后面的 be 动词。

6. You kept me on the straight path, one I think I still walk. 你使我一直走在正路上,我认为这仍是我在走的路。one(that) I think I still walk 是 path 的同位语,起补充说明的作用。修饰 one 的定语从句省略了关系代词 that。I think 是插入语,表达作者的观点。

7. There was nothing quite so humbling as... 最为丢脸的事莫过于…… 在英语中,否定词 + so + 形容词/副词 + as 表示"最…"的意思。

8. ... seeing you come walking down the hall. ……看到你沿着走廊走过来。在英语中,感官动词 see, feel, watch 等跟不带 to 的不定式作宾语补足语。

9. ... and I often managed to get sent outside class for something. ……而我竟然常常因为犯事被赶出教室。此句中的 manage 意为"竟然搞得、竟做出"。又如:I don't know how I managed to arrive so late. 我也不知道我怎么竟然会到得这么晚。

10. ... you weren't afraid to remind me... ……你也不怕提醒我…… afraid 用于结构 be afraid of 和 be afraid to do,前者表示怕做某事,而后者侧重表示因为担心后果严重而不敢也不愿做某事。

11. For that I thank you. 为此我感谢你。本句倒装,句型 thank sb. for sth. 中的介词结构 for that 置于句首是为了与上文更紧密。同样的例子还有 11 段中的 for that I am grateful.

12. But you were never too busy to help with a problem, or just give a hand. 然而即使再忙你也总能帮着我做题,或助我一臂之力。句型 too... to 表示"太…以至于不能"。

13. ... during the time I was on my own it kept me from going hungry. ……这使我在独自一人时不致挨饿。句型 keep sb. from doing 使某人不做某事。go 作联系动词,表示过程。

14. You taught by example... 你以身作则,身教重于言教。

15. I can see how much easier it is with my own daughter to be the best model I can be. 我看到我多么容易就成了自己女儿的最佳楷模。how much easier it is... 是感叹句,it 是形式主语,真正的主语是后面的 to be the best model (that) I can be 不定式短语。形容词的比较级 easier 之前用 much 修饰,表示容易得多。

Exercises

Reading Aloud

1 Read the following paragraphs until you have learned them by heart.

There are so many reasons to say thank you, it's hard to begin. I'll always remember you were there when you were needed.

When I was a child, as happens with young boys, there were cuts and bumps and scrapes that always felt better when tended by you.

You kept me on the straight path, one I think I still walk.

There was nothing quite so humbling as standing outside my elementary school classroom and seeing you come walking down the hall. You were working at the school and I often managed to get sent outside class for something. Your chiding was gentle, but right to the point.

Understanding the Text

2 Answer the following questions.

1. What important things do many of us forget?
2. What does the writer ask his mother to forgive?
3. What happened to the writer as a boy?
4. What was the most humbling thing to happen to the writer in his childhood (童年)?
5. What does the writer think of his mother's chiding?
6. What did the writer's mother remind him of even after he grew bigger than her?
7. What did the writer's mother do for her children at home?
8. What does the writer benefit from (得益于) learning the basics in the kitchen?
9. How did the writer's mother teach him?
10. How does the writer judge his mother?

3 Topics for Discussion.

1. What do you think of your mother? Does she stand with the best?
2. What is your mother's way of chiding? Is it right to the point?

Reading Analysis

4 Read Text A again and complete the following table.

Part	Topic	Paragraph	Main Idea
I	Reasons for writing the letter	1-2	We should never forget to say "_____" to our mothers no matter _____.
II	My letter	3-4	The writer expresses the ever-present gratitude (感激) that he has for _____.
		5-7	The writer recalls how his mother took great care of him when _____.
		8-11	The writer lists the things that his mother did for him when _____.
		12-13	The writer praises his mother and expresses _____.

Now retell the main idea of the passage by using the information in the table you have completed.

Vocabulary

5 Fill in the blanks with the words given below. Change the forms where necessary.

tend	everyday	business	reflect	greet	forgive
reason	path	remind	grateful	pride	judge

1. I need some time alone to _____ on what has just happened.

2. He has a _____ to hate her because she is responsible for him losing his job.

3. It was a difficult _____ getting everything ready in time.

4. When I was a child, my parents always told me that hard work is the only _____ to success.

5. Thank you for _____ me that someone is waiting for me in the office.

6. People like this film because it is about their _____ life.

7. I _____ you this time, but please don't let it happen again.

8. She _____ to spend too much time playing computer games.

9. I am _____ to my parents for all that they have done for me.

10. I can't _____ whether he was right or wrong, so I have to ask someone else.

11. I was filled with _____ after I achieved great success through hard work.

12. He _____ me in the street with a friendly wave of the hand.

6 Fill in the blanks with the expressions given below. Change the forms where necessary.

be (get) caught up in	on the occasion of	feel free to do sth.
walk down	to the point	be in charge
give a hand	be on one's own	look back
go hungry		

1. He didn't speak for long, but everything he said was _____.

2. With no one taking care of him, the boy had to _____ after his father's death.

3. He is welcome everywhere, for he is ready to _____ to anyone in need.

4. When I _____, I still remember my high-school days which were among the happiest in my life.

5. This was given to me as a present _____ my graduation from high school.

6. Many people in the world have more than enough to eat, but many others often _____.

7. Last night the man drank too much and _____ the street shooting（射
   击）his gun into the air.

8. In my family my parents are like our friends, so we _____ to ask them
   any questions.

9. The monitor（班长）_____ when the teacher leaves the classroom.

10. Bob knew that one day he would _____ the war, like all his friends.

Structure

7 Rewrite the following sentences according to the model, using the "There be
no... + so + a./ad. + as" structure.

Model:

> The most humbling thing was standing outside my elementary school class-
> room and see you come walking down the hall.
>
> →There was **nothing** quite **so** humbling **as** standing outside my elementary
> school classroom and seeing you come walking down the hall.

1. The most terrible thing is arriving five minutes late for a plane that has just taken off.

   _____

2. My mother worked very hard to send me to school, so I believe that for everyone the
   greatest person in the world is their mother.

   _____

3. Sometimes the most difficult thing is to decide what to do next.

   _____

4. The tallest building in this city is the hotel we are staying in now.

   _____

Translation

8 Translate the following sentences into English.

1. 回首往事,他对父母充满了感激之情。

   _____

2. 母亲从来不忘记提醒我她是家里的主管,而且每当需要她时,她总会助我一臂
   之力。

   _____

3. 这个小男孩独自一人时往往会挨饿,因为他不会做饭。

_____

4. 在母亲的生日之际,我请母亲原谅我因常常被日常事务缠住而忘记对她说一声
"谢谢你。"

_____

5. 学生都很喜欢这位年轻老师,因为她不仅言传身教,而且说话温和而中肯。

_____

Grammar Review

动词时态(Verb Tenses) (3)

The Simple Future and the Future in the Past(一般将来时和过去将来时)

一般将来时表示将要发生的动作或情况,一般由助动词 shall /will + 动词原
形构成,助动词 shall 用于主语是第一人称时,will 用于主语是第二、第三人称时。
美国英语则不管什么人称,一律用 will。

过去将来时表示过去将要发生的动作或情况,一般由助动词 should/would +
动词原形构成。

一般将来时(**The Simple Future**)

用　　法	例　　句
1. 表示将要发生的动作或 情况	I shall/will attend the meeting tomorrow. 我明天要参加会议。 The workers will build a school here next year. 工人们明年将在这儿盖一所学校。
2. 表示一种倾向或对未来 的预见	You'll feel better if you take this medicine. 你吃了这种药以后就会感觉好一些的。 Do you think it will rain tomorrow? 你认为明天会下雨吗?

其他表示将来的方法

用 法	例 句
1. 用 be going to + 动词原形,表示打算、计划、最近或将来要做的某事	I'm going to see a movie tonight. 今晚我打算看电影。 How long are you going to stay here? 你打算在这儿待多久?
2. be about to + 动词原形,表示即将、正要,强调马上要做的事	Please get everything ready. The experiment is about to start. 请做好一切准备,实验就要开始了。 Don't worry. I am about to make a close examination of you. 别担心,我马上就给你做一次仔细的检查。

过去将来时(**The Future in the Past**)

用 法	例 句
1. 表示从过去的某个时间看将要发生的事	I said on Thursday I should see my friend the next day. 我星期四说过我将于第二天拜访我的朋友。 I thought he would not attend that evening party. 我认为他不会去参加那个晚会。
2. 用 would + 动词原形表示过去的习惯动作	When we were children, we would go swimming every summer. 我们小的时候,每年夏天都去游泳。 Whenever he had time, he would go fishing at the lake. 过去他只要有空,就会去湖边钓鱼。
3. 表示意愿或许诺等,如用于否定句,则表示不会、不可能	We knew he would never permit such a thing. 我们知道他绝不会允许这类事发生。 He promised he would send a postcard from Egypt. 他答应一定从埃及寄一张明信片来。

其他表示过去将来时间的方法

用　　法	例　　　　句
1. 用 was/were going to + 动词原形表示过去某时间内计划、打算的动作	They <u>were going to have</u> a meeting to discuss the matter. 他们打算开个会讨论那件事。 Last Sunday we <u>were going to go</u> for a picnic but it rained. 上周日我们本打算去野餐的,可下雨了。
2. 用 was/were about to + 动词原形,表示过去某时间内即将、正要做的事	I <u>was about to go out</u> when a friend of mine dropped in. 我刚要出去,这时我的一个朋友来了。 We <u>were about to set off</u> when it began to rain. 我们正准备出发时开始下雨了。

9 Complete each of the following sentences with the correct form of the word given.

A. Fill in the blanks with the right tenses of the verbs given in braclets.

1. Johnson then said to the crowd, "Friends, I _____ (eat) now _____ my first tomato."

2. Tom bought a plane ticket for New York. He told Anna, "I _____ (go) to New York next week." Anna said. "That's a good idea. I _____ (go) with you."

3. I _____ (study) French next year. I've already paid for the lessons.

4. "Do you want some money? Ask Sarah. Perhaps, she _____ (give) you $5."

5. — _____ (call) I _____ you on Friday?
   — Ok, I _____ (give) you my phone number.

6. Our computer was broken and we hoped the new one _____ (arrive) soon.

7. During the winter I decided that I _____ (grow) tomatoes when summer came.

8. The performance _____ (begin) when someone started crying.

B. *The following is an excerpt* (摘录) *from* Rainbow (《虹》), *one of D. H. Lawrence's most outstanding novels. Fill in the blanks with the right tenses of the verbs given in brackets.*

She dreamed how she (1)＿＿＿＿＿＿＿＿ (make) the little, ugly children love her. She (2)＿＿＿＿＿＿＿＿ (be) so personal (有人情味的). Teachers (3)＿＿＿＿＿＿＿＿ (be) always so hard and impersonal. There (4)＿＿＿＿＿＿＿＿ (be) no vivid relationship. She (5)＿＿＿＿＿＿＿＿ (make) everything personal and vivid, she (6)＿＿＿＿＿＿＿＿ (give) herself, she (7)＿＿＿＿＿＿＿＿ (give), give, give all her great stores of wealth to her children, she (8)＿＿＿＿＿＿＿＿ (make) them so happy, and they (9)＿＿＿＿＿＿＿＿ (prefer) her to any other teacher on the face of the earth.

Practical Writing

Application Forms

10 The following is part of an application form. Fill in the form with the information given below in Chinese. Some parts have been done for you.

刘佳妮，女，上海人，生于 1982 年 11 月 20 日。现为上海电机技术高等专科学校 (Shanghai College of Electricity and Machinery Technology) 财务管理专业 (Financial Management) 学生。应聘上海某跨国公司客户服务部兼职秘书。

联系地址(永久地址)：上海浦东崂山西路 1090 号 1102 室　　　邮政编码：200122
家庭电话：86-21-58697078　　　　寝室电话：86-21-58733018
手机：13912239398　　　　E-mail：jianiliu@163.com

Application Form

Job Title: Part-time Secretary — Consumer Services Department

Please complete this form and return it to the Human Resources Department by **March 20th, 2004.**

PERSONAL INFORMATION			
Name:			
Date of Birth:		Age: 22	Place of Birth:
Nationality at Birth: *Chinese*		Nationality:	*Chinese*
Address:			
Zip Code:			
Tel(home):		Tel(dorm):	
E-mail:		Tel(mobile):	

EDUCATION			
Dates		College or Polytechnic(理工专科学校)	Major (专业)
From	To		
Sept., 2001	*present* (迄今)		

QUALIFICATIONS(资历)

Give details of your membership in professional organizations, examinations taken and results achieved:

Qualified Accounting Computerization License   *October, 2002*

Qualified Assistant Public Accountant License   *September, 2003*

Give details of any other knowledge or experience that you consider relevant to your application:

Good command of both spoken and written English.

Skilled in computer software such as Windows XP, Office 2000, Internet, etc.

11 Fill in the following application form for a course(课程)with your own information.

APPLICATION FORM

COURSE DESCRIPTION
Course Level: Intermediate (中级)
Course Name: Communication Technology (信息技术)

PERSONAL INFORMATION
Name:
ID Card No. (身份证号): Sex:
Date of Birth: Age:
Tel(Home): Tel(Office): Fax:
Mobile Phone: E-mail Address:
Address:

EDUCATION

Year	Name of School/Institution	Level

DECLARATION

(a) I DECLARE that all information given in this Application Form is true and correct to the best of my knowledge.

(b) I understand that this data will become part of my student record and used for all purposes relating to my studies.

Signature: _____ Date: _____

Text B

His Life's Work

Wyverne Flatt

W hen his wife died, the baby was two. They had six other children — three boys and three girls, ranging in age from 4 to 16.

2　A few days after he became a widower, the man's parents and his wife's parents came to visit.　　　　　　　　　　　　　　5

3　"We've been talking," they said, "about how to make this work. There's no way you can take care of all these children and work to make a living. So, we've arranged for each child to be placed with a different uncle and aunt. We're making sure that all of your children will be living right here in the neighborhood, so you　　10 can see them anytime... "

4　"You have no idea how much I appreciate your thoughtfulness," the man said. "But I want you to know," he smiled and continued, "if the children should interfere with my work, or if we should need any help, we'll let you know. "　　　　　　　　15

5　Over the next few weeks the man worked with his children, assigning them chores and giving them responsibilities. The two older girls, aged 12 and 10, began to cook and do the laundry and household chores. The two older boys, 16 and 14, helped their father with farming.　　　　　　　　　　　　　　　20

6　But then another blow came. The man developed arthritis. His hands swelled, and he was unable to use his farm tools. The children shouldered their loads well, but the man could see that he would not be able to continue in this way. He sold his farming equipment, moved the family to a small town and opened a small　　25 business.

7　The family was welcomed into the new neighborhood. The man's business flourished. He derived pleasure from seeing people

and serving them. Word of his pleasant personality and excellent customer service began to spread. People came from far and wide to do business with him. And the children helped both at home and at work. Their

father's pleasure in his work brought satisfaction to them, and he drew pleasure from their successes.

8   The children grew up and got married. Five of the seven went off to college, most after they were married. Each one paid his or her own way. The children's collegiate successes were a source of pride to the father. He had stopped at the sixth grade.

9   Then came grandchildren. No one enjoyed grandchildren more than this man. As they became toddlers, he invited them to his workplace and his small home. They brought each other great joy.

10   Finally, the youngest daughter — the baby who had been two years old at her mother's death — got married.

11   And the man, his life's work completed, died.

12   This man's work had been the lonely but joyful task of raising his family. This man was my father. I was the 16-year-old, the oldest of seven.

(460 *words*)

New Words

★range /reɪndʒ/ *vi.*	vary or extend between specified limits(在一定范围内)变动,变化;显示不等
◆widower /ˈwɪdəʊə/ *n.*	man whose wife has died 鳏夫
★living /ˈlɪvɪŋ/ *n.*	means of keeping alive or of living in a certain style 生计;生活(方式)
a.	alive 活的,活着的
★arrange /əˈreɪndʒ/ *v.*	prepare; make plans; put into some kind of order 准备,安排;筹划;整理;排列

★neighborhood /ˈneɪbəhʊd/ n.   (people living in a) district; area near a parti-
                                 cular place 地区,地段;四邻,街坊;邻近地区

★appreciate /əˈpriːʃɪeɪt/ vt.   be grateful for (sth.); understand and enjoy;
                                 value highly 为…表示感激;理解并欣赏;重视

* thoughtful /ˈθɔːtfl/ a.   showing thought for the needs of others; consid-
                                 erate; thinking deeply; absorbed in thought 关
                                 心别人的,体贴的;考虑周到的;思考的,沉
                                 思的

* interfere /ˌɪntəˈfɪə/ vi.   妨碍,干扰;干涉,介入

* assign /əˈsaɪn/ vt.   give as a share of work to be done; name
                                 (sb.) for a task or position; appoint 分配(工
                                 作);布置(作业);指派;选派

◆chore /tʃɔː/ n.   small, dull piece of work, esp. one which one
                                 would like to avoid(常指单调乏味的) 日常零
                                 星活儿;[~ s]家庭杂务

★responsibility /rɪsˌpɒnsəˈbɪlətɪ/ n.   thing for which one is responsible 职务,任务

★household /ˈhaʊshəʊld/ n.   all the people, esp. a whole family, who live
                                 in one house 一家人;家庭,户

                    a.   connected with looking after a house and the
                                 people in it; domestic 家庭的;家用的

★blow /bləʊ/ n.   hard hit or stroke; shock; unfortunate happen-
                                 ing 重击;捶打;打击;灾祸

◆arthritis /ɑːˈθraɪtɪs/ n.   关节炎

◆swell /swel/ (swelled, swollen   become bigger because of liquid, inflamma-
/ˈswəʊlən/ or swelled) vi.   tion, etc. inside 膨胀;肿胀

★unable /ʌnˈeɪbl/ a.   not able (to do sth.)不能的,不会的

★shoulder /ˈʃəʊldə/ n.   肩;肩膀

                    vt.   put (sth.) on one's shoulder(s) ; accept or take
                                 on (a job, duty, etc.)肩起,挑起;担负,承担
                                 (工作、责任等)

* load /ləʊd/ n.   thing that is being carried or to be carried 负
                                 荷,负担

                    vt.   put (a load) in or on 装,装载;把(货物或人)
                                 装上

★equipment /ɪˈkwɪpmənt/ *n.*　things needed for a particular purpose 装备；设备；器材

◆flourish /ˈflʌrɪʃ/ *vi.*　grow or develop well; prosper 茂盛；兴旺，繁荣

★derive /dɪˈraɪv/ *vt.*　obtain; get 得到；获取

★serve /sɜːv/ *v.*　为…服务；为…服役；为…尽职责；服务；服役；供职

◆personality /ˌpɜːsəˈnælətɪ/ *n.*　characteristics and qualities of a person seen as a whole 人格；个性

★excellent /ˈeksələnt/ *a.*　very good; of very high quality 极好的；优秀的；卓越的

★customer /ˈkʌstəmə/ *n.*　person who buys sth. from a shop, etc. 顾客；主顾

★service /ˈsɜːvɪs/ *n.*　服务

★satisfaction /ˌsætɪsˈfækʃn/ *n.*　state of being satisfied 满意；满足

◆collegiate /kəˈliːdʒɪət/ *a.*　of or relating to a college or its students 大学（生）的；学院的

★source /sɔːs/ *n.*　place where a river begins; place / thing / person from which sth. starts or comes 源头；来源；根源；出处；消息来源；提供消息者

◆sixth /sɪksθ/ *a.*　第六的

　　　　　　n.　第六；六分之一；月的第六日

◆toddler /ˈtɒdlə/ *n.*　child who has only recently learnt to walk 刚学会走路的孩子

★invite /ɪnˈvaɪt/ *vt.*　ask (sb.) in a friendly way to go somewhere or do sth. 邀请

★joy /dʒɔɪ/ *n.*　feeling of great happiness 欢乐；喜悦

★lonely /ˈləʊnlɪ/ *a.*　unhappy and needing a friend, etc. when alone; far from other people or places 孤独的，寂寞的；荒凉的，人迹稀少的

◆joyful /ˈdʒɔɪfl/ *a.*　causing great joy; filled with joy 使人高兴的；高兴的，快乐的

★task /tɑːsk/ *n.*　piece of work, usu. one that is hard or unpleasant but must be done 任务，工作

生词量	总词数	生词率	B 级词(*)	A 级词(★)	纲外词(◆)
36	460	7.8%	20	6	10

Phrases & Expressions

There's no way (that)…	[infml] It is impossible (that)… …没有可能。
make a living	earn one's livelihood 谋生;挣钱
arrange for	make (sth.) happen; ensure that (sth.) happens 为…作准备,安排
make sure	do sth. to ensure that sth. happens 确保
interfere with	distract or hinder 干扰;妨碍
far and wide	everywhere; in all directions 到处,各处;四面八方
do business with	和…做生意
pay one's way	support oneself with money one has earned 支付自己应承担的费用

Proper Name

Wyverne Flatt /ˈwaɪvən ˈflæt/	怀维恩·弗拉特

Notes on the Text

1. … ranging in age from 4 to 16. ……年龄从 4 岁到 16 岁不等。本句中,现在分词短语作后置定语,起解释说明作用。

2. We've been talking about how to make this work. 我们一直在讨论这事怎么办才好。"疑问词 + 动词不定式"结构具有名词的性质,在本句中作介词 about 的宾语。动词 make 后跟不带 to 的不定式作宾语补足语。

3. … we've arranged for each child to be placed with a different uncle and aunt. 我们已在安排把每个孩子安置在一个叔叔、阿姨家。

4. … if the children should interfere with my work, or if we should need any help, we'll let you know. 万一孩子们妨碍了我的工作,万一我们需要任何帮助,我会告诉你们的。本句中,条件从句中用了虚拟式 should + 动词原形,表示发生这种情况的可能性很小。

5. Over the next few weeks the man worked with his children, assigning them chores

and giving them responsibilities. 在以后的几个星期里,那人跟他的孩子们一起干活。他给他们分配杂活儿,让他们承担职责。本句中,现在分词短语 assigning them chores and giving them responsibilities 作方式状语。

6. ... aged 12 and 10 ... aged 12 and 10 作后置定语,起解释说明作用。

7. He derived pleasure from seeing people and serving them. 他从接待人们并为他们服务中得到了快乐。本句中,动名词短语 seeing people and serving them 作介词 from 的宾语。

8. Word of his pleasant personality and excellent customer service began to spread. 关于他为人和蔼可亲,对顾客服务细致周到的口碑开始传了出去。本句中,word 作不可数名词,表示消息、传闻。

9. No one enjoyed grandchildren more than this man. 没有哪个爷爷比这个男人更喜欢孙子辈的小孩了。在英语中,否定词 + 形容词/副词比较级(+ than)表示"再也没有…(比得过)"的意思。

10. Finally, the youngest daughter — the baby who had been two years old at her mother's death — got married. 两个破折号之间的短语 the baby who had been two years old at her mother's death 是同位语,解释了上文的 the youngest daughter。

11. And the man, his life's work completed, died. 本句中,his life's work completed 是一个独立结构,表示 after his life's work was completed。独立结构从属于主句,但带有自己的主语,通常在句中起状语从句的作用。

Exercises

12 Answer the following questions.

1. How many children did the man have and how old were they when his wife died?
2. How did the man's parents and his wife's parents arrange the matter of the children for the man?
3. How did the man reply to them?
4. How did the man make a living with his children?
5. What happened to the man then?
6. What did the man do since he was unable to farm?
7. Why did the man's business flourish?
8. How did the man feel about his children's collegiate successes?

9. When did the man die?

10. Who was the man?

13 Fill in the blanks with the words given below. Change the forms where necessary.

range	work(*v.*)	appreciate	continue	assign	unable
equipment	excellent	service	source	invite	task

1. They _____ to talk even though I told them to keep quiet.

2. Prices in this shop _____ from 5 dollars to 100 dollars to meet the needs of different customers.

3. As colleges and universities receive more and more students many young people are _____ to get jobs after finishing their studies.

4. Not having seen her for more than 20 years, he _____ her to dinner last night.

5. Without the right _____, the worker couldn't repair the car.

6. He won the first prize for his _____ work, and both his parents and friends were very happy.

7. The food is good at the restaurant, but the _____ is poor: sometimes you have to wait a long time.

8. In our factory, the hardest work is often _____ to the strongest workers.

9. For many old people their grandchildren's success is the only _____ of their pride and pleasure.

10. How did you manage to accomplish the _____ in two hours?

11. I didn't sleep very well last night so my brain doesn't seem to be _____ today.

12. We deeply _____ your kindness and thoughtfulness.

14 Fill in the blanks with the expressions given below. Change the forms where necessary.

There is no way...	make a living	arrange for	make sure
interfere with	far and wide	do business with	pay one's way

1. It's still very hard for some farmers to _____.

2. My husband was very busy at his company, so he had to _____ a car to pick me up at the station.

3. He's going to have an important examination next Monday morning, so he doesn't let anything _____ his study.

4. Known to people _____ for his book about the history of time, Stephen Hawking is a star scientist in more ways than one.

5. Many people came to _____ him because of the low prices and good services he offered.

6. Every night father _____ that all the lights are turned off before he goes to bed.

7. The young man was the son of a poor farmer so he worked to _____ through college.

8. She married again after her husband's death because _____ she could send all her children to school.

Text C

The Odd Couple （奇特的一对夫妻）

Lisa Giacomo

I have always wondered how my parents were attracted to each other. Their personalities, temperaments, and attitudes toward money are all *opposite* （相反的）. The saying that "opposites attract" certainly holds true for them.

5　　*2* Their personalities are quite different. My mother is *outgoing* （爽直的） and friendly. She enjoys people because, to her, they are the most interesting form of life. When she meets new people, she greets them as if they were old friends, whether they are first-time *clients* （顾客） at her *beauty shop* （美容院） or acquaintances

10　（熟人） of someone she already likes. She loves to socialize. Making *conversation* （交谈） with any *type* （类型） of personality comes easily to her — it's a natural *quality* （品质）.

3 My father, on the other hand, is *conservative* (保守的) and shy. Socializing is not easy for him. 15 His shyness may give the *impression* (印象) that he's cold, but once he gets to know you, his warmth and *sincerity* (真诚) *emerge* (显现出来).

4 When it comes to controlling 20 one's *temper* (脾气), my mother clearly *outdoes* (胜过) my father. She will *tolerate* (容忍) a lot before she gets angry and prefers to *rationalize* (自我辩解) rather than lose her temper. However, my father's temper is like a short *fuse* (导火线) on a stick of *dynamite* (炸药). He will *flare up* (勃然大怒) 25 *immediately* (立刻) when something is said or done wrongly. Also very *stubborn* (固执的), he always *insists* (坚持) that he is right. Our dinners often turn into *debates* (争论), with the *issue* (问题) usually being money.

5 My mother is not a *bargain* (便宜货) shopper. She does not 30 cut out *coupons* (赠券) or *compare* (比较) products or prices; she is impatient — if she likes something, she buys it. My father, *therefore* (因此), has always done our food shopping. He compares products and prices, looks for *sales* (廉价出售) and bargains, and buys only what he needs. He has also always taken care of our 35 household *finances* (财政) and is the bookkeeper and *accountant* (会计) of the family. My father says that my mother has *champagne* (香槟酒) *tastes* (品味) with a *beer* (啤酒) pocketbook, and she says that he's cheap, but there is a happy *compromise* (妥协) — she spends and he saves. 40

6 "It must be love," I say about this odd couple. They may be very different, but they are also very *compatible* (和谐的). Learning from each other *ensures* (确保) the success of their *partnership* (夫妻关系).

(355 *words*) 45

Comprehension of the Text

15 Choose the best answer for each of the following multiple choice questions.

1. The writer's parents are different in all the following aspects（方面）except
   _____.

    A) personalities　　　　　　　　B) attitudes toward each other

    C) temperaments　　　　　　　　D) attitudes toward money

2. The writer's mother enjoys socializing with _____.

    A) old friends

    B) first-time clients

    C) acquaintances of someone she already likes

    D) anyone she meets

3. We know from the text that the writer's father is not a _____ person.

    A) conservative　　　　　　　　B) shy

    C) cold　　　　　　　　　　　　D) warm

4. Which of the following is true about the mother's temper?

    A) She never gets angry.

    B) She always insists that she is right.

    C) She thinks it better to rationalize.

    D) She has to tolerate her husband although she doesn't like it.

5. The sentence "my father's temper is like a short fuse on a stick of dynamite" means
   that the writer's father _____.

    A) gets angry easily

    B) is angry for a short while

    C) gets angry only when something is said or done wrongly

    D) gets angry about the issue of money

6. The reason why the writer's father does food shopping is that _____.

    A) he is the bookkeeper and accountant of the family

    B) he compares products and prices

    C) he knows what they need

    D) he buys everything he likes

7. The sentence "my father says that my mother has champagne tastes with a beer pocketbook" means that the writer's father thinks _____.

A) she likes champagne more than beer

B) she likes beer more than champagne

C) she buys the things that are too expensive for them

D) she spends more money than he saves

8. It can be learned from the text that the writer thinks that ＿＿＿＿＿＿.

A) it is important for a couple to make compromises

B) his parents are an odd couple because they love each other but never feel attracted to each other

C) couples of different personalities are less compatible than couple of the same
personalities

D) "opposites attract" certainly holds true for everyone

Basic Reading Skills

Understanding Signal Words (1)

作者写文章时按一定的思路或顺序展开,领悟作者的思路有助于我们理解作者的文章。英语中有一类词叫作 Signal Words(信号词),这些词能帮助我们理解文章思路的发展,了解句子与句子、段落与段落之间的关系。

表示"递进"关系的 Signal Words 有 and, also, first, second, next, besides, fur-thermore, moreover, in addition (to), again, likewise(同样地;也)和 what is more 等。

比如:

I'll always remember you were there when you were needed.

…

I **also** remember that even after I grew bigger than you, you weren't afraid to re-mind me who was in charge.

前一句表示作者记得某桩事,后一句用 also 表示还记得另一桩事。

16 Read the following paragraph from Text C. Identify the signal word that the writer uses to add something more about the father's temper.

However, my father's temper is like a short fuse on a stick of dynamite. He will flare up immediately when something is said or done wrongly. Also very stubborn, he always insists that he is right. Our dinners often turn into debates, with the issue usual-ly being money.

UNIT 4

Highlights

Preview

In this unit, you are going to learn about running and walking and what benefits you can get from each exercise. In the Listening and Speaking section, you will learn how to express personal interests and state likes and dislikes. In the Reading and Writing section, two basic skills needed for running are discussed in Text A; Text B describes what exercise can do for us; and, while most people believe that running is a better exercise than walking, Text C offers a quite different view.

Listening & Speaking

Expressing Personal Interests

1 You are going to listen to two students talking about their personal interests. Listen carefully and fill in the blanks with the missing words.

Wang Ying: You know what I like? I like music. It can make me _____. It can make me _____. It can also make me _____ ____. Wherever I go, I'll take music _____. I listen to it while walking, riding on the bus, even while reading somewhere. Music is _____ in the world.

Li Ming: Oh, I love outdoor(户外) sports. I _____ in the suburbs(郊外) on weekends. I often run alone. I'm _____ nature while running. I can _____. I can _____. And I can _____. I am crazy(热衷的) about nature. Outdoor sports make me _____ nature.

2 Now you can tell your classmates about your personal interests using the structures given below.

> 1. I like…
> 2. I love…
> 3. I enjoy DOING…
> 4. I'm fond of…
> 5. I'm crazy about…
> 6. I'm into…

Expressing Likes and Dislikes

3

1) *Before you listen to the first conversation, read the following words and expressions which may be new to you.*

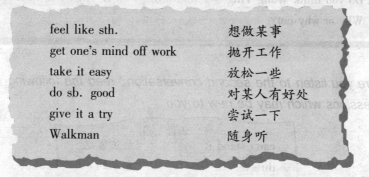

feel like sth.	想做某事
get one's mind off work	抛开工作
take it easy	放松一些
do sb. good	对某人有好处
give it a try	尝试一下
Walkman	随身听

Listen to the conversation twice and fill in the blanks with the missing words.

Li Ming:	I feel like a really good run this weekend. It'll get my mind off work. How _____?
Wang Ying:	Well, I think I'll take it easy. I'll _____ to get some information.
Li Ming:	Come on. You need physical exercise. You need fresh air. It'll _____.
Wang Ying:	I _____ running. It's boring.
Li Ming:	Oh yeah? But I _____ when I run in the suburbs. I'm sure you will.
Wang Ying:	I don't think I'll _____.
Li Ming:	Oh, yes, you can take your Walkman with you. _____ while you are running.
Wang Ying:	Good idea. I'll _____.
Li Ming:	Good. See you then.
Wang Ying:	See you.

Now listen to the conversation again and answer the following questions.

> 1. What is Li Ming doing this weekend?
> 2. What is Wang Ying planning to do this weekend?
> 3. What does Li Ming ask Wang Ying to do?
> 4. What does Wang Ying think of running?
> 5. Do you think Wang Ying is going to run with Li Ming this weekend?
>   Why or why not?

2) *Before you listen to the second conversation, read the following words and expressions which may be new to you.*

| can't stand it | 无法容忍 |
| direct | 直率的 |

Listen to the conversation twice and fill in the blanks with the missing words.

Li Ming: What do you think of the movie?

Wang Ying: That _____! But I can't stand it when _____ during a movie.

Li Ming: I feel the same way. You know, I can't stand it when _____.

Wang Ying: You're talking _____, right?

Li Ming: Well.

Wang Ying: It's OK. _____ when people are direct.

Li Ming: You want _____?

Wang Ying: Yes, please.

Now listen to the conversation again and answer the following questions.

1. Where have Wang Ying and Li Ming been?
2. How was the movie?
3. What does Wang Ying dislike?
4. What does Li Ming dislike?
5. Who do you think is direct?

4 Make a dialogue in class, asking for personal interests and expressing your likes and dislikes. Try to use the structures given below.

1. Do you take much interest in...?
2. Are you interested in...?

1. I like it when people....
2. It makes me happy when a friend/someone....
3. I can't stand it when people....
4. It really bothers(烦扰) me when someone/a person....

Listening Practice

5 Listen to people speaking and decide what they are talking about.

1. A) A job.   B) A vacation(假期).
   C) A newspaper.   D) A movie.
2. A) Music.   B) Weather.
   C) Food.   D) Flowers.
3. A) Classmates.   B) Homework.
   C) Housework.   D) Parents.
4. A) Making a plan.   B) Going to the movies.
   C) Doing homework.   D) Watching TV.

5. A) Music.   B) Love.
   C) People.   D) Friends.

6 Listen to five questions and choose the appropriate answers.

1. A) Here we are.   B) There you go.
   C) Oh, where are you going?   D) Oh, where have you been?
2. A) Yes, I know.   B) No problem.
   C) Yes, that's fine.   D) As soon as possible.
3. A) They like stories.   B) They hate money.
   C) They are students.   D) They are friendly(友好).
4. A) Huh? Why not?   B) Well, it's the wrong size.
   C) Are you sure? Let me see.   D) That's O. K. Don't worry about it.
5. A) Well, do something.   B) No, I don't mind.
   C) Of course I do.   D) Oh, yes, it is.

7 Listen to five short dialogues and choose the appropriate answers.

1. A) The man is leaving.   B) The man is arriving late.
   C) The woman is coming soon.   D) The woman is late for the party.
2. A) Being rich.   B) Being direct.
   C) Being friendly.   D) Being wonderful.
3. A) Shopping.   B) Watching TV.
   C) Having a party.   D) Moving around.
4. A) Few do.   B) Some do.
   C) Many of them do.   D) All of them do.
5. A) She exercises.   B) She watches TV.
   C) She listens to music.   D) She makes phone calls.

8 Listen to the following short talk and fill in the blanks with the missing
    words. The talk is given twice.

On a windy day, it may seem to you that the wind is blowing _____.
Then you hear the weather report, and it says, "Winds of 10 to 15 miles per hour." It's

easy for us to _____ about the speed of the wind. But the exact (精确的) wind speed _____ to many people, so there are scientific (科学的) ways of measuring the wind.

The first tool for measuring the speed of the wind _____ in 1667 by an Englishman named Robert Hooke. The tool is called an anemometer (风速机). There are _____ of anemometers, but the most common type now used has _____ aluminum (铝) cups on a spindle (杆). They are free to turn _____, and the harder the wind blows, the faster the cups _____. By counting the number of turns made by the cups in a given time, _____ may be measured.

(155 *words*)

9 Listen to the talk again and then answer the following questions orally.

> 1. How do we usually know about wind speed?
> 2. What is important to many people?
> 3. Where was the first tool for measuring the speed of the wind invented?
> 4. What is the tool made up of?
> 5. How can we measure the speed of the wind?

10 Think about your living environment — its places and people — and tell your classmates about your likes and dislikes using the language you learned in Exercises 2 & 4.

Reading & Writing

Text A

For many of us, running like the wind sounds like a dream that may never come true. How fast can you run? Talk to your classmates and find out who is the best runner. Ask the best runner to tell you how he or she manages to do it.

The name of the best runner is _____.

He/She can run 100 meters in _____ seconds.

He/She can run so fast because _____.

Now read the following passage and find out what advice the author gives us in order to run fast.

Text

Run Like the Wind

Kristen Hoel

Not many kids know this, but a person can actually learn how to run faster. It's true. Even the slowest person on the playground can become a fast runner by learning and practicing running techniques. Here's how!

The Basic Skills

2   There are two basic skills needed for running: speed and endurance.

3   Speed is the measure of how fast a person can run.

4   Endurance is the measure of how far a person can run.

5

10   *5* Most sports require athletes to be skilled at both speed and endurance. Football players, for example, use speed when making a play and endurance to **15** be able to run up and down the field for an entire game. Both speed and endurance can be learned.

The Secrets of Speed

20   *6* To run fast, an athlete must use a special running technique known as sprinting. Here's how it works:

     7 First, think of the foot as four separate parts: 1. heel, 2. arch, 3. pad, 4. toes.

     8 When sprinting, the athlete uses only two parts, the pad **25** and the toes. The athlete strikes the ground with the pad of the foot, then pushes off with the toes. (The heels never touch the ground!) By using only these two parts, the steps are quicker, and the speed is increased.

     9 Another part of sprinting technique is the use of the arms. It **30** may sound silly, but the arms actually do help us run faster.

     10 A young athlete can increase his speed by practicing the sprinting technique in his backyard or playground. It may take some time to perfect, but as with any other athletic skill, the more often one practices, the better one becomes!

35   ### The Keys to Endurance

     11 The second running skill is endurance. An athlete needs good endurance to be able to run for a long time without getting tired. This is a very important skill in most sports.

     12 The key to endurance running is to conserve energy. This **40** means using as little energy as needed to move oneself forward. As with sprinting, there is a technique runners use to help them become better endurance runners. This technique is known as the gravity pull technique. Here's how it works:

13 First, the athlete leans forward just enough so that he has to keep stepping forward to keep from falling. Second, he swings 45 his arms long, to keep his balance. Finally — and here's the tricky part — he stays in that position for the entire course of the run!

14 It takes quite a bit of practice to become skilled at this technique. However, by running this way, the athlete uses the pull of gravity to move forward, rather than having to use his own ener- 50 gy to push himself forward. Isn't that clever?

Conclusion

15 Athletes in nearly every sport use both speed and endur-ance. The nice thing is that anybody can become a better athlete by studying and practicing these running techniques. The funny 55 thing is that hardly anyone knows this!

(483 *words*)

New Words

* kid /kɪd/ *n.*	child or young person 小孩;年轻人
* actually /'æktʃʊəlɪ/ *ad.*	really; in fact 实际上
* playground /'pleɪgraʊnd/ *n.*	area of land where children play, e.g. as part of a school(学校的)操场,运动场
◆runner /'rʌnə/ *n.*	person or animal that runs; one taking part in a race 奔跑的人(或动物);赛跑的人(或动物)
* technique /tek'niːk/ *n.*	method of doing or performing sth. 技术,技能;技巧;手段,方法
* speed /spiːd/ *n.*	rate at which sb./sth. moves; quickness of movements 速度;迅速,快
◆endurance /ɪn'djʊərəns/ *n.*	state or power of enduring 忍耐力;耐力
* measure /'meʒə/ *vt.*	find the size, length, volume, etc. of (sth.) by comparing it with a standard unit 量,测量
n.	(量得的)尺寸,大小,分量;量度,测量
* require /rɪ'kwaɪə/ *vt.*	need; demand (sth.) as obligatory; stipulate 需要;要求;规定
★athlete /'æθliːt/ *n.*	person who trains to compete in physical exercises and sports 运动员

* skilled /skɪld/ *a.*	having skill; skilful 有技能的;熟练的
* entire /ɪnˈtaɪə/ *a.*	with no part left out; whole; complete 全部的,整个的;完全的
* special /ˈspeʃl/ *a.*	of a particular or certain type; not common, usual or general; designed or arranged for a particular purpose 特殊的;特别的;专门的
◆sprint /sprɪnt/ *v. /n.*	(短距离的)全速奔跑;冲刺
* separate /ˈseprət/ *a.*	different; not together; divided 不同的;分开的;分隔的
/ˈsepəreɪt/ *v.*	divide; (cause to) come apart (使)分开;(使)分隔
* heel /hiːl/ *n.*	back part of the human foot 脚后跟
◆arch /ɑːtʃ/ *n.*	足弓;拱;拱门;拱形结构
◆pad /pæd/ *n.*	足垫;垫;衬垫;拍纸簿
* toe /təu/ *n.*	each of the five divisions of the front part of the human foot 脚趾
* touch /tʌtʃ/ *v.*	be or come together with (sth.) so that there is no space between; press or strike lightly, esp. with the hand 触,接触;触摸;轻碰
n.	触,碰;触摸;触觉
* increase /ɪnˈkriːs/ *v.*	become or make (sth.) greater in number, quantity, size, etc. 增加;增大;增长;增强
/ˈɪnkriːs/ *n.*	增加;增大;增长;增强
* yard /jɑːd/ *n.*	院子;天井;庭院;码(英美长度单位,1 码 = 3 英尺,合 0.9144 米)
◆backyard /ˈbækˈjɑːd/ *n.*	后院
* perfect /ˈpɜːfɪkt/ *a.*	not having any mistakes, faults, etc.; ideal; complete 完美的,完善的;理想的;完全的
/pəˈfekt/ *vt.*	make perfect or complete 使完美;使完全;完成
◆athletic /æθˈletɪk/ *a.*	运动的,体育的;运动员的
★conserve /kənˈsɜːv/ *vt.*	prevent (sth.) from being changed, lost or destroyed 保护;保藏;保存
* energy /ˈenədʒɪ/ *n.*	精力;干劲;活力;能;能量;能源
* forward /ˈfɔːwəd/ *ad.*	towards the front 向前

◆gravity /'grævətɪ/ *n.*　　　　　　万有引力;地心引力;重力

★lean /li:n/ *vi.*　　　　　　　　　be in a sloping position; bend 倾斜;弯曲;屈身

★swing /swɪŋ/ (swung /swʌŋ/) *v.*　(使)摆动,(使)摇动

　　　　　　　　　　　n.　　　　　摆动,摇摆;秋千

★balance /'bæləns/ *n.*　　　　　　平衡,均衡;天平;秤

　　　　　　　　　　vt.　　　　　使平衡;(用天平)称;权衡

◆tricky /'trɪkɪ/ *a.*　　　　　　　difficult to answer or deal with 难以回答的;难对付的;棘手的

* position /pə'zɪʃn/ *n.*　　　　　　particular way of standing, sitting, etc.; place where sb. /sth. is; person's rank or place; person's job or responsibility 姿势,姿态;位置;地位;职位

★conclusion /kən'klu:ʒən/ *n.*　　　opinion, decision or judgement arrived at after some thought 结论

* funny /'fʌnɪ/ *a.*　　　　　　　causing amusement, laughter, etc.; strange 滑稽的,可笑的;奇怪的

* anyone /'enɪwʌn/ *pron.*　　　　　any person 任何人

生词量	总词数	生词率	B 级词(*)	A 级词(★)	纲外词(◆)
37	483	7.7%	22	6	9

Phrases & Expressions

for example　　　　　　　as an example 例如

up and down　　　　　　　来来回回,往返地;沿…来来回回

be known as　　　　　　　be regarded or called as 被认为是;被叫作,被称作

keep one's balance　　　　keep steady; remain upright 保持身体平衡

quite a bit　　　　　　　a fairly large amount, or to a fairly large degree 相当数量;相当程度

rather than　　　　　　　instead of 不是…(而是)

keep from　　　　　　　stop or prevent oneself from (doing sth.); hold oneself back from 阻止,防止;克制,抑制

Proper Name

Kristen Hoel /ˈkrɪstən ˈhəʊəl/   克里斯坦·赫尔

Notes on the Text

1. Even the slowest person on the playground can become a fast runner by learning and practicing running techniques. 即使运动场上跑得最慢的人也可以通过学习和练习跑的技术成为一个跑得快的人。此句中由 by 引导的-ing 分词短语结构作状语表示方式。课文中多处使用这种结构。如第八段：中 By using only these two parts，the steps are quicker, and the speed is increased. 第十段中：A young athlete can increase his speed by practicing sprinting technique in his backyard or playground. 以及最后一段中：The nice thing is that anybody can become a better athlete by studying and practicing these running techniques.

2. Football players, for example, use speed when making a play and endurance to be able to run up and down the field for an entire game. 例如,足球运动员在做动作时要用速度,而要在整场比赛中能在球场上来回奔跑则需要耐力。此句中 when making a play 实际上是一个省略了主语和连系动词的状语从句,即应为 when they are making a play,表示时间。使用此种结构,从句中被省略的主语就是主句的主语。课文中相似的例子还有第八段：When sprinting, the athlete uses only two parts, the pad and the toes.

3. It may sound silly, but the arms actually do help us run faster. 这可能听上去很愚蠢,但双臂实际上的确能帮助我们跑得更快。sound 在该句中用作连系动词,意为"听起来、似乎"。句中 do 表示强调,意为"的确、确实"。

4. It may take some time to perfect, but as with any other athletic skill, the more often one practices, the better one becomes! 要达到技术娴熟的水平可能要花费一些时间,但如同任何运动技术一样,练习越经常,技术越熟练! the more… the more 相当于汉语中的"越… 越…",表示两个过程按比例同时增减。这种句型的前一个the more… 结构是从句,后 一个 the more… 结构是主句。

5. The key to endurance running is to conserve energy. This means using as little energy as needed to move oneself forward. 耐力跑的要诀是保存能量。这意思是说用所需的最小能量使自己向前移动。后句中第一个 as 为副词,第二个 as 为连接词,连接一个省略了 it is 的句 子,即：This means using as little energy as it is needed to move oneself forward.

6. First, the athlete leans forward just enough so that he has to keep stepping forward to

keep from falling. 首先,运动员前倾的幅度不要太大,只要使他不停地向前跨步使自己不致摔倒即可。

7. However, by running this way, the athlete uses the pull of gravity to move forward, rather than having to use his own energy to push himself forward. 然而,用这种方式跑,运动员就可以运用重力的引力向前跑,而无须非凭借自身的体力不可。

8. The nice thing is that anybody can become a better athlete by studying and practicing these running techniques. The funny thing is that hardly anyone knows this! 令人高兴的是,任何人都可以通过学习和练习这些跑的技术成为一名更好的运动员。奇怪的是,几乎没有人知道这一点!

Exercises

Reading Aloud

1 Read the following paragraphs until you have learned them by heart.

The second running skill is endurance. An athlete needs good endurance to be able to run for a long time without getting tired. This is a very important skill in most sports.

The key to endurance running is to conserve energy. This means using as little energy as needed to move oneself forward. As with sprinting, there is a technique runners use to help them become better endurance runners. This technique is known as the gravity pull technique. Here's how it works:

First, the athlete leans forward just enough so that he has to keep stepping forward to keep from falling. Second, he swings his arms long, to keep his balance. Finally — and here's the tricky part — he stays in that position for the entire course of the run!

It takes quite a bit of practice to become skilled at this technique. However, by running this way, the athlete uses the pull of gravity to move forward, rather than having to use his own energy to push himself forward. Isn't that clever?

Understanding the Text

2 Answer the following questions.

1. What are the two basic skills needed for running?
2. What is speed? And what is endurance?

3. How do athletes, such as football players, use speed and endurance in sports?

4. Which parts of the foot do runners use when employing the sprinting technique? What is the effect(效果,作用)of it?

5. Does sprinting technique only involve(包含)the right use of one's foot?

6. How can athletes perfect their sprinting skill?

7. Why is good endurance important in running?

8. What is the key to endurance running?

9. What is the gravity pull technique? How does it work?

10. What is the nice thing and the funny thing about the two running techniques?

3 Topics for Discussion.

1. Do you like running? Why or why not?

2. Running, especially distance running, is a test of one's endurance. Is endurance also important in doing other things? Discuss the importance of endurance in your work and study.

Reading Analysis

4 Read Text A again and complete the following table.

Part	Topic	Paragraph(s)	Main Idea
I	Introduction	1	All people can run faster if _____.
II	Two basic skills	_____	_____ are the two basic skills that athletes need to succeed.
III	_____	6-10	Using the sprinting technique helps athletes _____.
IV	The key to endurance	_____	Using the gravity pull technique helps athletes _____.
V	_____	15	_____ if he or she has learnt the running techniques.

Vocabulary

5 Fill in the blanks with the words given below. Change the forms where necessary.

actually	energy	entire	increase	position	require
secret	separate	skilled	special	speed	touch

1. Those buildings are so tall that they seem to _____ the sky.

2. We need someone with _____ and enthusiasm(热情) to do this job.

3. He was driving at a _____ of 90 miles per hour on his way home.

4. Of course he is our landlord(房东); he owns the _____ building.

5. Is there anything _____ that you'd like to do this afternoon, Peter?

6. China's GDP(国内生产总值) _____ by 9. 1 percent in 2003.

7. Believe it or not, our foreign teacher is quite _____ at cooking Chinese dishes.

8. She seems so quiet, but _____ she likes to talk.

9. This word has four _____ meanings.

10. You are _____ by law to stop your car after an accident(事故).

11. What's your _____ for looking so young?

12. I go to sleep on my back but I always wake up in a different _____ .

6 Fill in the blanks with the expressions given below. Change the forms where necessary.

keep from	keep one's balance	known as	quite a bit (of)
rather than	think of... as	up and down	

1. She was running _____ outside her house, shouting for help.

2. The noise from the next door _____ me _____ sleeping last night.

3. The disease is more commonly _____ Mad Cow Disease.

4. He is having _____ trouble with his car, isn't he?

5. The little girl had to hold onto the railings(扶手) to _____ .

6. I prefer to live near my work _____ spend a lot of time travelling every day.

7. I used to _____ him _____ someone who would always help me, but I was wrong.

Structure

7 Complete the following sentences by translating the Chinese in brackets into English, using "the more... the more" structure .

Model:

> **The more** often one practices, **the better** one becomes!

1. _____ , the more likely you are to win the race. (你跑得越快)
2. Actually the less she worried, _____ . (她干得越好)
3. _____ , the easier things are. (人们掌握的信息越多)
4. The more I read the poem(诗) , _____ . (我越喜欢它)

8 Rewrite the following sentences according to the model, omitting what can be omitted.

Model:

> When he is sprinting, the athlete uses only two parts, the pad and the toes.
> →**When sprinting**, the athlete uses only two parts, the pad and the toes.

1. Though it is small, the restaurant offers nice food and good service.

_____

2. While I was sitting there, I examined every part of the room.

_____

3. When he was crossing the street, Tom was hit by a car.

_____

4. The teacher spoke slowly as if she was trying to impress every word on our minds.

_____

Translation

9 Translate the following sentences into English.

1. 汤姆的故事很滑稽,我们都忍不住笑了起来。

_____

2.德语系和英语系分处两幢楼,而不是在同一幢楼里。

_____

3.伍兹(Woods)具备什么其他高尔夫球运动员(golfer)不具备的特殊技巧呢?

_____

4.跑步是最大众化的运动方式,因为它不需要什么训练或器材(equipment)。

_____

5.需要相当多的练习才能在速度和耐力两方面均技术娴熟。

_____

6.他被认为是我们学校跑得最快的人,尽管他对跑步的技巧一无所知。

_____

Grammar Review

动词时态(Verb Tenses)(4)

The Present Perfect and the Past Perfect(现在完成时和过去完成时)

　　现在完成时表示动作发生在过去,但与现在情况有关系。现在完成时由助动词 have/has 加动词-ed 分词构成。

过去完成时主要表示过去某时前已发生的动作或情况(也可说是"过去的过去")。

过去完成时由 had 加动词-ed 分词构成。

现在完成时(**The Present Perfect**)

用　　法	例　　　　　　句
1. 表示动作到现在为止已经完成	The taxi has arrived. 出租车已经到了。 Her bicycle has been broken. 她的自行车已经坏了。
2. 表示过去的一个动作,但其发生的时间不确切或不知道	Linda still hasn't finished her assignment. 琳达还没完成她的功课。 Have you ever been to Paris? 你去过巴黎吗?

用　　法	例　　　　句
3. 表示过去反复发生的动作	I have been to the post office twice today. 我今天都到邮局去过两次了。 Jenny has taken several courses this year. 珍妮今年已经修了几门课程了。
4. 表示从过去延续至今的动作、状态,常与 for 和 since 引导的短语或从句连用	We have lived here since 1982. 从 1982 年以来,我们就一直住在这儿。 Our family has owned that house for generations. 这房子已经属于我们家好几代人了。

过去完成时(The Past Perfect)

用　　法	例　　　　句
1. 表示过去某时前已发生的动作或情况	We had already learned two thousand words by the end of last year. 到去年年底我们已经学了 2 000 个单词。 Until then, his family hadn't heard from him for six months. 到那时为止,他家里已经有 6 个月没得到他的消息了。
2. 与由 when/before/after/ until 等连词引导的分句连用,表示过去某一动作之前的动作	When we arrived at the theatre, they had waited for more than twenty minutes. 我们到达剧院的时候,他们已经等了 20 多分钟。 The train had left before I reached the station. 我到达车站的时候火车已经开走了。
3. 动词 expect, hope, think, want 等用过去完成时,表示过去的愿望、预期或意图等没有实现	They had wanted to help but couldn't get there in time. 他们本想帮忙的,但未能及时赶到那儿。 I had hoped that we would be able to leave tomorrow, but it's beginning to look difficult. 我曾希望我们能在明天离开,但现在看来很难做到。

用　　　法	例　　　　句
4. 用于 if, as if, I wish 引导的分句中,表示与过去事态相反的主观设想	If you <u>had walked</u> faster, you wouldn't have missed the train. 如果你当初走快一些,你就不会搭不上火车了。 I <u>wish</u> I <u>hadn't said</u> that. 我真希望自己没有说过这样的话。

10 Complete each of the following sentences with the verbs given in their right tenses.

A. *Use the proper tenses of verbs given to fill in the blanks.*

1. When we were kids, we _____ (go) to Beijing for our holidays, but I _____ (not be) there for years.

2. We _____ (live) in Hunan from 1995 to 2001, but we _____ (move) to Hainan now.

3. They _____ (not come) to our party yesterday, even though we _____ (send) them a special invitation.

4. I _____ (be) late for the film. It _____ (start) half an hour before.

5. Nobody _____ (see) Boris Norman since last Saturday. He _____ (leave) the house in the middle of the night.

6. Mary _____ (work) for Mr. and Mrs. Norman for six months now. She _____ (clean) Mrs. Norman's room every day.

7. Her father _____ (die) in 1988. He _____ (be) ill since 1986.

8. Gloria _____ (return) to Scotland in 1987. She _____ (live) in the USA for five years.

B. *The following is a simplified excerpt from* Of Human Bondage (《人生的枷锁》), *one of Somerset Maugham's most outstanding novels. Fill in the blanks with the verbs given in their right tenses.*

　　Philip walked out of the house. His school-days were over, and he (1)_____ (be) free; but the wild joy which he (2)_____ (expect) at that moment (3)_____ (be) not there. He walked round the school slowly, and a deep regret seized him. He wished now that he (4)_____ (not be) foolish. He did not want to go, but he knew he could never bring himself to go to the headmaster and tell him he (5)_____ (stay). That was a shame he could never put upon himself. He wondered whether he (6)_____ (do) right. He asked himself whether you wished that you (7)_____ (not get) your way after you (8)_____ (get) it.

Practical Writing

Business/Name Cards

11 Please write an English business card for Mr. Chen Yang based on the Chinese one given below.

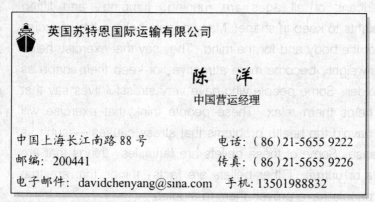

英国苏特恩国际运输有限公司

陈　洋
中国营运经理

中国上海长江南路 88 号　　　　　　电话：(86)21-5655 9222
邮编：200441　　　　　　　　　　　传真：(86)21-5655 9226
电子邮件：davidchenyang@sina.com　手机：13501988832

SUTON

_____
　　　　　　　　　　Operations Manager, China

Suton International Shipping Limited
Representative Office

Add: _____　　Tel: _____
Zip code: _____　　Fax: _____
Email: _____　Mobile: _____

12 Write a business card in English according to the information given below.

Mr. James Green works for Green Industries Inc.
He is the General Manager (总经理) of the company.
His telephone number is (01)306-824-4556.

His fax number is (01)306-821-9866.

His company is located at 999 Park Avenue, Rockford, IL 61265, USA.

His e-mail is gj@ green. industries. com.

Text B

Exercise: What Can It Do for You?

Author Unknown

Americans of all ages are running, jumping, and lifting weights to keep in shape. Many people believe that exercise is good for the body and for the mind. They say that exercise helps them lose weight, become more attractive, or keep their shape as they get older. Some people who have very stressful lives say that   5 exercise helps them relax. These people think that exercise will help them avoid the health problems that stress causes — such as heart disease. Some of these beliefs are fantasies: things that are impossible or untrue. Other beliefs are facts: things that are true because people have proven them in studies.   10

2　What are the facts about exercise? Can you actually change the shape of your body simply by exercising? Can any woman look like Jane Fonda if she works out? Can any man look like Arnold Schwarzenegger if he lifts weights long enough? As a matter of   15 fact, the answer is no, not really. Genetics determined the number of fat cells you have and your muscle definition (how visible your muscles are) before you were born, so there is a limit to how much your body can   20 change now with exercise. However, you can lose weight by burning (using up) more calories than you take in. Exercise combined with dieting can

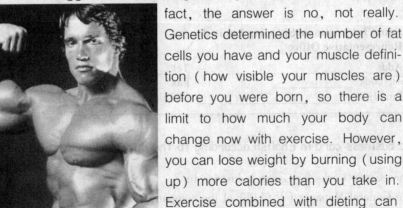

25 help, but you probably won't look like Ms. Fonda unless you did before you started. Also, you can strengthen and enlarge your muscles; this can improve your overall appearance, but it probably won't make you

30 look like Mr. Schwarzenegger unless you were born with his kind of muscle definition.

3 What about reducing stress by exercising? In fact, studies have shown that doing aerobic exercise (exercise that increa-

35 ses your heart rate) causes the brain to release endorphins, a chemical in your body that reduces pain and relaxes the body. Again, there is no guarantee that exercise will prevent a heart attack or a stroke, especially if members of your family have had

40 these diseases. But if you exercise, have a good diet, don't smoke, and have a relaxed, positive attitude, you will reduce your chances of getting stress-related illnesses.

(354 *words*)

New Words

* weight /weɪt/ *n.*	how heavy sb. or sth. is when measured by a particular system 重量
* attractive /əˈtræktɪv/ *a.*	having the power to attract; pleasant to look at; pretty; handsome 有吸引力的;妩媚动人的;漂亮的;英俊的
* stress /stres/ *n.*	force that puts pressure on sb. /sth. ; continuous feelings of worrying about one's work or personal life, that prevent one from relaxing 压力;紧张
◆ stressful /ˈstresfl/ *a.*	压力重的;紧张的
* relax /rɪˈlæks/ *v.*	make or become less tight, stiff, etc.; (make sb.) rest after work or effort(使)松弛,(使)放松;(使)休息;(使)轻松
* avoid /əˈvɔɪd/ *vt.*	get or keep away from; stop (sth.) happening;

prevent 避开;避免;防止

* cause /kɔːz/ *n.*   event, act, person, etc. that makes sth. happen or leads to a certain result; reason 原因,起因;理由

  vt.   be the cause of; make happen 使产生,使发生,引起

* disease /dɪ'ziːz/ *n.*   (cause of) illness of the body, of the mind or of plants caused by infection or internal disorder 疾病;病害

* belief /bɪ'liːf/ *n.*   fact of believing (in sb./sth.); thing, idea that one believes 相信,信任;信念;看法

◆fantasy /'fæntəsɪ/ *n.*   imagination or fancy, esp. when completely unrelated to reality; product of the imagination; wild or unrealistic notion 想象;幻想;想象的产物;荒诞的念头;怪念头

* impossible /ɪm'pɒsəbl/ *a.*   that cannot be done; not possible 办不到的;不可能的

◆untrue /ˌʌn'truː/ *a.*   not true; contrary to fact 不真实的;与事实相反的;假的

* prove /pruːv/ *vt.*   show that (sth.) is true or certain by means of argument or evidence 证明,证实

* simply /'sɪmplɪ/ *ad.*   merely; only; in an easy way; in a plain way; completely 仅仅,只不过;简单地;简朴地;完全地

◆genetics /dʒɪ'netɪks/ *n.*   scientific study of the ways in which characteristics are passed from parents to their offspring 遗传学

* determine /dɪ'tɜːmɪn/ *v.*   fix (sth.) precisely; decide; make up one's mind about (sth.) 确定;决定;下决心

* cell /sel/ *n.*   细胞;小牢房,单身牢房;电池

* muscle /'mʌsl/ *n.*   肌肉

★definition /ˌdefɪ'nɪʃn/ *n.*   定义;释义;(轮廓、线条等的)清晰

* visible /'vɪzəbl/ *a.*   that can be seen; in sight; that can be noticed; apparent 看得见的,可见的;易觉察的;明显的

* limit /'lɪmɪt/ *n.*   point or line beyond which sth. does not extend; greatest or smallest degree 范围；限度；极限

◆calorie /'kælərɪ/ *n.*   unit for measuring a quantity of heat 卡路里，卡（热量单位）

* combine /kəm'baɪn/*v.*   (cause things to) join or mix together to form a whole(使)结合；(使)联合；(使)混合

* probably /'prɒbəblɪ/ *ad.*   almost certainly；very likely 大概；很可能

◆Ms /mɪz/ *abbr.*   title that comes before the (first name and the) surname of a woman whether married or unmarried 女士(冠于已婚或未婚女子姓或姓名前的称呼)

* strengthen /'streŋθn/ *v.*   (cause sb./sth. to) become stronger 加强；巩固；变强

* enlarge /ɪn'lɑːdʒ/ *v.*   (cause sth. to) become large (使)变大；扩大；放大

* improve /ɪm'pruːv/*v.*   (cause sth. to) become better(使)变得更好；改进，改善

◆overall /ˌəʊvər'ɔːl/*a.*   including everything；total 包括一切的；总的；全面的

★appearance /ə'pɪərəns/ *n.*   coming into view；arrival；what sb./sth. appears to be 出现；来到；外貌；外观

* reduce /rɪ'djuːs/ *vt.*   make (sth.) smaller in size, number, degree, price, etc. 减少；缩小；削减；降低

◆aerobic /eə'rəʊbɪk/*a.*   增氧健身的

* rate /reɪt/ *n.*   比率，率；速率，速度；等级

* brain /breɪn/ *n.*   organ of the body that controls thought, memory and feeling, consisting of a mass of soft grey matter in the head；mind or intellect；intelligence 脑；头脑；智力

★release /rɪ'liːs/ *vt.*   free；set free；allow to leave；publish, usu. in newspapers, on television, etc. 解放；释放；放开；发布；公开发行

◆endorphin /en'dɔːfɪn/ *n.*   内啡肽

★guarantee /ˌgærən'tiː/ *n.*   保证，担保

	vt.	undertake to be legally responsible for 保证,担保
* prevent /prɪˈvent/	*vt.*	stop (sth.) happening; stop (sb. from doing sth.) 预防;防止
* attack /əˈtæk/	*n.*	violent attempt to hurt and/or defeat; strong criticism in speech or writing; sudden start of an illness, etc. 攻击;进攻;抨击;(疾病的)突然发作
	v.	make an attack; criticize severely 攻击;进攻;抨击
* stroke /strəʊk/	*n.*	act or process of striking; blow; sudden attack of illness in the brain that can cause loss of the power to move, speak clearly, etc. 击,打;打击;中风
* especially /ɪˈspeʃəlɪ/	*ad.*	in particular; specially 尤其;特别
* positive /ˈpɒzətɪv/	*a.*	certain about one's opinion; providing help; constructive; showing confidence and optimism 有把握的;有助益的;建设性的;有信心的;乐观的
* attitude /ˈætɪtjuːd/	*n.*	way of thinking or behaving 看法;态度
* relate /rɪˈleɪt/	*vt.*	tell; see, show the relation between 讲;叙述;使互相关联;证明…之间的联系
* illness /ˈɪlnɪs/	*n.*	state of being ill in body or mind 病;疾病

生词量	总词数	生词率	B 级词(*)	A 级词(★)	纲外词(◆)
45	354	12.7%	32	4	9

Phrases & Expressions

in shape	fit; in a good state or condition 健康;处于良好状况;处于良好的健康状况
lose weight	become lighter in weight 减轻体重;变瘦
work out	have or take exercise 锻炼,训练
as a matter of fact	actually; in reality; in fact 事实上;其实
not really	事实上不是
use up	use until nothing is left; spend or consume completely 用完,用光;耗尽

take in	absorb (sth.) into the body 吸收；摄取
What about…?	(used to ask for information or make a sugges-tion)(询问消息或提出建议)…怎么样？
in fact	in truth; really 实际上；事实上；其实

Proper Names

| Jane Fonda /dʒeɪn ˈfɒndə/ | 简·方达(1937—)(美国著名电影女演员；1980 年代所撰写、录制的有关健美的书和录像带很畅销,影响很大) |
| Arnold Schwarzenegger /ˈɑːnəld ˈʃvɑːtsəndʒə/ | 阿诺德·施瓦辛格(1947—)(奥裔美国电影演员,动作片巨星,曾在国际健美比赛中多次胜出;2003 年竞选加州州长并当选) |

Notes on the Text

1. Americans of all ages are running, jumping, and lifting weights to keep in shape. Many people believe that exercise is good for the body and for the mind. 各种不同年龄的美国人都在跑步、跳跃和举重,以保持身体健康。很多人相信,运动对身心有好处。

2. Some of these beliefs are fantasies: things that are impossible or untrue. Other beliefs are facts: things that are true because people have proven them in studies. 这些信念中有些是幻想:不可能或不真实的东西。其他的信念则是事实:真实的东西,因为人们在研究中已经证实了它们。

3. Genetics determined the number of fat cells you have and your muscle definition (how visible your muscles are) before you were born, so there is a limit to how much your body can change now with exercise. 在你出生前,遗传性就决定了你的脂肪细胞数和你的肌肉线条(你肌肉的显露程度),所以,你的身体现在通过运动能改变多少是有一个限度的。

4. Exercise combined with dieting can help, but you probably won't look like Ms. Fonda unless you did before you started. 运动与节食相结合能有所帮助,但你大概不会看上去像方达女士那样身段优美,除非你在开始运动前已经身材优美。unless you did before you started 中 did 是 looked like Ms. Fond 的省略表示。

5. In fact, studies have shown that doing aerobic exercise (exercise that increases your heart rate) causes the brain to release endorphins, a chemical in your body that re-duces pain and relaxes the body. 实际上,研究已经表明,做有氧运动(加快心率的

运动)能促使脑释放内啡肽，这是你身体内的一种减轻痛苦、使身体放松的化学物质。a chemical in your body that reduces pain and relaxes the body 是 endorphins 的同位语，对 endorphins 起解释作用。

Exercises

13 Answer the following questions.

1. For what purpose do Americans of all ages exercise?
2. Why do people who lead stressful lives exercise?
3. Are these people's beliefs about exercise facts or fantasies?
4. Why can't any woman look like Jane Fonda by doing exercise?
5. How can a woman lose weight if she wishes to?
6. Can exercise help reduce stress? If so, how?
7. Can exercise prevent a heart attack or a stroke?
8. How can we reduce our chances of getting stress-related illnesses?

14 Fill in the blanks with the words given below. Change the forms where necessary.

appearance	avoid	determine	especially	impossible	improve
limit	positive	prove	relax	release	stress

1. It is almost _____ for me to stay in the same position for the entire course of the run.
2. After work she _____ with a cup of tea and the newspaper.
3. I try to _____ the playground when running — it's always so crowded.
4. People under a lot of _____ may experience headaches and sleeping difficulties.
5. Your health is _____ in part by what you eat and how you exercise.
6. Studies have _____ that exercise helps reduce stress.
7. I think we ought to put a strict _____ on the amount of time we can spend on the project(项目).

8. Her health has _____ greatly since she increased her exercise and started on the new diet.

9. You can change the whole _____ of your room simply by decorating it with one or two beautiful pictures.

10. The contraction(收缩) of muscles uses energy and _____ heat.

11. John is very fond of ball games, _____ football and basketball.

12. It's great being with her because she's got such a _____ attitude towards everything.

15 Fill in the blanks with the expressions given below. Change the forms where necessary.

as a matter of fact	in fact	(keep) in shape	lose weight
not really	take in	use up	what about

1. Many pregnant(怀孕的) moms enjoy swimming to _____, but have trouble finding anything fashionable to wear.

2. — Have you always lived here?
   — _____, I've only lived here for the last three years.

3. I did _____ but found that the weight returned as soon as I returned to my normal diet.

4. — I've invited John and Mary to your birthday party.
   — _____ Tom and Linda? Shall we invite them?

5. Many people think that exercise helps prevent a heart attack or a stroke, but this is _____ the case.

6. Don't worry if you _____ the shampoo(洗发液) — I'm going shopping tomorrow.

7. When running we _____ a lot more oxygen(氧气), our blood pressure rises and our brains release a chemical which relaxes our body.

8. These running techniques sound easy to learn and practice, but _____ they're rather difficult.

Text C

Walk, Don't Run

Christine Gorman

You want to get healthy. You know you need to exercise more. But if you're not ready to take part in intense physical activities, don't *despair*(绝望). There's growing agreement among exercise researchers(研究者) that, in fact, the best thing most of us can do may be to just walk.   5

2   Yes, walk. Not run or *jog*(慢跑) or sprint. Just walk five or six times a week. You may not feel the *benefits*(好处) all at once, but the *evidence*(证据) suggests that *over the long term*(从长远来说), a regular walking routine can do a world of good to your health.

3   *Brisk*(轻快的) walking is known to be good for the heart,   10 which *makes a lot of sense*(很有道理). The heart is a muscle, after all, and anything that makes the blood flow faster through a muscle helps keep it in shape. But regular walking benefits the heart in other ways as well. It lowers blood pressure, which helps *decrease*(减少) the stress on the *arteries*(动脉).   15

4   Walking is also a great way to lose body fat, though most people find they have to do it for at least an hour a day in order to lose weight. The body doesn't really start burning its fat stores until after 30 minutes of activity. Exercising too intensely can actually work against you by interfering with the body's ability to pull energy   20 from fat cells. You are more likely to maintain any weight loss you achieve if you take a walk regularly every day.

5   Walking won't *cure*(治愈) everything that troubles you, of course, and nothing happens overnight. "People who have never exercised regularly should not think that in a week they'll *solve*(解   25 决) their problems by walking," says Dr. David Curb of the University of Hawaii. But they can expect a regular walking program to serve them well into old age.

6   When you are ready to begin, the following two

30   pieces of advice can help you get the most out of your walking routine.

7   First, pay attention to your shoes. Walkers spend

35   more time with the entire foot

on the ground, so shoes for walking need to have more room at the front for the feet to spread.

8   Second, set *realistic*(现实的) *goals*(目标). Some people find that walking at a specific time each day works best for them.

40   Others do the walking exercise by making some adjustments in their daily routines, such as parking the car a few *blocks*(街区) away from their office, taking the stairs instead of the *elevator*(电梯) or going out for a walk rather than having a cup of coffee during the time for break.

(423 *words*)

Comprehension of the Text

16 Choose the best answer for each of the following multiple choice questions.

1. If you are not physically prepared for vigorous exercise, you can _____ instead.

   A) jog   B) run

   C) walk   D) sprint

2. According to the author, a regular walking routine _____.

   A) benefits people of old age rather than those who are young

   B) works even better for those who are not physically active

   C) solves all the problems that troubles us in a week's time

   D) does a whole lot of good to our health in the long run

3. Walking keeps the heart in shape in all the following ways except that
  _____.

  A) it increases the speed of blood flow through the heart

  B) it makes sense to a lot of muscles of the body

  C) it brings the blood pressure to a lower level

  D) it reduces the stress on the arteries

4. Most people find they have to walk a certain length of time each day in order to lose
  weight. This is because _____.

  A) it is after 30 minutes of exercise that the body begins to burn its fat stores

  B) it takes quite a bit of time and effort to maintain any weight loss achieved

  C) short-time walking prevents the body from pulling energy from fat cells

  D) walking is not thought of as intense when compared with other forms of exercise

5. By saying that "they can expect a regular walking program to serve them well into old
  age" (Lines 5-6, Par. 5), Dr. David Curb implies that _____.

  A) the benefits of walking will show up when people get old

  B) walking, a light form of exercise, suits people of all ages

  C) walking is a lifelong exercise people can choose

  D) walking is an age-old(古老的)exercise people can benefit from

6. Which of the following statements is true according to the passage?

  A) Shoes for walking need to have more room at the heel rather than the front.

  B) To get the most from walking, walkers should set a fixed time for it each day.

  C) Whether or not people can benefit from a regular walking routine is undecided yet.

  D) Walking, like anything else, won't cure everything that bothers you overnight.

Basic Reading Skills

Understanding Signal Words (2)

有些 Signal Words 表示的是"转折"关系,这些词语有: but, however, although, nevertheless, otherwise 和 yet 等。

下面是 A 篇课文中的句子:

Not many kids know this, **but** a person can actually learn how to run faster.

"知道这一点的孩子并不多"和"实际上一个人可以学会跑得更快"这两个ideas用 but 连接,表示一种转折。再如:

A young athlete can increase his speed by practicing sprinting technique in his backyard or playground. It may take some time to perfect, **but** as with any other athletic skill, the more often one practices, the better one becomes!

同样,作者用 but 连接了 It may take some time to perfect 和 as with any other athletic skill, the more often one practices, the better one becomes 这两个 ideas。

再看下面一段:

When it comes to controlling one's temper, my mother clearly outdoes my father. She will tolerate a lot before she gets angry and prefers to rationalize rather than lose her temper. **However**, my father's temper is like a short fuse on a stick of dynamite. (Text C, Unit 3)

作者谈到在 controlling one's temper 方面,她的母亲显然比她的父亲做得好。She will tolerate a lot before she gets angry and prefers to rationalize rather than lose her temper,而 my father's temper is like a short fuse on a stick of dynamite。在两个句子中间,作者用 However 这个信号词表示了一种转折与对比关系。

在阅读时,利用这些 Signal Words,可以帮助我们提高阅读速度,加深对文章的理解。

17 Read the following excerpts from your textbook. Identify the signal words that the writers use to express shift in thought.

1. ... so there is a limit to how much your body can change with exercise. However, you can lose weight by burning (using up) more calories than you take in. (Text B, Unit 4)

2. It takes quite a bit of practice to become skilled at this technique. However, by run-

ning this way, the athlete uses the pull of gravity to move forward, rather than having to use his own energy to push himself forward. (Text A, Unit 4)

3. Again, there is no guarantee that exercise will prevent a heart attack or a stroke, especially if members of your family have had these diseases. But if you exercise, have a good diet, don't smoke, and have a relaxed, positive attitude, you will reduce your chances of getting stress-related illnesses. (Text B, Unit 4)

Fun Time

 Crossword

When you go to a zoo, you may see a lot of animals there. Can you spell these animals? Here are some clues for you to follow:

Down
1. a little green animal living in water that can jump
2. a kind of sea animal that children like to play with
3. a kind of horse with stripes

Across
4. the king of animals
5. a dangerous big animal living in water

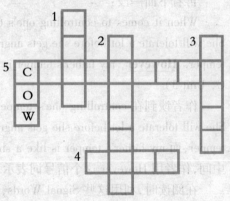

Answers: 1. frog 2. dolphin 3. zebra 4. lion 5. crocodile

UNIT 5

Highlights

Preview

Very often old stories teach us various lessons when we read them. This unit contains some stories that have something to do with fortune. In the Listening and Speaking section, you will pick up the language for making requests and learn how to do it. In the Reading and Writing Section, Text A tells us how a father helps his sons to make their fortune after his death; Text B tells about the bad end of a greedy person; Text C is a little story about the wisdom of Nasrudin, who always helps the poor out of their miseries.

Listening & Speaking

The Language for Making Requests

1 You are going to listen to an instructor talking about making requests. Listen carefully and fill in the blanks with the missing words.

Instructor: In our daily life, we need to make requests(要求). In other words, we need to ask somebody to _____. We can make polite, hesitant(犹豫的), formal(正式的), and direct requests. How to make a request depends on whom _____. You can use the following correct language in different situations:

1. Could you _____, please? (polite)
2. Would you _____, please? (polite)
3. Do you think you could _____? (polite)
4. Would you mind _____? (polite)
5. I wonder if you could possibly _____. (hesitant)
6. Can you _____? (direct)
7. Will you _____? (direct)
8. Do me a favor and _____, will you? (direct)

2 Now you can make requests using the structures you have just picked up in Exercise 1. Practice with a partner and use the appropriate responses given below.

1. OK. 2. Sure. No problem. 3. Yes, of course. 4. I'd be glad to. 5. All right. 6. Never mind.	1. I'm sorry. But… 2. Oh, but… 3. Well, but…

Making Requests

3

1) *Before you listen to the first conversation, read the following words which may be new to you.*

do	[用于加强语气]确实
dorm	宿舍

Listen to the conversation twice and fill in the blanks with the missing words.

Li Ming: Excuse me.

Wang Ying: Yes?

Li Ming: I was wondering _____ lend me your dictionary — I'm _____.

Wang Ying: I'm sorry. I'm using it _____. Maybe later.

Li Ming: Oh, that's OK. Thanks anyway.

Wang Ying: _____ you could get one at the bookstore?

Li Ming: Oh, I do have one. But I _____ in the dorm.

Wang Ying: I see.

Now listen to the conversation again and answer the following questions.

1. Where could Wang Ying and Li Ming be?
2. What did Li Ming ask Wang Ying to do?
3. What did Wang Ying do with the request?
4. What did Wang Ying ask Li Ming to do?
5. Did Li Ming do it at Wang Ying's request? Why or why not?

2) *Before you listen to the second conversation, read the following words and expressions which may be new to you.*

| stereo | 立体声 |
| apartment | 公寓 |

Listen to the conversation twice and fill in the blanks with the missing words.

Tom Chang: (*Li Ming opens the door.*) Hi. I'm your new neighbor, Tom Chang. _____.

Li Ming: Oh, hi. I'm Li Ming. _____?

Tom Chang: Yes. Last week.

Li Ming: _____?

Tom Chang: Not right now. But thanks anyway.

Li Ming: Uh, any problems?

Tom Chang: Well, _____? The walls are really thin, so the sound goes through to my apartment. _____.

Li Ming: Oh, I'm sorry. I didn't know that. _____.

Tom Chang: I appreciate that.

Li Ming: Sure.

Now listen to the conversation again and answer the following questions.

> 1. Where is Tom Chang living now?
> 2. What is Li Ming doing now?
> 3. Why is Tom Chang having a word with Li Ming?
> 4. What is Li Ming going to do right now?
> 5. Do you think Tom made a polite request? And why?

4 Write a dialogue with your partner like the ones in Exercise 3. Begin with Part A and let your partner play the role of Part B. After that, practice the dialogue in class, stating a problem and making a request using the language you learned in Exercise 1.

Listening Practice

5 Listen to people speaking and decide what they are talking about.

1. A) A park.
   B) A view(景色).
   C) A country.
   D) A window.
2. A) A word.
   B) A problem.
   C) A trip.
   D) Difficulties.
3. A) Weather.
   B) Snow.
   C) Vacation.
   D) Hometown.
4. A) Children.
   B) Education
   C) School.
   D) Pictures.
5. A) Noise.
   B) Neighbors.
   C) Neighborhood(居住区).
   D) Campus(校园).

6 Listen to five questions and choose the appropriate answers.

1. A) Take it easy.
   B) Turn it down.

C) Oh, which one?   D) Sure. What is it?

2. A) Oh great.   B) Of course.

   C) That's right.   D) What's that?

3. A) I'd love to.   B) Yes, it does.

   C) No, help yourself.   D) Sorry, I didn't know.

4. A) Yeah, I'm sure.   B) Oh, that's OK.

   C) Maybe, I'll.   D) Sure do.

5. A) Everything seems to be going fine.

   B) That's what I want to say.

   C) I agree with you.

   D) That's for sure.

7 Listen to five short dialogues and choose the appropriate answers.

1. A) A customer and a waitress.

   B) A boss and a secretary(秘书).

   C) A librarian and a student.

   D) A teacher and a student.

2. A) Milk.   B) Sugar.

   C) Medicine.   D) Humor(幽默).

3. A) Next to the sign.   B) Behind the sign.

   C) Behind the man.   D) In front of the man.

4. A) He's asking somebody to do something.

   B) He's talking with his mother.

   C) He's picking up his things.

   D) He's talking on the phone.

5. A) Sleep.   B) Study.

   C) Noise.   D) Heat(热).

8 Listen to the following short talk and fill in the blanks with the missing words. The talk is given twice.

In almost all cultures around the world throughout history, gold has been valued and sought as a precious (珍贵的) metal (金属) and a commodity (商品).

_____ a symbol(象征) of power, wealth(财富) and success.

One of the most exciting events in Californian(美国加州的) history occurred on January 24, 1848. John Sutter had a huge land grant(授予物) at the junction(汇合处) of the American and Sacramento Rivers. He hired James Marshall to build a sawmill(锯木厂) _____ the Indians called Coloma. On that cold January morning, Marshall _____ shining up from the millrace(推动水车的水流). He picked up _____. Were these small nuggets(小块) really gold? He tested one by smashing it _____. It flattened(变平) but didn't break. The woman who cooked for the construction(建造) people _____ in a pot(罐) of lye(碱液). It was gold! With this chance discovery of a few, small gold nuggets on the American River, _____ in California. Sutter had hoped to keep the news of _____ quiet while completing his construction. But there was no controlling gold fever(发烧)! People flocked(拥向) to California's gold. _____ the California Gold Rush.

(184 *words*)

9 Listen to the talk again and then answer the following questions orally.

1. What is gold?
2. What happened in California in 1848?
3. How did Marshall know what he had found was gold?
4. What did Sutter hope to do when Marshall had found gold?
5. What happened after the chance discovery of gold?

10 Move around the classroom, making three requests of each person. Try to use a variety of expressions. Then discuss a free talk on the topic given below.

How to make a polite request.

Reading & Writing

Text A

Starter

What is wealth and what kind of wealth do dying people hope to leave their children? With your classmates, discuss the best replies to these two statements.

Wealth is:
1.
2.
3.

Dying people hope to leave their children:
1.
2.
3.

Now read the following passage and find out what treasure the gardener left in the orchard for his children.

Text

The Treasure in the Orchard

Author Unknown

A n old gardener who was dying sent for his two sons to come to his bedside, as he wished to speak to them. When they came in answer to his request, the old man, raising himself on his pillows, pointed through the window towards his orchard.

5   *2* "You see that orchard?" said he.

    3 "Yes, Father, we see the orchard. "

    4 "For years it has given the best of fruit — golden oranges, red apples, and cherries bigger and brighter than rubies!"

    5 "To be sure, Father. It has always been a good orchard!"

10   *6* The old gardener nodded his head, time and time again. He looked at his hands — they were worn from the spade that he had used all his life. Then he looked at the hands of his sons and saw that their nails were polished and their fingers as white as those of any fine lady's.

15   *7* "You have never done a day's work in your lives, you two!" said he. "I doubt if you ever will! But I have hidden a treasure in my orchard for you to find. You will never possess it unless you dig it up. It lies midway between two of the trees, not too near, yet not too far from the trunks. It is yours for the trouble of digging

20   — that is all!"

    8 Then he sent them away, and soon afterwards he died. So the orchard became the property of his sons, and

25   without any delay, they set to work to dig for the treasure that had been promised them.

9   Well, they dug and dug, day after day, week after week, going down the long alleys of fruit trees, never too near yet never too far from the trunks. They dug up all the weeds and picked out 30 all the stones, not because they liked weeding and cleaning, but because it was all part of the hunt for the buried treasure. Winter passed and spring came, and never were there such blossoms as those which hung the orange and apple and cherry trees with curtains of petals pale as pearls and soft as silk. Then summer threw 35 sunshine over the orchard, and sometimes the clouds bathed it in cool, delicious rain. At last the time of the fruit harvest came. But the two brothers had not yet found the treasure that was hidden among the roots of the trees.

10   Then they sent for a merchant from the nearest town to buy 40 the fruit. It hung in great bunches, golden oranges, red apples, and cherries bigger and brighter than rubies. The merchant looked at them in open admiration.

11   "This is the finest crop I have yet seen," said he. "I will give you twenty bags of money for it!" 45

12   Twenty bags of money were more than the two brothers had ever owned in their life. They struck the bargain in great delight and took the money-bags into the house, while the merchant made arrangements to carry away the fruit.

13   "I will come again next year," said he. "I am always glad 50 to buy crop like this. How you must have dug and weeded and worked to get it!"

14   He went away, and the brothers sat eyeing each other over the tops of the money-bags. Their hands were rough and toil-worn, just as the old gardener's had been when he died. 55

15   "Golden oranges and red apples and cherries bigger and brighter than rubies," said one of them, softly. "I believe that this is the treasure we have been digging for all year, the very treasure our father meant!"

(591 *words*)

New Words

★treasure /ˈtreʒə/ n.　　　　　　　(store of) gold, silver, jewels, etc. 金银财宝;
　　　　　　　　　　　　　　　　　财富

◆orchard /ˈɔːtʃəd/ n.　　　　　　　piece of land in which fruit trees are grown 果园

◆gardener /ˈgɑːdnə/ n.　　　　　　person who works in a garden, either for pay or as
　　　　　　　　　　　　　　　　　a hobby 园丁;园艺家

＊request /rɪˈkwest/ n.　　　　　　　act of asking for sth., esp. politely 要求;请求
　　　　　　　　vt.　　　　　　　　ask for (sth.) politely; ask (sb. to do sth.)请
　　　　　　　　　　　　　　　　　求;要求

◆pillow /ˈpɪləʊ/ n.　　　　　　　　枕头

＊golden /ˈgəʊldən/ a.　　　　　　　of gold or like gold in value or color 金的,金制
　　　　　　　　　　　　　　　　　的;金色的;像黄金一样贵重的

◆cherry /ˈtʃerɪ/ n.　　　　　　　　樱桃;樱桃树

◆ruby /ˈruːbɪ/ n.　　　　　　　　　红宝石

＊nod /nɒd/ v.　　　　　　　　　　move (the head) up and down quickly as a greet-
　　　　　　　　　　　　　　　　　ing or to show agreement, etc. 点(头)(致意或表
　　　　　　　　　　　　　　　　　示同意等)

＊spade /speɪd/ n.　　　　　　　　tool for digging with a wooden handle and a broad
　　　　　　　　　　　　　　　　　metal blade 锹,铲

★nail /neɪl/ n.　　　　　　　　　　指甲;钉子

＊polish /ˈpɒlɪʃ/ vt.　　　　　　　　cause the surface of (sth.) to be smooth and
　　　　　　　　　　　　　　　　　shiny by rubbing 擦光;擦亮

＊hide /haɪd/ (hid /hɪd/,　　　　　　put or keep out of sight 把…藏起来,隐藏
　　hidden /ˈhɪdn/) vt.

＊possess /pəˈzes/ vt.　　　　　　　have (sth.) as one's belonging; own 占有,拥有

★dig /dɪg/ (dug /dʌg/) vt.　　　　　(use a tool such as a spade to) turn over (land)
　　　　　　　　　　　　　　　　　in (a place) 掘,挖

◆midway /ˈmɪdˌweɪ/ ad.　　　　　in the middle; halfway 当中;中间;半途

◆trunk /trʌŋk/ n.　　　　　　　　main stem of a tree, from which the branches
　　　　　　　　　　　　　　　　　grow 树干

★afterwards /ˈɑːftəwədz/ ad.　　　at a later time 以后,过后,后来

＊property /ˈprɒpətɪ/ n.　　　　　　thing or things that sb. owns 财产,资产;所有物

＊delay /dɪˈleɪ/ n.　　　　　　　　延迟;拖延;耽搁

◆alley /'ælɪ/ n.   path bordered by trees in a garden(花园中两边有树的)小径

◆weed /wiːd/ n.   wild plant that is not wanted in a garden, field, etc. 野草,杂草

* hunt /hʌnt/ v.   follow after, catch and sometimes kill (wild animals); search carefully (for); try to find 追猎,猎取;打猎;寻找;搜寻

          n.   打猎;寻找;搜寻

* bury /'berɪ/ vt.   put (a dead person) in a grave; hide (sth.) in the earth 埋葬;掩埋;埋藏

◆blossom /'blɒsəm/ n.   flower, esp. of a fruit tree(尤指果树的)花;(一棵树上开出的)全部花朵

* hang /hæŋ/ (hung /hʌŋ/) v.   悬挂,吊

* curtain /'kɜːtn/ n.   帘;窗帘;门帘;(舞台上的)幕,帷幕;帘状物;幕状物

◆petal /'petl/ n.   花瓣

* pale /peɪl/ a.   (of a person, his face, etc.) having little color; (of a color) not bright or vivid(指人、面色等)苍白的,灰白的;(指颜色)浅的,淡的

◆pearl /pɜːl/ n.   珍珠

* silk /sɪlk/ n.   丝;丝绸

* sunshine /'sʌnʃaɪn/ n.   light and heat of the sun 日光,阳光

★bathe /beɪð/ vt.   给…洗澡;使沐浴

* delicious /dɪ'lɪʃəs/ a.   having a very pleasant taste; very pleasant (when tasted, smelled, etc.)美味的,可口的;芬芳的,怡人的

* harvest /'hɑːvɪst/ n.   cutting and gathering of grain and other food crops; (amount of the) crop obtained 收割;收获;收成

* root /ruːt/ n.   part of a plant that is under the ground; the real cause, reason for sth. (植物的)根;根部;根源;根由,原因

★merchant /'mɜːtʃənt/ n.   trader 商人

◆bunch /bʌntʃ/ n.   number of things (usu. of the same kind) growing, fastened or grouped together 束;串;扎;捆

◆admiration /ˌædməˈreɪʃn/ n.　feeling of respect, warm approval or pleasure 钦佩;赞赏;羡慕

＊bargain /ˈbɑːgɪn/ n.　agreement (to buy, sell, exchange, etc.), usu. made after some discussion; thing bought or sold cheaply(买卖等双方的)协议;交易;便宜货

＊delight /dɪˈlaɪt/ n.　great pleasure; joy 快乐;高兴

◆arrangement /əˈreɪndʒmənt/ n.　安排

＊rough /rʌf/ a.　having a surface that is not even, regular or smooth(表面)不平滑的;粗糙的

◆toil-worn /ˈtɔɪlwɔːn/ a.　worn or worn out by toil 劳累的;疲惫不堪的

生词量	总词数	生词率	B级词(＊)	A级词(★)	纲外词(◆)
44	591	7.4%	22	6	16

Phrases & Expressions

send for　send sb. to fetch 派人去请,派人去叫,派人去拿

in answer to　as an answer to 作为对…的回答(或响应)

to be sure　without a doubt; certainly; of course; one must admit that 毫无疑问;无疑地;当然;必须承认

time and time again　many times; repeatedly 多次;一再,反复地

all one's life　for the whole of one's life 一辈子,毕生

dig up　remove from the ground by digging 掘起;挖掘出

send away　cause to depart 使离去,把…打发走

set to　begin doing sth. in an eager or a determined way 开始起劲地做某事

day after day　continuously; for many days 日复一日,一天又一天

pick out　remove by picking 拣出

carry away　take away 拿走,搬走,运走

Notes on the Text

1. When they came in answer to his request, the old man, raising himself on his pillows, pointed through the window towards his orchard. 两个儿子应他的要求来了,

老人坐直身子靠在枕头上,指向窗外的果园。动词 raise 的现在分词 raising 修饰句中谓语动词 pointed,表示伴随该动作发生的状态。

2. For years it has given the best of fruit — golden oranges, red apples, and cherries bigger and brighter than rubies! 多年来,它一直出产最好的水果——黄澄澄的橘子,红艳艳的苹果,还有比红宝石还要大还要晶莹鲜亮的樱桃! 状语 for years 前置,起强调作用。破折号后面的部分是 fruit 的同位语。

3. … without any delay, they set to work to dig for the treasure that had been promised them. ……他们毫不迟延,立即开始工作,挖掘、寻找已经答应给他们的财宝。set to work(开始工作)中的 work 是名词,不是动词;set to 后不可以直接跟动词,只可以跟动名词。promise 后应跟双宾语,即 promise sb. sth.。在 that 引导的这句定语从句里,sb. 是 them, sth. 则是定语从句的先行词 treasure。

4. They dug up all the weeds and picked out all the stones, not because they liked weeding and cleaning, but because it was all part of the hunt for the buried treasure. 他们锄去所有的杂草,拣出所有的石块;不是因为他们喜欢除草和清理石块,而是因为这是寻找埋藏的财宝必须做的事情。这句中的 it 指代 weeding and cleaning 这件事。

5. Winter passed and spring came, and never were there such blossoms as those which hung the orange and apple and cherry trees with curtains of petals pale as pearls and soft as silk. 冬去春来,橘子树上、苹果树上和樱桃树上开出了花,花瓣淡雅如珍珠,柔软如丝绸,像窗帘般挂在树上,那花朵从来没有这样盛开过。否定词never 提前,起强调作用,句子中的主谓结构 there were 要倒装。

6. How you must have dug and weeded and worked to get it! 你们肯定花了大力气挖地、除草、干活才种出这样的水果吧! 这是一句感叹句。句中的结构 must have done 是情态动词的一种用法,表示对过去事情的推测。

7. He went away, and the brothers sat eyeing each other over the tops of the money-bags. 商人走了。两兄弟坐在那儿,目光越过钱袋顶看着对方。eye 用作动词,表示"看、注视"。

8. I believe that this is the treasure we have been digging for all year, the very treasure our father meant! 我想这就是我们整整一年来一直在挖掘、寻找的财宝,也正是我们父亲所指的财宝。句中 very 是形容词,意思是"同一的、正是的"。又如: This is the very book I want! 这正是我想要的书。You're the very person we need for the job. 你正是我们这份工作所需要的人。

Exercises

Reading Aloud

1 Read the following paragraphs until you have learned them by heart.

An old gardener who was dying sent for his two sons to come to his bedside, as he wished to speak to them. When they came in answer to his request, the old man, raising himself on his pillows, pointed through the window towards his orchard.

"You see that orchard?" said he.

"Yes, Father, we see the orchard."

"For years it has given the best of fruit — golden oranges, red apples, and cherries bigger and brighter than rubies!"

"To be sure, Father. It has always been a good orchard!"

The old gardener nodded his head, time and time again. He looked at his hands — they were worn from the spade that he had used all his life. Then he looked at the hands of his sons and saw that their nails were polished and their fingers as white as those of any fine lady's.

Understanding the Text

2 Answer the following questions.

1. How did the gardener feel about his orchard?
2. What were the differences between the father's and the sons' hands?
3. How often did the sons work before the gardener died?
4. Why did the sons dig so hard?
5. What treasure did they find after a year's hard digging?
6. What did they get from one year's hard work?
7. How did they feel when the merchant gave them twenty bags of money?
8. Were they angry not to find any treasure in the orchard?
9. What did they learn about the treasure in the end?

3 Topics for Discussion.

1. What do you think of the treasure the father left his sons? Is it more valuable than money?
2. What kind of treasure do you want your parents to leave you?

Reading Analysis

4 Read Text A again and complete the following table.

Part	Topic	Paragraph	Main Idea
I	_____ last words	1-7	The dying old man told his sons to _____ in the orchard in the hope that _____.
II	The sons' search (搜寻) for treasure	_____	The two brothers worked hard in the orchard in order to _____.
III	The finest crop	10-13	Because of all the _____, the two brothers made a lot of _____ from the finest crop that had yet resulted.
IV	The truth(真相) _____	14-15	The two brothers finally understood _____ before his death.

Vocabulary

5 Fill in the blanks with the words given below. Change the forms where necessary.

bury	delay	delicious	delight	harvest	hide
hunt	merchant	nod	possess	property	request

1. Though he _____ several big farms in the south of the country, he left nothing to his children.

2. The family were very sad because they lost all their _____ in the fire.

3. Can I have another piece of the cake? It's simply _____.

4. He got a great deal of _____ from his children.

5. The farmers are expecting a good _____ this year.

6. She was born in 1432, the daughter of a wealthy London _____, whose business was selling shoes.

7. They _____ their gold in the garden where they hoped nobody would be able to find it.

8. They have turned down our repeated _____ for a crosswalk (人行横道) near the school.

9. After a long _____, they finally found a house they liked.

10. When the son asked his dying mother if she wanted some water to drink, she _____ her head by way of(作为) saying "Yes."

11. Because of some problems with the engine, there will be a _____ of ten minutes before the plane takes off.

12. Lily used to _____ her diary under her pillow.

6 **Fill in the blanks with the expressions given below. Change the forms where necessary.**

all one's life	carry away	day after day	dig up
in answer to	pick out	send away	send for
set to	to be sure	time and time again	

1. Suddenly a fight started and the restaurant owner had to _____ the police.

2. Tom is clever, _____, but not very hard-working.

3. I've told you _____ not to play with fire, but you never listen to me.

4. As soon as David arrived in Beijing he fell in love with the city and decided that he would live there _____.

5. He was trying to explain but she became impatient(不耐烦) and _____ him _____.

6. We must _____ those weeds by the roots.

7. He was the fastest worker and _____ work right away, not stopping until he was tired out.

8. The same problem seemed to come up _____ but neither the father nor

the son knew what to do.

9. How could he _____ the best tomatoes _____ for himself and leave the rest to his parents?

10. _____ the students' request, the teacher has begun to give them more chances to speak in class.

11. Several houses _____ when the river suddenly changed its course during a flood(洪水) last summer.

Structure

7 Complete the following sentences by translating the Chinese in brackets into English.

Model:

> They dug up all the weeds and picked out all the stones, not because they liked weeding and cleaning, **but because** it was all part of the hunt for the buried treasure.

1. We're not going on holiday this year, not because we don't have money, _____. (而是因为我们没有时间)

2. He lent you his car yesterday, not because he wanted to, _____ _____. (而是因为他妈妈要他这样做)

3. We didn't consider him for the job, _____, but because he didn't do well in the test. (不是因为他没有经验)

4. She's in a bad mood _____, but because her father won't let her go to the party tonight. (不是因为她有门考试没过)

5. We come here today _____. (不是因为我们喜欢这个聚会,而是因为我们想对他说声谢谢)

8 Study the following example and then translate each of the sentences into English using the "This is + the superlative + sb. has yet done" structure with the adjective provided.

Model:

> This is **the finest** crop I **have yet seen**.

1. 这是我吃过的最好吃的中餐。(delicious)

_____

2. 这是他做过的最难的练习。(difficult)

_____

3. 这是我们听到过的最动听的音乐。(beautiful)

_____

4. 这是她玩过的最有趣的游戏。(interesting)

_____

5. 这是他们试过的最好的方法。(good)

_____

Translation

9 Translate the following sentences into English.

1. 看到老人奄奄一息,邻居们一刻也没有耽误,马上请来医生。

_____

2. 一个漂亮的果园要人付出辛勤劳动,要日复一日地浇水、除草、清除石块。不过丰收的时刻总是让人愉快的。

_____

3. 他一辈子都富有,但他从没为他所拥有的财产开心过。

_____

4. 在搜寻的过程中,他们不断以为自己找到了埋在地里的财宝,结果一无所获。

_____

5. 应商人的要求,那家餐馆打发走了其他客人,着手为他一人准备美味的食物。

_____

6. "我可以把这些旧报纸搬走吗?"工人问。"当然可以,"他点点头。

_____

Grammar Review

基本句型(Sentence Pattern)

英语句子有长有短,有简有繁,似乎千变万化,难以捉摸,但其实只有五种基本句型。所有英语句子都可以看成是这五种基本句型的扩大、组合、省略或倒装。掌

握这些句型,是掌握各种英语句子结构的基础。这五种句型列表如下:

用　　法	句 型 特 点	例　　　　　句
SV(主—动)	由主语 + 不及物的谓语动词构成,常用来表示主语的动作	The moon rose. 月亮升起了。 What he said does not matter. 他所讲的不重要。 Great minds think alike. 英雄所见略同。
SVC (主—动—表)	由主语 + 系动词 + 表语组成,主要用以说明主语的特征、属性、状态、身份	Everything looks different. 一切看来都不同了。 The flowers smell sweet. 花散发着香味。 The trouble is that they are short of money. 麻烦的是他们缺钱。
SVO (主—动—宾)	由主语 + 及物动词 + 宾语组成,谓语动词是主语产生的动作,宾语为动作的承受者	He enjoys reading. 他喜欢看书。 Who knows the answer? 谁知道答案? All of us believe that you are an honest man. 我们大家都相信你是个诚实的人。
SVoO (主—动—间宾—直宾)	由主语 + 及物动词 + 双宾语组成,这两个宾语一个是动作的直接承受者(多指物),即直接宾语;另一个是间接承受者(多指人),即间接宾语	I showed him my pictures. 我给他看我的照片。 She cooked her husband a delicious meal. 她给丈夫做了一顿美餐。 I told him that the bus was late. 我告诉他汽车晚点了。

用　法	句型特点	例　　句
SVOC （主—动— 宾—宾补）	由主语＋及物动词＋宾语 ＋宾语补语组成,宾语补 语用来补充说明宾语的特 征、属性、状态	We found the hall full. 我们发现礼堂坐满了。 Make my house your home. 别客气/请随意。（主语省略） He makes his parents happy. 他使他的父母很快乐。

10 Translate the following sentences into Chinese and point out the pattern of each sentence.

A.

1. We elected John captain of our football team.

_____

2. Things of that sort are happening all over the world every day.

_____

3. They have carried out the plan successfully.

_____

4. She ordered herself a new dress.

_____

5. The most important thing is knowing what to do next.

_____

B.

1. Teach fish to swim.

_____

2. Seeing is believing.

_____

3. Keep your sword bright.

_____

4. Money can't buy time.

_____

5. Friends must part.

_____

Practical Writing

Greeting Cards

11 This Sunday will be your friend's birthday. Write a greeting card to express your sincere wishes to him/her.

_____,

_____

_____

                                                    Love,

                                        _____

12 Christmas Day is approaching. Write a greeting card to your teacher to express your gratitude to him/her.

_____,

_____

_____

                                                    Yours,

                                        _____

Text B

The Golden Carambola Tree

Mrs. Nguyen

Long, long ago there lived a rich family of four people: a father, a mother and two sons. When the parents died they left their fortune of gold, houses and land to their sons but the older boy cheated his brother and took almost everything for himself. The only thing he left the younger brother was a carambola tree.

2 The younger brother, who was gentle and calm, was not upset by his older brother's greedy, dishonest behaviour. He found himself a job and spent his spare time caring for the carambola tree. Whenever he looked at it, it reminded him of his father and mother. He hoped it would bear a rich crop of fruit for him to sell at the market and so earn some extra money.

3 One morning, just as the fruit was ripening, a phoenix flew down and began to eat the best carambolas. "Please don't eat them," said the young man. "I must sell them at the market. I really need the money. Perhaps I can offer you something else to eat." The phoenix replied, "I will pay you in pure gold for what I eat. Get a bag ready and when I have finished eating you can have a fortune in gold pieces to replace your carambolas."

4 The young man fetched a bag and, when the phoenix had eaten its fill, it carried him on its back far over the sea to an island where gold coins lay thickly on the ground. The young man took a gold coin for every piece of fruit the phoenix had eaten and then the great bird carried him and his bag full of gold back to his home.

5 The young man bought a new house and filled it with expensive furniture. Then he bought some businesses and settled down to enjoy the life of a rich man. Very soon he invited his brother to share a fine meal with him to celebrate his changed fortune.

6 The older brother was amazed to find his brother so wealthy. "How did you become rich so quickly?" he asked very anxiously. The young man told him the story of the phoenix and the tree, and straight away the older brother wanted to exchange the carambola tree for the gold, houses and land his parents had left. The younger brother, who felt he had already more than enough wealth to last him all of his life, agreed to the exchange.

7 When the fruit of the carambola was ripening once more, the phoenix returned to eat it. The older brother demanded to be paid for his fruit and the phoenix agreed. "Get a bag to carry the gold and you shall be paid," it said.

8 When the phoenix carried the older brother to the island, the greedy man was not content to replace each piece of fruit with a gold coin but seized handfuls of coins, and packed the bag full. On the way back from the island, the bag was so heavy that even the great phoenix could not bear the weight. It dropped both the man and the bag into the ocean. The older brother drowned and the gold was lost at the bottom of the sea.

(535 *words*)

New Words

◆carambola / ˌkærəmˈbəʊlə/ *n.* 　五敛子，杨桃

* fortune /ˈfɔːtʃən/ *n.* 　large amount of money; wealth; chance; luck; fate 大笔的钱；财产；运气；命运

* land /lænd/ *n.* 　ground, esp. when used for farming; solid part of the earth's surface 地；土地；陆地

* cheat /tʃiːt/ *vt.* 　act in a dishonest way towards (sb.) 欺骗(某人)

* calm /kɑːm/ *a.* 　not excited; quiet; untroubled 不激动的；平静的；镇静的，镇定的

* upset /ʌpˈset/ *vt.* 　cause (sb.) to be unhappy or distressed 使(某

人)不高兴;使(某人)心烦意乱;使(某人)苦恼

* greedy /ˈgriːdɪ/ *a.*　showing or filled with too great a desire for food, money, power, etc. 贪食的,贪嘴的;贪婪的

◆ dishonest /dɪsˈɒnɪst/ *a.*　not honest; intended to deceive or cheat 不老实的,不诚实的;骗人的;欺骗性的

* behaviour /bɪˈheɪvjə/ *n.*　way of acting or doing things 行为;举止

* spare /speə/ *a.*　not needed immediately but ready to be used when needed; not being used for anything; free 备用的;多余的;空闲的

★ whenever /wenˈevə/ *conj.*　at any time; every time that 任何时候;每当

* bear /beə/ (bore /bɔː/,　produce (fruit, etc.); give birth to (a baby);
borne /bɔːn/) *vt.*　put up with; be able to tolerate; take (responsibility, etc.) on oneself 结(果实);生(孩子);忍受,容忍;承担(责任等)

* earn /ɜːn/ *vt.*　get (money, one's living, etc.) by working; gain (sth.) as a reward for what one has done 赚(钱),挣(钱);谋(生);获得,博得

* extra /ˈekstrə/ *a.*　beyond the usual amount, number, etc. ; additional 额外的;外加的;附加的

* ripe /raɪp/ *a.*　(of fruit, grain, etc.) ready to be gathered and used, esp. for eating(指水果、谷物等)成熟的

◆ ripen /ˈraɪpən/ *v.*　(cause to) become ripe(使)成熟

◆ phoenix /ˈfiːnɪks/ *n.*　凤凰;长生鸟

* pure /pjʊə/ *a.*　not mixed with any other substance; without harmful substances; without any faults or immorality; complete 纯的;纯净的; 无瑕的;完美的

* replace /rɪˈpleɪs/ *vt.*　provide a substitute for; take the place of; put (sth.) back in its place 替换;代替;接替;把…放回原处

★ fetch /fetʃ/ *vt.*　go for and bring back(去)拿来;请来;接来

* coin /kɔɪn/ *n.*　money made of metal 硬币

* furniture /ˈfɜːnɪtʃə/ *n.*　things needed in a house, office, room, etc. such as tables, chairs, beds and desks 家具

* celebrate /ˈselɪbreɪt/ *vt.*　mark (a happy or important day, event, etc.) by doing sth. enjoyable 庆祝

* amaze /ə'meɪz/ *vt.*	fill (sb.) with great surprise or wonder 使(某人)大为惊奇;使(某人)惊愕
◆wealthy /'welθɪ/ *a.*	having wealth; rich 富的;有钱的
* anxious /'æŋkʃəs/ *a.*	worried; uneasy; eager; wanting sth. very much 焦虑的;不安的;急切的;渴望的
* exchange /ɪks'tʃeɪndʒ/ *vt.*	change (one thing for another); give (sth.) in order to get sth. else 交换;调换
n.	交换;调换
* wealth /welθ/ *n.*	large amount of money, property, etc. ; riches 财产;财富
* demand /dɪ'mɑːnd/ *vt.*	ask for, claim, in a determined way; require; need 要求,请求;强要;需要
* content /kən'tent/ *a.*	satisfied with what one has; not wanting more; happy 满意的;满足的;乐意的
* seize /siːz/ *vt.*	take hold of (sth.) suddenly and violently; grab 抓住,捉住;攫取
◆handful /'hændfʊl/ *n.*	as much or as many as can be held in one hand; small number 一把;少数,少量
* pack /pæk/ *v.*	put (sth.) into a container; fill (a container) with sth. 把…装箱;把…打包;把东西装进(容器)
* ocean /'əʊʃn/ *n.*	mass of salt water that covers most of the earth's surface 洋;海洋;大海
* drown /draʊn/ *v.*	(cause to) die in water because not able to breathe(使)淹死
* bottom /'bɒtəm/ *n.*	lowest or deepest part (of sth.)底;底部

生词量	总词数	生词率	B级词(*)	A级词(★)	纲外词(◆)
36	535	6.7%	28	2	6

Phrases & Expressions

long, long ago	a very long time ago 很久、很久以前
care for	look after; take care of; attend to 照顾;照料
remind sb. of sb./sth.	cause sb. to remember sb./sth. 使(某人)想起(某人/某事)
eat one's fill	eat as much as one can 吃个饱
settle down	begin to live a regular life 安顿下来;过安定的生活
straight away	immediately; without delay 立即,马上;毫不耽搁地
agree to	say "yes" to; consent to 同意;赞同
once more	again; one more time 重新;再一次

Proper Name

Nguyen /əŋˈəʊˈjen/	阮

Notes on the Text

1. The only thing he left the younger brother was a carambola tree. 他留给弟弟的唯一一样东西是一棵杨桃树。句子的主语是 the only thing,谓语是 was。he left the younger brother 是定语从句,修饰、限定 thing。

2. He found himself a job and spent his spare time caring for the carambola tree. 他找到一份工作,业余时间则照料那棵杨桃树。find 跟双宾语时,表示给某人(自己)找到什么。

3. I will pay you in pure gold for what I eat. Get a bag ready and when I have finished eating you can have a fortune in gold pieces to replace your carambolas. 我吃的杨桃我会用纯金来偿付你的。准备好一只袋子,等我吃完,你就可以有一大笔金币补偿你的杨桃了。

4. The young man took a gold coin for every piece of fruit the phoenix had eaten and then the great bird carried him and his bag full of gold back to his home. 年轻人为凤凰吃的每一只杨桃拿了一枚金币,然后那只大鸟又驮着他和那只装满金币的口袋回到他的家。full of gold 是后置形容词短语,修饰名词 bag。

5. Very soon he invited his brother to share a fine meal with him to celebrate his

changed fortune. 很快他便邀请哥哥来共享美餐,庆祝自己时来运转。

6. The younger brother, who felt he had already more than enough wealth to last him all of his life, agreed to the exchange. 弟弟觉得自己已经有了一辈子也用不完的财富,便同意交换。

7. ... seized handfuls of coins, and packed the bag full. …… 抓起一把一把的金币,把口袋装得满满的。full 是动词 pack 的宾语补足语。

Exercises

13 Answer the following questions.

1. Did the younger brother feel angry when the older brother cheated him? Why or why not?

2. Why did the younger brother take good care of the carambola tree?

3. Did the younger brother want the phoenix to eat the carambolas at the beginning? Why or why not?

4. What did the phoenix offer to do for the younger brother?

5. Was the younger brother greedy when he took the gold coins? Why or why not?

6. What kind of life did the younger brother live after he got rich?

7. How did the older brother feel when he found his brother had become so rich?

8. What did the older brother want to do after he heard the story?

9. How greedy was the older brother when he took the gold coins?

10. How did the older brother die and why?

14 Fill in the blanks with the words given below. Change the forms where necessary.

amaze	behaviour	cheat	content	demand	earn
exchange	extra	fortune	replace	seize	spare

1. Her uncle made a great _____ in the oil business and left it all to her instead of his own son.

2. We _____ to see John looking so well so soon after he came back from the hospital.

3. Tim was very angry, saying that he _____ by his greedy uncle.

4. Mary bought a red T-shirt yesterday, but then she went back to the store and wanted to _____ it for a white one.

5. The poor workers _____ higher pay and better working conditions, but the boss refused to listen.

6. If you are not _____ with the way the computer operates, bring it back and we will look at it again.

7. The greedy boy _____ the bag of sweets in both hands and would not let go(松手).

8. His _____ in school is beginning to improve; he used to be such a bad boy that nobody liked him.

9. She _____ some money by playing the piano in a bar, but it's far from enough to support her family.

10. They did a lot of _____ work but refused to take any _____ pay.

11. He likes to read English novels in his _____ time.

12. The old bridge is unsafe. They're going to _____ it with a new one made of stone.

15 Fill in the blanks with the expressions given below. Change the forms where necessary.

agree to	care for	eat one's fill	long, long ago
once more	remind... of	settle down	straight away

1. He wants me to give up my job when we're married, but I could never _____ that.

2. No more cookies(小甜饼,曲奇), thank you. _____ and don't have any room for any more.

3. The hospital needs more nurses to _____ those people who were injured in the serious accident(事故).

4. _____, there lived a girl called Cinderella.

5. _____ he wrote to her asking her to marry him, but again she refused him.

6. I'm tired of traveling; I'd like to _____ — probably in a small town.

7. Looking down on the water, he _____ suddenly _____ his

childhood days playing in the river.

8. Time is running out. We'd better start work _____.

Text C

A Dinner of Smells

Author Unknown

One day a poor man came into a little town. He was very hungry. Every time he saw food, his mouth watered. But he had no money.

2   The poor man stopped outside a fine restaurant. The food at the restaurant smelled delicious. He *sniffed*(闻) and sniffed the   5 wonderful smell.

3   The *owner*(老板) of the restaurant came into the street.

4   "Hey! You!" the owner called. "I saw what you did! You smelled my excellent food! You *stole*(偷) the smell of my food. Are you going to pay for it?"   10

5   The poor man replied, "I cannot pay. I have no money. I took nothing!"

6   The owner of the restaurant did not listen to him. "I'm taking you to the judge," he said. And he took the poor man to court.

7   The judge listened to the story. "This is very unusual," he   15 said. "I want to think about it. Come back tomorrow."

8   The poor man was very worried. He had no money. "What can I do?" he asked himself. He could not sleep at all.

9   The next morning the man got up and said his *prayers*(祈祷). Then he went slowly back to the court. On the way he met the   20 wise *mullah*(毛拉), Nasrudin.

10   "Nasrudin," the poor man cried. "Please help me. People say that you are very clever. I am very unhappy and very worried." He told Nasrudin his story.

11   "Well, well," wise Nasrudin said. "Let's see what hap-   25

pens. " The two men went to court.

    12   The judge was already there. He was with the owner of the restaurant. They looked very friendly with each other. When the poor man arrived, the judge began to speak. He said the poor man *owed*(欠)the restaurant owner a lot of money.

    13   Nasrudin stepped forward. "This man is my friend," he said. "Can I pay for him?" He held out a bag of money.

    14   The judge looked at the restaurant owner. "Can Nasrudin pay?" he asked.

    15   "Yes," the restaurant owner said. "Nasrudin has money. The poor man does not. Nasrudin can pay!"

    16   Nasrudin smiled. He stood next to the restaurant owner. Nasrudin held the bag of money near the restaurant owner's ear. He *shook*(摇)it so the coins made a noise.

    17   "Can you hear the money?" he asked.

    18   "Of course I can hear it," the restaurant owner said.

    19   "That is your payment," the mullah said. "My friend smelled your food, and you heard his money."

    20   And that is the end of the story.

(405 *words*)

Comprehension of the Text

16 Choose the best answer for each of the following multiple choice questions.

1. The poor man stopped outside a fine restaurant because he _____.

    A) wanted to eat without paying

    B) was attracted by the smell

    C) wanted to steal the smell

    D) was reminded of home

2. The owner of the restaurant took the poor man to court in order to _____.

    A) teach him a lesson

    B) trouble the judge

    C) get back the stolen smell

    D) get some money from the poor man

3. In the sentence "This is very unusual," the word "unusual" means _____.

    A) strange

    B) difficult

    C) new

    D) different

4. The poor man asked Nasrudin for help because he believed that Nasrudin _____.

    A) was a powerful official

    B) could find a way out

    C) had money to pay for him

    D) could fight against the judge

5. Nasrudin smiled when the restaurant owner allowed him to pay for the poor man. The reason is that he _____.

    A) wanted to be friendly

    B) was not afraid of the judge

    C) knew he could help the poor man

    D) was proud he had money to pay

6. The restaurant owner was paid with _____.

    A) a bag of real money

    B) the sound of money

    C) the smell of money

    D) the smell of food

Basic Reading Skills

Understanding Signal Words（3）

　　有些 Signal Words 表示的是"因果"关系，表示原因的词语有：because, since, as, because of, thanks to 等，表示结果的词语有：so, consequently（因此，所以），thus, therefore, as a result 等。

　　下面本单元是 A 篇课文中的句子：

They dug up all the weeds and picked out all the stones, not **because** they liked weeding and cleaning, but **because** it was all part of the hunt for the buried treasure.

　　他们为什么 dug up all the weeds and picked out all the stones 呢？原因不是 they liked weeding and cleaning，而是 it was all part of the hunt for the buried treasure。作者用 because 表示了这种"因果"关系。

　　再看下面一段：

My mother is not the bargain shopper. She does not cut out coupons or compare products or prices; she is impatient — if she likes something, she buys it. My father, **therefore**, has always done our food shopping. He compares products and prices, looks for sales and bargains, and buys only what he needs. He has also always taken care of our household finances and is the bookkeeper and accountant of the family. My father says that my mother has champagne tastes with a beer pocketbook, and she says that he's cheap, but there is a happy compromise — she spends and he saves. (Text C, Unit 3)

　　作者的母亲不是一位 bargain shopper，她不剪优惠券（coupons），也不比较商品价格，而父亲很会精打细算，所以（therefore），他 has always done our food shopping。作者用 therefore 表示了这种因果关系。

17 Reread the following sentences from your textbook. Identify the signal words that are used to express a cause and effect relationship.

1. She enjoys people because, to her, they are the most interesting form of life. (Text C, Unit 3)

2. Other beliefs are facts: things that are true because people have proven them in studies. (Text B, Unit 4)

3. Since the automobile manufacturers wouldn't build the engine, the brothers talked to Charles Taylor. (Text C, Unit 2)

Fun Time

Idiom

> ### "Better Late Than Never" (迟总比不好)
>
> **"Better late than never"** means that it is **better** to do something **late than** to **never** do it at all. Example: "The movie has already started. Do you still want to go in?" Reply: "Sure. **Better late than never!**"("电影已经开始了。你还想进去吗?""当然进去。迟到总比不看好呀!")
>
> **"Better late than never"** is often used as a polite way to respond when a person says sorry for being **late**. Example: "Sorry I was late for the meeting today. I got stuck in traffic." Reply: "That's okay. **Better late than never.**"("对不起,今天开会我迟到了。路上堵车。""没关系。迟到总比不来好。")
>
> **"Better late than never"** means that even if you are going to be **late** you should still go ahead and do the thing, because it is **better** to do it **late than** to **never** do it at all. Example: "I'm sorry it has taken me so long to return this book." Reply: "**Better late than never.**"("对不起,过了这么长时间才还书。""迟还总比不还好。")

UNIT 6

Highlights

Preview Churchill once said, "Courage is the first of human qualities." In the Listening and Speaking section of this unit, you will pick up language for building self-confidence and learn how to encourage people to do it. In the Reading and Writing section, the author of Text A learned through her own experience what courage meant to ordinary people. Text B is a touching story about the world-famous miler Glenn Cunningham. The Wisdom of Socrates in Text C may help anyone who wants to do something well.

Listening & Speaking

The Language for Building Self-confidence

1 You are going to listen to an instructor talking about building self-confidence. Listen carefully and fill in the blanks with the missing words.

Instructor: Self-confidence(自信) is the key to your success. Without self-confidence you'll never _____. Every successful person will tell you that they only achieved their goals because they always _____. But no one is born _____. Self-confidence is something you _____ and perfect. But sometimes people tend to lose confidence and complain. They say:

1. I can't take _____ of it.
2. I'm sick and tired of _____.
3. It makes me sick the way they _____.
4. It makes my blood boil(沸腾) when _____.
5. I'm finished. (我完蛋了。)

You can help people build confidence and change the way their minds focus(集中) on things by saying:

1. Cheer up. It is not the _____.
2. _____. Every cloud has a silver lining. (黑暗中总有一丝希望。)
3. Come on! It can't be _____ all that.
4. Try and look on _____.
5. Hey look, why don't we _____?
6. Well, maybe _____ to look at it.
7. Don't _____ get to(使沮丧) you.

2 Now work in pairs. One has lost confidence, while the other helps build his/her partner's confidence. Use the language you have just learned in Exercise 1.

Building Self-confidence

3

1) Before you listen to the first conversation, read the following words and expressions which may be new to you.

It takes a while to...	做…要花一些时间
get it right	把它弄对
vocabulary	词汇

Listen to the conversation twice and fill in the blanks with the missing words.

Wang Ying: So how's your English class going?

Li Ming: I can't take any more of it. _____ the pronunciation difficult.

Wang Ying: Well, take it easy. It takes a while to _____.

Li Ming: I don't think I'm the right person for _____.

Wang Ying: Come on. Don't say that. I know _____ for you.

Li Ming: And I always seem to forget new words. _____ new vocabulary?

Wang Ying: I learn new words by writing them on pieces of paper and sticking them _____. I look at them every night before I _____.

Li Ming: Maybe I should try something _____!

Wang Ying: Why not? If I can do it, you _____.

Now listen to the conversation again and answer the following questions.

1. What are Wang Ying and Li Ming talking about?
2. What did Li Ming say about learning English?
3. What did Wang Ying encourage Li Ming to do?
4. How does Wang Ying learn new words?
5. What will Li Ming do next?

2) *Before you listen to the second conversation, read the following words and expressions which may be new to you.*

get sb. down	使某人沮丧
I'll tell you what.	你听我说。
make-up test	补考
make it	成功

Listen to the conversation twice and fill in the blanks with the missing words.

Li Ming:	Why the long face?
Wang Ying:	_____.
Li Ming:	What's the matter? Want to talk about it? _____.
Wang Ying:	My career is over before it has started.
Li Ming:	_____.
Wang Ying:	Yeah, I'm finished.
Li Ming:	Oh, come on, it can't be as bad as all that. _____.
Wang Ying:	Thanks.
Li Ming:	I'll tell you what, you can have a make-up test. _____.
Wang Ying:	You're right. I should believe in myself.
Li Ming:	Hey, look, why don't you listen to some music? _____.
Wang Ying:	You won't believe it, but I feel much better already!

Now listen to the conversation again and answer the following questions.

1. What has gotten Wang Ying down?
2. Is it true that Wang Ying's finished?
3. What did Li Ming say?
4. Do you think Wang Ying's going to make it in the make-up test? Why or why not?
5. How is Wang Ying feeling now?

4 Write a dialogue with your partner like the ones in Exercise 3. Begin with Part A and let your partner play the role of Part B. After that, practice the dialogue in class, using the the language you learned in Exercise 1.

Listening Practice

5 Listen to people speaking and decide what they are talking about.

1. A) A chance.   B) A person.
   C) A country.   D) A city.
2. A) A dinner party.   B) A job interview(求职面试).
   C) A past thing.   D) A future plan.
3. A) Courses.   B) Jobs.
   C) Likes.   D) Dislikes.
4. A) An English course.   B) A piece of information.
   C) A long weekend.   D) A new class.
5. A) Age.   B) Marriage.
   C) Health.   D) People.

6 Listen to five questions and choose the appropriate answers.

1. A) I sure do.   B) Sure I am.
   C) Surely I did.   D) Certainly I will.

2. A) You're right.   B) Not at all.
   C) I think so.   D) You, too.
3. A) Yes, I did.   B) Yes, I will.
   C) No, I didn't.   D) No, I haven't.
4. A) Yes. Tea would be nice. Thanks.   B) Thanks God! I'm hungry.
   C) Let's see what we can do.   D) I guess you're right.
5. A) What do you suggest?   B) Can you tell how?
   C) Sorry about that!   D) Hmm... so do I.

7 Listen to five short dialogues and choose the appropriate answers.

1. A) In a restaurant.   B) In the library.
   C) In a hotel.   D) On a bus.
2. A) The man is good at basketball.
   B) The woman is good at volleyball(排球).
   C) The man is a poor basketball player.
   D) The woman is a poor volleyball player.
3. A) The one wearing glasses.   B) The one talking to a man.
   C) The tall one by the window.   D) The short one sitting at the table.
4. A) In winter.   B) In spring.
   C) In summer.   D) In all seasons.
5. A) It's rush hour.   B) It's raining hard.
   C) The taxi is broken.   D) The bus will arrive late.

8 Listen to the following short talk and fill in the blanks with the missing words. The talk is given twice.

TWO FROGS(青蛙) — a big one and a small one — hopped into a pail(桶) of milk. The _____ were shiny and smooth(光滑). The frogs were swimming round and round without being able _____ the pail again, and every time they lifted their mouths to catch a little air to breathe, down _____. They kept on swimming and gasping(喘气) like this till the big frog _____ and drowned(溺死). Then the little frog said to himself, "Well, well. I will hang on(坚持)as long as _____, too." It kept on for hours, when suddenly it found something solid _____ — the milk had churned(搅拌) into butter(黄油)! _____

the little frog!

(116 *words*)

9 Listen to the talk again and then answer the following questions orally.

> 1. How many frogs hopped into the pail of milk?
> 2. Why was it so difficult for the frogs to jump out of the pail?
> 3. What happened to the big frog?
> 4. What did the little frog do?
> 5. What can we learn from the story?

10 Have an open discussion on the topic given below.

> Self-confidence is the key to success.

Reading & Writing

Text A

Starter

You must have watched some races or ball games and you must have heard people cheering and shouting on these occasions. They may cheer for the winner as well as for the loser. Now make a list of the reasons why people do both.

Reasons people cheer for the winner:
1.
2.
3.

Reasons people cheer for the loser:
1.
2.
3.

Now read the following passage and try to find out why the crowd cheered for the writer.

The reason why the crowd cheered for the writer:

Text

Tracking Down My Dream

Ashley Hodgeson

It was the district track meet — the one we had been training for all season. My foot still hadn't healed from an earlier injury. As a matter of fact, I had debated whether or not I should attend the meet. But there I was, preparing for the 3,200-meter run.

2   "Ready... set...." The gun popped and we were off. The other girls darted ahead of me. I realized I was limping and felt humiliated as I fell farther and farther behind.

3   The first-place runner was two laps ahead of me when she crossed the finish line. "Hooray!" shouted the crowd. It was the loudest cheer I had ever heard at a meet.

4   "Maybe I should quit," I thought as I limped on. "Those people don't want to wait for me to finish this race." Somehow, though, I decided to keep going. During the last two laps, I ran in

pain and decided not to compete in track
15 next year. It wouldn't be worth it, even if
my foot did heal. I could never beat the
girl who had lapped me twice.

5 When I finished, I heard a cheer —
just as enthusiastic as the one I'd heard
20 when the first girl passed the finish line.
"What was that all about?" I asked myself. I turned around and, sure enough,
the boys were preparing for their race.
"That must be it; they're cheering for the
25 boys."

6 I went straight to the bathroom where a girl bumped into
me. "Wow, you've got courage!" she told me.

7 I thought, "Courage? She must be mistaking me for some
one else. I just lost a race!"

30 *8* "I would never have been able to finish those two miles if I
were you. I would have quit on the first lap. What happened to your
foot? We were cheering for you. Did you hear us?"

9 I couldn't believe it. A complete stranger had been cheering
for me — not because she wanted me to win, but because she wan-
35 ted me to keep going and not give up. Suddenly I regained hope. I
decided to stick with track next year. One girl saved my dream.

10 That day I learned two things:

11 First, a little kindness and confidence in people can make
a great difference to them.

40 *12* And, second, strength and courage aren't always measured in medals and victories. They are measured in the struggles
we overcome. The strongest people are not always the people who
win, but the people who don't give up when they lose.

13 I dream only that someday — perhaps as a senior — I will
45 be able to win a race with a cheer as big as the one I got when I
lost that race as a freshman.

(451 *words*)

New Words

★track /træk/ n.　　　　　足迹;踪迹;小道,小径;路径;跑道;径赛运动;田径运动

　　　　　vt.　　　　　　　跟踪;追踪

★district /ˈdɪstrɪkt/ n.　　part of a country or town; area of a country or town treated as an administrative unit 区;地区;行政区

◆heal /hiːl/ v.　　　　　　(cause to) become healthy again(使)愈合;(使)痊愈;(使)康复

* injury /ˈɪndʒərɪ/ n.　　　instance of harm to one's body or reputation(对身体的)伤害;(对名誉的)损害

★debate /dɪˈbeɪt/ vt.　　　think (sth.) over in order to decide; discuss (sth.) formally 考虑,盘算;讨论;争论

* attend /əˈtend/ vt.　　　be present at; go regularly to (a place) 出席,参加;上(学等)

* pop /pɒp/ n.　　　　　　short sharp explosive sound 砰的一声,啪的一声

　　　　　vi.　　　　　　　make a short sharp explosive sound 发出砰(或啪)的响声

◆dart /dɑːt/ vi.　　　　　move or run suddenly and quickly 猛冲;飞奔

* realize /ˈrɪəlaɪz/ vt.　　understand; be/become fully aware of; turn into a reality 明白,理解;认识到;体会到;实现

◆limp /lɪmp/ vi.　　　　　walk unevenly, as when one foot or leg is hurt or stiff 跛行;一拐一拐地走

◆humiliate /hjuːˈmɪlɪeɪt/ vt.　make (sb.) feel ashamed or disgraced 使(某人)感到羞耻(或不光彩);使丢脸

◆lap /læp/ n.　　　　　　single circuit of a track or racecourt(跑道的)一圈

　　　　　vt.　　　　　　　be one or more laps ahead of (another competitor) in a race 比…领先一圈(或数圈)

◆hooray /hʊˈreɪ/ int.　　(used to express joy, pleasure, enthusiasm, etc.)(表示高兴、欢快、热情等的呼喊声)好,好哇;万岁

* cheer /tʃɪə/ n.　　　　　shout of joy, praise, support or encouragement 欢

	呼声;喝彩声
v.	give shouts of joy, praise, support or encouragement to (sb.) 向(某人)欢呼;为(某人)喝彩
* quit /kwɪt/ (quit, quit *or* quitted) *v.*	give up or resign (one's job or position); stop (doing sth.); stop trying; accept or acknowledge defeat 放弃;辞去;停止(做某事);停止努力;认输
* race /reɪs/ *n.*	contest of speed between runners, horses, etc. (速度的)比赛,赛跑
* somehow /'sʌmhaʊ/ *ad.*	in some way; by some means; for a reason that is unknown or unspecified 以某种方式;用某种方法;不知怎么地
* worth /wɜːθ/ *a.*	having the value of; good enough to deserve (to be done) 值…钱;有…价值;值得…
◆enthusiastic /ɪnˌθjuːzɪ'æstɪk/ *a.*	full of enthusiasm 热情的;热心的,热烈的
◆wow /waʊ/ *int.*	(used to express astonishment or admiration) (表示惊奇或钦佩等)哇,呀
* courage /'kʌrɪdʒ/ *n.*	quality of mind or strength of purpose that a person has to help face or handle fear, danger, pain, etc.; bravery 勇气;胆量
◆regain /rɪ'geɪn/ *vt.*	get (sth.) back again after losing it 重新获得
* kindness /'kaɪndnɪs/ *n.*	quality of being kind 仁慈,好意
* confidence /'kɒnfɪdəns/ *n.*	belief or faith in one's own or others' ability 信任;信心;自信
* difference /'dɪfrəns/ *n.*	state or way in which two people or things are not the same; amount or degree in which two things are not the same; disagreement 差别,差异;不同之处;差距;差额;(意见的)分歧,不和
* strength /streŋθ/ *n.*	quality of being strong; degree of intensity of this 力量;力气;强度
* medal /'medl/ *n.*	flat round piece of metal with words and/or a picture on it, given to sb. as a reward for success in a sports competition, being brave during a battle, etc. 奖牌;奖章;勋章;纪念章

* victory /ˈvɪktərɪ/ *n.*	success in a war, contest, game, etc. 胜利;成功
* struggle /ˈstrʌgl/ *n.*	fight; great effort 斗争,搏斗;奋斗,努力
vi.	fight (with sb.); move one's body vigorously; try to overcome difficulties, etc.; make great efforts (与某人)斗争,搏斗;挣扎;奋斗,努力
* overcome /ˌəʊvəˈkʌm/ *vt.*	win a victory over (sb./sth.); defeat 战胜;克服
◆ someday /ˈsʌmdeɪ/ *ad.*	at some time in the future 将来某一天;总有一天
★ senior /ˈsiːnɪə/ *n.*	older person; person higher in rank; [AmE] a student in his/her last year of high school or university 较年长者;地位(级别)较高者;(美国四年制大学或中学的)高年级生

生词量	总词数	生词率	B级词(*)	A级词(★)	纲外词(◆)
32	451	7.1%	18	4	10

Phrases & Expressions

track down	find (sb./sth.) by following her / his / its track; find by searching 跟踪找到;追捕到;搜寻到
prepare for	make oneself mentally or physically ready for 为…作好准备
fall behind	fail to stay (with the group); be slower than (the rest) 落在…后面
in pain	painfully; with pain 痛苦地
worth it	certain or very likely to repay the money, effort or time given 值得的;值得花费金钱(或努力、时间)的
even if	in spite of the fact that 即使
turn around / round	face about 转身
sure enough	as expected 果然
mistake... for...	think wrongly that (sb./sth.) is (sb./sth. else) 把…误认为…
happen to	befall 临到;发生于;落到…头上
make a difference to	have an effect on; be important to 对…有影响;对…起重要作用

Proper Name

Ashley Hodgeson /ˈæʃlɪ ˈhɒdʒsn/   阿什利·霍奇森

Notes on the Text

1. As a matter of fact, I had debated whether or not I should attend the meet. 实际上，我一直在考虑是否应该参加这次运动会。debate 这儿解释为"考虑"。

2. But there I was, preparing for the 3,200-meter run. 但我还是去了，准备好参加3 200米跑。there I was 是倒装句。

3. Those people don't want to wait for me to finish this race. 那些人并不想等着我跑完全程。to finish this race 是不定式短语，充当"me"的宾语补足语。

4. It wouldn't be worth it, even if my foot did heal. 即使我的脚真的好了，这也不值得。worth it 意为"值得"，did 起强调作用。

5. When I finished, I heard a cheer — just as enthusiastic as the one I'd heard when the first girl passed the finish line. 当我跑完时，我听到了一片欢呼声——就像第一个女孩冲过终点线时我听到的欢呼声一样热烈。本句有 4 个从句，按顺序为：When I finished 时间状语从句；as the one I'd heard 比较状语从句；I'd heard 定语从句（省略了连接代词 that）；when the first girl... 时间状语从句。

6. What was that all about? 这是怎么回事？

7. I turned around and, sure enough, the boys were preparing for their race. 我转过身去，果然，是男孩子们正在准备开始比赛。sure enough 果然，又如：He said he'd left the book on the desk, and sure enough, there it was. 他说他已经把书留在书桌上了，果然，书就在那里。

8. I would never have been able to finish those two miles if I were you. 如果我是你的话，我绝不可能跑完那两英里。本句用虚拟语气：从句中用过去时，表示事实与现在相反；主句用过去将来完成时，表示事实与过去相反。

9. First, a little kindness and confidence in people can make a great difference to them. 第一，对别人表示一点好意和信任可以对他们产生很大的影响。make a great difference to：对…产生很大影响。

10. I dream only that someday — perhaps as a senior — I will be able to win a race with a cheer as big as the one I got when I lost that race as a freshman. 我只是梦想将来某一天——也许在大四时——我能赢得比赛，得到与我在大一输掉比赛时得到的同样热烈的欢呼。本句中 that 引导一个宾语从句。在这个宾语从句中，又包含有一个比较状语从句，一个定语从句和一个时间状语从句。

Exercises

Reading Aloud

1 Read the following paragraphs until you have learned them by heart.

That day I learned two things:

First, a little kindness and confidence in people can make a great difference to them.

And, second, strength and courage aren't always measured in medals and victories. They are measured in the struggles we overcome. The strongest people are not always the people who win, but the people who don't give up when they lose.

I dream only that someday — perhaps as a senior — I will be able to win a race with a cheer as big as the one I got when I lost that race as a freshman.

Understanding the Text

2 Answer the following questions.

1. How long did the writer train for the track meet?
2. What event did the writer take part in?
3. How was the writer running?
4. Why did she feel humiliated?
5. How fast was the first-place runner?
6. What was the crowd's response?
7. What decision did the writer make during the last two laps?
8. What happened when the writer finished?
9. What did the writer think of the cheer?
10. Whom did the writer meet in the bathroom?
11. What did the writer and the girl talk about?
12. Why did the crowd cheer for the writer?
13. What decision did the writer make after the conversation with the girl?
14. What did the writer learn that day?
15. What has been the writer's dream since then?

3 Topics for Discussion.

1. If you were the writer, what decision would you have made during the race? Tell us

why you would make such a decision?

2. Whatever we do, among other things, we need courage of our own and encouragement from others. In your opinion, which is more important? Why?

Reading Analysis

4 Read Text A again and complete the following table.

Part	Paragraph	Key Words	Main Ideas
Part One	Paragraphs 1-4	limping, humiliated, quit	I fell behind in a race and was thinking of quitting.
Part Two	Paragraph 5		
Part Three	Paragraphs ___		
Part Four	Paragraphs ___		

Now retell the story, using the information in the table you have completed.

Vocabulary

5 Fill in the blanks with the words given below. Change the forms where necessary.

injury	debate	attend	realize	quit	somehow
worth	courage	measure	overcome	race	kindness

1. The soldier showed great _____ in the battle.
2. I've voiced my opinion at every meeting I've _____.
3. A friend of mine has recently decided to _____ his highly-paid but demanding job in an American company.
4. In the crash the taxi driver received serious _____ to his head and arms.
5. It's taken me a while but at last I've managed to _____ my fear of public speaking.
6. _____, though, he managed to pass all his final exams.

7. He was not feeling well that morning and was _____ whether or not he should go to work.

8. He helped us entirely out of _____, not for the money.

9. As he watched the TV play, he suddenly _____ that he'd seen it before.

10. When he was young, my father ran in the cross-country _____ every year and often won.

11. The English dictionary cost me a lot of money, but it's certainly _____ it.

12. Education shouldn't be _____ purely by examination results.

6 Fill in the blanks with the expressions given below. Change the forms where necessary.

track down	prepare for	fall behind	in pain
even if	turn around	sure enough	mistake... for...
happen to	make a difference to		

1. I often _____ her _____ her sister on the phone.

2. Take these tablets if you are _____.

3. Did you hear what _____ David last night?

4. I _____ quickly to see if someone was following.

5. Tom spent an hour in the library and finally _____ the book he wanted.

6. Exercise can _____ your state of health.

7. Will you help me _____ the old classmates' reunion(重聚联欢会)?

8. He said he would come with his wife, and _____ he did.

9. I wouldn't lose courage _____ I should fail ten times.

10. After five miles, Tara was tired and started to _____.

Structure

7 Complete the following sentences by translating the Chinese in brackets into English using "as... as" structure.

Model:

I will be able to win a race with a cheer **as** big **as** the one I got when I lost that race as a freshman.

1. This book is _____. (和我上星期读的那本一样有趣)

2. He is painting a picture _____. (和你在他办公室里

看到的那张一样美)

3. The computer on display is _____. (和约翰昨天买
   的那台一样先进)

4. This singer is _____. (与去年获奖的那位齐名)

5. The newly built school is _____. (和玛丽上过的那
   所一样大)

6. George has just passed an exam _____. (和他去年
   通过的那次考试一样难)

8 Translate each of the following sentences into English according to the model.

Model:

> 要是有时间我一定去。
>
> I **would** certainly **go** if I **had** the time.

1. 要是你能多呆些时候多好！

_____

2. 如果我是你,我肯定会接受这份工作。

_____

3. 我要是问南希,她会怎么说?

_____

4. 要是你处在他的地位,你会怎么办?

_____

Translation

9 Translate the following sentences into English.

1. 事实上,她曾考虑过是否该出国。

_____

2. 这是我看过的最感人(touching)的电影。

_____

3. 我一瘸一拐地走向教室,在那儿碰到了汤姆。

_____

4. 他娶艾丽斯不是因为她美丽,而是因为她有钱。

_____

5. 衡量一个学生的学习不能只看他的分数,还要看他解决问题的能力。

_____

6. 最快乐的人不一定是有很多钱的人,而是那些乐于助人的人。

_____

Grammar Review

主谓一致(Subject-verb Agreement)(1)

主谓一致是指谓语动词在人称和数上必须与主语一致。主谓一致有许多原则,概括起来主要有三种,即语法形式一致,意义一致(语言内容上一致),毗邻一致(谓语动词的单复数形式和紧位于其前的主语一致)。列表如下:

原　则	说　明	例　句
语法形式一致	按主语的单复数形式确定谓语动词的单复数形式	My favorite book is *Gone with the Wind*. 我最喜爱的书是《飘》。 My favorite books are *David Copperfield*, *Wuthering Heights* and *The Gadfly*. 我最喜爱的书是《大卫·科波菲尔》、《呼啸山庄》和《牛虻》。
意义一致	谓语动词的单复数形式由主语所表达的单、复数意义决定	Chinese is a difficult language. 汉语是一门很难的语言。 The Chinese are kind and friendly. 中国人善良而友好。
毗邻一致	谓语动词的人称和数要在形式上与最靠近它的那个名词或代词取得一致	Either John or his brothers are waiting in the room. 不是约翰就是他的几个兄弟正在房间里等候。 Neither you, nor I, nor anybody else knows anything about it. 你、我或其他任何人都不知道这件事。

语法形式一致

用　　法	例　　　句
1. 可数名词单数、不可数名词、单个动词不定式、动名词短语或句子作主语时,谓语动词用单数形式	To learn English well <u>is</u> difficult. 学好英语是困难的。 Why she did this <u>is</u> not known. 还不清楚她为什么做这件事。
2. 可数名词复数、有表示数量的复数名词修饰的不可数名词、用 and 连接的动词不定式、动名词短语或句子作主语时,谓语动词用复数形式	Playing basketball and swimming <u>are</u> my favorite sports. 打篮球和游泳是我最喜爱的运动。 In the past few years 5 <u>million square meters</u> of housing <u>have been</u> constructed in Shanghai. 在过去几年中上海修建了 500 万平方米的住房。 What I say and think <u>are</u> none of your business. 我说什么、想什么都与你无关。
3. and 连接的两个名词指同一个人或同一件事(and 后的名词前没有冠词)时,谓语动词用单数形式	The secretary and cashier of the hotel <u>is</u> absent today. 这家旅馆的秘书兼收银员今天没有来。 This bread and butter <u>is</u> too thick. 这片涂黄油的面包太厚了。 比较: The bread and the butter <u>are</u> on sale. 正在优惠出售黄油和面包。
4. 由 as well as, with, like, together with, rather than, including 等引导的结构作插入语时,主语如果是单数,其谓语动词仍用单数形式	John, together with his family, <u>is</u> flying to Paris. 约翰将和家人一起乘坐飞机去巴黎。 <u>This man</u>, as well as his sons, always <u>catches</u> the largest fish. 这个人和他的几个儿子一样,总是能钓到最大的鱼。

用　　法	例　　句
5. 由 either, neither, each, one, the other, another, somebody, someone 等指代单数可数名词的代词作主语,或作某个名词的限定词时,谓语动词用单数形式	Each drank a cup of tea. 每个人都喝了一杯茶。 Neither of them is going to give up his/her chance of education. 他们俩都不想放弃受教育的机会。
6. 由 both, few, many, several 等不定代词作主语, 或作某个名词的限定词时,谓语动词用复数形式	Both of them have gone to London. 他们俩都到伦敦去了。 Few of my family really understand me. 家里几乎没人真正理解我。
7. 由 all of, most of, a lot of, some of, none of, plenty of 等加名词作主语时,谓语动词的单复数形式应与名词的单复数一致	None of the evidence points to his guilt. 没有哪一件证据能指证他的罪行。 None of my friends are here. 我的朋友都不在这儿。
8. 由分数或百分数 + of + 名词作主语时,谓语动词的单复数形式应与 of 后的名词的单复数一致	Half of my spare time is spent on my hobby. 我一半的业余时间都花在业余爱好上了。 Three-fourths of the workers in the factory are women. 这个工厂四分之三的工人是女工。
9. 定语从句中谓语动词的单复数形式与先行词一致	A person who has many friends enjoys life more. 朋友多的人更能享受生活。 Charles is one of those persons who always think they are right. 查尔斯是那种自以为是的人。

10 Choose the correct verbal form in the brackets to complete each of the following sentences.

1. Walking ＿＿＿＿＿＿ (is, are) good exercise.
2. Several of the students ＿＿＿＿＿＿(was, were) absent.
3. One of my friends ＿＿＿＿＿＿ (needs, need) some help.
4. Mike, rather than his brothers, ＿＿＿＿＿＿ (is, are) responsible for the loss.
5. Most of the book ＿＿＿＿＿＿ (was, were) interesting.
6. The writer and poet ＿＿＿＿＿＿ (is, are) here.
7. That I shall work with you ＿＿＿＿＿＿ (is, are) a great pleasure.
8. What he says ＿＿＿＿＿＿ (does, do) not agree with what he does.
9. This is one of the rooms that ＿＿＿＿＿＿ (was, were) damaged in the war.
10. We went to two restaurants. Neither of them ＿＿＿＿＿＿ (was, were) expensive.

Practical Writing

Thank-you Notes

11 Read these two thank-you notes. Which one is to a friend? Which one is to a new business partner (伙伴)?

---

21 August, 2003

Dear Mr. Smith,

I'm writing to thank you for your hospitality during my recent trip to Germany.

It's always very useful to meet one's business partners face to face, and I think we had some interesting discussions.

I look forward to seeing you when you visit London in September.

Yours sincerely,
Mark Howard

---

29 September, 2003

Dear Peter,

This is just a short note to thank you for a very pleasant evening while I was in New York.

It is always good to see old friends again and it was very useful to exchange ideas.

Please give me a ring the next time you come to London. Perhaps we can meet for lunch.

Best wishes.
Mark

12 Write a note to Oliver and Jennifer thanking them for inviting you to a dinner party held at their home on January 8, 2004.

Text B

From Crutches to a World-class Runner

Author Unknown

A number of years ago in Elkhart, Kansas, two brothers had a job at the local school. Early each morning their job was to start a fire in the potbellied stove in the classroom.

2 One cold morning, the brothers cleaned out the stove and loaded it with firewood. Grabbing a can of kerosene, one of them   5
doused the wood and lit the fire. The explosion rocked the old building. The fire killed the older brother and badly burned the legs of the other boy. It was later discovered that the kerosene can had

accidentally been filled with gasoline.

3   The doctor attending the injured boy recommended amputating the young boy's legs. The
parents were very sad. They had already lost one
son, and now their other son was to lose his legs.
But they did not lose their faith. They asked the
doctor for a postponement of the amputation. The
doctor consented. Each day they asked the doctor for a delay, praying that their son's legs would
somehow heal and he would become well again. For two months,
the parents and the doctor debated on whether to amputate. They
used this time to instill in the boy the belief that he would someday
walk again.

4   They never amputated the boy's legs, but when the bandages were finally removed, it was discovered that his right leg was
almost three inches shorter than the other. The toes on his left foot
were almost completely burned out. Yet the boy was fiercely determined. Though in great pain, he forced himself to exercise daily
and finally took a few painful steps. Slowly recovering, this young
man finally threw away his crutches and began to walk almost normally. Soon he was running.

5   This determined young man kept running and running and
running — and those legs that came so close to being amputated
carried him to a world record in the mile run. His name? Glenn
Cunningham, known as the "World's Fastest Human Being," and
named athlete of the century at Madison Square Garden.

(337 *words*)

New Words

◆crutch /krʌtʃ/ *n.*	one of a pair of sticks put under the armpit to help a lame person to walk 拐杖
* pot /pɒt/ *n.*	round container for holding things for cooking in, etc. 罐;壶;锅
◆belly /'belɪ/ *n.*	front of the human body from the waist to the groin

肚子

◆potbellied /ˌpɒtˈbelɪd/ *a.*   (of a person) having a fat round belly; (of a container) curving out below the middle(指人)大腹便便的;(指容器)下部向外鼓的

＊stove /stəʊv/ *n.*   device for cooking things on; similar thing for heating rooms, etc. 炉子;火炉

◆firewood /ˈfaɪəwʊd/ *n.*   wood used for lighting fires or as fuel 木柴

◆grab /græb/ *vt.*   get hold of (sb./sth.) in a sudden, rough and usu. rude way 抓取;攫取

◆kerosene /ˈkerəsiːn/ *n.*   煤油

◆douse /daʊs/ *vt.*   put… into water, etc.; put water, etc. on 把…浸入水(或其他液体中);浇(或泼)水(或其他液体)在…上

◆explosion /ɪkˈspləʊʒn/ *n.*   (loud noise caused by) sudden and violent bursting 爆炸(声)

＊badly /ˈbædlɪ/ *ad.*   in an unsatisfactory or unsuccessful way; to a great or serious degree 坏,差;拙劣地;严重地;厉害地

◆accidentally /ˌæksɪˈdentəlɪ/ *ad.*   unexpectedly; by chance 意外地;偶然地

＊attend /əˈtend/ *vt.*   take care of; look after 照料;看管

＊recommend /ˌrekəˈmend/ *vt.*   suggest; advise; praise (sth.) as suitable for a purpose; praise (sb.) as suitable for a post 建议;劝告;推荐;称赞

◆amputate /ˈæmpjʊteɪt/ *vt.*   cut off (an arm, leg, etc.)切断,截(肢)

＊faith /feɪθ/ *n.*   strong belief; trust; unquestioning confidence 信念;信任;信心

＊postpone /ˌpəʊsˈpəʊn/ *vt.*   arrange (sth.) at a later time; delay (doing sth.) until a later time 使延期;推迟

◆postponement /ˌpəʊsˈpəʊnmənt/ *n.*   延期;推迟

◆amputation /ˌæmpjʊˈteɪʃn/ *n.*   切断(术);截肢(术)

★pray /preɪ/ *v.*   speak to God to give praise, ask for sth., etc. 祈祷;祈求

◆instill /ɪnˈstɪl/ *vt.*   put (an idea, feeling, virtue, etc.) (in or into

	sb. or sb.'s mind)(向某人或某人的头脑)逐步灌输(思想、感情、美德等)
◆bandage /ˈbændɪdʒ/ n.	strip of material used for binding round a wound or an injury(包扎伤口或患处的)绷带
* remove /rɪˈmuːv/ vt.	take away from one place to another; dismiss from a post, etc.; take off from the body; get rid of 移开;挪走;把…免职;脱下;摘下;去掉,除去
* inch /ɪntʃ/ n.	measure of length equal to 2.54cm or one twelfth of a foot 英寸(长度单位,等于2.54厘米或1/12英尺)
* complete /kəmˈpliːt/ a.	having all its parts; whole 完整的,完全的;整个的
vt.	finish; make whole or perfect 完成;使完整;使完善
* force /fɔːs/ vt.	make (sb./oneself) do sth. he/one does not want to do; compel 强迫;迫使
n.	力,力量;力气;武力;暴力
* daily /ˈdeɪlɪ/ ad.	every day 每日,天天
a.	done, produced or happening every day 每天的;日常的
n.	daily newspaper 日报
◆painful /ˈpeɪnfl/ a.	causing mental pain; having or producing pain 令人痛苦的;令人疼痛的;疼的
* recover /rɪˈkʌvə/ v.	get well, strong, etc. again; find again (sth. stolen, lost, etc.); regain possession of; get back the use of (one's faculties, health, etc.)痊愈;康复;重新找到;重新获得;恢复(能力、健康等)
* normally /ˈnɔːməlɪ/ ad.	in a usual way; usually 正常地;通常
* human /ˈhjuːmən/ a.	of or referring to a person or people in general 人的;人类的
* century /ˈsentʃərɪ/ n.	one hundred years; any of the periods of 100 years before or after the death of Jesus Christ 百年;世纪

生词量	总词数	生词率	B 级词(＊)	A 级词(★)	纲外词(◆)
32	337	9.5%	16	1	15

Phrases & Expressions

a number of	several; a large quantity of 若干;许多
clean out	clean the inside of (sth.) thoroughly 把…打扫干净;把…出空
burn out	completely destroy (sth.) by burning 烧光;烧毁
throw away	get rid of as worthless or unnecessary 扔掉,抛弃

Proper Names

Elkhart /ˈelkhɑːt/	埃尔克哈特(美国堪萨斯州一城镇)
Kansas /ˈkænsəs/	堪萨斯州(美国中部一州)
Glenn Cunningham /ˌglen ˈkʌnɪŋhæm/	格伦·坎宁安
Madison /ˈmædɪsn/ Square Garden	麦迪逊广场花园(纽约市曼哈顿的大型室内运动、娱乐和集会中心)

Notes on the Text

1. Early each morning their job was to start a fire in the potbellied stove in the classroom. 每天清晨,他们的工作就是给教室里的大腹取暖炉生火。

2. Grabbing a can of kerosene, one of them doused the wood and lit the fire. 两兄弟中的一个抓起一罐煤油,把它浇在木柴上,然后便点着了火。

3. It was later discovered that the kerosene can had accidentally been filled with gasoline. 后来才发现,原来煤油罐里偶然装满了汽油。"It"作形式主语,替代 that 引导的从句。

4. The doctor attending the injured boy recommended amputating the young boy's legs. 为受伤男孩治疗的医生建议给他截肢。

5. Each day they asked the doctor for a delay, praying that their son's legs would somehow heal and he would become well again. 每天他们都要求医生延期,同时祈盼儿子的双腿会不治而愈,他会重新康复。

6. They used this time to instill in the boy the belief that he would someday walk again. 他们用这段时间向男孩灌输这一信念:总有一天他会重新行走的。

7. ... it was discovered that his right leg was almost three inches shorter than the other. ······人们发现他的右腿比左腿短了差不多有三英寸。

8. Though in great pain, he forced himself to exercise daily and finally took a few painful steps. 虽然疼痛难熬,但他仍强迫自己每天锻炼,最后终于痛苦地走了几步。

9. ... and those legs that came so close to being amputated carried him to a world record in the mile run. ······而那两条差一点就被切除的腿竟然使他创造了一项一英里跑的世界纪录。

Exercises

13 Answer the following questions.

1. What was the two brothers' job?
2. What happened one cold morning?
3. What caused the accident?
4. What was the doctor's recommendation?
5. What belief did the parents instill in the boy?
6. What did they discover when the bandages were finally removed?
7. After hard exercises, what could the boy do at last?
8. Who was known as the "World's Fastest Human Being"?

14 Fill in the blanks with the words given below. Change the forms where necessary.

rock	explosion	badly	recommend	force
attend	recover	determined	faith	belief

1. It was the parents' firm _____ that their son would someday walk again.
2. I have great _____ in you — I'm sure you will succeed.
3. The explosion, which _____ the city, killed a number of passers-by and damaged many buildings.
4. I am _____ in need of your advice.
5. At 9:30 there was a terrible _____ at the other side of the square.

6. The doctors tried to _____ the worst injured soldiers first.

7. The doctor _____ that I take more exercise and stop smoking immediately.

8. It took her a long while to _____ from her heart operation.

9. Nobody _____ me — it was my own decision.

10. I think she will get the job that she wants — she is a very _____ person.

15 **Fill in the blanks with the expressions given below. Change the forms where necessary.**

> clean out   a number of   throw away
> burn out   instill in

1. They decided not to go to the party for _____ reasons.

2. It is part of a teacher's job to _____ self-confidence _____ his or her students.

3. It is time you _____ the drawers(抽屉) of your desk.

4. After the fire the factory was completely _____.

5. When are you going to _____ those old magazines of yours?

Text C

Socrates(苏格拉底)

Retold by Eric Saperston

There once was an *eager*(热切的) student who wanted to gain wisdom and *insight*(智慧和悟性). He went to the wisest of the town, Socrates, to seek his *counsel*(建议). Socrates was an old *soul*(人) and had great knowledge of many things. The boy asked the town *sage*(智者) how he too could acquire such mastery. Being a man of few words, Socrates chose not to speak, but to *illustrate*(用事例说明).

5

2 He took the child to the beach and, with all of his clothes still on, walked straight out into the water. He loved to do curious

10 things like that, especially when he was trying to prove a point. The pupil carefully followed his instruction and walked into the
sea, joining Socrates where the water was
just below their *chins*(下巴). Without saying
15 a word, Socrates reached out and put his
hands on the boy's shoulders. Looking deep
into his student's eyes, Socrates pushed the
student's head under the water with all his
might(力气).

20 *3* A struggle followed, and just before the boy's life was taken
away, Socrates released him. The boy raced to the surface and,
gasping for air and *choking*(呛) from the salt water, looked around
for Socrates in order to seek *retaliation*(报复) on the sage. To the
student's *bewilderment*(困惑), the old man was already patiently
25 waiting on the beach. When the student arrived on the sand, he
angrily shouted, "Why did you try to kill me?" The wise man calmly
retorted(反驳) with a question of his own: "Boy, when you were
underneath the water, not sure if you would live to see another day,
what did you want more than anything in the world?"

30 *4* The student took a few moments to reflect, then went with
his *intuition*(直觉). Softly he said, "I wanted to breathe." Socrates, now *illuminated*(容光焕发) by his own huge smile, looked at
the boy comfortingly and said, "Ah! When you want wisdom and
insight as badly as you wanted to breathe, then you shall have
35 them."

(323 *words*)

Comprehension of the Text

16 Choose the best answer for each of the following multiple choice questions.

1. Why did the student go to visit Socrates?
   A) Because he wanted to become a wise man, too.
   B) Because he wanted to challenge him.

C) Because he wanted to beat him.

D) Because he wanted to seek his advice.

2. How did Socrates answer the student's question?

   A) He didn't tell the student anything.

   B) He drove the student away.

   C) He tried to illustrate his idea.

   D) He told the answer to the student directly.

3. What did Socrates do to the student when they reached where the water was below their chins?

   A) He tried to push the student's head under the water with all his strength.

   B) He wanted to kill the student.

   C) He asked the student himself to put his head under the water.

   D) He gave a lesson to the student.

4. How did the student feel when he saw Socrates waiting patiently on the beach?

   A) Angry.   B) Puzzled.

   C) Wild.   D) Curious.

5. What did the student want to do when his head was pushed under the water?

   A) Become a wise man.

   B) Get as much knowledge as possible.

   C) Breathe.

   D) Gain wisdom and insight.

6. What was the author's reaction to Socrates' answer?

   A) It was ambiguous(模棱两可的).

   B) It was intelligent.

   C) It was hard to understand.

   D) Socrates didn't answer the student's question at all.

Basic Reading Skills

Understanding Signal Words（4）

有些 Signal Words 表示的是一种"归纳"或"小结"，当你读到这些 Signal Words 时，作者可能要概括要点或用最简单的话表达自己的思想了。表示"归纳"或"小结"的词语有：in conclusion，to sum up，to summarize，to conclude，in short，in a word 等。

最典型的要数第 4 单元 A 篇课文了：作者用小标题标出 Conclusion，说明下面一段文字是对全文的小结。

Conclusion

Athletes in nearly every sport use both speed and endurance. The nice thing is that anybody can become a better athlete by studying and practicing these running techniques. The funny thing is that hardly anyone knows this!

17 Read the following paragraphs. Identify the signal words that the writers use to express a conclusion.

1. The children could play as long as they liked, they had no work to do, and nobody scolded(责骂) them; in short, they were happy.

2. John is smart, polite and well-behaved(行为端正). In a word, he is admirable(值得赞美的).

3. However, television can also be harmful. Watching TV too much not only hurts our eyes, but also has a bad effect on our sleep and work; it also cuts down on children's study time. In short, we should take television as our assistant(助手) not as our master.

4. In conclusion, walking is a cheap, safe, enjoyable and readily available form of exercise.

Fun Time

Riddles

1. What will you break once you say it?
2. If the green house is on the right side of the road, and the red house is on the left side of the road, where is the white house?
3. What two words contain thousands of letters?
4. Why is the bride unhappy on her wedding day?
5. How many feet are there in a yard?
6. What's the poorest bank in the world?

Answers:
1. *Silence.*
2. *In Washington, D.C.*
3. *Post office.*
4. *Because she didn't marry the best man* (要结的人；最好的人). (新郎娶错了).
5. *It depends on how many people stand in the yard.*
6. *The river bank.*

UNIT 7

Highlights

Preview

Listening & Speaking

About Compliments

Giving Compliments
   and Replying to
   Compliments

Listening Practice

Reading & Writing

Text A

The Smile

Grammar Review

Subject-verb Agreement (2)

Practical Writing

Note of Congratulation

Text B

Blameless

Text C

A Lady Named Lill

Basic Reading Skills

Reading for the Main Idea:
   Topic Sentence (2)

Preview

Feeling low today? This unit is the chicken soup for your soul. In the Listening and Speaking section, you will learn about compliments and how to give and reply to them. In the Reading and Writing section, Text A tells a miraculous story about how a smile saved a person's life. Text B teaches us not to blame, however bad the situation may be. And Text C shows the great power that words of encouragement can have on people.

Listening & Speaking

About Compliments

1 You are going to listen to an instructor talking about compliments. Listen carefully and fill in the blanks with the missing words.

Instructor: Usually, you compliment someone if you notice _____ about the person's appearance: new eyeglasses, _____ or an article (件) of clothing. You may also compliment a person on his or her _____: "Gee, you really look good today" or "_____ terrific these days." It's common to compliment a person on a recently bought thing: "Hey, I really like _____" or "That new gadget (小玩意) is lovely." When you visit someone's apartment for the first time, you may give a general compliment like this: "What a beautiful apartment you have." When a host (主人) _____ for you, you usually offer a general compliment, such as "The meal was delicious, especially the _____." When you _____, you can say: "What a cute (漂亮的) baby!"

2 Now you can walk around the classroom, giving compliments to your classmates on their general appearance using the language you have just learned.

Giving Compliments and Replying to Compliments

.3

1) *Before you listen to the first conversation, read the following words and expressions which may be new to you.*

CD player	= diskman CD(激光)机
Not too bad.	还可以。
Lucky you!	你真幸运!
admire	羡慕

Listen to the conversation twice and fill in the blanks with the missing words.

Wang Ying: Hi, Li Ming, how are you?

Li Ming: Not too bad. How about you?

Wang Ying: Not too bad either. What's the gadget _____?

Li Ming: Oh, it's a CD player. It's a _____ from my uncle.

Wang Ying: Lucky you! I was just admiring it. It _____.

Li Ming: Why don't you give it _____?

Wang Ying: Thanks. Wow, it's great. _____ than my Walk-man.

Li Ming: Glad you like it. I can lend it to you _____.

Wang Ying: Oh, thank you so much. Well, I have _____. See you around.

Li Ming: So long.

Now listen to the conversation again and answer the following questions.

1. What is the gadget Li Ming is playing?
2. What is the gadget Wang Ying has?
3. What's Wang Ying's compliment?
4. What's Li Ming's reply to the compliment?
5. Do you think Li Ming is a nice young man? And why?

2) *Before you listen to the second conversation, read the following words and expressions which may be new to you.*

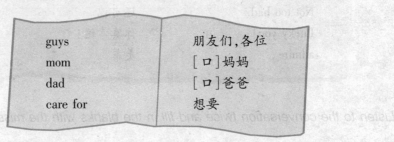

guys	朋友们,各位
mom	[口]妈妈
dad	[口]爸爸
care for	想要

Listen to the conversation twice and fill in the blanks with the missing words.

(*The doorbell rings.*)

Wang Ying: Hi! _____.

Li Ming, Michael Lu & Paul Li: Hi, Wang Ying. Happy birthday to you. This is our gift for you. _____.

Wang Ying: Wow, it's a CD player! _____! Thank you so much.

Li Ming: It's nothing.

Wang Ying: Oh, you guys, this is my mom and my dad.

Mr. & Mrs. Wang: Welcome. _____. And you must be Li Ming. Right?

Li Ming: Yeah. _____. What a lovely home you have!

Wang Ying: Thanks. I'm so glad you could come. _____.

Michael Lu: Good idea. We can admire the view from here.

Paul Li: Wang Ying, you've got a beautiful view. _____.

Wang Ying: Hey, guys, would you care for a drink? _____.

Now listen to the conversation again and answer the following questions.

> 1. Whose birthday party was it?
> 2. What did the boys bring to Wang Ying?
> 3. What did Wang Ying do about the gift?
> 4. What was Li Ming's compliment?
> 5. What was Paul Li's compliment?

4 Make a list of five situations in which you might compliment someone. After that practice the dialogue in class, giving compliments and replying to them using the structures given below.

Compliments	Responses
1. I'd like to compliment you on...	1. Thank you.
2. I think your... is very nice.	2. Thank you. It's nice of you to say so.
3. I just love your...	3. I'm glad you like it.
4. The... is nice/beautiful/great.	4. Thank you. Yours is even nicer.
5. What a nice... you've got!	5. Thank you, but it really isn't anything
6. That's nice/great/terrific.	special.

Listening Practice

5 Listen to people speaking and decide what they are talking about.

1. A) A plant.   B) A garden.
   C) A rose.   D) A room.
2. A) A hair style(发型).   B) A nice place.
   C) A cooking style.   D) A new dress.
3. A) A day.   B) A cook.
   C) A dish.   D) A dinner.

4. A) A race.   B) A path.
   C) A place.   D) A performance(演出).
5. A) A present.   B) A dress.
   C) A shop.   D) A movie.

6 Listen to five questions and choose the appropriate answers.

1. A) Yes. I've lived here for years.   B) Yes, I'm fine, thanks.
   C) Yes. It's really nice.   D) Yes, it is. Thanks.
2. A) We had a wonderful time.   B) I don't think so.
   C) I'll do that.   D) It's mine.
3. A) Yes, I will.   B) No. Go ahead.
   C) Yes, let me do it.   D) No, thanks. I can manage it.
4. A) Better than yours.   B) It's pretty(相当) good.
   C) I'd like to compliment you on it.   D) Thanks, but it's really nothing great.
5. A) No, it isn't.   B) That's right.
   C) You're so kind.   D) Thank you. Yours is even nicer.

7 Listen to five short dialogues and choose the appropriate answers.

1. A) In the street.   B) In the office.
   C) At the dinner party.   D) In the supermarket(超市).
2. A) The car is not his.   B) The car runs well.
   C) The car is nothing great.   D) The car is nicer than the woman's.
3. A) The man enjoys living in the city.
   B) The woman wants to move to the city.
   C) The man hates living in the center of the city.
   D) The woman lives near the shopping center.
4. A) He worried about something last night.
   B) He didn't get enough sleep last night.
   C) He had a bad dream last night.
   D) He had a sleepless night.
5. A) They're going to get married.   B) They are going to meet again.
   C) They're going to work together.   D) They're going to call on someone.

8 Listen to the following short talk and fill in the blanks with the missing words. The talk is given twice.

Throughout human history, the smile has carried great significance(意义). And today, a healthy, attractive smile continues to be _____. You meet people _____. You wear a smile while giving and responding to compliments. Sometimes, you just smile _____. A smile is worth(值) a thousand words.

Luckily, smiling is a universal(世界的) language. Wherever you go in the world, you can _____. People can understand you _____. Even when everything else in life is amiss(出错), a smile is the one thing we _____. And, best of all, smiling is contagious(感染的). _____ like the flu(流感). If you smile at someone, he or she is very likely to _____. Smiling is free and has no negative side effects(副作用). A day without laughter is _____. For success _____!

(150 *words*)

9 Listen to the talk again and then answer the following questions orally.

1. How long is the history of a smile?
2. Why do we smile without a word sometimes?
3. Why is smiling a universal language?
4. Why is smiling contagious?
5. How important is smiling in our life?

10 Think about the relationship between a smile and a compliment. Tell your classmates your understanding about it. Then have an open discussion on the topic given below.

A smile is worth a thousand words.

Reading & Writing

Text A

We meet people everyday. A nice relationship with those around us may make our day joyful. What do you usually do

1. when you meet your professor on campus,
2. when you return books to the librarian in your school library,
3. when you see your neighbour in the morning,
4. when a passenger has shown you the way to somewhere,
5. when someone thanks you for your help?

While answering the above questions, how many times did you mention "smile"? Do you think that smiling can help improve human relationships? Do you believe that a smile can not only solve many of your problems, but also even save your life? Read the following text and you may be convinced.

Text

The Smile

Hanock McCarty

Smile at each other, smile at your wife, smile at your husband, smile at your children, smile at each other — it doesn't matter who it is — and that will help you to grow up in greater love for each other.

Mother Teresa

Many Americans are familiar with *The Little Prince*, a wonderful book by Antoine de Saint-Exupery. Far fewer are aware of

Saint-Exupery's other writings, novels and short stories.

5   **2**   Saint-Exupery was a fighter
pilot who fought against the Nazis
and was killed in action. Before
World War Ⅱ, he fought in the
Spanish Civil War against the fas-
10   cists. He wrote a very interesting

story based on that experience entitled *The Smile*. It is this story
that I'd like to share with you now.

        3   He said that he was captured by the enemy and thrown into
a jail cell. From the contemptuous looks and rough treatment he re-
15   ceived from his jailers, he was sure that he would be executed the
next day.

        4   "I was sure that I was to be killed. I became terribly nerv-
ous and upset. I fumbled in my pockets to see if there were any
cigarettes which had escaped their search. I found one but I had
20   no matches.

        5   "I looked through the bars at my jailer. He did not make
eye contact with me. I called out to him, 'Have you got a light,
sir?' He looked at me for a while and came over to light my
cigarette.

25   **6**   "As he came close and lit the match, our eyes met. At that
moment, I smiled. I don't know why I did that. Perhaps it was nervousness, or perhaps it was because when you get very close,
one to another, it is very hard not to smile. In any case, I smiled.
In that instant, it was as though a spark jumped across the gap be-
30   tween our two hearts. I know he didn't want it, but my smile leaped
through the bars and generated a smile on his lips, too. He lit my
cigarette but stayed near, looking at me directly in the eyes and
continuing to smile.

        7   "I kept smiling at him, now aware of him as a person and
35   not just a jailer. And his looking at me seemed to have a new dimension, too. 'Do you have kids?' he asked.

8 " 'Yes, here, here,' I took out my wallet and nervously fumbled for the pictures of my family. He, too, took out the pictures of his children and began to talk about his plans and hopes for them. My eyes filled with tears. I said that I feared I'd never see   40 my family again, never have the chance to see them grow up. Tears came to his eyes, too.

9 "Suddenly, without another word, he unlocked my cell and silently led me out. Out of the jail and out of the town, and there, at the edge of town, he released me. And without another word, he   45 turned back toward the town.

10 "My life was saved by a smile."

11 Yes, the smile — the unaffected, unplanned, natural connection between people.

(532 *words*)

New Words

* prince /prɪns/ *n.*	son of a king or queen 王子
* aware /əˈweə/ *a.*	knowing; conscious of 知道的;意识到的
* writing /ˈraɪtɪŋ/ *n.*	thing that is written; activity of writing 作品;写作
* novel /ˈnɒvl/ *n.*	long story about imaginary or historical people (长篇)小说
◆fighter /ˈfaɪtə/ *n.*	战斗机;战士
* pilot /ˈpaɪlət/ *n.*	person trained to control an aircraft; person trained to direct ships into or out of a harbor, etc. 飞行员;引航员
* action /ˈækʃn/ *n.*	fighting in a war, etc.; process of doing sth.; activity; thing done; deed; act 战斗,作战;行动(过程);活动;行为
◆civil /ˈsɪvl/ *a.*	of or relating to the citizens of a country; connected with the people who live in a country 公民的;国内的
◆fascist /ˈfæʃɪst/ *n.*	person who supports fascism 法西斯主义者,法西斯分子

	a.	法西斯主义的
* base /beɪs/ *n.*		bottom of sth. ; foundation; basis 底部;基底; 基础;根据
	vt.	use (sth.) as grounds, evidence, etc. for sth. else 以…为…的基础(或根据)
* experience /ɪkˈspɪərɪəns/ *n.*		(process of gaining) knowledge or skill acquired from seeing and doing things; event or activity that affects one in some way 经验;体验;经历,阅历
◆ entitle /ɪnˈtaɪtl/ *vt.*		give a title to (a book, etc.) 给(书等)题名, 定名
★ capture /ˈkæptʃə/ *vt.*		make (sb.) a prisoner; catch (a wild animal, etc.) and put (it) in a cage, etc. 俘房;捕获
◆ jail /dʒeɪl/ *n.*		prison building 监狱
* cell /sel/ *n.*		small room in which one or more prisoners are kept 小牢房;单人牢房
◆ contemptuous /kənˈtemptʃʊəs/ *a.*		feeling or showing contempt 鄙视的;表示轻蔑的
◆ treatment /ˈtriːtmənt/ *n.*		process or way of treating sb. or sth. 对待;待遇;治疗;疗法
◆ jailer /ˈdʒeɪlə/ *n.*		person in charge of a jail and the prisoners in it 监狱看守,狱卒
★ execute /ˈeksɪkjuːt/ *vt.*		kill (sb.) as a legal punishment; carry out; perform; put into effect 将(某人)处死;实行,执行;履行;实施
* nervous /ˈnɜːvəs/ *a.*		tense; anxious; afraid; of the nervous 神经紧张的;情绪不安的;提心吊胆的;神经的
◆ fumble /ˈfʌmbl/ *vi.*		feel with one's hands in an uncertain way 乱摸;摸索
* cigarette /ˌsɪɡəˈret, ˈsɪɡəret/ *n.*		香烟
* escape /ɪˈskeɪp/ *v.*		get free; get away (from sb. /sth.); find a way out (of sth.); get away from; avoid 逃跑;逃走;逃出;逃脱;逃避;避免
* search /sɜːtʃ/ *v.*		try to find sb. /sth. by looking in places, ex-

n.

amining sth. , etc. 搜寻;搜索;搜查

act of searching 搜寻;搜索;搜查

* bar /bɑː/ *n.*

narrow piece of wood or metal placed as an obstacle in a doorway, window, etc. (门、窗等的)闩;(用作栅栏、杠杆等的)杆,棒

* contact /ˈkɒntækt/ *n.*

state of touching; communication; instance of meeting or communicating 接触;联系;交往

* moment /ˈməʊmənt/ *n.*

very brief period of time; exact point in time 片刻,瞬间;时刻,时候

* instant /ˈɪnstənt/ *n.*

precise point of time; short space of time; moment 时刻;瞬息,顷刻,刹那

◆ spark /spɑːk/ *n.*

very small piece of burning material, etc. that suddenly jumps out from a fire or that is produced when hard objects hit each other 火花,火星

* gap /gæp/ *n.*

opening, break or empty space in sth. or between two things; difference (of opinions, views, etc.) between two groups of people 缺口;裂口;间隔;差距,分歧

★ leap /liːp/ *vi.*

jump or move very quickly 跳,跳跃;迅速移动

* generate /ˈdʒenəreɪt/ *vt.*

cause (sth.) to exist or happen; produce 使存在;引起;使产生;使发生

* lip /lɪp/ *n.*

either the top or bottom edge of the mouth 嘴唇

* directly /dɪˈrektlɪ/ *ad.*

in a direct line or manner; straight 径直地;直接地;直率地

★ dimension /dɪˈmenʃn/ *n.*

measurement of length, width, height, thickness, etc. ; aspect or factor 尺寸;长度;宽度;高度;厚度;方面;因素

◆ wallet /ˈwɒlɪt/ *n.*

small flat folding case, usu. made of leather, carried in the pocket and used for holding banknotes, credit cards, etc. 钱包,皮夹

* lock /lɒk/ *n.*

device used with a key to fasten a door, etc. 锁

vt.

fasten (a door, etc.) with a lock 锁,锁上

◆ unlock /ʌnˈlɒk/ *vt.*

unfasten the lock of (a door, etc.) using a key 开…的锁

* silent /ˈsaɪlənt/ *a.*	making no or little sound; absolutely quiet 安静的;寂静无声的
* edge /edʒ/ *n.*	outside limit or boundary of a solid (flat) object, surface or area 边;边界;边缘
◆unaffected /ˌʌnəˈfektɪd/ *a.*	free from affectation; sincere 不矫揉造作的;真挚的
◆unplanned /ˌʌnˈplænd/ *a.*	not planned 无计划的;未经筹划的
* natural /ˈnætʃrəl/ *a.*	of, produced by, nature and not people; normal; to be expected 自然的,非人为的;正常的;合乎常情的
◆connection /kəˈnekʃn/ *n.*	connecting or being connected 连接,连结;联系

生词量	总词数	生词率	B 级词(*)	A 级词(★)	纲外词(◆)
44	532	8.3%	25	4	15

Phrases & Expressions

in action	taking part in a battle 在战斗中
call out	shout; speak loudly 叫喊;大声地说
come over	move from some distance 走过来
in any case	whatever happens or may have happened 无论如何,不管怎样;总之
as though	with the appearance of; apparently 好像;似乎;仿佛
look (at) sb. in the eye(s)	look directly at sb.'s eyes without shame, etc. (心地坦然地)直视某人,正视某人

Proper Names

Hanock McCarty /ˈhænɒk məˈkɑːtɪ/	汉诺克·麦卡蒂
Mother Teresa /təˈriːzə/	特蕾莎嬷嬷(1910—1997,天主教修女,1979 年诺贝尔和平奖获得者。因其国际性慈善活动受到世人尊敬)
Antoine de Saint-Exupery /æntˈwɑːn də sæŋtegzjuːpeɪˈriː/	安托万·德·圣埃克苏佩里(1900—1944,法国小说家)

Notes on the Text

1. Saint-Exupery was a fighter pilot who fought against the Nazis and was killed in action. 圣埃克苏佩里是一位战斗机驾驶员, 曾与纳粹分子作战并在战斗中阵亡。who 引导的定语从句有两个谓语动词:fought against 和 was killed。

2. He wrote a very interesting story based on that experience entitled *The Smile*. 他根据这番经历写了一篇很有趣的故事, 题目叫《微笑》。两个过去分词词组 based on that experience 和 entitled *The Smile* 都是 story 的定语。

3. It is this story that I'd like to share with you now. 我现在要对你们讲的就是这个故事。这是一个强调句型 (emphatic structure), 结构为 It is/was... that ...。被强调的部分放在 is 或 was 后面, 再如: It is this book that I'm looking for. 我找的正是这本书。It was in this very house that he was born. 他就出生在这所房子里。

4. From the contemptuous looks and rough treatment he received from his jailers, he was sure that he would be executed the next day. 从狱卒们轻蔑的脸色和他受到的粗暴对待判断, 他确信第二天他就会被处决。that 引导的从句是 he would be executed the next day, that 和从句之间的 from the contemptuous looks and rough treatment he received from his jailers 是状语。

5. In that instant, it was as though a spark jumped across the gap between our two hearts. 在那一瞬间, 就仿佛有一粒火星跳过了我们两颗心之间的鸿沟。as though 的意思是"好像、仿佛"。如:Look at the dark clouds. It looks as though it's going to rain. 和 He said goodbye to me quickly as though he was in a hurry. 如果 as though 后面的情形不是真实的, 那么要用虚拟语气。如:She looks as though she had seen a ghost. 和 Why is he looking at me as though he knew me? I've never seen him before.

6. I know he didn't want it, but my smile leaped through the bars and generated a smile on his lips, too. 我知道他并不想微笑, 但我的微笑越过了牢房的栅栏, 让他的双唇也露出了一丝微笑。I know he didn't want it = I know he didn't want to smile。

7. And his looking at me seemed to have a new dimension, too. 而他看我的样子也似乎有了一种新的特点。

Exercises

Reading Aloud

1 Read the following paragraph until you have learned it by heart.

As he came close and lit the match, our eyes met. At that moment, I smiled. I don't know why I did that. Perhaps it was nervousness, perhaps it was because, when you get very close, one to another, it is very hard not to smile. In any case, I smiled. In that instant, it was as though a spark jumped across the gap between our two hearts. I know he didn't want it, but my smile leaped through the bars and generated a smile on his lips, too. He lit my cigarette but stayed near, looking at me directly in the eyes and continuing to smile.

Understanding the Text

2 Answer the following questions.

1. Who was Saint-Exupery?
2. Did Saint-Exupery make up the story entitled "The Smile"?
3. What happened to Saint-Exupery during the Spanish Civil War?
4. Why did he think that he was going to be killed?
5. How did he feel in the jail cell and what did he do to deal with this feeling?
6. Why did he call out to the jailer?
7. What did he do when the jailer lit his cigarette? Why did he do so?
8. How did the jailer respond to his smile?
9. What did the two people do after they exchanged smiles?
10. What did Saint-Exupery say that moved the jailer to tears?
11. What did the jailer do after he heard Saint-Exupery's words?
12. What can a smile do to people who are strangers to each other?

3 Topics for Discussion.

1. Do you think the jailer did the right thing by releasing his prisoner secretly? Would

you have done the same if you had been the jailer?

2. What might have happened to the jailer the next day?

3. What do you think made the jailer decide to release Antoine de Saint-Exupery?

Reading Analysis

4 Read Text A again and complete the following table.

Part	Topic	Paragraph	Main Idea
I	Introducing Antoine de Saint-Exupery	1-2	Antoine de Saint-Exupery was a _____ and the author of _____.
II	Saint-Exupery's story: _____	3	During the Spanish Civil War, Saint-Exupery _____.
		4	Thinking _____, Saint-Exupery looked for a cigarette to overcome his nervousness.
		5	He then asked the jailer if _____.
		6	As the jailer came close, Saint-Exupery _____, and the jailer _____.
		7-8	The two of them showed each other _____ and talked about _____.
		9-10	Moved by Saint-Exupery's words, the jailer _____, which all started with a smile.
III	Closing remarks	11	The smile reveals the _____ between people.

Now retell the story by using the information you have completed in the table.

Vocabulary

5 Fill in the blanks with the words given below. Change the forms where necessary.

aware	writing	novel	experience	capture	execute	nervous
upset	escape	search	gap		contact	instant	edge

1. Children's-Voice is a publishing house that mainly publishes children's
   _____.

2. I got terribly _____ and dropped a spoon on the floor.

3. The citizens were warned of the trouble that the _____ monkeys might cause.

4. We are fully _____ of the problem, why it exists(存在) and what we can do about it.

5. I did a quick _____ on the Internet for some local bookstores and theatres.

6. These were lonely people and you could see they were longing for _____ with other human beings.

7. My girlfriend is really _____ with me for leaving her alone while she was ill.

8. The London Bridge Hotel, which opened in 1998, is located at the _____ of London.

9. Please take a seat. Dinner will be ready in an _____.

10. The man asked for forgiveness(宽恕) before he was _____ for murder(谋杀).

11. They are debating whether the _____ between the rich and the poor is becoming wider.

12. I'll always smile when I think of my first year's _____ in college.

13. He went out hunting alone and _____ some wild birds.

14. *The Old Man and the Sea* is a _____ about an old fisherman and his fight with a huge marlin(枪鱼).

6 Fill in the blanks with the expressions given below. Change the forms where necessary.

in action	based on	call out	come over
in any case	as though	take out	turn back

1. The Stones had three sons, two of whom were killed _____ during World War Ⅱ.

2. He spoke _____ he knew all about our plans when in fact he knew nothing at all.

3. The other day my mother _____ and spent the whole morning cleaning my room.

4. He _____ to the waiter, "Please bring me a cup of water to drink."

5. Finally he stopped the car, _____ a map, and found the right way.

6. Knowing that the film was _____ a true story made it even more enjoyable.

7. If we can't reach there before dark, we'd better _____ now while there's still time.

8. _____, we'll finish the work today.

Structure

7 Complete the following sentences by translating the Chinese in brackets into English.

Model:

In that instant, it was **as though** a spark jumped across the gap between our two hearts.

1. My parents used to arrange everything for me, _____ ____. (好像我还是个孩子一样)

2. He looked confused. It was as though _____. (就好像没看到刚才发生的事情一样)

3. You look perfect in that dress, _____. (像是专门为你做的一样)

4. Her body was shaking. It was _____. (好像她经历了什么可怕的事情)

8 Rewrite the following sentences according to the model using the emphatic structure "It is/was... that ..." (强调句).

Models:

I'd like to share <u>this story</u> with you now.

→*It is this story that I'd like to share with you now.*

1. I want to show you this picture.

   _____

2. He was captured by the enemy in the Spanish Civil War.

   _____

3. This desire to live on supports his fight against the terrible disease.

   _____

4. The weather began to cool down by the end of September.

   _____

5. I can't endure most her contemptuous look.

   _____

Translation

9 Translate the following sentences into English.

1. 这部小说讲述了她如何逃脱纳粹的搜查,是根据她的亲身经历写成的。

   _____

2. 当陌生人直视我的时候我会感到紧张,所以我尽量不接触他的目光。

   _____

3. 就在那一刻,黑暗中有个像火花一样的东西吸引了我的视线。

   _____

4. 父母和孩子都应该明白他们之间有隔阂,但他们不必难过,因为这种隔阂不是不可逾越的。

   _____

5. 无论如何,这个决定必须明天执行,哪怕会招来多数人的反对(objection)。

   _____

6. 她在讲述自己受到的粗暴待遇时越来越激动,好像到了发火(explosion)的边缘。

   _____

Grammar Review

主谓一致(Subject-verb Agreement)(2)

意义一致

语　法　形　式	例　　　　　句
1. 集合名词如 crowd, family, team, group, government, class, school, staff, public 作主语时,其作为一个整体,谓语动词用单数形式,若视为一个个成员,则谓语动词用复数形式	The audience was large. 观众很多。 The audience were greatly moved by his words. 听众们被他的话深深地打动了。
2. 有些集合名词如 people, police, cattle,形式上是单数,而意义上却是复数,则谓语动词用复数形式	The Chinese people are brave and hardworking. 中国人民勤劳勇敢。 The cattle are grazing in the sunshine. 牛群在阳光下吃草。
3. 以-ics 结尾的学科名称,如 economics, physics, mechanics, politics 等作主语时,谓语动词用单数形式	Physics is an important subject in middle school. 物理是中学一门重要的科目。 Mathematics is the study of numbers. 数学是对数字的研究。
4. 表示时间、重量、长度、价值的复数名词作主语时,如果当作一个整体看待,则谓语动词用单数形式	Four hours is needed to complete the work. 完成这项工作需要4个小时。 Twenty miles is a long way to walk. 20英里的路程很长。

语　法　形　式	例　　　　　　句
5. 国家、单位和书报的名称作主语时，谓语动词用单数形式	The United Nations is trying to find a better way to bring the two parties together. 联合国正在寻求更有效的方法来调停双方。 *War and Peace* is the longest book I've ever read. 《战争与和平》是我看过的最长的书。

毗邻一致

语　法　形　式	例　　　　　　句
1. 由连词 or, neither… nor …, either… or, not only … but also…, nor 等连接的并列主语，谓语动词的单复数形式通常与贴近它的主语一致	Not only you but also he is wrong. 不仅是你，他也错了。 My brothers or my father is likely to be at home. 我的兄弟或我爸爸可能在家。
2. 在 there be 结构中，谓语动词的单复数形式一般也与贴近它的名词一致	There was a radio and several books on the table. 桌上有一只收音机和一些书。 There are a few envelops, a pen and some paper in her bag. 她的包里有一些信封、一支笔和一些纸。

10 Underline the errors in agreement between subject and verb. Write the correct forms. If there is no error, write none at the end of each sentence.

1. Two million tons of coal were exported last year.
2. Neither the quality nor the prices has changed.
3. The family are the basic unit of our society.
4. The president, together with his wife and children, are going to visit us.
5. Five thousand miles is too far to travel.
6. General Motors have brought us fresh thinking from around the world.
7. Five hours of sleep are not enough.

8. The United States is the country with people of various origins.

9. Politics is often a topic for discussion among us.

10. They believe neither answer are correct.

Practical Writing

Notes of Congratulation

11 Suppose your business partner Mr. Anderson has been promoted (晋升) to the post of President of Howard Joys, Inc. Fill in the following note of congratulation, containing:

- Your warmest congratulations and best wishes for his every success.
- Your hope that your business relationship will continue to develop.

Dear Mr. Anderson,

    I have just learned of your promotion _____.
Please accept _____.

    I hope that with you at the head of HJ, _____
_____ in the same pleasant and trusting manner.

Sincerely yours,

Frank Clark

---

12 Suppose your friend David has been promoted to the Regional Manager (地区经理) for China. Write a note of about 50 words congratulating him. Contain the following:

- Your sincere congratulations on his promotion.
- Your wish for his success in his future work.

Text B

Blameless

Kathy Johnson Gale

I was a freshman in college when I met the Whites. They were completely different from my own family, yet I felt at home with them instantly. Jane White and I became friends at school, and her family welcomed me, an outsider, like a long-lost cousin.

5   *2*   In my family, when anything bad happened, it was always important to place blame.

3   "Who did this?" my mother would yell about a mess in the kitchen.

4   "This is all your fault, Katharine," my father would insist
10   when the cat got out or the dishwasher broke.

5   But the Whites didn't worry about who had done what. They picked up the pieces and moved on with their lives. The beauty of this was driven home to me the summer that Jane died.

6   Mr. and Mrs. White had six children: three sons and three
15   daughters. One son had passed away in childhood, which may be why the surviving five children remained so close.

7   In July, the White sisters and I decided to take a car trip from their home in Florida to New York. The two oldest, Sarah and Jane, were college
20   students, and the youngest, Amy, had recently turned sixteen. The proud possessor of a brand-new driver's license, Amy was excited about practicing her driving on the trip. With her giggle, she showed off her
25   license to everyone she met.

8   The big sisters shared the driving of Sarah's new car during the first part of the trip, but when they reached less populated areas, they let Amy take over. Somewhere in South Carolina, we pulled off the highway to eat. After lunch, Amy got behind the wheel. She came to an intersection with a stop sign for her direction only. Whether she was nervous or just didn't see the sign no one will ever know, but Amy continued into the intersection without stopping. The driver of a large truck, unable to brake in time, ran into our car.

9　Jane was killed instantly.

10　I survived the accident with only a few bruises. The most difficult thing that I've ever done was to call the Whites to tell them about the accident and that Jane had died. As painful as it was for me to lose a good friend, I knew that it was far worse for them to lose a child.

11　When Mr. and Mrs. White arrived at the hospital, they found their two surviving daughters sharing a room. Sarah's head was wrapped in bandages; Amy's leg was in a cast. They hugged us all and cried tears of sadness and of joy at seeing their daughters. They wiped away the girls' tears and teased a few giggles out of Amy as she learned to use her crutches.

12　To both of their daughters, and especially to Amy, over and over they simply said, "We're so glad that you're alive."

13　I was astonished. No accusations. No blame.

14　Later, I asked the Whites why they never talked about the fact that Amy was driving and had run a stop sign.

15　Mrs. White said, "Jane's gone, and we miss her terribly. Nothing we say or do will bring her back. But Amy has her whole life ahead of her. How can she lead a full and happy life if she feels we blame her for her sister's death?"

16　They were right. Amy graduated from college and got married several years ago. She works as a high school teacher. She's also a mother of two little girls of her own, the oldest named Jane.

17　I learned from the Whites that blame really isn't very important. Sometimes, there's no use for it at all.

(*603 words*)

New Words

* blame /bleɪm/ *n.*   responsibility (for a mistake, etc.); criticism for doing sth. wrong(过错等的)责任;指责,责备

         vt.   put the blame (for sth.) on (sb./sth.); put the blame for (sth.) on sb./sth. 指责,责备;把…归咎(于)

◆ blameless /'bleɪmlɪs/ *a.*   free from blame; innocent 无可指责的;无过错的

◆ outsider /ˌaʊt'saɪdə/ *n.*   person who is not a member of a society, group, etc. 外人,组织之外的人

* cousin /'kʌsn/ *n.*   child of one's uncle or aunt 堂兄弟(或姐妹);表兄弟(或姐妹)

◆ yell /jel/ *v.*   shout loudly; give a loud cry 叫喊,叫嚷;号叫

◆ mess /mes/ *n.*   dirty or untidy state 脏乱状态,零乱状态

* fault /fɔːlt/ *n.*   responsibility for a mistake; thing that is (done) wrong; imperfection or flaw 过失;过错;缺点;毛病;故障

* insist /ɪn'sɪst/ *v.*   state strongly and continuously; demand or urge strongly 坚持说;坚决要求;一定要

◆ dishwasher /'dɪʃwɒʃə/ *n.*   machine or person that washes dishes 洗碟机;洗碟工

* beauty /'bjuːtɪ/ *n.*   combination of qualities that pleases one's eyes, ears, mind, etc.; person or thing that is beautiful 美,美丽;美人;美的东西

* childhood /'tʃaɪldhʊd/ *n.*   condition or period of being a child 儿童状态;童年,幼年

* survive /sə'vaɪv/ *v.*   continue to live or exist; not be killed by (sth.); remain alive after (sb.) 活下来;幸存;继续存在;从…中逃生;经历…后继续存在;比…活得长

* remain /rɪ'meɪn/ *v.*   continue to be; stay in the same condition; stay; not go away 仍然是;保持不变;留下,逗留

* recently /'riːsntlɪ/ *ad.*   not long ago or before; lately 最近;新近

* sixteen /ˌsɪkˈstiːn/ *n.*	number 16　十六
◆ possessor /pəˈzesə/ *n.*	person who possesses sth. 拥有者,持有人;所有人
★ brand /brænd/ *n.*	particular make of goods or their trade mark(商品的)牌子;商标
◆ brand-new /ˈbrændˈnjuː/ *a.*	completely new 全新的,崭新的
* license /ˈlaɪsns/ *n.*	official document showing that permission has been given to own, use or do sth. 执照;许可证
* excited /ɪkˈsaɪtɪd/ *a.*	feeling or showing excitement 兴奋的,激动的
◆ giggle /ˈɡɪɡl/ *n.*	nervous or silly laugh 咯咯的笑;傻笑
* everyone /ˈevrɪwʌn/ *pron.*	each or every person 每人,人人
◆ populate /ˈpɒpjʊleɪt/ *vt.*	live in (a place) and form its population 居住于,生活于;构成…的人口
* area /ˈeərɪə/ *n.*	extent or measurement of a surface; part of the earth's surface; district of a city, etc. 面积;地域;地区
* highway /ˈhaɪweɪ/ *n.*	main public road 公路
★ wheel /wiːl/ *n.*	轮;车轮;方向盘,驾驶盘
◆ intersection /ˌɪntəˈsekʃn/ *n.*	place where two or more roads intersect; cross-roads 道路交叉口;十字路口
* sign /saɪn/ *n.*	mark, symbol, etc. used to represent sth.; board, notice, etc. that directs sb. towards sth., gives a warning, advertises a business, etc. 符号,记号;标志;牌;指示牌;招牌
* direction /dɪˈrekʃn/ *n.*	course along which sb./sth. moves, points, looks, etc. 方向
◆ brake /breɪk/ *n.*	device for reducing the speed of or stopping a car, cycle, train, etc. 制动器;闸;刹车
v.	(cause sth. to) stop by using a brake 刹(车)
* accident /ˈæksɪdənt/ *n.*	event that happens unexpectedly and causes damage, injury, etc. 意外;事故
◆ bruise /bruːz/ *n.*	injury caused by a blow to the body or to a fruit, discoloring the skin but not breaking it(人体跌、碰后产生的)青肿,挫伤;(水果等的)伤痕

★wrap /ræp/ *vt.*   cover or enclose (sth.) in soft or flexible material
包;裹;包扎;缠绕

★cast /kɑːst/ *n.*   casing put round a broken bone while it heals 固
定用敷料;石膏绷带

◆hug /hʌg/ *vt.*   put the arms round (sb.) tightly, esp. to show
love 拥抱

＊wipe /waɪp/ *vt.*   clean or dry (sth.) by rubbing it with a cloth,
piece of paper, etc. 擦,拭;抹;擦净;揩干

◆tease /tiːz/ *vt.*   戏弄,逗弄;取笑;惹

＊alive /əˈlaɪv/ *a.*   living; not dead 活着的

★astonish /əˈstɒnɪʃ/ *vt.*   surprise greatly 使惊讶

◆accusation /ˌækjuːˈzeɪʃn/ *n.*   指责;指控

生词量	总词数	生词率	B级词(＊)	A级词(★)	纲外词(◆)
40	603	6.6%	20	5	15

Phrases & Expressions

be/feel at home   be/feel comfortable and relaxed (as if in one's
own home)(像在自己家里一样)舒适自在;无
拘束

pick up the pieces   try what one can to get the situation back to normal again after a setback, disaster, etc. 收拾残
局;恢复正常

move on   proceed; continue one's journey 继续前进;继续
行进

drive sth. home (to sb.)   make (sb.) realize or understand sth. 使(某人)
充分认识(或理解)某物

pass away   [euph.] die[婉]去世

show off   display with pride; display one's own abilities,
etc. in order to impress people 炫耀,卖弄;表现
自己

take over   take charge or responsibility; take control or pos-
session of 接管,接任;接收,接办

pull off	drive a motor-vehicle off (a road) into a lay-by, etc. 把机动车驶离(道路)进入路旁停车处
at/behind the wheel	driving or steering (a car or ship) 在驾驶;在操纵
run into	collide with or crash into 与…相撞;撞在…上
wipe away	clear or remove by wiping 擦掉,擦去
over and over (again)	many times; repeatedly 一再地,再三地
bring back	cause (sb.) to return 使(某人)回来;使(某人)死而复生
of one's own	belonging to oneself 属于自己的

Proper Names

Kathy Johnson Gale /ˈkæθɪ ˈdʒɒnsn ˈgeɪl/	凯西·约翰逊·盖尔
White /waɪt/	怀特(姓氏)
Jane /dʒeɪn/	简(女子名)
Katharine /ˈkæθərɪn/	凯瑟琳(女子名)
Florida /ˈflɔːrɪdə/	佛罗里达州(美国东南部一州)
New York /ˌnjuːˈjɔːk/	纽约州(美国东部一州)
	纽约市(美国纽约州东南部港市)
Sarah /ˈseərə/	萨拉(女子名)
Amy /ˈeɪmɪ/	艾米(女子名)
South Carolina /ˌsauθ ˌkærəˈlaɪnə/	南卡罗来纳州(美国东南部一州)

Notes on the Text

1. The beauty of this was driven home to me the summer that Jane died. 在简去世的那年夏天,我充分理解了这一境界的崇高之美。

2. One son had passed away in childhood, which may be why the surviving five children remained so close. 一个儿子小时候就去世了,这也许就是为什么活下来的五个孩子一直如此亲密无间。which 指的是 one son had passed away in childhood 这件事。

3. The proud possessor of a brand-new driver's license, Amy was excited about practicing her driving on the trip. 艾米自豪地拿到一张崭新的汽车驾照,对于一路上可以练习驾驶技术很是激动。the proud possessor of a brand-new driver's license

是主语 Amy 的同位语。

4. Whether she was nervous or just didn't see the sign no one will ever know, ... 是她紧张呢,还是压根儿没看到那个标志呢,永远没有人会知道了……。whether 引导的从句是动词 know 的宾语从句,在句中被提前到句首,有强调的意味。

5. The most difficult thing that I've ever done was to call the Whites to tell them about the accident and that Jane had died. 我生平所做的最困难的事情就是给怀特夫妇打电话,把发生车祸及简已经去世的消息告诉他们。

6. As painful as it was for me to lose a good friend, I knew that it was far worse for them to lose a child. 如同我失去一位好友非常痛苦一样,我知道对他们来说失去一个子女更要痛苦得多。

7. Later, I asked the Whites why they never talked about the fact that Amy was driving and had run a stop sign. 后来,我问怀特夫妇,为什么他们从不谈起艾米开车闯了停车标志这件事。

Exercises

13 **Answer the following questions.**

1. How did the writer feel about the White family?
2. Name one difference between the writer's family and the Whites.
3. How many people were there in the White family before Jane died?
4. How many people took that car trip to New York in July? Who were they?
5. Why was Amy excited?
6. When was Amy allowed to drive?
7. What caused the car accident?
8. What was the most difficult thing that the writer had ever done?
9. What did the Whites do when they met their daughters in the hospital?
10. Why was the writer astonished?
11. Why didn't the Whites talk about the fact that Amy had run a stop sign?
12. What has the writer learned from the Whites?

14 Fill in the blanks with the words given below. Change the forms where necessary.

blame	fault	childhood	remain	recently	license	area
highway	survive	accident	excite	simply	cousin	alive

1. I love to visit my aunt's family for I have three _____ there to play with me.
2. Even after so many years, her dream of becoming a pilot is still _____.
3. I'm sorry. It's my _____ for having led the topic (话题) to the wrong direction.
4. They'll be upset if you _____ say no to them without an excuse.
5. The soldiers stood next to their guns, ready for action, but the night _____ quiet.
6. He _____ the fire but had some serious burn injuries.
7. I drove on the _____, and my speed was 70... 80... 90... 100 kilometers per hour!
8. You've got to teach her to take responsibility for her actions. She's always trying to put the _____ on someone else.
9. A number of factories have moved from the central _____ to the edge of the city.
10. Have you seen any good films _____?
11. The law (法律) requires that you should get a _____ for your business first.
12. Do you know the feeling of seeing a long-lost _____ friend?
13. The students were _____ about the results of the experiment (实验).
14. There's no one to blame and nothing to blame. It was just an _____.

15 Fill in the blanks with the expressions given below. Change the forms where necessary.

at home	move on	drive... home to	pass away	show off
take over	pull off	run into	wipe away	bring back
of one's own				

1. For the past five years she has been saving to buy a house _____.
2. At noon they _____ the main road to avoid the burning sun.

3. He felt _____ in Shanghai the minute he arrived.

4. The old lady mistakenly stepped on the accelerator(加速器) instead of the brake and _____ a tree.

5. They were married 74 years when his wife _____ at the age of 92.

6. I tried to _____ him again and again that his children needed him more than anything or anyone else in the world.

7. I think the only thing you can do is let go of this romance(恋情) and _____ with your life.

8. The team has been winning one game after another since he _____.

9. She came with a mop(拖把) and easily _____ the water on the floor.

10. More games and less homework may help _____ the joy of learning for bored children.

11. A group of young people raced by on their bikes. One or two of them even _____ their skills by riding on only one wheel.

Text C

A Lady Named Lill

James M. Kenmedy and James C. Kennedy

Kind words can be short and easy to speak, but their echoes(反响) are truly endless.

Mother Teresa

Lillian was a young French Canadian girl who grew up on a farm in *Ontario*(安大略省). At the age of 16, her father thought "Lill" had had enough schooling, and she was forced to drop out of school. In 1922, with English as her second language

5   and limited education and skills, the future didn't look bright for Lill.

   2   Her father was a strict man who seldom took no for an answer and never accepted excuses. He demanded that Lill find a job. But her limitations left her with little confidence, and she didn't

know what work she could do.

3   With small hope of gaining *employment*(雇用), she would still ride the bus daily into the "big cities" of Windsor or Detroit. But she couldn't *muster*(鼓起) the courage to respond to a *Help Wanted ad*(招工广告); she couldn't even bring herself to knock on a door. Each day she would just ride to the city, walk *aimlessly*(无目的地) about and at *dusk*(黄昏) return home. Her father would ask, "Any luck today, Lill?"

4   "No... no luck today, Dad," she would respond *meekly*(温顺地).

5   As the days passed, Lill continued to ride and her father continued to ask about her *job-hunting*(找工作). The questions became more *demanding*(苛求的), and Lill knew she would soon have to knock on a door.

6   On one of her trips, Lill saw a sign at the Carhartt Overall Company in *downtown*(市中心)Detroit. "HELP WANTED," the sign said, "*SECRETARIAL*(秘书的). APPLY WITHIN."

7   She walked up the long flight of stairs to the Carhartt Company offices. Cautiously, Lill knocked on her very first door. She was met by the office manager, Margaret Costello. In her broken English, Lill told her she was interested in the secretarial position, falsely stating that she was 19. Margaret knew something wasn't right, but decided to give the girl a chance.

8   She guided Lill through the old business office of the Carhartt Company. With *rows*(一排排) and rows of people seated at rows and rows of *typewriters*(打字机), Lill felt as if a hundred pairs of eyes were staring at her. With her eyes staring down, the farm girl followed Margaret to the back of the room. Margaret sat her down at a typewriter and said, "Lill, let's see how good you really are."

9   She asked Lill to type a single letter, and then left. Lill

10

15

20

25

30

35

40

looked at the clock and saw that it was 11:40 A. M. Everyone would be leaving for lunch at noon. She thought that she could slip away in the crowd then. But she knew she should at least *attempt*(尝试) the letter.

10　On her first try, she got through one line. It had five words, and she made four mistakes. She pulled the paper out and threw it away. The clock now read 11:45. "At noon," she said to herself, "I'll move out with the crowd, and they will never see me again. "

11　On her second attempt, Lill got through a full paragraph, but still made many mistakes. Again she pulled out the paper, threw it out and started over. This time she completed the letter, but her work was still full of mistakes. She looked at the clock: 11:55 — five minutes to freedom.

12　Just then, the door at one end of the office opened and Margaret walked in. She came directly over to Lill, putting one hand on the desk and the other on the girl's shoulder. She read the letter and *paused*(停顿). Then she said, "Lill, you're doing good work!"

13　Lill was *stunned*(震惊). She looked at the letter, then up at Margaret. With those simple words of encouragement, her desire to escape vanished and her confidence began to grow. She thought, "Well, if she thinks it's good, then it must be good. I think I'll stay!"

14　Lill did stay at Carhartt Overall Company... for 51 years, through two world wars and a *Depression*(大萧条), through 11 presidents and six prime *ministers*(总理) — all because someone had the *insight*(洞察力) to give a shy and uncertain young girl the gift of self-confidence when she knocked on the door.

(690 *words*)

Comprehension of the Text

16 Choose the best answer for each of the following multiple choice questions.

1. Lill dropped out of school at age 16 because _____.
   - A) she had had enough schooling
   - B) she had limited learning skills
   - C) her father wanted her to do so
   - D) the future didn't look bright

2. As Lill rode to the city, she was almost sure that she wouldn't _____.
   - A) find a job
   - B) see any job ads
   - C) like the city life
   - D) be accepted by the citizens

3. What did Lill often do in the city?
   - A) Looking for Help Wanted ads.
   - B) Knocking at doors for work.
   - C) Walking about in the streets.
   - D) Shopping in the stores.

4. When Lill knocked at the door of Carhartt Overall Company, it was mainly because _____.
   - A) she was good at secretarial work
   - B) it was the first Help Wanted sign she saw
   - C) the company was located in the downtown area
   - D) her father pushed her harder on job-hunting

5. When Lill was seated at the typewriter, she wanted to _____.
   - A) stay in the company
   - B) escape from the office
   - C) finish typing before noon
   - D) make no typing mistakes

6. How many times did Lill attempt to complete the letter?
   - A) One.   B) Two.
   - C) Three.   D) Four.

7. How old was Lill when she stopped working for Carhartt Overall Company?

A) 51.   B) 60.

C) 67.   D) 70.

8. What is the main idea of this passage?

A) Education is important to everybody.

B) Confidence is the key to career success.

C) Opportunity is critical(关键的) in job-hunting.

D) Encouragement is a valuable gift one can give.

Basic Reading Skills

Reading for the Main Idea: Topic Sentence (2)

　　有时,主题句并没有出现在段落的开头,这时候就要注意概括段落中心思想的句子是否在段落的结尾。如第四单元 B 篇课文的第三段:

What about reducing stress by exercising? In fact, studies have shown that doing aerobic exercise (exercise that increases your heart rate) causes the brain to release endorphins, a chemical in your body that reduces pain and relaxes the body. Again, there is no guarantee that exercise will prevent a heart attack or a stroke, especially if members of your family have had these diseases. But if you exercise, have a good diet, don't smoke, and have a relaxed, positive attitude, you will reduce your chances of getting stress-related illnesses.

　　作者一开始提出"通过运动来减轻压力又怎么样呢?"接着用研究成果来说明"做有氧运动能减轻疼痛,放松身体",当然作者也说"不能保证运动会防止心脏病发作或中风"。在段落的结尾,作者概括了这一段的中心思想:But if you exercise, have a good diet, don't smoke, and have a relaxed, positive attitude, you will reduce your chances of getting stress-related illnesses.

　　再如第三单元 C 篇课文的第一段:

I have always wondered how my parents were attracted to each other. Their personalities, temperaments, and attitudes toward money are all opposite. The saying that "opposites attract" certainly holds true for them.

　　段落结尾的一句话概括了这一段的中心思想。

17 Reread the following paragraphs from your textbook and identify the topic sentence of each paragraph.

1. My mother is not a bargain shopper. She does not cut out coupons or compare products or prices; she is impatient — if she likes something, she buys it. My father, therefore, has always done our food shopping. He compares products and prices, looks for sales and bargains, and buys only what he needs. He has also always taken care of our household finances and is the bookkeeper and accountant of the family. My father says that my mother has champagne tastes with a beer pocketbook, and she says that he's cheap, but there is a happy compromise — she spends and he saves. (Text C, Unit 3)

2. "It must be love," I say about this odd couple. They may be very different, but they are also very compatible. Learning from each other ensures the success of their partnership. (Text C, Unit 3)

Fun Time

Poem

Only a Smile

Don't go for looks(外表), they can deceive(欺骗);
Don't go for wealth, even that fades away(消失).
Go for someone who makes you smile,
Because it takes only a smile
To make a dark day seem bright.

UNIT 8

Highlights

Preview

This is the last unit of Book One. In the Listening and Speaking section, you will learn how to give suggestions. In the Reading and Writing section, Text A offers some effective study skills and strategies for improved learning; Text B tells learners of English how to maintain learning progress while Text C distinguishes successful language learners as those who learn independently, actively and purposefully.

Listening & Speaking

The Language of Giving Suggestions for Travel

1 You are going to listen to two college students giving travel suggestions. Listen carefully and fill in the blanks with the missing words.

Wang Ying： My favorite city in our country is Beijing.
It's ＿＿＿＿＿＿＿ with many places of
interest(名胜古迹). It's one of ＿＿＿＿＿＿＿
for tourism(旅游). You should go to the
Great Wall. It's ＿＿＿＿＿＿＿. Oh,
you shouldn't miss the Forbidden City(紫
禁城). It's ＿＿＿＿＿＿＿. By the
way, you should try Peking duck. A trip
to Beijing ＿＿＿＿＿＿＿ is tasteless.
You could go there ＿＿＿＿＿＿＿.

Li Ming： Well, my favorite city is Shanghai. It's a
modern city and ＿＿＿＿＿＿＿. It's one of the best places
＿＿＿＿＿＿＿. You name it, and you'll ＿＿＿＿＿＿＿. Of
course, there're ＿＿＿＿＿＿＿ worth visiting. You should spend a
morning at the Bund(外滩). It has ＿＿＿＿＿＿＿. Then you can go
to the People's Square and visit the Shanghai Museum there, and you
shouldn't miss the Grand Theater(大剧院). They're ＿＿＿＿＿＿＿.
Oh, you can go to the Yu Garden(豫园), and should try some snacks(小
吃) there. I'm sure you'll ＿＿＿＿＿＿＿. You can visit the city of
Shanghai anytime. The weather is ＿＿＿＿＿＿＿.

2 Now you can tell the class where you come from and, using the language you
have just learned in Exercise 1 give suggestions to those who might like to
visit your hometown/city.

Giving Suggestions

3

1) *Before you listen to the first conversation, read the following words and expressions which may be new to you.*

> 'cause   [口] = because
> the Temple of Heaven   天坛
> fall   秋天

Listen to the conversation twice and fill in the blanks with the missing words.

Peter: Where are you from, Wang Ying?

Wang Ying: I'm from Beijing.

Peter: Oh, I've _____. What's it like?

Wang Ying: It's a fairly big city, and it's very interesting. There're many places

                       _____.

Peter: Oh, really? What should I see there?

Wang Ying: Well, first of all, _____ the Great Wall

                       and visit the Forbidden City. They're very interesting 'cause they have

                       _____.

Peter: What else?

Wang Ying: Oh, _____ the Temple of Heaven. It's

                       a beautiful place.

Peter: Any special foods?

Wang Ying: Oh, yeah. _____ Peking duck. It's delicious.

Peter: Mm, it all sounds really exciting! And what's a good time

                       _____?

Wang Ying: I think fall is the perfect season. The weather is _____

                       _____ then.

Now listen to the conversation again and answer the following questions.

1. What does Peter learn about Beijing?
2. What should Peter visit there, according to Wang Ying?
3. What shouldn't Peter miss there?
4. What should Peter try there?
5. What time of year should Peter go?

2) *Before you listen to the second conversation, read the following words and expressions which may be new to you.*

harbor	港口
the Statue of Liberty	自由女神像
the Empire State Building	帝国大厦
the Metropolitan Museum of Art	大都会艺术博物馆
the United Nations Headquarters	联合国总部
Central Park	中央公园
pizza	比萨饼

Listen to the conversation twice and fill in the blanks with the missing words.

Li Ming: Where in the United States are you from, Sally?

Sally: I'm from New York.

Li Ming: Oh, I've never been there. _____?

Sally: It's a modern city, like Shanghai. _____.

Li Ming: Well, when is a good time to visit?

Sally: _____. So, I would say spring and fall are nice seasons for a visit.

Li Ming: Oh, good! _____?

Sally: Well, you can see the Statue of Liberty and visit the Empire State Building.

Li Ming: _____?

Sally: No. There're many interesting places, such as the Metropolitan Museum of Art and the United Nations Headquarters. Oh, you should spend a day at the Central Park, especially on the weekend. _____. It's very interesting.

Li Ming: It all sounds really exciting! And are there any special foods there?

Sally Sure. _____.

Li Ming: Mm, I love pizza.

Now listen to the conversation again and answer the following questions.

1. What's New York like?
2. What's the weather like there?
3. When is a good time to visit the city?
4. What should a visitor see?
5. What shouldn't a visitor miss?

4 Make dialogues in class, asking and telling your classmates what to see in their hometowns/cities, using the structures given below.

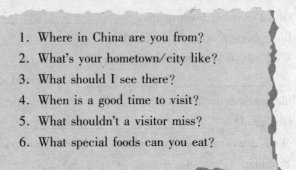

1. Where in China are you from?
2. What's your hometown/city like?
3. What should I see there?
4. When is a good time to visit?
5. What shouldn't a visitor miss?
6. What special foods can you eat?

Listening Practice

5 Listen to people speaking and decide what they are talking about.

1. A) Living in a city.   B) Traveling by air.
   C) Traveling abroad(国外).   D) Eating fast food.

2. A) Weather.   B) Happiness.
   C) Health.   D) Work.

3. A) A weekend.   B) A beach(海滩).
   C) A kid.   D) A vacation.

4. A) The Statue of Liberty.   B) The Great Wall.
   C) The Forbidden City.   D) The People's Square.

5. A) A dinner.   B) A book.
   C) An invitation.   D) An appointment(约会).

6 Listen to five questions and choose the right answers.

1. A) Anytime.   B) Sure I can.
   C) Oh, really?   D) Sure. I'd love to.

2. A) How about you?   B) Are you all right?

C) How do you know that?   D) What do you want to know?

3. A) Yes, everything will be fine.   B) I know what you mean.

   C) Well, if you want to.   D) No, I don't mind.

4. A) I think you can go anytime.

   B) It all sounds really exciting.

   C) What would you like to know?

   D) Why don't we spend a morning in the park?

5. A) Yes, please.   B) OK, I'll take it.

   C) Oh, sorry, I can't.   D) No, I'm afraid not.

7 Listen to five short dialogues and choose the right answers.

1. A) They're going to meet someone.   B) They're going to visit a place.

   C) They're going to ask the way.   D) They're going to have a ride.

2. A) At home.   B) In the dorm.

   C) In the library.   D) In the classroom.

3. A) She needs to relax.   B) She needs to work better.

   C) She needs to study harder.   D) She needs to finish her homework.

4. A) Leave.   B) Rest in bed.

   C) Stay for dinner.   D) Have a good idea.

5. A) It's exciting.   B) It's crowded.

   C) It's interesting.   D) All of the above.

8 Listen to the following short talk and fill in the blanks with the missing words. The talk is given twice.

One story Einstein liked to tell about his childhood was of a "wonder" he saw when he was four or five years old: a magnetic compass(磁罗盘). The needle's invariable(永恒的) northward swing(摆动), _____ an invisible(看不见的) force, greatly impressed the child. The compass convinced him that there had to be "_____, something deeply hidden." Even as a small boy Einstein was self-sufficient and thoughtful. According to family legend(传说) he was a slow talker at first, pausing(停顿) to consider _____. His sister remembered the concentration(专心) and perseverance(毅力) with which he would build houses of cards

_____. The boy's thought was stimulated(刺激) by his uncle, an engineer, and by a medical student who ate dinner _____ at the Einsteins'.

(125 *words*)

9 Listen to the talk again and then answer the following questions orally.

> 1. What was the "wonder" little Einstein saw?
> 2. What was little Einstein convinced of?
> 3. What kind of a boy was Einstein?
> 4. Who stimulated the boy's thought?
> 5. What can we learn from the story?

10 Your vacation is just around the corner. Ask for or give suggestions about what to do and where to travel during the vacation, using the language you learned in Exercises 1 & 4.

Reading & Writing

Text A

Starter

As a student who has almost finished the first semester at college, have you ever had any difficulties or problems with your studies? How do you usually deal with them? Try to list these difficulties or problems together with your solutions. Share this list with your classmates.

Your difficulties or problems 　　　　　　　Your solutions

1. _____　　　　　　　　　　_____

2. _____　　　　　　　　　　_____

3. _____　　　　　　　　　　_____

4. _____

5. _____

Learning to Learn

Author Unknown

E ffective study skills and strategies are the basis of effective
learning. They give you an opportunity to learn systematically and independently. By always using good study habits and
learning to work like a successful student, you can become one.

5   *2*   Learning is a very personal matter. There isn't one study
skill or learning strategy that works for every person in every situation. Therefore, you must learn what you know, what you don't
know, and what to do about it. Don't always wait for others to tell
you what to learn or how to do it.

10   *3*   ***Know Yourself***   Begin by honestly assessing your strengths
and weaknesses in basic college skills and identify your learning
style. Consider whether you learn most effectively by reading, watching, listening, or doing. You must also become familiar with your
teachers' teaching styles; adjusting your learning style to theirs will

15 be to your advantage. In addition,
consider when and where you are at
your best for learning. (Are you a
morning person or a night owl? Do you
like to be alone or with others? Do you

20 concentrate best in a bright room with
noise or in a quiet corner?)

    4   ***Manage Your Time and Life***
Learn to manage your time and control
your own life. Identify what your goals

are and then establish priorities to help you reach them. If you   25
aren't spending time on your priorities, you must make the necessary adjustments or you won't reach your goals. If school learning
and good grades are priorities, then you must make and follow a
schedule that gives enough time for class and study.

    5 *Improve Your Concentration*   As a good student, you will   30
not necessarily study more than a poor student, but you will certainly use your study time more effectively. Learn to keep your attention focused on the task at hand. When you are in class or ready
to study, give it your full attention. (How well you learn something,
not how fast you learn it, is the critical factor in remembering. You   35
must "get" something before you can "forget" it.)

    6 *Know What Study Means & How to Do It*   Learning takes
more than just going to class and doing homework. It is really a
four-part cycle:

            preview →class →review →study →   40
When you establish a learning-cycle routine you will be able to learn
more in less time.

    7 *Become An Active Reader*   To learn from reading or stud-
ying, you must be an active, thinking participant in the process
(not a passive bystander). Always preview the reading and make   45
sure you have a specific purpose for each assignment. Read actively to fulfil your purpose and answer questions about the material. Keep involved by giving yourself frequent tests on what you've
read.

    8 *Build Listening & Notetaking Skills*   Carefully listening to a   50
lecture and deciding what is important are two aspects that must be
mastered before you worry about how to take notes. Again, being
an active participant is the key to your success.

    9   True education is not about cramming material into your
brain. Instead, true education is a process of expanding your ca-   55
pabilities, of bringing yourself into the world. Professors can only
set the stage for you to create learning through your own actions.

                                                    (531 *words*)

New Words

* effective /ɪˈfektɪv/ a.   having an effect; producing the desired result 有效的；产生预期结果的

★strategy /ˈstrætədʒɪ/ n.   (art of) planning and directing an operation in a war or campaign; (skill of) planning or managing any affair well 战略；策略

* basis /ˈbeɪsɪs/ n.   thing on which sth. is based; foundation 基础

* opportunity /ˌɒpəˈtjuːnətɪ/ n.   favorable time, occasion, chance, etc. for doing sth. 机会，时机

★systematic /ˌsɪstəˈmætɪk/ a.   done or acting according to a system or plan 系统的

* habit /ˈhæbɪt/ n.   thing that one does normally or regularly (and often cannot change easily) 习惯

* personal /ˈpɜːsənl/ a.   of or belonging to a particular person; private 个人的；私人的

* situation /ˌsɪtʃʊˈeɪʃn/ n.   set of circumstances or state of affairs, esp. at a certain time 状况，处境；局面，形势

* therefore /ˈðeəfɔː/ ad.   for that reason; so 因此，所以

★assess /əˈses/ vt.   decide or fix the amount or value of (sth.); evaluate 估定…的数额（或价值）；估价

* identify /aɪˈdentɪfaɪ/ vt.   show, prove, etc. who or what (sb./sth.) is; recognize (sb./sth. as being the specified person or thing) 鉴定（或证明）（某人／某事物）；认出，识别

* style /staɪl/ n.   manner of writing or speaking; manner of doing anything 文体；风格

* adjust /əˈdʒʌst/ vt.   change (sth.), usu. a little, in order to fit in (with sth. else); make suited (to new conditions) 调节；改变…以适应

* advantage /ədˈvɑːntɪdʒ/ n.   condition or circumstance that gives one superiority or success; benefit; profit 有利条件；优点；好处，利益

◆owl /aʊl/ n.   猫头鹰

* concentrate /ˈkɒnsntreɪt/ v.   focus one's attention, effort, etc. exclusively and intensely (on sth.) 全神贯注,专心致志

* establish /ɪˈstæblɪʃ/ vt.   set up; give a firm and permanent basis to (a rule, a business, etc.); prove the truth of (sth.) 建立,设立;确立;证实

★priority /praɪˈɒrəti/ n.   (state of) being more important; right to have or do sth. before others; thing that is (regarded as) more important than others 优先;重点;优先权;优先考虑的事

* schedule /ˈʃedjuːl, US ˈskedʒuːl/ n.   timetable; program of work to be done or of planned events 时间表;日程安排表

* necessarily /ˈnesəsərəli; US ˌnesəˈserəlɪ/ ad.   as an inevitable result 必然,必定

* attention /əˈtenʃn/ n.   action of applying one's mind to sb./sth. 注意;专心

* focus /ˈfəʊkəs/ v.   concentrate (one's attention, etc.) on (sth.) 将(注意力等)集中于(某事物)

* critical /ˈkrɪtɪkl/ a.   decisive; crucial; looking for faults; pointing out faults; of or at a crisis 决定性的;关键的;批评的;危机中的;危急时刻的

* factor /ˈfæktə/ n.   fact, circumstance, etc. that helps to produce a result 因素

* cycle /ˈsaɪkl/ n.   series of events that are regularly repeated in the same order 循环;周期

◆preview /ˈpriːvjuː/ v.   预习

* review /rɪˈvjuː/ vt.   go over (work already learnt) in preparation for an exam 复习(功课)

* active /ˈæktɪv/ a.   积极的;主动的;活跃的

★participant /pɑːˈtɪsɪpənt/ n.   person who takes part or becomes involved in an activity 参加者

* process /ˈprəʊses/ n.   series of actions or operations performed in order to do, make or achieve sth. 过程,进程;步骤,程序

* passive /ˈpæsɪv/ a.   not active; submissive 被动的;消极的

◆bystander /ˈbaɪstændə/ *n.*　　person standing near, but not taking part, when sth. happens; onlooker 旁观者

∗ specific /speˈsɪfɪk/ *a.*　　detailed, precise and exact; relating to one particular thing, etc.; not general 明确的,确切的;特定的;具体的

∗ purpose /ˈpɜːpəs/ *n.*　　thing that one intends to do, get, be, etc.; intention 目的;意图

∗ fulfil(l) /fʊlˈfɪl/ *vt.*　　perform (sth.); bring (sth.) to completion; satisfy (sth.) 履行;实现;满足

∗ material /məˈtɪərɪəl/ *n.*　　substance or things from which sth. else is or can be made; thing with which sth. is done; pieces of information that can be used to prepare a book, report, etc. 材料;原料;素材;资料

∗ involve /ɪnˈvɒlv/ *vt.*　　cause (sb./sth.) to take part in (an activity or a situation); bring (sb./sth.) into (a difficult situation); include (sth.) as a necessary part 使参与;使陷入;使卷入;牵涉;包含,含有

∗ frequent /ˈfriːkwənt/ *a.*　　happening often; habitual 时常发生的,频繁的;经常的,惯常的

∗ lecture /ˈlektʃə/ *n.*　　talk giving information about a subject to an audience or a class, often as part of a teaching program 演讲;讲课

∗ aspect /ˈæspekt/ *n.*　　particular part or side of sth. being considered 方面

∗ master /ˈmɑːstə/ *n.*　　man who has others working for him or under him; employer; skilled worker in a trade 主人;雇主;师傅;能手

　　　　　　　　vt.　　gain considerable knowledge of or skill in (sth.) 掌握,精通

◆cram /kræm/ *vt.*　　push or force too much of (sth.) into; fill (all the available space of sth.) (with people or thing)把…塞进;把…塞满

∗ expand /ɪksˈpænd/ *v.*　　(cause sth. to) become greater in size, number or importance 扩大;扩充;扩展

◆capability /ˌkeɪpəˈbɪlətɪ/ n.   quality of being able to do sth.; ability 能力；才能

＊professor /prəˈfesə/ n.   (title of a) university teacher of the highest rank (大学)教授

生词量	总词数	生词率	B 级词(＊)	A 级词(★)	纲外词(◆)
45	531	8.2%	35	5	5

Phrases & Expressions

to sb.'s advantage	with results which are profitable or helpful to sb. 对某人有利
at its/one's best	in the best state or form 处于最佳状态
focus on	concentrate (one's attention, etc.) on 把(注意力等)集中于
at hand	near; closely; about to happen 近在手边；在附近；即将发生
worry about	be anxious about 对…担忧,对…担心
take notes	write notes 作记录,记笔记
set the stage for	prepare for; make it possible or easy for (sb.) to do sth. 为…创造条件,为…作好准备;使成为可能

Notes on the Text

1. By always using good study habits and learning to work like a successful student, you can become one. 始终运用良好的学习习惯,学会像一名成功的学生那样学习,你也能成为一名成功的学生。本句中,介词 by 表示通过…方式。同样的例子还有第三段中的 Begin by honestly assessing your strengths and weaknesses…。

2. Don't always wait for others to tell you what to learn or how to do it. 不要老是等着别人告诉你学习什么或怎么学习。本句是祈使句的否定形式,表示劝告、建议、命令等语气。本文中有许多祈使句。

3. You must also become familiar with your teachers' teaching styles; adjusting your learning style to theirs will be to your advantage. 你还必须熟悉教师们的教学风格;调整自己的学习风格与之相适应对你将是有利的。

4. Consider whether you learn most effectively by reading, watching, listening, or doing. 要考虑你学习效果最佳的手段是阅读、观察、听课还是实际操作。连词 whether 通常与 or 连用,表示选择。

5. ... consider when and where you are at your best for learning. = ... consider when you are at your best for learning and where you are at your best for learning. ……还要考虑你在什么时候、什么地方处于最佳学习状态。这是一个省略句。如果一个句子中有两个并列的名词性从句,从句相同而 wh-连词不同,则可省略第一个分句,只保留连词。

6. ... you must make the necessary adjustments or you won't reach your goals. ……你必须做必要的调整,否则你就不会实现你的目标。本句中,连词 or 表示"否则、要不然"。

7. If school learning and good grades are priorities, then you must make and follow a schedule that gives enough time for class and study. 如果在校学习和好成绩是你优先考虑的目标,那你就必须制订一个给上课和学习足够时间的时间表,并照着这个时间表去做。英语的 if... then...结构通常从句以 if 开头,主句以 then 开头。If 从句表示说话人所做的一个假设,then 主句陈述了逻辑推理关系的结果。

8. ... keep your attention focused on the task at hand. ……把注意力一直集中在手头的任务上。句型"keep + 名词/代词 + 过去分词/现在分词/形容词/副词/介词短语",表示"使…保持某一状态"。

9. How well you learn something, not how fast you learn it, is the critical factor in remembering. 记忆的关键因素不是你对某样东西学得多么快,而是你学习得多么好。本句的主语是由 how 引导的名词从句。名词从句可充当主语、宾语、同位语和表语。

10. Keep involved by giving yourself frequent tests on what you've read. 要经常就已读过的内容考考自己,从而使自己一直全神贯注。名词从句 what you've read 在句中作介词宾语。

11. Carefully listening to a lecture and deciding what is important are two aspects that must be mastered before you worry about how to take notes. 仔细听课并决定哪些内容重要是必须先掌握的两个方面,然后再考虑怎么去记笔记。本句的主语是动名词短语 Carefully listening to a lecture and deciding what is important。

Exercises

Reading Aloud

1 Read the following paragraphs until you have learned them by heart.

Effective study skills and strategies are the basis of effective learning. They give you an opportunity to learn systematically and independently. By always using good study habits and learning to work like a successful student, you can become one.

Learning is a very personal matter. There isn't one study skill or learning strategy that works for every person in every situation. Therefore, you must learn what you know, what you don't know, and what to do about it. Don't always wait for others to tell you what to learn or how to do it.

Understanding the Text

2 Answer the following questions.

1. What are the basis of effective learning? Why?
2. How can one become a successful student?
3. What are the things one must learn, since learning is a very personal matter?
4. How many study skills and strategies does the writer offer? What are they?
5. How can one know oneself?
6. How can one manage one's time and life?
7. In what way is a good student different from a poor student?
8. What is the critical factor in remembering?
9. What does learning really mean?
10. What must one do to learn from reading or studying?
11. What must one master when taking notes?
12. What is true education?

3 Topics for Discussion.

1. In the text, the writer presents several study skills and strategies. Among them, which do you think are the most effective for your studies? Do you have any other ef-

fective study skills and strategies ? If yes, please introduce them to the class.

2. Have you experienced any difficulties in learning? How have you managed to conquer them?

Reading Analysis

4 Read Text A again and complete the following table.

Part	Topic	Topic Sentence	Details
1	The basis of _____ _____	Effective study skills and strategies are the basis of effective learning.	They help you to learn _____ and _____. You can become a successful student by _____.
2	Different people learn differently	_____ _____ _____	Different people need different study skills and strategies. Do what you must and don't wait for other people to _____.
3	_____ _____ _____	(Begin by) honestly assess(ing) your strengths and weaknesses in basic college skills and identify your learning style.	Consider how you can learn most effectively. Be familiar with _____. Know your best _____ for learning.
4	Manage your time and life	_____ _____ _____	Identify your goals and establish priorities. Make necessary adjustments to reach your goals.
5	Improve your concentration	_____ _____ _____	You must use your time more effectively than others. Give your _____ to whatever you do.

Part	Topic	Topic Sentence	Details
6	_____ _____	It is really a four-part cycle.	Learning means more than just _____. Following the learning-cycle will help you to _____.
7	Become an active reader	_____ _____ _____	Always _____. Read actively and answer questions. _____.
8	Build listening & notetaking skills	Carefully listening to a lecture and deciding what is important are _____ that must be mastered before you worry about _____.	To succeed, you must be an active participant.
9	The essence (要素) of _____ _____	True education is a process of expanding your capabilities, of bringing yourself into the world.	Don't just cram material into your brain. Professors set the stage, but you _____.

Vocabulary

5 Fill in the blanks with the words given below. Change the forms where necessary.

basis	opportunity	therefore	necessarily
process	fulfil	involve	master
establish	attention	effective	purpose

1. Once you have made a promise, you should _____ it.
2. Applying (申请) to enter a university is a complicated _____ with many steps to follow.
3. You must give your full _____ to what you are doing.
4. Although the brightest students do not _____ make the best teachers, most teachers were good students.
5. He was so _____ in reading the book that he didn't even hear the knock at the door.
6. We have to have a(n) _____ plan if we are to deal with this serious problem.
7. John has _____ a close relationship(关系) with some of his classmates.
8. If you understand a foreign language and can make yourself understood when speaking and writing, you have _____ it.
9. Getting rich seems to be his only _____ in life.
10. Don't miss this _____ : it may never come again.
11. He works hard and _____ has a good chance of winning the prize.
12. The _____ of their friendship is a common interest in sports.

6 Fill in the blanks with the expressions given below. Change the forms where necessary.

| adjust... to | at one's best | focus... on | at hand |
| worry about | take notes | set the stage for | to sb.'s advantage |

1. Most athletes are _____ during their youth.
2. If you feel cold, you can _____ the temperature in the room _____ your taste.
3. Mary _____ on everything that's said in class and reviews them in the evening.
4. This weekend's talks between the two leaders have _____ a peace agreement to be reached.
5. I'm so tired that I can't _____ my attention _____ anything.
6. He has the good habit of keeping a dictionary _____ when he's reading or writing.
7. Your parents _____ you; do write to them.
8. You will find it _____ to learn French before you visit France.

Structure

7 Rewrite the following sentences according to the model.

Model:

> If you want to reach your goals, you must make the necessary adjustments.
>
> →You must make the necessary adjustments **or** you won't reach your goals.

1. If I don't want to be late for class, I must go now.

   _____

2. If he didn't want to go hungry, he had to have a job.

   _____

3. Put on your coat if you don't want to catch cold.

   _____

4. If you don't want to feel sorry, take care what you say.

   _____

5. You have to go early if you want to get a seat.

   _____

8 Study the following example and then complete the following sentences by translating the Chinese into English.

Example:

> **If** school learning and good grades are priorities, **then** you must make and follow a schedule that gives enough time for class and study.

1. _____, then you can be a successful student. (如果你掌握了有效的学习技能和策略)

2. If the book isn't in your bag, _____. (那它肯定在桌子上)

3. _____, then let's try something else. (如果他们到星期五还没有作出决定的话)

4. If you have a headache and feel weak, _____. (那你肯定是病了)

5. _____, then one of them must be lying. (如果两个

人都说没有拿过钱)

Translation

9 Translate the following sentences into English.

1. 如果你把注意力集中在学习上,你肯定能实现你的目标,成为一名成功的学生。

   _____

2. 好学生知道如何更有效地利用他的学习时间。这就是他能在较少的时间里学到更多东西的原因。

   _____

3. 如果你手头有很多任务,你必须确定优先考虑的目标,否则你将一事无成。

   _____

4. 对别人有效的学习策略不一定对你也有效,因此要作出必要的调整以达到最佳效果。

   _____

5. 扩展自己的能力而不是把知识塞进脑子里才是你成功的关键。

   _____

6. 要在学习上做得好,你就必须在学习过程中成为一名积极的参与者,而不是一名消极的旁观者。

   _____

Grammar Review

动词不定式(The Infinitive)

　　动词不定式是一种非谓语动词的形式,可在句中担任除谓语外的其他任何成分。除不定式外,动词的非谓语形式还有动名词和分词。

　　动词不定式分为带 to 的不定式(to-infinitive)和不带 to 的不定式(bare infinitive)。带 to 的不定式由 to + 动词原形构成,不带 to 的不定式为动词原形。不定式的形式变化和用法列表如下:

不定式的形式变化(以 write 为例)

时 态	主动形式	被动形式
一般时	to write	to be written
进行时	to be writing	
完成时	to have written	to have been written
完成进行时	to have been writing	

不定式的用法

用 法	例 句
1. 作主语：当主语较长时，常用 it 做形式主语,而将不定式放到句子后部	To master a language is not an easy thing. 掌握一门语言不是一件容易的事情。 To teach English is my favorite. 教英语是我的最爱。 It's necessary for you to have a good sleep before the test. 考试前一定要睡个好觉。
2. 作宾语：主要结构为"动词 + 不定式","动词 + wh-词 + 不定式"	I like to help others if I can. 我愿意尽力帮助别人。 Have you decided where to go for a picnic? 你们决定好到哪儿去野餐了吗？
3. 作宾语补语：在 let, make, have, hear, look at, see, feel 等动词后面作宾语补语时,用不带 to 的不定式	We expect you to be with us. 我们期待你和我们在一起。 The doctor advised me to quit smoking. 医生劝我戒烟。 Father had my younger brother wash the car today. 今天爸爸让弟弟洗车。 I heard him speak in the next room. 我听到他在隔壁房间里讲话。

用　　法	例　　句
作表语	What I should do is to finish the task soon. 我应该做的是赶快完成任务。 The most urgent thing is to see a doctor. 当务之急是马上去看病。
作定语:通常放在其所修饰的名词或代词之后	I have no desire to travel. 我没有旅行的愿望。 He is always the last one to leave the office. 他总是最后一个离开办公室的人。
作状语:可以表示原因、目的和结果等	He got up early to review his lessons. 他早起是为了复习功课。 She was too tired to walk. 她累得走不动了。

10 Translate the Chinese in the brackets into English.

1. It's necessary for us _____(互相帮忙).

2. I can tell you _____(到哪找这本书).

3. We are sorry _____(让你久等了).

4. What you should do is _____(尽快地完成工作).

5. I think he is _____(做好这份工作的人的最佳人选).

6. I like _____(出去散步) in the warm sunshine in spring.

7. I am sorry _____(没有按时完成作文).

8. He gets up early _____(是为了赶上第一班公共汽车).

9. I don't know _____(怎样给他回信).

10. I didn't expect _____(被邀请).

Practical Writing

Notices

11 Please write notice in English for the Department Office based on the Chinese one given below.

通　　知

　　本系全体教师、学生 1 月 16 日(星期五)2：00 在会议室听时事报告，望届时参加。

系办公室

2004 年 1 月 12 日

---

12 The English reading-room is now ready to open, please write a notice using the information given below in Chinese.

- 阅览室新进了一些英文小说，欢迎大家借阅。
- 英语墙报将出新版（edition），欢迎大家写文章或读书报告。
- 上学期借书未还的同学请办理续借（renew）或还书手续，否则，将不准使用本阅览室。

Text B

Maintaining Progress in Your English Studies

Author Unknown

Languages are for communication so if you always work alone on your lessons, you are denying yourself the opportunity to put language into use. Working in pairs and small groups will give you more time to spend trying out new language skills. Don't worry if the teacher cannot hear and correct every mistake you make. Remember, mistakes disappear with time. Classes are a good way to meet other people who want to learn the same language as you, and you don't have to limit your contact to lesson times only. Why

5

10 not meet after class and help one another with review and testing? You can compare notes on things you found difficult and share information about the materials you have found useful. Your friends

15 can provide lots of ideas about different ways to learn as well as be sympathetic, supportive listeners when the going gets tough.

2 Maintaining motivation is critical for success in language learning and, as we said before, you should be ready to take the
20 rough with the smooth. During the course of your studies there may be periods when you'll experience negative feelings towards the language you are learning. These feelings will include: frustration, when your progress seems slow; uncertainty, when you don't fully understand things; annoyance, when you keep forgetting something
30 simple; boredom when you have to do the same thing over and over again; and *resentment*, that everything has to be so complicated and that English can't work in the same way as Chinese.

3 Obviously we aren't trying to put you off learning English, but as these feelings are likely to surface at different times, it's best to
35 be aware that they are quite normal and you won't be alone in feeling this way. Persevere. The feelings will pass and there will be many compensations along the way. Of course, at other times you'll feel: satisfaction, when you see yourself making progress; interest, as you learn more about the ways in which language operates; amuse-
40 ment, when you come across a novel phrase or expression; stimulation, when you encounter new ways of thinking and talking about the world; and pride, in your growing ability to understand the new language and express your thoughts and feelings.

4 As you experiment and discover the ways in which you
45 learn best, you will also feel a growing confidence in yourself and in your ability to learn successfully.

(405 *words*)

New Words

* progress /ˈprəugres/ *n.* — forward or onward movement; advance or development 前进;进步;进展

* communicate /kəˈmjuːnɪkeɪt/ *v.* — convey; pass on; transmit; exchange information, news, ideas, etc. 传送;传达;传递;传播;交流,交际

* communication /kəˌmjuːnɪˈkeɪʃn/ *n.* — act of communicating 传达;交流;通信

* deny /dɪˈnaɪ/ *vt.* — say that (sth.) is not true; refuse to give 否认,不承认;拒绝给予

* disappear /ˌdɪsəˈpɪə/ *vi.* — no longer be visible; vanish; stop existing 不见;消失;不复存在

* compare /kəmˈpeə/ *vt.* — examine (people or things) to see how they are alike and how they are different 比较

* information /ˌɪnfəˈmeɪʃn/ *n.* — facts told, heard or discovered (about sb./sth.) 消息;情报;资料;信息

* provide /prəˈvaɪd/ *vt.* — supply; make available 供给;提供

◆ sympathetic /ˌsɪmpəˈθetɪk/ *a.* — feeling or showing sympathy 同情的;表示同情的

◆ supportive /səˈpɔːtɪv/ *a.* — giving help, encouragement or sympathy 支持的;给予帮助、鼓励或同情的

★ tough /tʌf/ *a.* — difficult to cut or break; difficult or hard to do 坚韧的;牢固的;困难的;艰苦的

* smooth /smuːð/ *a.* — having an even surface without lumps, etc.; free from difficulties, problems, etc. 光滑的,平整的;顺利的

* period /ˈpɪərɪəd/ *n.* — amount of time; portion of time in the life of a person, nation or civilization; amount of time of a lesson at school (一段)时间;时期;时代;课时

* negative /ˈnegətɪv/ *a.* — expressing denial or refusal; indicating "no" or "not"; lacking in definite, constructive or helpful qualities or characteristics 否定的;反面的;消极的

* feeling /ˈfiːlɪŋ/ *n.* — ability to feel; emotion 感觉;感情

﹡ include /ɪnˈkluːd/ *vt.*	have (sb./sth.) as part of a whole 包括,包含
◆frustration /frʌˈstreɪʃn/ *n.*	(state of) being frustrated; example of feeling frustrated 受挫;挫折;沮丧;失望
◆uncertainty /ʌnˈsɜːtntɪ/ *n.*	state of being uncertain 不确定,无把握
◆annoyance /əˈnɔɪəns/ *n.*	being annoyed 烦恼;恼怒
◆boredom /ˈbɔːdəm/ *n.*	state of being bored 厌烦;厌倦
◆resentment /rɪˈzentmənt/ *n.*	愤恨,怨恨
﹡ obvious /ˈɒbvɪəs/ *a.*	easily seen, recognized or understood; clear 显然的,明显的
﹡ likely /ˈlaɪklɪ/ *a.*	probable 可能的
﹡ surface /ˈsɜːfɪs/ *n.*	outside of an object (物体的) 表面
vi.	come to the surface of a body of water; appear or emerge 浮出水面;出现;浮现
﹡ normal /ˈnɔːml/ *a.*	conforming to the standard; usual; regular(符合)标准的;通常的;正常的
◆persevere /ˌpɜːsɪˈvɪə/ *vi.*	continue trying to do sth., esp. in spite of difficulty 坚持不懈,锲而不舍
★compensate /ˈkɒmpenseɪt/ *vt.*	give (sb.) sth. good to balance the bad effect of damage, loss, injury, etc. 补偿;赔偿;报偿;报酬
﹡ interest /ˈɪntrɪst/ *n.*	desire or willingness to know or learn (about sb./sth.) 兴趣
﹡ operate /ˈɒpəreɪt/ *vi.*	work, perform or function 工作;运转;运行;起作用
★amuse /əˈmjuːz/ *vt.*	make (sb.) laugh or feel happy; make time pass pleasantly for (sb.) 逗笑;逗乐;给…提供娱乐
﹡ novel /ˈnɒvl/ *a.*	new and strange; of a kind not known before 新奇的;新颖的
﹡ expression /ɪkˈspreʃn/ *n.*	action or process of expressing; word or phrase 表达;词语;表达方式
★stimulate /ˈstɪmjʊleɪt/ *vt.*	make more active or alert; arouse the interest and excitement of (sb.) 刺激;激励;激发(某人的)兴趣;使兴奋
◆encounter /ɪnˈkaʊntə/ *vt.*	meet (sb.), esp. by chance; meet or experience

(danger, difficulty, etc.)意外遇见;偶尔碰到;遭到,受到

* express /ɪkˈspres/ vt.   show or make known (a feeling, an opinion, etc.) by words, looks, actions, etc.表示,表露,表达

* thought /θɔːt/ n.   idea or opinion produced by thinking 想法,见解

* experiment /ɪkˈsperɪmənt/ n.   test or trial done carefully in order to study what happens and gain new knowledge 实验;试验

                 vi. make an experiment 进行实验(或试验)

生词量	总词数	生词率	B 级词(*)	A 级词(★)	纲外词(◆)
37	403	9.1%	24	4	9

Phrases & Expressions

put... into use   use 使用,应用

in pairs   in twos; two at a time 成对地,成双地;两个一组;一次两个

try out   use experimentally; test 试用;试

compare notes   exchange ideas or opinions 交换意见

take the rough with the smooth   accept what is unpleasant or difficult as well as what is pleasant or easy; patiently accept bad things as well as good ones 既能享受顺境,又能承受逆境;既能享乐也能吃苦;好事坏事都接受

put sb. off sth. / doing sth.   cause sb. to lose interest in sth. 使某人对(做)某事失去兴趣

at other times   on other occasions 在别的时候

come across   meet or find by chance 偶然遇见;碰上

Notes on the Text

1. ... you are denying yourself the opportunity to put language into use. ……你就自动放弃了使用语言的机会。

2. Working in pairs and small groups will give you more time to spend trying out new language skills. 两个人或一个小组在一起学习就会使你有更多的时间花在试

用新学的语言上。本句的主语是动名词短语 Working in pairs and small groups。

3. Why not meet after class and help one another with review and testing? 为什么不能课后见面,在复习和测试方面互相帮助呢? 句型 Why not do sth.? 是 Why don't you do sth.? 的简略形式,表达说话人的建议。

4. You can compare notes on things you found difficult and share information about the materials you have found useful. = You can compare notes on things (that) you found difficult and share information about the materials (that) you have found useful. 你们可以就一些困难的地方交换意见,并就一些有用的资料互通信息。本句中,名词 things 和 materials 分别由两个定语从句修饰,省略了引导从句的关系代词 that。

5. Your friends can provide lots of ideas about different ways to help you learn as well as be sympathetic, supportive listeners when the going gets tough. 你的朋友们不仅可以在你进展艰难之时充满同情地听你倾诉,给予你支持,而且还可以提供许多不同的方法帮助你学习。going 一词在本句中表示"进展"。

6. Maintaining motivation is critical for success in language learning and, as we said before, you should be ready to take the rough with the smooth. 保持学习的积极性是语言学习取得成功的关键,而且正如我们前面说到的,你应该准备好顺利艰难都能承受。

7. During the course of your studies there may be periods when you'll experience negative feelings towards the language you are learning. 在你的学习过程中可能会有一些时期你会对正在学习的语言产生一些消极的情绪。本句中,修饰 periods 的定语从句由关系副词 when 引导,相当于 in which。

8. ... when you keep forgetting something simple...: ……在你老是忘记一些简单的东西时…… 短语 keep doing sth. 表示"继续做某事,不断或反复做某事"。

9. Obviously we aren't trying to put you off learning English... 我们显然不是要使你对学习英语失去兴趣……

10. ... see yourself making progress. ……你看到自己取得进步。在英语中,一些动词如 hear, see, feel, watch 等可跟分词短语作宾语补足语。不定式作宾补与现在分词均可作这些动词的宾补,它们的区别在于:现在分词强调动作正在发生,而不定式指事情的全过程,表示动作已经结束。

Exercises

13 Answer the following questions.

1. What does the writer suggest learners do to put language into use?
2. How can learners help each other in learning a language?
3. What is critical for success in language learning?
4. What negative feelings will a learner experience during the course of his or her studies?
5. When does a learner experience these negative feelings?
6. What should a learner do when these negative feelings appear? Why?
7. When does a learner feel satisfied, interested, amused, stimulated and proud?
8. What does a learner feel when he discovers the ways in which he learns best?

14 Fill in the blanks with the words given below. Change the forms where necessary.

progress	deny	provide	include	obviously	likely
normal	operate	express	disappear	thought	information

1. A society couldn't _____ well if its members were allowed to pay no attention to its rules.
2. No one should be _____ a good education.
3. He seems to be able to put complicated _____ into simple words.
4. Eight people, _____ two women, were injured in the explosion.
5. _____ he was very nervous since for some minutes he just stood there, not knowing what to say.
6. Children who are interested in learning are more _____ to do well in school than children who are not interested in learning.
7. Although the boy spent every minute learning, he made little _____ in

his studies.

8. Group discussion _____ a good opportunity for us to practice oral English.

9. It's quite _____ that you make a lot of mistakes when beginning to learn a foreign language.

10. She _____ her thanks by sending them a bunch of flowers.

11. I can't find my keys anywhere — they've completely _____.

12. The tour guide will provide you with _____ about the area.

15 Fill in the blanks with the expressions given below. Change the form where necessary.

| put... into use | in pairs | try out | compare notes |
| put sb. off | at other times | come across | |

1. The scientists _____ the new medicine to see how well it works.

2. Do the exercise alone and then discuss your answers _____.

3. In some areas, rivers that are full of water during certain seasons of the year become dry _____, perhaps when water is most needed.

4. These problems have appeared because new techniques _____ without considering possible results.

5. As we were having dinner at a restaurant we _____ an old friend we hadn't seen for ages.

6. The fact that some people may disagree will not _____ doing what I think is right.

7. Managers of the company often get together and _____ on how to improve their work.

Text C

Successful Language Learners

Author Unknown

S ome people seem to have a *knack*(窍门)for learning languages. They can pick up new *vocabulary*(词汇), master rules
of *grammar*(语法), and learn to write in the new language more
quickly than others. They do not seem to be any more *intelligent*(聪
明的), so what makes language learning so much easier for them?   **5**
Perhaps if we take a close look at these successful language learners we may discover a few of the techniques which make language
learning easier for them.

   2   First of all, successful language learners are independent
learners. They do not *depend on* (依赖)the book or the teacher;   **10**
they discover their own way to learn the language. Instead of waiting for the teacher to explain, they try to find the patterns and the
rules for themselves. They are good *guessers* (猜测者)who look for
clues(线索)and form their own conclusions. When they guess
wrong, they guess again. They try to learn from their mistakes.   **15**

   3   Successful language learning is active learning. Therefore,
successful learners do not wait for a chance to use the language;
they look for chances. They find people who speak the language

and ask these people to correct
them when they make a mistake.   **20**
They will try anything to communicate. They are not afraid to repeat
what they hear or say strange
things; they are willing to make mistakes and try again. When commu-   **25**
nication is difficult, they can accept
information that is *inexact*(不准确的)

or *incomplete* (不完全的). It is more important for them to learn to think in the language than to know the meaning of every word.

30   **4** Finally, successful language learners are learners with a purpose. They want to learn the language because they are interested in the language and the people who speak it. It is necessary for them to learn the language in order to communicate with these people and to learn from them. They find it easy to practice the lan-
35   guage *regularly* (经常地) because they want to use it for learning.

5 What kind of language learner are you? If you are a successful language learner, you probably have been learning independently, actively, and *purposefully* (有目的地). On the other hand, if your language learning has been less than successful, you
40   might do well to try some of the techniques *outlined* (概述) above.

(370 *words*)

Comprehension of the Text

16 Choose the best answer for each of the following multiple choice questions.

1. In the sentence "Some people seem to have a knack for learning languages," the word "knack" means _____.
   A) purpose   B) ability
   C) interest   D) basis

2. Some people learn languages more successfully than others because they learn
   _____.
   A) independently   B) actively
   C) purposefully   D) All of the above.

3. It can be learned from the text that successful language learners _____.
   A) are more intelligent than others
   B) master rules of grammar more quickly
   C) write in the language better than others
   D) have a larger vocabulary

4. What does an independent learner do?
   A) He waits for the teacher to explain.
   B) He corrects every mistake he has made.

C) He never guesses wrong.

D) He finds the patterns and the rules for himself.

5. _____ is the most important for active learners.

A) Thinking in the language they are learning

B) Knowing the meaning of every word

C) Understanding information that is inexact or incomplete

D) Correcting mistakes

6. Which of the following is NOT true about active learners?

A) They will repeat what they hear.

B) They are willing to make mistakes.

C) They will not give up when communication is difficult.

D) They never communicate with each other in the language they are learning.

7. For what purpose do some people learn a foreign language successfully?

A) They want to go abroad.

B) They want to communicate with people who speak the language.

C) They want to be more successful than others.

D) They want to use the language regularly.

8. The purpose of the writer is to _____.

A) show that some people are born good at learning a foreign language

B) explain why some people find it easy to practice using the foreign language

C) introduce some techniques that make language learning easier

D) help the reader find out what kind of language learner he/she is

Basic Reading Skills

Reading for the Main Idea: Topic Sentence (3)

在有些英语段落中,我们会发现,作者在段落开头,同时又在段落结尾表达同样的中心思想。比如本单元 C 篇课文的第三段:

Successful language learning is active learning. Therefore, successful learners do not wait for a chance to use the language; they look for chances. They find people who speak the language and ask these people to correct them when they make a mistake. They will try anything to communicate. They are not afraid to repeat what they hear or say strange things; they are willing to make mistakes and try again. When communication is difficult, they can accept information that is inexact or incomplete. It is more important for them to learn to think in the language than to know the meaning of every word.

　　第一句是主题句,也是这一段要表达的中心思想:成功的语言学习是一种积极的学习。随后的五句说明成功的学习者是如何积极学习的。最后一句:对成功的学习者来说,学会用所学的语言思维比了解每一个词的意义更重要,实际上深化了第一句表达的思想。

| Successful language learning is active learning. |

| Therefore, successful learners do not wait for a chance to use the language; they look for chances. | They find people who speak the language and ask these people to correct them when they make a mistake. | They will try anything to communicate. | They are not afraid to repeat what they hear or say strange things; they are willing to make mistakes and try again. | When communication is difficult, they can accept information that is inexact or incomplete. |

| It is more important for them to learn to think in the language than to know the meaning of every word. |

17 Read Text C again and identify the topic sentence of each paragraph.

Glossary

New Words

* ability /əˈbɪlətɪ/ *n.* 能力　1B

* accident /ˈæksɪdənt/ *n.* 意外;事故　7B

◆ accidentally /ˌæksɪˈdentəlɪ/ *ad.* 意外地;偶然地　6B

★ accomplish /əˈkɒmplɪʃ/ *vt.* 完成;实现　1B

◆ accusation /ˌækjuːˈzeɪʃn/ *n.* 指责;指控　7B

* achieve /əˈtʃiːv/ *vt.* 得到;达到;完成,实现　1B

◆ acquire /əˈkwaɪə/ *vt.* (通过自己的能力或努力)获得;学到　1B

* action /ˈækʃn/ *n.* 战斗,作战;行动(过程);活动;行为　7A

* active /ˈæktɪv/ *a.* 积极的;主动的;活跃的　8A

* actually /ˈæktʃʊəlɪ/ *ad.* 实际上　4A

* addition /əˈdɪʃn/ *n.* 加;增加的人(或物)　1A

* adjust /əˈdʒʌst/ *vt.* 调节;改变…以适应　8A

◆ admiration /ˌædməˈreɪʃn/ *n.* 钦佩;赞赏;羡慕　5A

* advantage /ədˈvɑːntɪdʒ/ *n.* 有利条件;优点;好处,利益　8A

◆ aerobic /eəˈrəʊbɪk/ *a.* 增氧健身的　4B

★ afterwards /ˈɑːftəwədz/ *ad.* 以后,过后,后来　5A

◆ aha /ɑːˈhɑː/ *int.* 啊哈(表示惊讶、得意等)　2A

* ahead /əˈhed/ *ad.* & [一般作表语] *a.* 在前面,在前头　1A

* alive /əˈlaɪv/ *a.* 活着的　7B

◆ alley /ˈælɪ/ *n.* (花园中两边有树的)小径　5A

* allow /əˈlaʊ/ *vt.* 允许;容许　1B

★ alphabet /ˈælfəbet/ *n.* 字母表　2A

* amaze /əˈmeɪz/ *vt.* 使(某人)大为惊奇;使(某人)惊愕　5B

◆ amputate /ˈæmpjʊteɪt/ *vt.* 切断,截(肢)　6B

◆ amputation /ˌæmpjʊˈteɪʃn/ *n.* 切断(术);截肢(术)　6B

★ amuse /əˈmjuːz/ *vt.* 逗笑;逗乐;给…提供娱乐　8B

* announce /əˈnaʊns/ *vt.* 宣布,宣告　2B

◆ annoyance /əˈnɔɪəns/ *n.* 烦恼;恼怒　8B

* anxious /ˈæŋkʃəs/ *a.* 焦虑的;不安的;急切的;渴望的　5B

* anyone /ˈenɪwʌn/ *pron.* 任何人　4A

★ appearance /əˈpɪərəns/ *n.* 出现;来到;外貌;外观　4B

★ applause /əˈplɔːz/ *n.* 鼓掌;欢呼;喝彩　2B

* apply /əˈplaɪ/ *vt.* 应用;运用　1B

★appreciate /əˈpriːʃɪeɪt/ vt. 为…表示感激;理解并欣赏;重视 3B

◆arch /ɑːtʃ/ n. 足弓;拱;拱门;拱形结构 4A

＊area /ˈeərɪə/ n. 面积;地域;地区 7B

◆arrangement /əˈreɪndʒmənt/ n. 安排 5A

★arrange /əˈreɪndʒ/ v. 准备,安排;筹划;整理;排列 3B

◆arthritis /ɑːˈθraɪtɪs/ n. 关节炎 3B

＊aspect /ˈæspekt/ n. 方面 8A

★assess /əˈses/ vt. 估定…的数额(或价值);估价 8A

＊assign /əˈsaɪn/ vt. 分配(工作);布置(作业);指派;选派 3B

★assignment /əˈsaɪnmənt/ n. (分派的)任务;(指定的)作业 1A

◆assurance /əˈʃuərəns/ n. 把握;信心 1B

★astonish /əˈstɒnɪʃ/ vt. 使惊讶 7B

★athlete /ˈæθliːt/ n. 运动员 4A

◆athletic /æθˈletɪk/ a. 运动的,体育的;运动员的 4A

＊attack /əˈtæk/ n. 攻击;进攻;抨击;(疾病的)突然发作 v. 攻击;进攻;抨击 4B

＊attend /əˈtend/ vt. 出席,参加;上(学等) 6A

＊attend /əˈtend/ vt. 照料;看管 6B

＊attention /əˈtenʃn/ n. 注意;专心 8A

＊attitude /ˈætɪtjuːd/ n. 看法;态度 4B

＊attractive /əˈtræktɪv/ a. 有吸引力的;妩媚动人的;漂亮的;英俊的 4B

＊avoid /əˈvɔɪd/ vt. 避开;避免;防止 4B

＊aware /əˈweə/ a. 知道的;意识到的 7A

◆awl /ɔːl/ n. 锥子 2A

◆backyard /ˈbækˈjɑːd/ n. 后院 4A

＊badly /ˈbædlɪ/ ad. 坏,差;拙劣地;严重地;厉害地 6B

★balance /ˈbæləns/ n. 平衡,均衡;天平;秤 vt. 使平衡;(用天平)称;权衡 4A

◆bandage /ˈbændɪdʒ/ n. (包扎伤口或患处的)绷带 6B

＊bar /bɑː/ n. (门、窗等的)闩;(用作栅栏、杠杆等的)杆,棒 7A

＊bargain /ˈbɑːgɪn/ n. (买卖等双方的)协议;交易;便宜货 5A

＊base /beɪs/ n. 底部;基底;基础;根据 vt. 以…为…的基础(或根据) 7A

＊basic /ˈbeɪsɪk/ a. 基础的;基本的 n. 基本原理;基本因素;基本的东西 3A

＊basis /ˈbeɪsɪs/ n. 基础 8A

★bathe /beɪð/ vt. 给…洗澡;使沐浴 5A

＊bear /beə/ vt. 结(果实);生(孩子);忍受,容忍;承担(责任等) 5B

＊beauty /ˈbjuːtɪ/ n. 美,美丽;美人;美的东西 7B

＊behaviour /bɪˈheɪvjə/ n. 行为;举止 5B

＊belief /bɪˈliːf/ n. 相信,信任;信念;看法 4B

◆belly /ˈbelɪ/ n. 肚子 6B

★bite /baɪt/ v./n. 咬,叮 2B

*blame /bleɪm/ n. (过错等的)责任;指责,责备 vt. 指责,责备;把…归咎(于)   7B

◆blameless /'bleɪmlɪs/ a. 无可指责的;无过错的   7B

◆bless /bles/ vt. 赐福,保佑   3A

*blind /blaɪnd/ a. 瞎的,盲的   2A

◆blossom /'blɒsəm/ n. (尤指果树的)花;(一棵树上开出的)全部花朵   5A

★blow /bləʊ/ n. 重击;捶打;打击;灾祸   3B

◆blunt /blʌnt/ a. 钝的   2A

◆boredom /'bɔːdəm/ n. 厌烦;厌倦   8B

*bottom /'bɒtəm/ n. 底,底部   5B

*brain /breɪn/ n. 脑;头脑;智力   4B

◆brake /breɪk/ n. 制动器,闸;刹车 v. 刹(车)   7B

★brand /brænd/ n. (商品的)牌子;商标   7B

◆brand-new /'brænd'njuː/ a. 全新的,崭新的   7B

◆bruise /bruːz/ n. (人体跌、碰后产生的)青肿,挫伤;(水果等的)伤痕   7B

◆bump /bʌmp/ n. 肿块   3A

◆bunch /bʌntʃ/ n. 束;串;扎;捆   5A

*bury /'berɪ/ vt. 埋葬;掩埋;埋藏   5A

◆bushel /'bʊʃəl/ n. 蒲式耳(谷物、水果、蔬菜等的容量单位,1 蒲式耳在英国等于36.368升,在
            美国等于35.238 升)   2B

*business /'bɪznɪs/ n. 事务;事;买卖;商业;生意;商行;商店   3A

◆bystander /'baɪstændə/ n. 旁观者   8A

*calm /kɑːm/ a. 不激动的;平静的;镇静的,镇定的   5B

◆calorie /'kælərɪ/ n. 卡路里,卡(热量单位)   4B

◆capability /ˌkeɪpə'bɪlətɪ/ n. 能力;才能   8A

★capture /'kæptʃə/ vt. 俘虏;捕获   7A

◆carambola /ˌkærəm'bəʊlə/ n. 五敛子,杨桃   5B

*career /kə'rɪə/ n. 职业;生涯   1B

*case /keɪs/ n. 箱;盒;容器   2B

★cast /kɑːst/ n. 固定用敷料;石膏绷带   7B

◆catsup /'kætsəp/ n. 调味番茄酱   2B

*cause /kɔːz/ n. 原因,起因;理由 vt. 使产生,使发生,引起   4B

*celebrate /'selɪbreɪt/ vt. 庆祝   5B

*cell /sel/ n. 细胞;小牢房;单身牢房;电池   4B

*cell /sel/ n. 小牢房;单人牢房   7A

*central /'sentrəl/ a. 中心的;中央的;在中心的   2B

*century /'sentʃərɪ/ n. 百年;世纪   6B

*charge /tʃɑːdʒ/ n. 掌管;照管;价钱,费用;控告,指控;电荷,充电   3A

*cheat /tʃiːt/ vt. 欺骗(某人)   5B

*cheer /tʃɪə/ n. 欢呼声;喝彩声 v. 向(某人)欢呼;为(某人)喝彩   6A

★chemical /'kemɪkl/ a. 化学的 1B

◆cherry /'tʃerɪ/ n. 樱桃;樱桃树 5A

◆chiding /'tʃaɪdɪŋ/ n. 责备;责骂 3A

＊childhood /'tʃaɪldhʊd/ n. 儿童状态;童年,幼年 7B

◆chore /tʃɔː/ n. (常指单调乏味的)日常零星活儿;[~s]家庭杂务 3B

＊church /tʃɜːtʃ/ n. 教堂;教会 2A

＊cigarette /ˌsɪɡəˈret, ˈsɪɡəret/ n. 香烟 7A

◆civil /'sɪvl/ a. 公民的;国内的 7A

＊code /kəʊd/ n. 密码;电码;代码 2A

＊coin /kɔɪn/ n. 硬币 5B

◆collegiate /kə'liːdʒɪət/ a. 大学(生)的;学院的 3B

＊combine /kəm'baɪn/ v. (使)结合;(使)联合;(使)混合 4B

＊comfortable /'kʌmfətəbl/ a. 舒适的;安逸的;无忧无虑的 1A

＊communicate /kə'mjuːnɪkeɪt/ v. 传送;传达;传递;传播;交流,交际 8B

＊communication /kəmjuːnɪˈkeɪʃn/ n. 传达,交流;通信 8B

＊compare /kəm'peə/ vt. 比较 8B

★compensate /'kɒmpenseɪt/ vt. 补偿;赔偿;报偿;报酬 8B

＊compete /kəm'piːt/ vi. 竞争;对抗 1A

★complaint /kəm'pleɪnt/ n. 抱怨,诉苦;怨言;抱怨的缘由;申诉,投诉;控诉;控告 3A

＊complete /kəm'pliːt/ a. 完整的,完全的;整个的 vt. 完成,使完整,使完善 6B

＊complete /kəm'pliːt/ vt. 完成 1B

★complicated /'kɒmplɪkeɪtɪd/ a. (结构)复杂的;难懂的 2A

＊concentrate /'kɒnsntreɪt/ v. 全神贯注,专心致志 8A

＊concern /kən'sɜːn/ n. 关心;忧虑,挂念;关切的事;感兴趣的事;[常作~s]事物 3A

★conclusion /kən'kluːʒən/ n. 结论 4A

＊confidence /'kɒnfɪdəns/ n. 信任;信心;自信 6A

＊confuse /kən'fjuːz/ vt. 把(某人)弄糊涂;使困惑,使混乱,搞乱 1B

◆connection /kə'nekʃn/ n. 连接,连结;联系 7A

◆conquer /'kɒŋkə/ vt. 征服 2B

★conserve /kən'sɜːv/ vt. 保护;保藏;保存 4A

★consume /kən'sjuːm/ vt. 消耗,花费;耗尽 2B

＊contact /'kɒntækt/ n. 接触;联系;交往 7A

◆contemptuous /kən'temptʃʊəs/ a. 鄙视的;表示轻蔑的 7A

＊content /kən'tent/ a. 满意的;满足的;乐意的 5B

＊continue /kən'tɪnjuː/ vi. 继续(做某事);不停 1B

＊control /kən'trəʊl/ n. 控制;支配 1A

＊courage /'kʌrɪdʒ/ n. 勇气;胆量 6A

＊course /kɔːs/ n. 课程;科目 1A

＊courthouse /'kɔːthaʊs/ n. 法庭;法院;[美]县政府办公楼 2B

＊cousin /ˈkʌsn/ n. 堂兄弟(或姐妹);表兄弟(或姐妹) 7B

◆cram /kræm/ vt. 把…塞进;把…塞满 8A

＊create /kriːˈeɪt/ vt. 创造;创作;引起;产生 2A

＊critical /ˈkrɪtɪkl/ a. 决定性的;关键的;批评的;危机中的;危急时刻的 8A

◆crutch /krʌtʃ/ n. 拐杖 6B

＊curtain /ˈkɜːtn/ n. 帘;窗帘;门帘;(舞台上的)幕,帷幕;帘状物;幕状物 5A

★customer /ˈkʌstəmə/ n. 顾客;主顾 3B

＊cycle /ˈsaɪkl/ n. 循环;周期 8A

＊daily /ˈdeɪlɪ/ ad. 每日,天天 a. 每天的;日常的 n. daily newspaper 日报 6B

◆dart /dɑːt/ vi. 猛冲;飞奔 6A

★dash /dæʃ/ n. (莫尔斯电码的)划,长划;破折号(即—);猛冲,飞奔 2A

＊death /deθ/ n. 死;死亡 2B

★debate /dɪˈbeɪt/ vt. 考虑,盘算;讨论;争论 6A

＊decision /dɪˈsɪʒn/ n. 决定 1A

★decorate /ˈdekəreɪt/ vt. 装饰 2B

★definition /ˌdefɪˈnɪʃn/ n. 定义;释义;(轮廓、线条等的)清晰 4B

＊degree /dɪˈɡriː/ n. 学位;程度;度数 1B

＊delay /dɪˈleɪ/ n. 延迟;拖延;耽搁 5A

＊delicious /dɪˈlɪʃəs/ a. 美味的,可口的;芬芳的;怡人的 5A

＊delight /dɪˈlaɪt/ n. 快乐;高兴 5A

＊deliver /dɪˈlɪvə/ vt. 传送(信息等);投递(信件等);发表(演说等) 2A

＊demand /dɪˈmɑːnd/ vt. 要求,请求;强要;需要 5B

＊deny /dɪˈnaɪ/ vt. 否认,不承认;拒绝给予 8B

★dependent /dɪˈpendənt/ a. 依靠的;依赖的 1A

★derive /dɪˈraɪv/ vt. 得到;获取 3B

＊desire /dɪˈzaɪə/ n. 渴望;愿望 2A

◆desperate /ˈdespərət/ a. 绝望的;孤注一掷的,拼命的 2B

＊determine /dɪˈtɜːmɪn/ v. 确定;决定;下决心 4B

＊develop /dɪˈveləp/ v. 制订;研制;(使)形成;(使)成长;(使)发育;发展 2A

◆diet /ˈdaɪət/ n. 日常饮食,日常食物;(有助于减肥等的)特种饮食,规定饮食 2B

＊difference /ˈdɪfrəns/ n. 差别,差异;不同之处;差距;差额;(意见的)分歧,不和 6A

★dig /dɪɡ/ vt. 掘,挖 5A

★dimension /dɪˈmenʃn/ n. 尺寸;长度;宽度;高度;厚度;方面;因素 7A

＊direction /dɪˈrekʃn/ n. 方向 7B

＊directly /dɪˈrektlɪ/ ad. 径直地;直接地;直率地 7A

＊disappear /ˌdɪsəˈpɪə/ vi. 不见;消失;不复存在 8B

＊disease /dɪˈziːz/ n. 疾病;病害 4B

◆dishonest /dɪsˈɒnɪst/ a. 不老实的,不诚实的;骗人的;欺骗性的 5B

◆dishwasher /ˈdɪʃwɒʃə/ n. 洗碟机;洗碟工 7B

★district /'dɪstrɪkt/ n. 区;地区;行政区 6A

★dot /dɒt/ n. 点,圆点 2A

◆douse /daʊs/ vt. 把…浸入水(或其他液体中);浇(或泼)水(或其他液体)在…上 6B

＊drown /draʊn/ v. (使)淹死 5B

★due /djuː/ a. 到期的;应到的;应付的 3A

＊earn /ɜːn/ vt. 赚(钱),挣(钱);谋(生);获得,博得 5B

＊edge /edʒ/ n. 边;边界;边缘 7A

＊education /ˌedʒuːˈkeɪʃn/ n. 教育 1B

＊effective /ɪˈfektɪv/ a. 有效的;产生预期结果的 8A

★elementary /ˌelɪˈmentrɪ/ a. 初级的;基础的;基本的 3A

＊emotional /ɪˈməʊʃnəl/ a. 情感的 1A

◆encounter /ɪnˈkaʊntə/ vt. 意外遇见;偶尔碰到;遭到,受到 8B

◆endorphin /enˈdɔːfɪn/ n. 内啡肽 4B

◆endurance /ɪnˈdjʊərəns/ n. 忍耐力;耐力 4A

＊enemy /'enəmɪ/ n. 敌人 2A

＊energy /'enədʒɪ/ n. 精力;干劲;活力;能;能量;能源 4A

＊engineer /ˌendʒɪˈnɪə/ n. 工程师 1B

＊engineering /ˌendʒɪˈnɪərɪŋ/ n. 工程 1B

＊enlarge /ɪnˈlɑːdʒ/ v. (使)变大;扩大;放大 4B

＊enter /'entə/ vt. 进入 1A

◆enthusiastic /ɪnˌθjuːzɪˈæstɪk/ a. 热情的;热心的,热烈的 6A

＊entire /ɪnˈtaɪə/ a. 全部的,整个的;完全的 4A

◆entitle /ɪnˈtaɪtl/ vt. 给(书等)题名,定名 7A

＊environment /ɪnˈvaɪərənmənt/ n. 环境 1B

★equipment /ɪˈkwɪpmənt/ n. 装备;设备;器材 3B

＊escape /ɪˈskeɪp/ v. 逃跑;逃走;逃出;逃脱;逃避;避免 7A

＊especially /ɪˈspeʃəlɪ/ ad. 尤其;特别 4B

＊establish /ɪˈstæblɪʃ/ vt. 建立,设立;确立;证实 8A

＊everyday /'evrɪdeɪ/ a. 每天的,每天发生的;日常的 3A

＊everyone /'evrɪwʌn/ pron. 每人,人人 7B

★excellent /'eksələnt/ a. 极好的;优秀的;卓越的 3B

＊exchange /ɪksˈtʃeɪndʒ/ vt. 交换;调换 n. 交换;调换 5B

＊excited /ɪkˈsaɪtɪd/ a. 兴奋的,激动的 7B

★execute /'eksɪkjuːt/ vt. 将(某人)处死;实行,执行;履行;实施 7A

＊expand /ɪksˈpænd/ v. 扩大;扩充;扩展 8A

＊experience /ɪkˈspɪərɪəns/ n. 经验;体验;经历,阅历 7A

＊experiment /ɪkˈsperɪmənt/ n. 实验;试验 vi. 进行实验(或试验) 8B

＊explode /ɪkˈspləʊd/ v. (使)爆炸;(使)爆发 2B

◆explosion /ɪkˈspləʊʒn/ n. 爆炸(声) 6B

* express /ɪkˈspres/ *vt.* 表示,表露,表达　8B

* expression /ɪkˈspreʃn/ *n.* 表达;词语;表达方式　8B

* extra /ˈekstrə/ *a.* 额外的;外加的;附加的　5B

* factor /ˈfæktə/ *n.* 因素　8A

* faint /feɪnt/ *vi.* (因受热、受惊、失血等)昏厥,晕倒　2B

* faith /feɪθ/ *n.* 信念;信任;信心　6B

* familiar /fəˈmɪlɪə/ *a.* 熟悉的;通晓的　1B

◆ fantasy /ˈfæntəsɪ/ *n.* 想象;幻想;想象的产物;荒诞的念头;怪念头　4B

◆ fascist /ˈfæʃɪst/ *n.* 法西斯主义者,法西斯分子 *a.* 法西斯主义的　7A

* fault /fɔːlt/ *n.* 过失;过错;缺点;毛病;故障　7B

* fear /fɪə/ *n.* 恐惧;害怕　1A

* feeling /ˈfiːlɪŋ/ *n.* 感觉;感情　8B

★ fetch /fetʃ/ *vt.* (去)拿来;请来;接来　5B

◆ fighter /ˈfaɪtə/ *n.* 战斗机;战士　7A

* finally /ˈfaɪnəlɪ/ *ad.* 最终;最后　2B

◆ firewood /ˈfaɪəwʊd/ *n.* 木柴　6B

* fit /fɪt/ *vi.* 被容纳;(服装等)合身,合适;适合;适应 *a.* 适合的;健康的　2A

◆ flourish /ˈflʌrɪʃ/ *vi.* 茂盛;兴旺,繁荣　3B

◆ foam /fəʊm/ *vi.* 吐白沫;起泡沫　2B

* focus /ˈfəʊkəs/ *v.* 将(注意力等)集中于(某事物)　8A

* force /fɔːs/ *vt.* 强迫;迫使 *n.* 力,力量;力气;武力;暴力　6B

* forgive /fəˈgɪv/ *vt.* 原谅;饶恕;宽恕　3A

* fortune /ˈfɔːtʃən/ *n.* 大笔的钱;财产;运气;命运　5B

* forward /ˈfɔːwəd/ *ad.* 向前　4A

◆ French /frentʃ/ *a.* 法国的;法国人的;法语的 *n.* 法语　2A

* frequent /ˈfriːkwənt/ *a.* 时常发生的,频繁的;经常的,惯常的　8A

* freshman /ˈfreʃmən/ *n.* (中学或大学)一年级学生　1A

◆ frustration /frʌˈstreɪʃn/ *n.* 受挫;挫折;沮丧;失望　8B

* fulfil(l) /fʊlˈfɪl/ *vt.* 履行;实现;满足　8A

◆ fumble /ˈfʌmbl/ *vi.* 乱摸;摸索　7A

* funny /ˈfʌnɪ/ *a.* 滑稽的,可笑的;奇怪的　4A

* furniture /ˈfɜːnɪtʃə/ *n.* 家具　5B

* gain /geɪn/ *vt.* 得到;获得;赢得　1B

* gap /gæp/ *n.* 缺口;裂口;间隔;差距,分歧　7A

◆ gardener /ˈgɑːdnə/ *n.* 园丁;园艺家　5A

* generate /ˈdʒenəreɪt/ *vt.* 使存在;引起;使产生;使发生　7A

◆ genetics /dʒɪˈnetɪks/ *n.* 遗传学　4B

* gentle /ˈdʒentl/ *a.* 温和的;慈祥的;温柔的;和婉的　3A

◆ giggle /ˈgɪgl/ *n.* 咯咯的笑;傻笑　7B

* goal /gəʊl/ n. 目标;目的 1B
* golden /ˈgəʊldən/ a. 金的,金制的;金色的;像黄金一样贵重的 5A
◆ grab /græb/ vt. 抓取;攫取 6B
* graduate /ˈgrædʒʊeɪt/ vi. 毕业 1B
* graduation /ˌgrædʒʊˈeɪʃn/ n. (大学、中学等)毕业 1B
◆ grandchild /ˈgræntʃaɪld/ n. (外)孙女;孙子;外孙 3A
* grateful /ˈgreɪtfl/ a. 感激的;感谢的 3A
◆ gravity /ˈgrævɪtɪ/ n. 万有引力;地心引力;重力 4A
◆ greedy /ˈgriːdɪ/ a. 贪食的,贪嘴的;贪婪的 5B
* greet /griːt/ vt. 问候,迎接;招待 3A
★ guarantee /ˌgærənˈtiː/ n. 保证,担保 vt. 保证,担保 4B
* habit /ˈhæbɪt/ n. 习惯 8A
* hall /hɔːl/ n. 会堂,礼堂,大厅;门厅;[美](大楼)的过道,走廊 3A
◆ handful /ˈhændfʊl/ n. 一把;少数,少量 5B
* handle /ˈhændl/ vt. 处理,应付;管理;操纵,控制 1A
* hang /hæŋ/ v. 悬挂,吊 5A
* harvest /ˈhɑːvɪst/ n. 收割;收获;收成 5A
◆ heal /hiːl/ v. (使)愈合;(使)痊愈;(使)康复 6A
* heel /hiːl/ n. 脚后跟 4A
* hero /ˈhɪərəʊ/ n. 英雄;男主角;男主人公 2B
* hide /haɪd/ vt. 把…藏起来,隐藏 5A
* highway /ˈhaɪweɪ/ n. 公路 7B
* honor /ˈɒnə/ n. 崇敬;敬意;荣誉;名誉 vt. 向…表示敬意;给…以荣誉 2A
◆ hooray /hʊˈreɪ/ int. (表示高兴、欢快、热情等的呼喊声)好,好哇;万岁 6A
★ household /ˈhaʊshəʊld/ n. 一家人;家庭,户 a. 家庭的;家用的 3B
* however /haʊˈevə/ conj. 然而;可是 1A
◆ hug /hʌg/ vt. 拥抱 7B
* human /ˈhjuːmən/ a. 人的;人类的 6B
★ humble /ˈhʌmbl/ a. 地位低下的;卑贱的;谦逊的;谦虚的 vt. 使谦恭;羞辱;降低…的地位;
使卑贱 3A
◆ humiliate /hjuːˈmɪlɪeɪt/ vt. 使(某人)感到羞耻(或不光彩);使丢脸 6A
* hunt /hʌnt/ v. 追猎,猎取;打猎;寻找;搜寻 n. 打猎;寻找;搜寻 5A
◆ hurdle /ˈhɜːdl/ n. 难关;障碍 1A
* identify /aɪˈdentɪfaɪ/ vt. 鉴定(或证明)(某人 / 某事物);认出,识别 8A
* illness /ˈɪlnɪs/ n. 病;疾病 4B
* imitate /ˈɪmɪteɪt/ vt. 模仿,仿效,学…的样 2A
* impossible /ɪmˈpɒsəbl/ a. 办不到的;不可能的 4B
* improve /ɪmˈpruːv/ v. (使)变得更好;改进,改善 4B
* inch /ɪntʃ/ n. 英寸(长度单位,等于2.54厘米或1/12英尺) 6B

* include /ɪnˈkluːd/ *vt.* 包括,包含　8B

* increase /ɪnˈkriːs/ *v.* 增加;增大;增长;增强 /ˈɪnkriːs/ *n.* 增加;增大;增长;增强　4A

* independent /ˌɪndɪˈpendənt/ *a.* 独立的;自主的　1B

◆Indian /ˈɪndɪən/ *n.* 印第安人;印度人 *a.* 印第安人的;印度的;印度人的　2B

★infect /ɪnˈfekt/ *vt.* 传染;感染　2A

◆infection /ɪnˈfekʃn/ *n.* 传染;感染　2A

* information /ˌɪnfəˈmeɪʃn/ *n.* 消息;情报;资料;信息　8B

* injure /ˈɪndʒə/ *vt.* 伤害;损害　2A

* injury /ˈɪndʒərɪ/ *n.* (对身体的)伤害;(对名誉的)损害　6A

* insist /ɪnˈsɪst/ *v.* 坚持说;坚决要求;一定要　7B

* instant /ˈɪnstənt/ *n.* 时刻,瞬息,顷刻,刹那　7A

◆instill /ɪnˈstɪl/ *vt.* (向某人或某人的头脑)逐步灌输(思想、感情、美德等)　6B

* interest /ˈɪntrɪst/ *n.* 兴趣　8B

* interfere /ˌɪntəˈfɪə/ *vi.* 妨碍,干扰;干涉,介入　3B

◆intersection /ˌɪntəˈsekʃn/ *n.* 道路交叉口;十字路口　7B

★invite /ɪnˈvaɪt/ *vt.* 邀请　3B

* involve /ɪnˈvɒlv/ *vt.* 使参与;使陷入;使卷入;牵涉;包含,含有　8A

* item /ˈaɪtəm/ *n.* 条,项;项目;条款;(新闻等的)一条,一则　2A

◆jail /dʒeɪl/ *n.* 监狱　7A

◆jailer /ˈdʒeɪlə/ *n.* 监狱看守,狱卒　7A

★joy /dʒɔɪ/ *n.* 欢乐;喜悦　3B

◆joyful /ˈdʒɔɪfl/ *a.* 使人高兴的;高兴的,快乐的　3B

* judge /dʒʌdʒ/ *vt.* 判断,估计;评价;审判;裁决 *n.* 法官,审判员;仲裁人;裁判员;鉴定人　3A

★juice /dʒuːs/ *n.* (水果、蔬菜、肉的)汁;果汁;果汁饮料　2B

◆kerosene /ˈkerəsiːn/ *n.* 煤油　6B

* kid /kɪd/ *n.* 小孩;年轻人　4A

* kindness /ˈkaɪndnɪs/ *n.* 仁慈,好意　6A

* land /lænd/ *n.* 地;土地;陆地　5B

◆lap /læp/ *n.* (跑道的)一圈 *vt.* 比…领先一圈(或数圈)　6A

* laundry /ˈlɔːndrɪ/ *n.* 待洗衣物;已洗好的衣物;洗衣店,洗衣房　3A

★lean /liːn/ *vi.* 倾斜;弯曲;屈身　4A

★leap /liːp/ *vi.* 跳,跳跃;迅速移动　7A

◆leather /ˈleðə/ *n.* 皮革　2A

* lecture /ˈlektʃə/ *n.* 演讲;讲课　8A

* license /ˈlaɪsns/ *n.* 执照;许可证　7B

* likely /ˈlaɪklɪ/ *a.* 可能的　8B

* limit /ˈlɪmɪt/ *n.* 范围;限度;极限　4B

* limp /lɪmp/ *vi.* 跛行;一拐一拐地走　6A

* lip /lɪp/ *n.* 嘴唇　7A

★living /ˈlɪvɪŋ/ n. 生计;生活(方式) a. 活的,活着的 3B

＊load /ləud/ n. 负荷,负担 vt. 装,装载;把(货物或人)装上 3B

＊local /ˈləukl/ a. 地方性的;当地的,本地的 2B

＊lock /lɒk/ n. 锁 vt. 锁,锁上 7A

★lonely /ˈləunlɪ/ a. 孤独的,寂寞的;荒凉的,人迹稀少的 3B

＊maintain /meɪnˈteɪn/ vt. 保持;维持 1B

＊major /ˈmeɪdʒə/ n. (大学生的)主修科目;专业 1B

＊manage /ˈmænɪdʒ/ vt. 设法做到 1A

＊master /ˈmɑːstə/ n. 主人;雇主;师傅;能手 vt. 掌握,精通 8A

＊material /məˈtɪərɪəl/ n. 材料;原料;素材;资料 8A

＊measure /ˈmeʒə/ n. 措施;办法 vt. 量,测量;估量,衡量 2B

＊measure /ˈmeʒə/ vt. 量,测量 n. (量得的)尺寸,大小,分量;量度,测量 4A

＊medal /ˈmedl/ n. 奖牌;奖章;勋章;纪念章 6A

★merchant /ˈmɜːtʃənt/ n. 商人 5A

◆mess /mes/ n. 脏乱状态,零乱状态 7B

◆midway /ˈmɪdˌweɪ/ ad. 当中;中间;半途 5A

＊million /ˈmɪljən/ n. 百万 2B

＊minute /ˈmɪnɪt/ n. 分,分钟;片刻,一会儿 2B

＊model /ˈmɒdl/ n. 模范,榜样;模型;样式;模特儿 3A

＊moment /ˈməumənt/ n. 片刻,瞬间;时刻,时候 7A

◆mom /mɒm/ n. 妈;妈妈 3A

★motivate /ˈməutɪveɪt/ vt. 激起(某人的)兴趣;激发(某人)做某事 1B

◆Ms /mɪz/ abbr. 女士(冠于已婚或未婚女子姓或姓名前的称呼) 4B

＊muscle /ˈmʌsl/ n. 肌肉 4B

◆myth /mɪθ/ n. 神话;杜撰出来(或不可能)的人(或事物) 2B

★nail /neɪl/ n. 指甲;钉子 5A

＊natural /ˈnætʃrəl/ a. 自然的,非人为的;正常的;合乎常情的 7A

＊nearly /ˈnɪəlɪ/ ad. 几乎,差不多 2A

＊necessarily /ˈnesəsərəlɪ; US ˌnesəˈserəlɪ/ ad. 必然,必定 8A

＊negative /ˈnegətɪv/ a. 否定的;反面的;消极的 8B

★neighborhood /ˈneɪbəhud/ n. 地区,地段;四邻,街坊;邻近地区 3B

＊nervous /ˈnɜːvəs/ a. 神经紧张的;情绪不安的;提心吊胆的;神经的 7A

＊nod /nɒd/ v. 点(头)(致意或表示同意等) 5A

＊normal /ˈnɔːml/ a. (符合)标准的;通常的;正常的 8B

＊normally /ˈnɔːməlɪ/ ad. 正常地;通常 6B

＊novel /ˈnɒvl/ a. 新奇的;新颖的 8B

＊novel /ˈnɒvl/ n. (长篇)小说 7A

★objection /əbˈdʒekʃn/ n. 反对;异议 3A

＊obvious /ˈɒbvɪəs/ a. 显然的,明显的 8B

★occasion /əˈkeɪʒn/ n. (事情发生的)时刻,时候;场合;时机;机会   3A

* ocean /ˈəʊʃn/ n. 洋;海洋;大海   5B

* officer /ˈɒfɪsə/ n. 军官   2A

* operate /ˈɒpəreɪt/ vi. 工作;运转;运行;起作用   8B

* opportunity /ˌɒpəˈtjuːnɪti/ n. 机会,时机   8A

◆orchard /ˈɔːtʃəd/ n. 果园   5A

◆outsider /ˌaʊtˈsaɪdə/ n. 外人,组织之外的人   7B

◆overall /ˌəʊvərˈɔːl/ a. 包括一切的;总的;全面的   4B

* overcome /ˌəʊvəˈkʌm/ vt. 战胜;克服   6A

◆owl /aʊl/ n. 猫头鹰   8A

* pack /pæk/ v. 把…装箱;把…打包;把东西装进(容器)   5B

* pad /pæd/ n. 足垫;垫;衬垫;拍纸簿   4A

◆painful /ˈpeɪnfl/ a. 令人痛苦的;令人疼痛的;疼的   6B

* pale /peɪl/ a. (指人、面色等)苍白的,灰白的;(指颜色)浅的,淡的   5A

★participant /pɑːˈtɪsɪpənt/ n. 参加者   8A

* passive /ˈpæsɪv/ a. 被动的;消极的   8A

◆pastor /ˈpɑːstə/ n. 牧师   2A

* path /pɑːθ/ n. 小路,小径   3A

* patient /ˈpeɪʃənt/ n. 病人 a. 忍耐的;有耐心的   2B

◆pearl /pɜːl/ n. 珍珠   5A

* perfect /ˈpɜːfɪkt/ a. 完美的,完善的;理想的;完全的 /pəˈfekt/ vt. 使完美;使完全;完成   4A

* period /ˈpɪərɪəd/ n. (一段)时间;时期;时代;课时   8B

* persevere /ˌpɜːsɪˈvɪə/ vi. 坚持不懈,锲而不舍   8B

* personal /ˈpɜːsənl/ a. 个人的;私人的   8A

◆personality /ˌpɜːsəˈnælɪti/ n. 人格;个性   3B

◆perspective /pəˈspektɪv/ n. (观察问题的)视角;观点   1A

◆petal /ˈpetl/ n. 花瓣   5A

◆phoenix /ˈfiːnɪks/ n. 凤凰;长生鸟   5B

◆pillow /ˈpɪləʊ/ n. 枕头   5A

* pilot /ˈpaɪlət/ n. 飞行员;引航员   7A

* plan /plæn/ vt. 计划;打算   1B

* playground /ˈpleɪgraʊnd/ n. (学校的)操场,运动场   4A

◆poisonous /ˈpɔɪzənəs/ a. 有毒的   2B

* polish /ˈpɒlɪʃ/ vt. 擦光;擦亮   5A

* pop /pɒp/ n. 砰的一声,啪的一声 vi. 发出砰(或啪)的响声   6A

◆populate /ˈpɒpjʊleɪt/ vt. 居住于,生活于;构成…的人口   7B

* position /pəˈzɪʃn/ n. 姿势,姿态;位置;地位;职位   4A

* positive /ˈpɒzətɪv/ a. 有把握的;有助益的;建设性的;有信心的;乐观的   4B

* possess /pəˈzes/ vt. 占有,拥有   5A

◆possessor /pə'zesə/ n. 拥有者,持有人;所有人 7B

* postpone /ˌpəʊs'pəʊn/ vt. 使延期;推迟 6B

◆postponement /ˌpəʊs'pəʊnmənt/ n. 延期;推迟 6B

◆potbellied /pɒt'belɪd/ a. (指人)大腹便便的;(指容器)下部向外鼓的 6B

* pot /pɒt/ n. 罐;壶;锅 6B

★pray /preɪ/ v. 祈祷;祈求 6B

* pretty /'prɪtɪ/ a. 漂亮的,秀丽的 ad. 相当;颇 2B

★prevail /prɪ'veɪl/ vi. 普遍存在(或发生);盛行;流行 2B

* prevent /prɪ'vent/ vt. 预防;防止 4B

◆preview /'priːvjuː/ v. 预习 8A

* pride /praɪd/ n. 得意,自豪 3A

* prince /prɪns/ n. 王子 7A

★priority /praɪ'ɒrətɪ/ n. 优先;重点;优先权;优先考虑的事 8A

* prize /praɪz/ n. 奖赏;奖金;奖品 2B

* probably /'prɒbəblɪ/ ad. 大概;很可能 4B

* process /'prəʊses/ n. 过程,进程,步骤,程序 8A

* produce /prə'djuːs/ vt. 制造;生产;出产;引起;产生;生育 2B

* professor /prə'fesə/ n. (大学)教授 8A

* progress /'prəʊgres/ n. 前进;进步;进展 8B

* property /'prɒpətɪ/ n. 财产,资产;所有物 5A

* prove /pruːv/ vt. 证明,证实 4B

* provide /prə'vaɪd/ vt. 供给;提供 8B

* public /'pʌblɪk/ a. 公立的;公众的,公共的,公开的 n. 公众,民众 2A

* pure /pjʊə/ a. 纯的;纯净的;无瑕的;完美的 5B

* purpose /'pɜːpəs/ n. 目的;意图 8A

★pursue /pə'sjuː/ vt. 追求;从事 1B

* quantity /'kwɒntətɪ/ n. 量,数量;大量 2B

* quit /kwɪt/ v. 放弃;辞去;停止(做某事);停止努力;认输 6A

* race /reɪs/ n. (速度的)比赛,赛跑 6A

★range /reɪndʒ/ vi. (在一定范围内)变动,变化;显示不等 3B

* rate /reɪt/ n. 比率,率;速率,速度;等级 4B

* reality /rɪ'ælətɪ/ n. 现实,实际;真实,真实性 2A

* realize /'rɪəlaɪz/ vt. 明白,理解;认识到;体会到;实现 6A

* reason /'riːzn/ n. 原因,理由 3A

* recently /'riːsntlɪ/ ad. 最近;新近 7B

* recommend /ˌrekə'mend/ vt. 建议;劝告;推荐;称赞 6B

* recover /rɪ'kʌvə/ v. 痊愈;康复;重新找到;重新获得;恢复(能力、健康等) 6B

* reduce /rɪ'djuːs/ vt. 减少;缩小;削减;降低 4B

* reflect /rɪ'flekt/ v. 深思;反省;反射(光、热、声等);反映 3A

◆regain /rɪˈɡeɪn/ vt. 重新获得 6A

★regulate /ˈreɡjʊleɪt/ vt. 调整;调节(时间、速度等) 1A

* reject /rɪˈdʒekt/ vt. 拒绝;拒绝接受 2B

* relate /rɪˈleɪt/ vt. 讲;叙述;使互相关联;证明…之间的联系 4B

* relax /rɪˈlæks/ v. (使)松弛,(使)放松;(使)休息;(使)轻松 4B

★release /rɪˈliːs/ vt. 解放;释放;放开;发布;公开发行 4B

* remain /rɪˈmeɪn/ v. 仍然是;保持不变;留下,逗留 7B

* remind /rɪˈmaɪnd/ vt. 提醒;使想起 3A

* remove /rɪˈmuːv/ vt. 移开;挪走;把…免职;脱下;摘下;去掉,除去 6B

* replace /rɪˈpleɪs/ vt. 替换;代替;接替;把…放回原处 5B

* request /rɪˈkwest/ n. 要求;请求 vt. 请求;要求 5A

* require /rɪˈkwaɪə/ vt. 需要;要求;规定 4A

◆resentment /rɪˈzentmənt/ n. 愤恨,怨恨 8B

★responsibility /rɪsˌpɒnsəˈbɪlɪtɪ/ n. 职务,任务 3B

* responsible /rɪˈspɒnsəbl/ a. (法律上或道义上)需负责任的,承担责任的 1A

* review /rɪˈvjuː/ vt. 复习(功课) 8A

◆ripen /ˈraɪpən/ v. (使)成熟 5B

* ripe /raɪp/ a. (指水果、谷物等)成熟的 5B

* root /ruːt/ n. (植物的)根;根部;根源;根由,原因 5A

* rough /rʌf/ a. (表面)不平滑的;粗糙的 5A

★routine /ruːˈtiːn/ n. 惯常的程序;常规 1A

◆ruby /ˈruːbɪ/ n. 红宝石 5A

◆runner /ˈrʌnə/ n. 奔跑的人(或动物);赛跑的人(或动物) 4A

◆saddle /ˈsædl/ n. 鞍;马鞍;鞍具 2A

★satisfaction /ˌsætɪsˈfækʃn/ n. 满意;满足 3B

* schedule /ˈʃedjuːl, US ˈskedʒuːl/ n. 时间表;日程安排表 8A

◆scrape /skreɪp/ n. 擦伤;擦痕 3A

* search /sɜːtʃ/ v. 搜寻;搜索;搜查 n. 搜寻;搜索;搜查 7A

◆secondly /ˈsekəndlɪ/ ad. 第二;其次 1B

* secret /ˈsiːkrɪt/ a. 秘密的 n. 秘密 2A

* seize /siːz/ vt. 抓住,捉住;攫取 5B

★senior /ˈsiːnɪə/ n. 较年长者;地位(级别)较高者;(美国四年制大学或中学的)高年级生 6A

* separate /ˈseprət/ a. 不同的;分开的;分隔的 /ˈsepəreɪt/ v. (使)分开;(使)分隔 4A

* serve /sɜːv/ v. 为…服务;为…服役;为…尽职责;服务;服役;供职 3B

★service /ˈsɜːvɪs/ n. 服务 3B

* share /ʃeə/ vt. 与别人分享(或合用)(某物);把(某事)告诉(某人) 1A

* shock /ʃɒk/ vt. 使震惊,使惊愕 n. 冲击;震动;震惊 2B

* shortly /ˈʃɔːtlɪ/ ad. 不久;很快 1A

★shoulder /ˈʃəʊldə/ n. 肩;肩膀 vt. 肩起,挑起;担负,承担(工作、责任等) 3B

◆shriek /ʃriːk/ vi. 尖叫 2B

* sign /saɪn/ n. 符号,记号;标志;牌;指示牌;招牌 7B

* silence /ˈsaɪləns/ n. 寂静;无声;沉默 2B

* silent /ˈsaɪlənt/ a. 安静的;寂静无声的 7A

* silk /sɪlk/ n. 丝;丝绸 5A

◆simplify /ˈsɪmplɪfaɪ/ vt. 使简易;使简明;简化 2A

* simply /ˈsɪmplɪ/ ad. 仅仅,只不过;简单地;简朴地;完全地 4B

* situation /ˌsɪtʃʊˈeɪʃn/ n. 状况,处境;局面,形势 8A

* sixteen /ˌsɪkˈstiːn/ n. 十六 7B

◆sixth /sɪksθ/ a. 第六的 n. 第六;六分之一;月的第六日 3B

* skill /skɪl/ n. 技能;技艺;技巧 1B

* skilled /skɪld/ a. 有技能的;熟练的 4A

◆slip /slɪp/ vi. 滑;滑落;溜;悄悄地走 2A

* smart /smɑːt/ a. 聪明的 1A

* smooth /smuːð/ a. 光滑的,平整的;顺利的 8B

◆socialize /ˈsəʊʃəlaɪz/ vi. 与人交往;交际 1A

◆soldier /ˈsəʊldʒə/ n. 士兵 2A

◆someday /ˈsʌmdeɪ/ ad. 将来某一天;总有一天 6A

* somehow /ˈsʌmhaʊ/ ad. 以某种方式;用某种方法;不知怎么地 6A

★source /sɔːs/ n. 源头;来源;根源;出处;消息来源;提供消息者 3B

* spade /speɪd/ n. 锹,铲 5A

* Spanish /ˈspænɪʃ/ a. 西班牙的;西班牙人的;西班牙语的 n. 西班牙语 2B

* spare /speə/ a. 备用的;多余的;空闲的 5B

◆spark /spɑːk/ n. 火花,火星 7A

* special /ˈspeʃl/ a. 特殊的;特别的;专门的 4A

* specific /speˈsɪfɪk/ a. 明确的,确切的;特定的;具体的 8A

* speed /spiːd/ n. 速度;迅速,快 4A

* spread /spred/ v. (使)传开;传染;(使)蔓延 2A

◆sprint /sprɪnt/ v./n. (短距离的)全速奔跑;冲刺 4A

* stage /steɪdʒ/ n. 阶段,时期 1A

★stimulate /ˈstɪmjʊleɪt/ vt. 刺激;激励;激发(某人的)兴趣;使兴奋 8B

* stove /stəʊv/ n. 炉子;火炉 6B

★strategy /ˈstrætədʒɪ/ n. 战略;策略 8A

★strength /streŋθ/ n. 力量;力气;强度 6A

* strengthen /ˈstreŋθn/ v. 加强;巩固;变强 4B

* stress /stres/ n. 压力;紧张 4B

◆stressful /ˈstresfl/ a. 压力重的;紧张的 4B

* strike /straɪk/ vt. 打,击,敲;(时钟等)敲响报(时) n. 罢工 2B

* stroke /strəʊk/ n. 击,打;打击;中风 4B

* struggle /ˈstrʌgl/ n. 斗争,搏斗;奋斗,努力 vi. (与某人)斗争,搏斗;挣扎;奋斗,努力 6A
* style /staɪl/ n. 文体;风格 8A
* succeed /səkˈsiːd/ vi. 成功;达到目的 1A
* success /səkˈses/ n. 成功 1B
* successfully /səkˈsesfəlɪ/ ad. 成功地 1A
* sunshine /ˈsʌnʃaɪn/ n. 日光,阳光 5A
◆ supportive /səˈpɔːtɪv/ a. 支持的;给予帮助、鼓励或同情的 8B
* surface /ˈsɜːfɪs/ n. (物体的) 表面 vi. 浮出水面;出现;浮现 8B
* surround /səˈraʊnd/ vt. 包围;围住;环绕 1A
* survive /səˈvaɪv/ v. 活下来;幸存;继续存在;从…中逃生;经历…后继续存在;比…活得长 7B
◆ swell /swel/ vi. 膨胀;肿胀 3B
★ swing /swɪŋ/ (swung /swʌŋ/) v. (使)摆动,(使)摇动 n. 摆动,摇摆;秋千 4A
◆ sympathetic /ˌsɪmpəˈθetɪk/ a. 同情的;表示同情的 8B
* system /ˈsɪstəm/ n. 系统;制度;体系 2A
★ systematic /ˌsɪstəˈmætɪk/ a. 系统的 8A
◆ tardiness /ˈtɑːdɪnɪs/ n. 缓慢;迟;拖延 3A
★ task /tɑːsk/ n. 任务,工作 3B
◆ tease /tiːz/ vt. 戏弄,逗弄;取笑;惹 7B
* technique /tekˈniːk/ n. 技术,技能;技巧;手段,方法 4A
* tend /tend/ vi. [后接不定式]往往会;易于 vt. 照料;护理 3A
* therefore /ˈðeəfɔː/ ad. 因此,所以 8A
* thought /θɔːt/ n. 想法,见解 8B
* thoughtful /ˈθɔːtfl/ a. 关心别人的,体贴的;考虑周到的;思考的,沉思的 3B
◆ toddler /ˈtɒdlə/ n. 刚学会走路的孩子 3B
* toe /təʊ/ n. 脚趾 4A
◆ toil-worn /ˈtɔɪlwɔːn/ a. 劳累的;疲惫不堪的 5A
* tomato /təˈmɑːtəʊ/ n. 番茄,西红柿 2B
* touch /tʌtʃ/ v. 触,接触;触摸;轻碰 n. 触,碰;触摸;触觉 4A
★ tough /tʌf/ a. 坚韧的;牢固的;困难的;艰苦的 8B
◆ townsfolk /ˈtaʊnzfəʊk/ n. 镇民 2B
★ track /træk/ n. 足迹,踪迹;小道,小径;路径;跑道;径赛运动;田径运动 vt. 跟踪;追踪 6A
◆ transition /trænˈzɪʃn/ n. 过渡;转变 1A
★ treasure /ˈtreʒə/ n. 金银财宝;财富 5A
◆ treatment /ˈtriːtmənt/ n. 对待;待遇;治疗;疗法 7A
◆ tricky /ˈtrɪkɪ/ a. 难以回答的;难对付的;棘手的 4A
◆ trunk /trʌŋk/ n. 树干 5A
★ ultimately /ˈʌltɪmətlɪ/ ad. 最后,最终 1A
★ unable /ʌnˈeɪbl/ a. 不能的,不会的 3B

◆unaffected /ˌʌnəˈfektɪd/ *a.* 不矫揉造作的;真挚的 7A

◆uncertainty /ʌnˈsɜːtntɪ/ *n.* 不确定,无把握 8B

◆unlock /ʌnˈlɒk/ *vt.* 开…的锁 7A

◆unplanned /ˌʌnˈplænd/ *a.* 无计划的;未经筹划的 7A

◆untrue /ˌʌnˈtruː/ *a.* 不真实的;与事实相反的;假的 4B

*upset /ʌpˈset/ *vt.* 使(某人)不高兴;使(某人)心烦意乱;使(某人)苦恼 5B

★vacation /vəˈkeɪʃn/ *n.* 假期;休假 2A

*victory /ˈvɪktərɪ/ *n.* 胜利;成功 6A

*visible /ˈvɪzəbl/ *a.* 看得见的,可见的;易觉察的;明显的 4B

◆wallet /ˈwɒlɪt/ *n.* 钱包,皮夹 7A

*warn /wɔːn/ *vt.* 警告;告诫 2B

◆wary /ˈweərɪ/ *a.* 谨慎的;小心的;谨防的 2B

*wealth /welθ/ *n.* 财产;财富 5B

◆wealthy /ˈwelθɪ/ *a.* 富的;有钱的 5B

◆weed /wiːd/ *n.* 野草,杂草 5A

*weight /weɪt/ *n.* 重量 4B

★wheel /wiːl/ *n.* 轮;车轮;方向盘,驾驶盘 7B

★whenever /wenˈevə/ *conj.* 任何时候;每当 5B

◆widower /ˈwɪdəʊə/ *n.* 鳏夫 3B

*wipe /waɪp/ *vt.* 擦,拭;抹;擦净;揩干 7B

*wise /waɪz/ *a.* 英明的;明智的 1A

★workshop /ˈwɜːkʃɒp/ *n.* 车间;工场;作坊 2A

*worth /wɜːθ/ *a.* 值…钱;有…价值;值得… 6A

◆wow /waʊ/ *int.* (表示惊奇或钦佩等)哇,呀 6A

★wrap /ræp/ *vt.* 包;裹;包扎;缠绕 7B

*writing /ˈraɪtɪŋ/ *n.* 作品;写作 7A

*yard /jɑːd/ *n.* 院子;天井;庭院;码(英美长度单位,=3英尺,合0.9144米) 4B

◆yell /jel/ *v.* 叫喊,叫嚷;号叫 7B

Phrases & Expressions

agree to	同意;赞同	5B
ahead of	在…前面	1A
all one's life	一辈子,毕生	5A
a number of	若干,许多	6B
arrange for	为…做准备,安排	3B
as a matter of fact	事实上;其实	4B
as a result of	作为…的结果;由于	1B
as a result	结果	1A
as though	好像;似乎;仿佛	7A

as well	也,又,还	2B
at/behind the wheel	在驾驶;在操纵	7B
at first	起先,开始时	1A
at hand	近在手边;在附近;即将发生	8A
at its/one's best	处于最佳状态	8A
at other times	在别的时候	8B
be/feel at home	(像在自己家里一样)舒适自在;无拘束	7B
be/get caught up in	被卷入;陷入	3A
be known as	被认为是;被叫做,被称做	4A
be up to	取决于…的,须由…决定的	1A
bring back	使(某人)回来;使(某人)死而复生	7B
burn out	烧光;烧毁	6B
by oneself	单独地,独自地	1A
call out	叫喊;大声地说	7A
care for	照顾;照料	5B
carry away	拿走,搬走,运走	5A
clean out	把…打扫干净;把…出空	6B
come across	偶然遇见;碰上	8B
come over	走过来	7A
come to	(指主意)被想起	2A
compare notes	交换意见	8B
day after day	日复一日,一天又一天	5A
dig up	掘起;挖掘出	5A
do business with	和…做生意	3B
drive sth. home (to sb.)	使(某人)充分认识(或理解)某物	7B
eat one's fill	吃个饱	5B
even if	即使	6A
fall behind	落在…后面	6A
far and wide	到处,各处;四面八方	3B
feel free (to do sth.)	随意;请便;欢迎	3A
focus on	把(注意力等)集中于	8A
for example	例如	4A
for oneself	独自地;依靠自己	1A
give/lend a (helping) hand	给予帮助,助一臂之力	3A
go beyond	超过	1B
grow up	长大;成长;成熟	1A
happen to	临到;发生于;落到…头上	6A
have sth. under control	使某事恢复正常;使某事处于控制之下	1A
higher learning	高等教育;大学水平的学识	1B

hold up	举起;抬起	2B
in action	在战斗中	7A
in addition	另外;加之	1A
in answer to	作为对…的回答(或响应)	5A
in any case	无论如何,不管怎样;总之	7A
in charge (of sb. /sth.)	主管;负责;指挥	3A
in fact	实际上;事实上;其实	4B
in honor of	出于对…的敬意	2A
in pain	痛苦地	6A
in pairs	成对地,成双地;两个一组;一次两个	8B
in public	当众;公开地	2B
in shape	健康;处于良好状况;处于良好的健康状况	4B
in store	即将发生;等待着	1A
interfere with	干扰;妨碍	3B
keep from	阻止,防止;克制,抑制	4A
keep one's balance	保持身体平衡	4A
keep up with	跟上	1A
lead to	导致	2A
long, long ago	很久、很久以前	5B
look (at) sb. in the eye(s)	(心地坦然地)直视某人,正视某人	7A
look back	回顾,回忆	3A
look on/upon	(以特定目光或情绪)看;看待	1A
lose weight	减轻体重;变瘦	4B
make a difference to	对…有影响;对…起重要作用	6A
make a living	谋生;挣钱	3B
make history	创造历史;做出值得纪念的事情	1B
make one's way	前进,向前进;取得成功	2B
make... out of...	用…制造出…	2A
make sure	确保	3B
make up	组成,构成	2A
mistake... for...	把…误认为…	6A
move on	继续前进;继续行进	7B
not really	事实上不是	4B
of one's own	属于自己的	7B
once more	重新;再一次	5B
on one's own	独自一人;独力地;单独地	3A
on the occasion of	在…之际	3A
other than	除了	1B
over and over (again)	一再地,再三地	7B

pass away	[婉] 去世	7B
pay one's way	支付自己应承担的费用	3B
pick out	拣出	5A
pick up the pieces	收拾残局;恢复正常	7B
pick up	拿起;捡起;提起	2A
prepare for	为…做好准备	6A
pull off	把机动车驶离(道路)进入路旁停车处	7B
put… into use	使用,应用	8B
put sb. off sth. / doing sth.	使某人对(做)某事失去兴趣	8B
quite a bit	相当数量;相当程度	4A
rather than	不是…(而是)	4A
remind sb. of sb./sth.	使(某人)想起(某人/某事)	5B
run into	与…相撞;撞在…上	7B
send away	使离去,把…打发走	5A
send for	派人去请,派人去叫,派人去拿	5A
set the stage for	为…创造条件,为…作好准备;使成为可能	8A
settle down	安顿下来;过安定的生活	5B
set to	开始起劲地做某事	5A
set up	建立	1A
show off	炫耀,卖弄;表现自己	7B
straight away	立即,马上;毫不耽搁地	5B
sure enough	果然	6A
take care of	照料;负责	2A
take in	吸收;摄取	4B
take notes	作记录,记笔记	8A
take over	接管,接任;接收,接办	7B
take the rough with the smooth	既能享受顺境,又能承受逆境;既能享乐也能吃苦;好事坏事都接受	8B
take up	占去(时间或地方)	2A
There's no way (that)…	[口] …没有可能	3B
throw away	扔掉,抛弃	6B
time and time again	多次;一再,反复地	5A
to be sure	毫无疑问;无疑地;当然;必须承认	5A
to sb's advantage	对某人有利	8A
to the point	切题的(地);切中的(地);中肯的(地)	3A
track down	跟踪找到;追捕到;搜寻到	6A
try out	试用;试	8B
turn around/round	转身	6A
turn out	证明是	1A

up and down	来来回回,往返地;沿…来来回回	4A
use up	用完,用光;耗尽	4B
walk up	走上	2B
What about…?	(询问消息或提出建议)…怎么样?	4B
wipe away	擦掉,擦去	7B
work out	锻炼,训练	4B
worry about	对…担忧,对…担心	8A
worth it	值得的;值得花费金钱(或努力、时间)的	6A

Proper Names

Alexis Walton /əˈleksɪs ˈwɔːltn/ 亚历克西斯·沃尔顿 1B

Amy /ˈeɪmɪ/ 艾米(女子名) 7B

Antoine de Saint-Exupery /ænˈwɑːn də sæŋtegzjupeɪˈriː/ 安托万·德·圣埃克苏佩里(1900— 1944,法国小说家) 7A

Arnold Schwarzenegger /ˈɑːnəld ˈʃvɑːtsəndʒə/ 阿诺德·施瓦辛格(1947—)(奥裔美国电影演员,动作片巨星,曾在国际健美比赛中多次胜出;2003年竞选加州州长并当选) 4B

Ashley Hodgeson /ˈæʃlɪˈhɒdʒsn/ 阿什利·霍奇森 6A

Bob Burns /bɒb ˈbɜːnz/ 鲍勃·伯恩斯 3A

Central America 中美洲 2B

Charles Barbier /ˈtʃɑːlz bɑrˈbjeɪ/ 查尔斯·巴比埃 2A

Coupvray /ˈkuːpfreɪ/ 库普弗雷(法国城市) 2A

Ecuador /ˈekwədɔː(r)/ 厄瓜多尔(南美洲西北部国家) 2B

Elkhart /ˈelkhɑːt/ 埃尔克哈特(美国堪萨斯州一城镇) 6B

Europe /ˈjʊərəp/ 欧洲 2B

Florida /ˈflɔːrɪdə/ 佛罗里达州(美国东南部一州) 7B

France /frɑːns/ 法兰西,法国 2A

Glenn Cunningham /ˌglenˈkʌnɪŋhæm/ 格伦·坎宁安 6B

Hanock McCarty /ˈhænɒk məˈkɑːtɪ/ 汉诺克·麦卡蒂 7A

Jane /dʒeɪn/ 简(女子名) 7B

Jane Fonda /dʒeɪn ˈfɒndə/ 简·方达(1937—)(美国著名电影女演员;1980年代所撰写、录制的有关健美的书和录像带很畅销,影响很大) 4B

Jeanne K. Grieser /ˈdʒiːn keɪ ˈgriːzə/ 珍尼·K·格里泽 2A

Kansas /ˈkænsəs/ 堪萨斯州(美国中部一州) 6B

Katharine /ˈkæθərɪn/ 凯瑟琳(女子名) 7B

Kathy Johnson Gale /ˈkæθɪ ˈdʒɒnsn ˈgeɪl/ 凯西·约翰逊·盖尔 7B

Kristen Hoel /ˈkrɪstən ˈhəʊəl/ 克里斯坦·赫尔 4A

Louis Braille /lwiː ˈbreɪl/ 路易·布莱叶 2A

Madison /ˈmædɪsn/ Square Garden 麦迪逊广场花园(纽约市曼哈顿的大型室内运动、娱乐和集会中心) 6B

Mexico /ˈmeksɪkəʊ/　墨西哥(拉丁美洲国家)　2B

Michael Williams /ˈmaɪkəl ˈwɪljəmz/　迈克尔·威廉斯　2B

Mother's Day　(美国、加拿大等的)母亲节(5 月的第二个星期日)　3A

Mother Teresa /təˈriːzə/　特丽莎嬷嬷(1910—1997,天主教修女,1979 年诺贝尔和平奖获得者。
　因其国际性慈善活动受到世人尊敬)　7A

New Jersey /njuːˈdʒɜːzɪ/　新泽西州(美国东部一州)　2B

New York /ˌnjuːˈjɔːk/　纽约州(美国东部一州);纽约市(美国纽约州东南部港市)　7B

Nguyen /əŋˈəʊˈjen/　阮　5B

Paris /ˈpærɪs/　巴黎(法国首都)　2A

Peru /pəˈruː/　秘鲁(南美洲西部国家)　2B

Robert Johnson /ˈrɒbət ˈdʒɒnsən/　罗伯特·约翰逊　2B

Salem /ˈseɪləm/　塞勒姆(美国新泽西州城镇)　2B

Sarah /ˈseərə/　萨拉(女子名)　7B

South Carolina /ˌsaʊθ ˌkærəˈlaɪnə/　南卡罗来纳州(美国东南部一州)　7B

Spain /speɪn/　西班牙(欧洲西南部国家)　2B

White /waɪt/　怀特(姓氏)　7B

Wyverne Flatt /ˈwaɪvən ˈflæt/　怀维恩·弗拉特　3B

图书在版编目(CIP)数据

21 世纪大学实用英语综合教程. 第一册/翟象俊等主编.
—上海:复旦大学出版社,2006.7
(21 世纪大学实用英语)
ISBN 978-7-309-03990-0

Ⅰ. 2… Ⅱ. 翟… Ⅲ. 英语-高等学校-教材 Ⅳ. H31

中国版本图书馆 CIP 数据核字(2006)第 033019 号

21 世纪大学实用英语综合教程(第一册)
翟象俊 余建中 陈永捷 梁正溜 本册主编

出版发行	复旦大学出版社	上海市国权路 579 号 邮编 200433

86-21-65642857(门市零售)
86-21-65100562(团体订购) 86-21-65109143(外埠邮购)
fupnet@ fudanpress. com http://www. fudanpress. com

责任编辑	曹珍芬
出 品 人	贺圣遂

印 刷	浙江省临安市曙光印务有限公司
开 本	787×960 1/16
印 张	19.25
字 数	361 千
版 次	2009 年 5 月第一版第十八次印刷

书 号	ISBN 978-7-309-03990-0/H · 790
定 价	30.00 元